Reader's Raves

"A wonderful read, and with a powerful message: find your own heart code and use it as a mantra to guide your life's decisions."

HARALD – Pharmaceutical Executive

"Most teenage girls can relate when their mother has dreams for them that don't match what they want; and a father who can't get involved, for whatever reason. The lucky girls have a BFF who is their soul-sister, and a grandmother in their pocket. Some girls fall in love with an idea, perhaps the very well-orchestrated secret plan their mother was behind all the time. But hopefully, all girls find the strength to follow their heart, break free from the chains of tradition and do the right thing for themselves. In THE HEART CODE, Celeste is that girl in search of this truth. The kind of truth that is timeless and has the right stuff to deliver to the young women in the 21st Century, who are also caught in this emotional nightmare!"

ELLEN – Activist, Homemaker

"Chapter by chapter, a most engaging read … and the characters within will become your very good friends for a long time to come. A substantive and refractive work of Literary Art!"

JOHN – Strategist

"A beautiful period novel of a young girl coming of age, confronted and confounded with decisions and choices throughout. It's wonderful to read how she comes to find her own heart's desire."

JOLEEN – Chief Financial Officer

"This book has core. Like the inner muscles in the center of our body that drives our strength, THE HEART CODE works out the core muscles in the center of our heart: the seat of our soul. When I picked up this book, I had lost my self-confidence and was going through a divorce. THE HEART CODE empowered me to stand up, to be true to who I am. THE HEART CODE is the bible to my soul. I want this book to be the passenger in my car. If this book empowers anyone to do what is in their heart: then that's what's best about it. And the writing is clean. You see the characters as they are and bring your own interpretation, to see, feel, and determine for yourself what speaks to you."

JENNIFER – Marathoner, Race Director

"This book is an utterly captivating adventure – of the world and of the heart. The language is so evocative, you cannot help but be absolutely there every step of the way with these vividly drawn characters, and the story gallops along so deliciously that you simply cannot wait for the next chapter. Be prepared for plenty of late-night I can't stop now! I guarantee that when you finish this book, you'll be yearning for a sequel and a prequel. Laura Matson Hahn will be your favorite new author."

GERALD – Journalist

"Reading THE HEART CODE, I was in a movie. It was fresh with perfumes, colors and sounds. In the beginning, I lived with the characters in an ideal life, but I was waiting for a clash. Something between the two friends, the two 2 brothers … something was going to happen in the lives of all the people I met in this book. What are they going to understand or not understand? All the while, the grandmother shows the way. Gamma is very present in each person of the story. There is a lot of light. I liked the story of each person. I can see how they live and how they see their lives. I have different sun glasses for each of them. And through them I see all the times of my life: when I was younger, when I didn't know my heart voice, when I doubt, when I believe and when I doubt again. The characters are like onions, their skins peeling away, one after another, to arrive inside for the real one, for the mine. Not yours or his or hers or theirs: mine, my way. I kept reading and reading to know more about the heart voice."

ISABELLE – Nurse, Naturalist Health Care

"Everyone should be fortunate enough to have a Gamma. Everyone should have the opportunity to explore and inquire. Everyone who feels from the heart should read THE HEART CODE. Every woman should have a piece of Celeste in their being."

SHARYN – Educator

"THE HEART CODE is a richly, imagined novel of love and personal struggle. Laura Matson Hahn knows that all the things we ever will be, can be found in some forgotten fragment of our heart."

BARBARA – Equestrian

THE
HEART
CODE

A Novel

Laura Matson Hahn

Published by

Conversation Farm Books

The Heart Code is a work of historical fiction. Apart from the actual people, events and locales that figure into the narrative, all names, characters, places and incidents are the products of the author's imagination or are used fictitiously. Any resemblance to current events or locales, or to living persons, is entirely coincidental.

Published by Conversation Farm Books
65 West Ferry Street, New Hope, PA 18938
conversationfarm@gmail.com

Cover Art: Julie Costanzo

Interior Design and Production: Caryn Newton
Lantern Glow Design cnewton@lanternglowdesign.com

The Heart Code: Ancient Truth, Modern Wisdom
Fiction. Author: Laura Matson Hahn
ISBN 978-0-9890495-0-4
1. Fiction-Coming of Age 2. Fiction – Family Life 3. Fiction – Historical
4. Fiction- Romance – Historical 5. Fiction – Visionary & Metaphysical
Library of Congress Control Number: 2013904326

Grateful acknowledgement to Alfred Publishing Co. Inc for permission to re-print previously published material: BLUE MOON. Music by RICHARD RODGERS. Lyrics by LORENZ HART. @1934 (Renewed) METRO-GOLDWYN-MAYER INC. All Rights Controlled and Administered by EMI ROBBINS CATALOG INC. (Publishing) and ALFRED MUSIC PUBLISHING CO., INC. (Print) All Rights Reserved.

Summary
A young woman in 1930's Connecticut discovers a new way of thinking about her life from her Bohemian Grandmother, who believes each person's truth and life path is inscribed in their heart from birth, and is found by paying attention to what shows up and listening for the 'yes' inside one's heart.

Printed in the United States of America

Dedication

For John and Bucks:
My earthly guardian angels

and

In honor of my personal "Gammas"
who taught me much and loved me more

Sister Joal, Rita, Gail, Wynne and Aunt Therese

Contents

Part One

Chapter 1: Birch Bark Hat ◦ 17

Chapter 2: Sixteen ◦ 25

Chapter 3: The Gypsy ◦ 33

Chapter 4: Vojen Village ◦ 42

Chapter 5: The Howe's ◦ 53

Chapter 6: The Ball ◦ 60

Chapter 7: Ede ◦ 70

Chapter 8: Alchemy ◦ 77

Chapter 9: Traveling Blood ◦ 86

Chapter 10: Society ◦ 96

Chapter 11: Homecoming ◦ 104

Part Two

Chapter 12: Ron ◦ 119

Chapter 13: Dancing ◦ 127

Chapter 14: Estelle ◦ 139

Chapter 15: Legacy ◦ 147

Chapter 16: Graduation ◦ 158

Chapter 17: Dreams ◦ 170

Chapter 18: Choices ◦ 179

Chapter 19: James ◦ 194

Chapter 20: Truth ◦ 208

Chapter 21: Feelings ◦ 221

Chapter 22: Hollywood ◦ 228

Part Three

Chapter 23: Blue Moon ◦ 239

Chapter 24: Art ◦ 256

Chapter 25: Valentines ◦ 268

Chapter 26: Understandings ◦ 277

Chapter 27: Champion ◦ 288

Chapter 28: Clarity ◦ 301

Chapter 29: Conquests ◦ 313

Chapter 30: Connubial Mist ◦ 322

Chapter 31: Courage ◦ 334

Chapter 32: Hows and Means ◦ 343

Chapter 33: The Space In-Between ◦ 358

Chapter 34: Yes ◦ 369

Author's Note ◦ 385

Acknowledgements ◦ 387

Reader's Guide ◦ 389

Author's Biography ◦ 393

The country of Bohemia was established in 600 AD. It remained an independent country until after World War I, in 1919, when its boundaries and name were changed to Czechoslovakia. However, long before it became a recognized country in Eastern Europe, it was populated by the Boii Celts for hundreds, if not thousands, of years. Bohemia literally translates to: Home of the Boii.

POLAND

GERMANY

Elbe River

Elbe River

Prague

BOHEMIA
(600AD – 1919)

Nuremberg

Bohemian Mts.

Vltava River

Danube River

Danube River

AUSTRIA

Migration of the Boii Celts

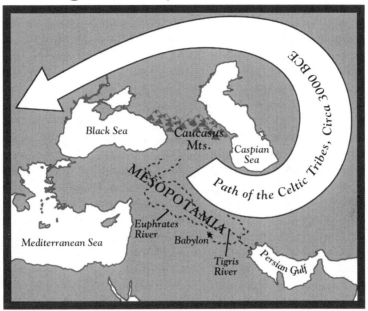

Linguists who study the origin of language have identified the root origin of many modern day languages to an area between the Black and Caspian Seas, under the Caucasus Mountains, where many tribes resided and influenced one another. In 3000 BCE, that territory became over populated and the tribes moved out to the north, south, east and west, spreading the commonalities of their language across the world.

CZECHOSLOVAKIA
(1919 – Now the Czech Republic)

HUNGARY

ROMANIA

Howe Family

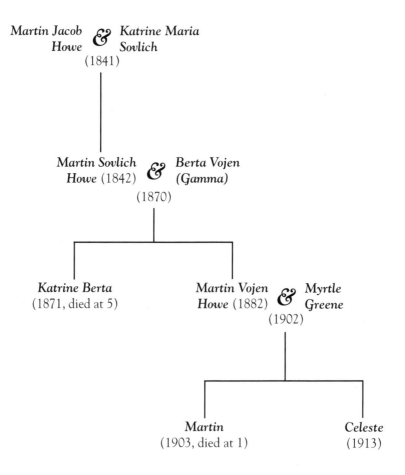

Martin Jacob Howe **&** Katrine Maria Sovlich
(1841)

Martin Sovlich Howe (1842) **&** Berta Vojen (Gamma)
(1870)

Katrine Berta
(1871, died at 5)

Martin Vojen Howe (1882) **&** Myrtle Greene
(1902)

Martin
(1903, died at 1)

Celeste
(1913)

Meaden Family

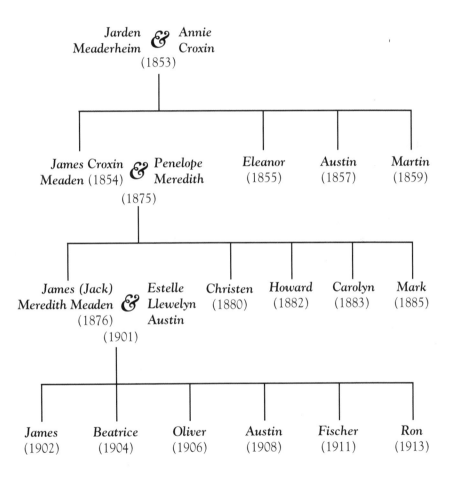

Jarden Meaderheim & Annie Croxin (1853)

James Croxin Meaden (1854) & Penelope Meredith (1875) — Eleanor (1855) — Austin (1857) — Martin (1859)

James (Jack) Meredith Meaden (1876) & Estelle Llewelyn Austin (1901) — Christen (1880) — Howard (1882) — Carolyn (1883) — Mark (1885)

James (1902) — Beatrice (1904) — Oliver (1906) — Austin (1908) — Fischer (1911) — Ron (1913)

The Facts Behind the Fiction

The genesis of this story was influenced by two key facts. One is the actual tribe of people who were the original Bohemians (circa 2000 BC). The other is the modern day scientific investigation into the separate intelligence that resides within the heart.

Bohemian: A Brief History.

The word Bohemian holds iconic stature in our society. While evoking disdain in some, to others it is an ideal state of being, defined as: a life unhampered by social convention, often artistic, with freedom to live as one chooses.

Where Did This Meaning Originate?

While used as a moniker for starving artists in 18th century Europe and a synonym for gypsy vagabonds, neither are the Bohemian beginning. The term was first recorded in 600 AD when the territory we now know as the Czech Republic was claimed by the Slavic people, who named it the Kingdom of Bohemia in honor of the Celtic tribe of Boii who first settled the land. The word Bohemia translates to "home of the Boii". Archeological and Linguistic researchers confirm a thriving Boii culture in the area around 750 BC, and some speculate they moved into the territory as early as 3000 BC.

Who Were The Original Bohemians?

By description, they dressed like modern day hippies in brightly colored garbs and ornamentation. By profession, they were highly skilled craftspeople and traders, among the first to create bronze out of tin and copper, among many other art forms. By culture they were independent and peaceful, expanding their families, businesses, and territory along the Vltava River, between Prague and the Danube River. By lore they were master storytellers whose tales traveled far, with some scribed by Greek scholars. And despite great population and political upheaval throughout Europe, their unique culture survived in that region until 50 BC, when they were attacked by a hired warring party (most likely Caesar's) and forced out of their homeland. Many fled west and south to Germany, France, Spain and Italy, where Boii populations continue today, confirmed by DNA. Some may have "jumped the pond," finding haven among the North Carolina Cherokee, where the "Celtic Axe" arrived to those Woodland Indians during that same timeframe. But it is also believed some of the original Bohemians must have stayed in their homeland, hidden away until the conquerors left. For how else would the land be named in honor of the Boii, 600 years after their supposed departure? The prevailing logic is when the Slavic people immigrated to the vacated

Boii land along the Vltava River; the remaining Boii emerged from the mountains to share their heritage and customs with their new neighbors, creating a valued bond. As a result, the land was named and remained Bohemia until 1919, when the spoils of World War One changed its name to Czechoslovakia.

What do Bohemians have to do With Modern Science's Study of a Heart's Code?

Documentation of the wide range of innovation the Boii Celt's created with their natural resources proves them to be a society that valued creativity. The longevity and prosperity of their culture suggests they encouraged tribe members to explore and develop unique skills and interests. If the culture's ethnology and folklore stands true, the original Bohemians represent the epitome of the universal ideal: "Follow Your Heart."

Fast forward to 1990, when scientists began an investigation of a separate intelligence residing in the heart and theorized that each heart contains a unique life map called: The Heart's Code. The theory began in early 1980 with the discovery of the mechanics of how atoms, cells and the heart stored coded information. That led to the question: could the heart cells learn and carry one's personal code? This theory was further supported though extensive clinical observations of heart transplant patients who admit to having dramatically new interests, tastes and preferences that identically matched the donor of their new heart (whom they'd never met). There is also the fact that in a fetus, the heart begins to beat on the 22nd day ... 180 days before the brain is fully formed ... and no one yet knows what causes the heart to start. Universally, our soul's wisdom has always been seated in the heart region, and, in a recent New York Times interview, TV host Dr. Oz considered the small white spot at the electrical center of the heart to be the soul.

Despite centuries of cultivating our brain smarts, many humans still cling to an ill-defined yet intrinsic stirring within our chest, believing it holds the magic potion for finding life's happiness. Science may now be catching up to our instincts, postulating a new revolution where the brain revolves around the heart, not the other way around.

Something, perhaps, the Boii Celts understood, long, long ago.

The human heart begins to beat
on its twenty-second day.

One hundred and eighty days
before the brain is fully formed.

No one yet knows the cause
of its spontaneous start.

Could there be a special intelligence
found only in the heart?

Extrapolated from:

The Heart's Code
Tapping the Wisdom and
Power of Our Heart Energy

By Paul Pearsall, Ph.D.

The Heart Code

Part One

1 Birch Bark Hat

May 27, 1920

Squatting on a crescent of rock jutting out from the creek's edge, six-year-old Celeste set down her collection of forest treasures while staring into the soft flowing gray-green water. Sniffing deeply, her nose filled with the scent of mud and new green as she wiggled her toes inside her shoes and looked up at her grandmother with hopeful eyes. "May I today, Gamma?" she asked.

Glancing at the houses on the hillcrest overlooking the creek, Gamma winced. News traveled fast in small towns. The ladies behind those glassy eyes would soon report them on the grassy slope, shoeless, sockless, skirts pulled up to their knees, splashing their feet, prompting yet another lecture from Myrtle on such dangers to her daughter's health. But none of that had ever stopped Gamma before, so she wrinkled her nose like a rabbit and nodded. Celeste's laugh gurgled in harmony with the stream as she unlaced her ankle-high shoes, pulled off her socks, rolled her canvas skirt above her knees and tiptoed into the creek, sucking small breaths at every step.

"Too cold?" Gamma asked, tucking the hem of her full length skirt into her waistband.

"Oh, noooo," Celeste said, biting her lower lip as Gamma stepped in. "Ouff! Is freezing! You make a joke of me!"

Squealing, Celeste clutched her sides, teetering in the water.

"Poof! What a pixie! Quick now, hand me the bark."

Still giggling, Celeste passed to her the long strip of birch bark they'd found on their walk through the woods and watched Gamma submerge it, gently working the edges underwater with her fingers, pulling and bending the bark to soften it. Lulled by the babbling water tumbling over the rock clusters, Celeste swayed to its melody.

"But in truth, I confess," Gamma broke the reverie as she lifted the bark out of the water, shaking off the drips: "To grandmamma, I make same joke, too."

Celeste cocked her head. "Here?"

"Ne. In Bohemia, where we live. Come close now. I measure."

Scooting over a rock, Celeste stood still as Gamma circled the bark around her head and marked her size by tearing a small notch in the bark. "But how will it stick?" she asked as they settled on the embankment.

"With notches." Gamma answered, setting the bark on her lap to adjust her eyeglasses. "Six notches of The Bohemian Way."

"Bo-MEEN-he-ahhhn," Celeste slowly ventured, hissing with the water.

"Bo-HE-me-ahn," Gamma corrected, positioning her fingers on the papery bark so Celeste could see. "One notch for each Way," she said and recited them with each tear. "Truth, Courage, Openness, Curiosity, Creativity, Love." She then offered the bark to Celeste. "Now you. Six notches on other side."

Drying her hands on her canvas jacket, Celeste studied Gamma's work before cautiously making her first tear."

"Good," Gamma nodded. "First for your Truth, which no one can know but you."

Celeste blinked a few times before making the second tear.

"Second for Courage, to follow the whispers of your heart."

Tentatively nodding, Celeste made the next tear.

"Third for Openness, to whatever comes your way."

Feeling warmth in her chest, Celeste made two tears in quick succession, but Gamma kept up with her.

"Fourth for Curiosity of what beckons you; and fifth for Creativity in all you do."

Celeste paused before making the last notch, feeling the roughness of the bark on her fingertips, her eyes twinkling. "Sixth for Love?"

Gamma smiled as her fingers ran down the row of notches. "Yah, sixth for Love; of yourself, first, from inside to out. These are the roots of our Bohemian Way, now notched in your bark hat for remembering always." She then showed Celeste how to interlock the notches, creating a circle of bark, which fit her head perfectly. "Now you add some fluff," Gamma pointed to the collection of forest treasures on the rock. "And a fine Bohemian Hat of ancient time you make."

Sliding off the bank, Celeste stood in the water surveying her cache on the quarter moon rock: a long vine, a few squiggly-edged leaves, three feathers from the geese who visit the creek, moss from the north side of a tree, and their prize: a translucent snakeskin, which they'd almost missed in the slant of afternoon sun. Carefully unhooking the notches, Celeste laid the bark flat, grabbed a fat, pointed stick and began boring holes along its edge. "Is this how you made clothes in Bohemia?" she asked.

Gamma looked at her skirt and laughed. "With bark? Ne. We use fabric and thread, same like here." In her mind's eye she saw herself as a girl, furiously working her needle in the dim glow of hearth and oil lamp, days before her departure to America. "But I was the sewing machine," she said, looking at her worn hands. "These very fingers."

"Me too," Celeste added, stripping the leaves off a vine and holding it up. "And this is my thread! Like Bohemian of ancient times!"

"Like Bohemian." Gamma trailed off as her mind flooded with images of the family she'd left behind so many years ago in the mountains beyond Prague. When she was too young to realize what she was trading away. When all she wanted was to flee the pain her carelessness had caused. Recalling the row of ancient stone shelters built on the ravine's crest with a sweet water creek at its bottom, her crystalline eyes misted, making Celeste and the creek a lovely blur. How odd to find herself so far from home, yet sitting beside a similar creek, with a blue-eyed granddaughter of her own.

"But what *is* a Bohemian?" Celeste asked.

Startled, Gamma shook herself out of her memory. Here it was, finally, the question she'd been hoping to hear and waiting to answer. She cleared her throat. "A Bohemian is a person who was born in the country of Bohemia, like me."

"Near New York?" It was the only place Celeste knew other than Connecticut.

"Ne, ne. Much more far. Across ocean," Gamma said, sighing deeply. "But sadly, is no more. Last year, after big war, they change our name from Bohemia to Czechoslovakia. But for me, is always Bohemia: home of the Boii, ancestors of our blood."

Celeste blinked. She didn't understand what Gamma had said, but she liked the tone of her voice; it was her storytelling voice when they snuggled up close at bedtime. "What's an-sess-tor?" she asked, weaving the vine through the holes in the bark.

As the afternoon sun melted in the treetops, casting long shadows across the hillside, Gamma shifted her hips. "Olden family of long ago time."

"Who's *my* olden family?" Celeste picked up the snakeskin.

"The same as me, Boii Celts."

"Boy kelp?"

Gamma laughed. "T, not P – Celt. Who live east of Europe …"

Celeste brightened. "Like Ede! She was born in Italy. That's in Europe! She showed us on the school map."

Gamma shook her head. "Yah, Italy is Europe, but our Celts first live more north and east, near the Mountains Caucasus and Caspian Sea. My grandfather tell many stories of how our first ancestors travel long long time to find a new home … in the land now called Bohemia."

"Like when you and Mama and Papa moved from New York?"

"Poofh," Gamma blew the air. "If only so easy. Our ancestors have much harder, more dangerous journey. You like to hear?"

Widening her blue eyes, Celeste nodded as she carefully slipped the edge of the snakeskin under the threaded vine while listening to Gamma's story of the Boii Celts' journey through deserts, around mountains and across snowy steppes until they came to a wide basin of beautiful land with bounteous plants, animals, rivers and forests.

"Bohemia?" Celeste deduced.

"Yah. Home of the Boii."

Holding up a feather, Celeste twirled it near her nose. It smelled wild. "What should I do with this?"

"How you like? Indian princess?"

Celeste smiled, and Gamma showed her where to bore the holes to hold it.

"But Gamma, where did they live? In a house like ours, or a castle?"

"Ha – a castle? Ne! In caves, I think at first."

Celeste's mouth dropped open. "Caves? With spiders and bugs?"

Gamma shrugged. "Out of wind and rain? Not so bad, eh? And what are castles? Big caves built by men."

Celeste thought of the castle in her storybook. "So did they build a castle?

"In time. But first a house with sticks, stone, mud and grass for roof."

"Grass for roof?!" Celeste peeled in laughter.

"Yah. They use what the land give. No hardware store like your Papa's to buy things. What they need, they make, from scratch, just like your hat."

"Just like my hat." Celeste repeated. "What should I do next?"

Leaning into the creek, Gamma drew a handful of musty-smelling mud. "Mud-glue for sticking," she said, plopping it on the rock and swirling it with her fingers.

Celeste wrinkled her nose at the musty smell and picked up a stick to stir it. "But Gamma, with no stores, what did they eat?"

"What earth provide: animal meat, goat's milk and cheese, plants from forest and field. Ah! Look!" Gamma pointed to a cluster of green across the creek. "The leaves, bouncing on the edge ... is watercress. In my creek it also grow. Quick now, get us some."

Yanking up her skirt, Celeste splashed to the bobbing cascade of small, round, tender greens. Easily ripping a handful from the mound, she hopped back.

Inhaling its fresh, woody smell, Gamma nibbled a few leaves. "Mmmmm, spring smell. Try some, my little Bohemian."

Sniffing, Celeste gave it a lick but wrinkled her nose. "I don't like it."

"Augh, the same, when I your age. But every day I must gather for supper."

With the tangle of stems still in hand, Celeste turned back to her rock table and stretched out the watercress in a long string, tucking it around the snakeskin. "I love making birch bark hats," she murmured.

"Is in your blood."

"Making hats?"

"Making beautiful things. Making art. From everything, Bohemians make art."

Celeste's face opened wide. "Like what?"

"Beads, sculptures, paintings, cloth, with bright colors ground from stones and crushed flowers. And carving designs on boats, tools, bowls. Everything they see and touch, Bohemians can't help but make more beauty, more art."

Celeste had stopped working on her hat to watch her grandmother speak. She liked how Gamma's eyes were sparkling. Then she sighed quietly, "I like Bohemia. Will you take me?"

"Oh yes, dítě. Is my great pleasure."

"When?"

"At sixteen your Papa I took."

Celeste's eyes clouded. Sixteen seemed forever away.

Gamma laughed. "Seems long, but I have many pillow stories to say before we go."

Celeste's eyes popped open, remembering the strange and magical images on Gamma's needlepoint pillows. "Like the singing goat, pooping little green hearts?"

"Yah, yah … goat, green hearts and more." Gamma lifted her arms overhead. "Like ancient ancestors, I call on Oghma, Bohemian god of wisdom, for guidance to tell you our history and the secret of heart's content."

Having finished mud-gluing the leaves on her hat, Celeste leaned down, washed her fingertips and sniffed them, making sure the mustiness was gone. "What's heart's content?" She asked.

Leaning forward, Gamma drew a circle around Celeste's chest. "In your heart are special clues for the life meant just for you. But speaks not in words, so you must learn how to listen for its voice, quiet and clear. And when you do, it help you find your deepest truth, from inside to out, and the quiet happiness of a life fulfilled. This is heart's content. This is Bohemian Way."

Celeste looked up at the pinkish clouds and deepening blue sky, trying to understand. Then she picked up her decorated hat and laid it on Gamma's lap.

"This is my heart's content," she said softly.

"The birch bark hat?"

"Making it," she said, admiring the feathers, leaves, snakeskin and vine.

"Ah, making it! In you, the Bohemian blood runs deep."

Sitting together, they silently admired the hat and each other as the sky's pink faded to soft gray. Then Gamma tapped Celeste's knee.

"Come now, put on shoes. Time to wear your hat home proud."

As the sun began setting Myrtle had been nervously scanning the hillside from her kitchen window and let out a big sigh when Gamma and Celeste finally appeared on the crest of the hill. Squinting in the waning light, she scrutinized their ambling figures and asked aloud: "What in heaven's name is on her head?"

Martin rose from the kitchen table to peer through the window. Seeing his mother and daughter heading toward the house, he knew instantly. "A bark hat. Made one as a boy."

Myrtle scoffed. "Where could you find bark on the docks of New York?"

Pulling his ear, Martin shook his head. "Every now and again Mother would take me to the country. When I was around Celeste's age, we found a creek and made a bark hat together. Took all day." Martin reached for a glass off the window sill and drew water from the kitchen tap. "She showed me how to curl the bark in the water as we stood in the creek." He gently inhaled, sucking air through his teeth, still able to smell the mix of grass, mud and bark from that day. "I loved that hat, but it got crushed on the trolley ride home. Never made another." Keeping time with the jaunty step of his daughter as she crossed the grass toward the house, he recited: "Truth, Courage, Openness, Curiosity, Creativity, Love." Sighing deeply, he returned to the kitchen table and opened his newspaper.

❦

"So did they live there forever?" Celeste swung her grandmother's arm.

"Who?"

"Our ancestors, the Bohemians."

"For long, long time, until, one day, some strangers – warriors – attack them."

"Meanies!" Celeste cried, thinking of the boy in kindergarten who smushed her painting.

"Big meanies! Who kill many of our ancestors and make the others run far away, to other countries. But some, they stay, hiding in the mountains until the warriors leave and it is safe again to live on the land they found. That is *our* family story, which I tell you, another day." As they came to the house, Gamma released Celeste's hand and shooed her in.

Holding on to her hat, Celeste carefully climbed the porch steps and ran into the kitchen, beaming. "Mama, Papa, look what we made today! A birch bark hat!"

Pushing aside his paper, Martin held out his arms, lifting his daughter to his lap. "Ah, you lucky girl. A Bohemian birch bark hat!" Closely examining her work, he named each treasure she'd used. "What a fine, fine job you've done, my dearest Celeste. Quite a talent you've got," kissing her cheek with a loud smack.

Giggling, Celeste slid off his lap and crossed to her mother at the stove. "And Gamma said she'll tell me all her story pillows and take me to Bohemia, when I'm older."

Myrtle smiled, cooing in return. "Very nice, I'm sure, but you'd best go wash for supper. Martin, would you help her, please?"

As Celeste scooted off hand-in-hand with her father, Myrtle's smile disappeared. Turning to her cooking pots, she vigorously stirred the soup, banging the wooden spoon against the tin sides. Stopping abruptly, she faced the table, "I won't have it," she spurted at Gamma, waving her spoon, "Filling my child's ears with your Bohemian nonsense. She's a modern girl in modern times who won't be needing any silly past, so I'll thank you not to talk about it, ever again."

Gamma's jaw dropped then promptly shut as her eyes steeled on her daughter-in-law. "What you say, Myrtle? Celeste should have no past? You erase your family and now her father's, too? So she come from nothing? No heritage? No ancestors? No stories for learning?"

"Ancestors? Ancestors!" Myrtle retorted, waving her spoon erratically. "What difference did they make to me? Vile memories I spit on. She don't need that blackness, and I'll not have it rob her chance for a better life – better than yours or mine. Better than a shopkeeper's wife. She's my daughter and I say: speak no more Bohemian bile."

Gamma pushed herself from the table, face empty of emotion and stepped towards Myrtle. "What you ask I cannot do. Your child she is, but Martin's, too. In their blood is history, beauty, knowledge that long survives on earth. As mother, is your right to raise her as you want. But grandmother has obligation, too."

Myrtle coiled for a fresh retort, but Gamma raised her hand for silence. "Between you and me, Myrtle, is not right, I know. Is not easy, living under my roof all your married life; but this is the fate of our hearts, which we can fight or make right. Celeste is yours to raise, but in other ways, she is mine. So only this promise I make: Your wishes for her I will not undo. But my heart demand I answer true, any questions she may ask."

The firm arch of Gamma's eyebrow caused Myrtle to blanch and purse her lips. Squeezing the spoon in her hand, she opened her mouth to reply but shut it just as quickly, turning back to the stove as the bathroom door banged open and Martin and Celeste returned with hands and faces bright.

❧

2 Sixteen

May 27, 1930

Leaning on her broom, Myrtle peered down the tree-lined street, watching Celeste meander across the Green, school satchel swinging, nose in the air, catching the sweet scent of linden flower now perfuming the town. "There she is," Myrtle said loud enough for her neighbor's ears. "There's my beautiful daughter."

Mrs. Harris stopped her sweeping, wiped her hands on her apron and squinted in the same direction. "Oh my, yes, hasn't she blossomed over the winter!"

Myrtle waved her arms to catch Celeste's eye. "Sixteen and nearly grown. Can you imagine? Where do the years go?"

Mrs. Harris shook her head. "Soon married with a brood of her own, and you a grandmother – ha ha! Any good prospects?"

"A few," Myrtle coyly twisted her head. "But we'll see what summer brings."

A block away, Celeste waved and hollered: "Mama, I'll be at church choir."

Myrtle nodded and ducked her head, returning to sweeping her walk. No longer interested in chatting, she wanted only to imagine the upcoming months, when her hopes and plans would finally converge. Never before had her dreams been so close to fulfillment. After years of false starts, slogging through the lower ranks of Gladdenbury's social fabric, she'd finally secured invitations to a selection of coveted summer parties that would place Celeste among the town's best set and win the most desired prize: an invitation to the Women's Club Fall Cotillion, where social merit was confirmed and rewarded with a proper introduction.

The Cotillion, Myrtle mused, sweeping harder. Where debutantes were presented and lifelong alliances forged. And, if the fates were kind, her own ascent up society's ladder, which had thus far eluded her anxious grasp. Although the season was weeks away, she could already smell the heady bloom of roses at the Conner's June soiree, feel the jazzy sway of the Club's midsummer dance and delight in the riot of hats at the August regatta. But the Cotillion! Ah, the Cotillion. If this one wish were granted, she would ask for nothing more. Her blood rushed at the thought of her daughter's prospects, so shiny, so bright, so far from her own tattered childhood. Everything she'd schemed for decades was now unfolding, and she couldn't wait for the festivities to begin.

"Excuse please, Myrtle?"

Myrtle's head jerked up at the old-country voice to see Gamma on the front porch.

"I like to make discussion with you. Please, you come soon?"

Myrtle forced a smile for Mrs. Harris's nosey eyes. As Gamma re-entered the house, Myrtle muttered, "Yes, your majesty," giving each step a hard sweep as she climbed the stoop. Leaving the broom by the door, she crossed through the parlor into the glass-walled conservatory where Gamma held court. The woody-green smell of the many plants assaulted her nose, along with a large frond of fern. Roughly pushing it aside, she heard a flutter of wings retreating from the six outdoor feeders and saw Gamma sitting on the wrought iron love seat, as she often did, calmly needle pointing. "I've got a lot to do today. What do you want?" Myrtle asked, trying to keep the irritation out of her voice.

Gamma's hands briefly stopped moving. "I have idea, for your agreement, something for Celeste; a promise made long ago, but now is time, I think. Please, sit."

Myrtle perched on the iron chair across from Gamma, wincing at its cool hardness. "Go on then. Supper won't start itself."

Gamma cleared her throat. "Ten year ago, I promise to show Celeste our roots in Bohemia. This summer I like to take her, as I am well enough and she 16 – same as her father was."

Myrtle's entire body flushed. "Roots? What are you talking about? No old roots are going to tangle my girl's shining future!" She couldn't believe her ears nor stop her rushing mind. "You want to dismiss all my hard work for *this* summer's plans? For some crusty old roots? What have they to do with our lives today? With *her life and future?*"

Myrtle's upset exploded well beyond her sense of reason. But having broken with her own past long ago, she knew of what she spoke. The first of too many children, she'd cut her teeth on want for something better, something more, and learned young how to snatch it, like apples off a cart. What else could she do? With a worthless father and haggard mother, living in the stench of New York City's Five Corners, polluted by fetid factories and savage people, she had no one to protect her from life's wretchedness. It exhausted and shamed her to recall any of it, but she'd vowed to escape her mother's washerwoman fate, and finally did, opting to roam the streets, searching for a smidgen of hope – when she spied young Master Howe, striding confidently in spats and spit-shine boots, posting notices for free tutoring. Fresh from college and eager to help those less fortunate, he was the sole heir to a small chain of hardware stores. From the moment Myrtle saw his softly tilted, handsome face and honest eyes, she recognized a means to a better tier of life where her old roots could be severed and her warehouse of want might be satisfied.

Clutching the cold, iron arm, Myrtle furiously shook her head. "No! You'll not steal my daughter's future. Not when it's her time to rise."

Gamma had anticipated such a response. "Hers – or yours, Myrtle?" she asked. "Celeste's future include her past. She has right to know from where she come."

"That makes no difference," Myrtle sputtered. "This is where she was born, not Bohemia or Ireland or some filthy New York alley. This is what she knows, and all she needs to know, for the life she was born to live, with people more like her than we'll ever be. Certainly more than backwoods strangers across the ocean."

Myrtle finished with a huff, still full of fury. From her first day in Gladdenbury she'd kept a gloved finger in the social pie, setting her sights on the *doyenne* with five sons a few blocks away. The time had finally come to reap what she'd carefully sown, to claim her dream, if only as mother of the most promising young woman about to enter the town's highest echelon. "No, Gamma, I won't abide your wish. It's been arranged. It's … all … been … *arranged*, and I won't let anything change it. You can't do that to … to … *her*. Not after all we've been through."

Gamma slowly wagged her head. "We? Did Celeste help make this choice?"

"She's *my* daughter," Myrtle shot back, "and I know what she needs," she popped up, spinning on her heel. "And I'll not have you filling her head with your Bohemian religion."

"*Ne!*" Gamma's raised voice arrested Myrtle's departure. "Is *not* religion. Is philosophy and history and art in the blood of her veins."

Myrtle jutted her chin "So you claim. But what does Martin say?"

Gamma blinked calmly. This, too, she expected. "I ask your blessing first."

"Well, I'll not give it. And let's just see what he has to say." Myrtle flicked her skirt as she turned to leave.

Gamma called after her. "What of Celeste's dreams and desires? Speak of those?"

Grasping the overhanging frond, her back to the old woman, Myrtle squeezed the foliage tight. "What can a child know at such an age?"

Gamma's eyes narrowed. "Much as you – when first you see my son."

Myrtle swiveled and locked eyes with Gamma, in mute defiance. After a long moment, Gamma spoke slowly.

"Her own heart voice she must know or have no compass to find her truth, for no one walks the same path."

"Poppycock!" Myrtle released the frond, ducked under the leaves and stomped out, untying her apron as she strode.

Gamma sank onto her chair. "*Bolení hlavy,*" she sighed, listening to her daughter-in-law pound across the parlor, rip open the coat closet, slam the glove box and bang the front door behind her. Through the conservatory's glass walls, she watched Myrtle flounce down the road toward town and their hardware store, hat bouncing with each step. Gamma shook her head. "Another headache," she translated for the birds re-clustering around the feeders. She knew Myrtle would badger Martin until he agreed to whatever his wife demanded, if only to regain peace. That's how it always was and this time would be no different – unless she put up a fight, a fight for her granddaughter's right to choose her own life.

Turning back to her needlepoint, Gamma tried to concentrate on the pillow in her lap. It was a gift for their distant kin, depicting Celeste's life and hopefully a map for her first campfire storytelling. She had not wanted to upset Myrtle, but time was not her friend. She'd learned first hand that too much could change too fast. But now supper would be smothered by angry silence. "And for what?" Gamma asked the birds. "A ticket to a dance?"

Had her husband lived, she'd still be in New York, running their three shops with closed eyes, for everything her husband knew, she knew as well, thanks to his blessed mother, Katrine. She'd hoped to do the same with Myrtle, despite their rocky start, until the sudden deaths led them to sell the stores and move to this town of glassy eyes and wagging tongues. Oh, how she missed New York's quirky imperfections, so unlike this hamlet where everyone strived to be the same; Myrtle most of all. Why was she so willing to become whatever she thought they wanted in exchange for acceptance and status?

Gamma sighed again, putting away her stitchery. Truth be told, she had failed her own son with the same blindness now driving Myrtle; guilty of putting her own wants ahead of her son's dreams. For that, she was deeply sorry. But it also was the reason she felt such urgency with Celeste. As the last of their Bohemian line, the girl was Gamma's only chance to honor the vow she'd made so many moons ago. If Celeste did not come to understand their Heart Code, no one would be left to pass it on. So no matter the discord, Celeste deserved more than an invitation to a cotillion by which to measure her self-worth.

◦◦◦

Brusquely opening the door of their hardware store and finding it empty, Myrtle brushed past the shop's counter and burst through the office door. Martin jumped in his seat, dropping his pencil.

"I refuse! Simply refuse!" Myrtle stamped her feet for emphasis. "To sacrifice my daughter to that old woman's ancient faith. What can Celeste gain among those ... those ... mountain people?"

"Jeepers, Myrtle, lower your voice," Martin cautioned, pulling off his green visor. He felt muddled by the sudden interruption after working on the shop's accounts all afternoon, and he hated arguing with anyone, especially in public.

"Don't you admonish me, Martin Howe, not after what I've been through. It's not you who has to spend all day dealing with your mother's foolishness."

Rubbing his face, Martin sank back into his chair. "Sit down. Calm down. What's the hoo-ha now?"

Pulling off her gloves, Myrtle perched on the chair alongside his desk. "If you don't put a stop to it, she'll ruin all our plans and our daughter's future."

Leaning back, Martin recalled a dozen instances of this same conflict flash through his mind. Since the move to Connecticut, his wife repeatedly clashed with his mother over the identical issue: Her lust for all things social, juxtaposed with his mother's ideology. "What is it today?" he asked quietly.

"The plans for this summer, to introduce Celeste to the right people so she'll have a chance – a chance I never had, until I met you. But times are different now. We must keep her on the right track."

"What?" Martin was baffled.

"Your mother wants to take Celeste to Bohemia *this summer*. The most important summer of her life! When they'll be choosing who to invite to the Cotillion! Everything I've worked for will piffle away!"

"The Women's Club Cotillion? In the fall?"

"Yes, in the fall, but if she isn't around this summer to make the proper impression, they won't even know she's alive. Don't you see? We can't miss this opportunity."

Martin rubbed his face again. Twenty-six years ago it seemed like a good idea to move to this small town to escape their losses: first his newborn son, then his father, then his youth, abruptly shunted aside to become head of household with a grieving mother, an inconsolable wife and three New York hardware stores to run. Barely 22 before his father died and still a boy in many respects, he was well educated but apprenticing the family business, with all the serious responsibilities still squarely on his father's shoulders. Only a few short years from his knock-about days on the docks of New York, dreaming of being a sailor like his Uncle Yazi, traveling the world with a yo-ho-ho and a bottle of rum. But then he met Myrtle and quickly eloped for reasons that now seemed hazy, yet instantly changed his whole world.

"What did Mother say?" he asked.

Myrtle knew he would check her every word. "She said she promised to take Celeste to Bohemia when she was 16 – same as you – and wants to do it this summer, in spite of knowing what a sacrifice it would mean for Celeste's future." She quickly rose, leaning on Martin's desk, her face close to his, her voice quiet and intense. "Can't you do something? Convince her that next year would be better, so as not to jeopardize our daughter's chances? Besides, how can we afford it after the crash and talk of depression?"

Martin shook his head. "Father willed Mother her own money."

Myrtle whirled around, dropping in her chair, summoning forced tears. "I can't believe you'd let all my hard work slip down the drain."

Martin stared at her contorted face. When they first met, her frailty had captivated him. She seemed the polar opposite of his mother and grandmother, the two towering pillars of strength that dominated his life. Her fearful nature, adoring eyes and neediness gave him a cause. Myrtle was someone *he* could protect. So, despite his Mother's probing and his own gnawing doubt, he followed Myrtle to a justice of the peace and became a young husband with a soon pregnant wife, living in his father's ample house and enjoying his mother's meals as he tested the sails and riggings of life. But with his father's sudden death, he was called on deck and thrusted the tiller before he even knew how to tie a proper knot. In that moment, trading New York for Connecticut seemed right, a place to begin anew. Before he truly knew his wife or welcomed the birth of his daughter; or held his breath through the "war to end all wars" or endured prohibition and the women's right to vote and the 1920's roar when Noel Coward's plays and Fitzgerald's books and Picasso's paintings ruled the day. Now, with Wall Street's debacle unhinging everyone's plans, Martin questioned what he'd done with his life. How changes he'd innocently set in motion nearly three decades before had come to impact everything he held most dear: his wife, his mother, his child, his heritage and especially – *especially* – the man he had hoped to become.

"We'll talk tonight," he offered, "and see what can be worked out."

After supper, when Celeste slipped off to do her homework and Myrtle began washing up, Martin broke the tense silence that had shrouded their meal. Stirring his coffee, he quietly asked, "Mother, how long were you thinking to be gone?"

Myrtle gasped, turning from the sink with soapy hands dripping on the floor. "But Martin, it's already settled. I've made the arrangements. We can't cancel now."

"Four weeks." Gamma ignored Myrtle's glare, stirring honey in her tea. "Six days on ship to London, then Paris and Prague, and six days back."

In the corner of his eye, Martin saw Myrtle vigorously shaking her head. "You promised me." Her voice shook. "There won't be another chance like this. Think of Celeste's future."

Gamma nodded slowly. "Yah, Myrtle is wise. Think of Celeste's future and the children she have one day. Who tell your grandchildren of Bohemian culture? Or will they know only Gladdenbury ways?"

Myrtle huffed. "You and that Bohemian piffle. It's your answer for everything."

"Myrtle…" Martin cautioned.

"What do you want from me, Martin? I've worked hard and long, and now you take it all away so she can traipse through the woods with… with…some hooligans across the sea! After all I've done to give our daughter the best possible life?"

Myrtle's puffy face saddened Gamma. Too much weary discord. "Myrtle," she began softly. "Is not your answer or mine that matters. Is the questions in Celeste heart and what she dream to follow."

Martin's head lowered and tilted to the left as he considered his mother's words.

Remembering his own trip to their homeland so many years ago, he'd never been able to explain to Myrtle how he felt among the Bohemian hills of their family's settlement, where the air felt soft despite the hard life the farmers led. Where laughter rang clear among his aunts, uncles and cousins, who wished each other well no matter what road they took. Nor had he told her how he felt growing up in New York, surrounded by his mother's varied friends who, like his Bohemian relatives, laughed and talked incessantly of questions and dreams. Where had his own dreams gone, he wondered? Did any embers of questions still hide in the recesses of his heart? Then he thought of Celeste. His body filled with unfettered love. Despite the losses, discarded dreams and disappointments in the ten long years before his daughter's miraculous birth, he'd repeat every step again, just to see her smile.

Looking at his scowling wife, hands planted on her hips, and then at his mother's placid face, he realized it was probably too late for his own questions and dreams, but not for his daughter's. Downing his coffee, he squared his shoulders, faced his wife's glare and then his mother's attentive gaze.

"I think this is the time for Celeste," he said, enunciating the words that would reverberate for hours. "Take her, Mother. Take Celeste to Bohemia for as long as you like and show her all she needs to know." And silently, he finished the thought to himself: "*Maybe she'll do what I could not and follow her heart's call.*"

❧

3 The Gypsy

August 1930

After six days of crossing the Atlantic, and four nights of London theater, and a sail across the English Channel, and a train to Paris for four more days of shopping, touring and dining, Gamma and Celeste were both near collapse as they trundled into a private sleeper on the overnight train to Nuremberg. Aroused in the blue-black, predawn light to change trains for the final leg of the journey to Prague, they crossed the German border into the foothills of the Bohemian Forest, where Gamma sighed deeply.

"Such green air smell!" She nudged Celeste, slumped on the seat.

"All I smell is stinky train," Celeste muttered, rubbing her nose as she hid under her coat. "How much longer will it be?" Then fell back asleep.

As the train chugged between the rolls of her beloved mountains, Gamma vigilantly watched as the countryside unfolded its sweet arms of boughs and streams. The gradual change from hills to plain, with glimpses of the Vltava River as they meandered through her homeland, warmed her heart and fired memories all the way to Prague.

"Is time now, wake up." Gamma shook Celeste.

Struggling and cranky, Celeste shuffled onto the platform behind Gamma, following a porter who transferred their luggage to a taxi, where she slumped again as Gamma gave directions in her native tongue and the motorcar pulled away. Seeing her granddaughter's eyes closed, Gamma poked her. "*Dítě*, look and see."

Celeste opened one eye. "What?"

"Prague in early light. We not here again this hour." She then arched one eyebrow, and Celeste bolted upright.

Traversing through the streets, Gamma pointed out the monuments, museums and churches, the castle on the hill and all the people attending their early morning duties. Unable to follow half of what Gamma was saying, Celeste almost quipped: *the butcher, the baker, the candlestick maker.* But she refrained from the flippancy and dutifully watched as the city awoke before her eyes in a soothing, cool wash of golden light. Soon they were in the countryside, riding in silence as the sun rose higher, banishing shadows from the few houses dotting the roadside.

"How far now?" Celeste asked, stifling a yawn. "And when can we eat?"

From her pocket, Gamma fished a dinner roll, wrapped in her hanky. "Eat this, but soon, more food than you can dream."

As the taxi labored up a hill, Celeste heard bleating and looked out the window. "Look, Gamma, goats! Just like you said."

"Likely your cousin, going to pasture."

"But why go to pasture? There's plenty of grass right there."

"Grass, yah, but something extra they need. Remember Paris goat cheese?"

Celeste thought for a moment. "The savory sweet one?"

"Yah. Is by goats eating special things in pastures like ours."

"Like what?"

"Soon you see. And much more, too," Gamma added with a mysterious nod.

The taxi suddenly turned off the road and bounced up a rutted driveway, shrouded by tall pines, until the view opened onto a field of waving grain. In the distance, they saw a cluster of thatch-roof houses.

"Are we home?" Celeste asked.

"Home we are," Gamma answered with moist eyes.

As the taxi stopped, a whoop came from the barn and a bell rang out, followed by a swarm of dogs and people running from all directions, calling Gamma's name. "Bertra Vojen! … Bertra Vojen! … Bertra Vojen!" were the only words Celeste understood as men, women and children of all ages rushed to greet them. Their words in a strange language tumbled past her like cartwheels of happiness as the clan clustered around, everyone talking, grabbing their bags, stroking their hair, touching their garments and pinching their cheeks. Gamma introduced Celeste to everyone, but she barely heard their names before she and Gamma were swept into the biggest house, where a table was piled with more food than Celeste had ever seen.

Gamma's elbow nudged her. "See? Like I say."

The aroma was intoxicating, teasing her nose with sweet and savory wafts. Without another thought, Celeste sat down and heaped a plate with sliced sausages and ham and fresh-baked bread slathered with butter and jam and a hard-boiled egg and a bowl of fresh berries doused with cream, while Gamma laughed and talked with her kin. Between bites, Celeste looked around the hearth room, as Gamma had called it. One big everything room surrounding the fireplace. She gazed across the blackened kitchen pots hanging from the rafters interspersed with bundles of drying herbs, leading her eye to the long window with a cozy seat – where she spied a cluster of needlepoint pillows and her heart leapt. Gamma's story pillows! Warmth washed over her chest. Many were the same as they had at home, depicting the stories of Gamma's life: her travel to America, her home in New York, their Connecticut house and Celeste's birth. Oh, it felt good to see something familiar so far away.

Then she saw a pillow she didn't recognize, one depicting a large green heart with a copper arrow piercing it and fat strings of tears gushing from its puncture wound. Although very much in Gamma's style, it was unlike any Celeste had seen, and she wondered what story it told. Rising from the table, she walked toward the window seat for a closer look, when a gust of laughter erupted among her relatives. Turning, she saw Gamma holding out a package to an old woman and waving for Celeste to come.

"Celeste, meet my niece Lidia."

Celeste blinked. The woman was much older than Gamma; at least much more wrinkly. Celeste's confused expression made the others in the room laugh, and her face flushed hot with embarrassment.

"Yah, clear you see. Lidia older to me."

Someone translated what Gamma said and Lidia scoffed.

"Still, she is niece," Gamma continued. "Daughter of my eldest sister, who marry before I born."

Celeste nodded, still a little confused, then turned and smiled sweetly at the old woman who viewed her with cold, narrow eyes.

Lidia nodded gravely as she inspected her young cousin.

"Now, she village elder. So to her we present our gift," Gamma summarized as she handed the package to Lidia for unwrapping. Then she whispered into Celeste's ear: "Maybe is time, you tell pillow's story?"

Celeste blanched, shaking her head. It was too frightening to speak in front of so many people. Plus how could they understand? She spoke only English and maybe a little French. "I don't think so," she whispered back, then tugged at Gamma's sleeve to ask about the crying-heart pillow. But when she turned to point it out, it had vanished. Leaving the group, Celeste looked all around the window seat but could find it nowhere.

Laughter burst out again as Gamma held up the new pillow, showing their Gladdenbury life: the creek, the church choir and their hardware store, centered around the town green. In her old language, with an exuberance of sounds Celeste had never heard before, Gamma told the story of each image. It made her feel a little homesick, and she forgot about the crying-heart pillow.

When Gamma finished, everyone applauded and began to depart, returning to their daily chores, leaving Gamma and Celeste to go up to their room, change out of their travel clothes, wash up and nap. A couple of hours later, they rose and dressed in slacks and sturdy shoes to walk about the farm.

"And the goat pasture?" Celeste reminded.

"Yah, if not too tired."

"Oh, I'm not tired."

But by the time they'd climbed the hill to the pasture, Celeste had to lie down in the middle of some wildflowers to catch her breath. The sweet scents enveloping her matched the delicate flowers floating around her face. "You did this everyday?"

"Um-hm, only faster; because the goats like to run." Opening the paper sack she'd brought along, Gamma spread out a cloth napkin and placed on it cheese, bread and dried apples. "Eat some, you feel better."

As they snacked, the sun began to wane and a light wind rustled the trees.

"You hear?" Gamma tilted her head. "Is forest name: *Šumava*."

"Shoo-mava," Celeste repeated, trying to memorize everything.

"Means: noise of trees in wind. Shooooooo-Maaaahhh-Vaaaaaa."

The sound washed over them, reminding Celeste of the ocean sucking at the sand, but soon she grew restless. "Shouldn't we get back?"

"*Ne*. Over the hill we go now," Gamma answered, gathering up their picnic. "To meet old friend."

Celeste brushed off her slacks. "A childhood friend?"

"First I know her mother – when I a young girl. And now I am friend with her daughter. Their Gypsy family come here every summer."

"Gypsies!" Celeste interrupted. "Aren't they bad people who rob and steal?"

"Celeste!" Gamma's voice sharpened. "Every people have bad seed. But gypsies are feared because they are strangers, traveling place to place. My friend and her family come to Šumava every summer, long before I born. I meet her here, this very pasture, and learn much things. Things no one else could say."

"Like what?"

Gamma squeezed Celeste's leg. "Like you coming to us, four years before you born."

Celeste face twisted. "Like a witch?"

"*Ne*," Gamma shook her head. "Not spells. She has gift of Second sight, of prophecy, as does her daughter, who now we go to see. To hear story of our ancestors. The first Bohemians."

"Why don't *you* tell me that?"

"Because you hear better this way. Like London theater."

Celeste giggled nervously.

"And *dítě*, listen well, for her talk is odd, but truth she tell." Gamma said, standing and tucking the paper sack under her belt, then picked up her walking stick and led Celeste across the field. As they marched along, she pointed out the thistle and laurel and lavender that made the goat's cheese taste so nice. Down a hill and across a stream and up the other side they walked as the sky darkened, giving Celeste a creepy feeling, until she saw a glow at the top of the path. Scuttling to catch up with Gamma, Celeste took her hand as they approached a circle of wagons. Gamma paused and yelled: "Hooo Ahhhh!" Then nudged Celeste to sidle between two wagons into a clearing where a roaring bonfire danced.

"*Hooo Ahhhh!*" A gypsy woman answered, whirling her skirt as she came toward the sweet-faced adolescent and white-haired woman entering their camp. Nodding respectfully to the older woman, the gypsy grasped the girl's chin, pulling her close and peering into her face before exclaiming: "Ahh, yes. *The cut of jaw, the lifted cheeks, the kind-filled eyes – is Vojen clan.*"

As twilight faded, the gypsy led Celeste and Gamma to the campfire, pointing to a log for them to sit on, then clapped the air, bangles clashing down both arms, bidding her family to join them. "*Brothers, sisters, come quick! As prophesized by our great Madre' – God rest her soul – to our hearth the young one has arrived. From across the ocean she come, to learn her spirit roots. Behold – the beauty of Madre's vision – sixteen years from birth.*"

The gypsy gazed at Celeste and then Gamma. Two peas in a pod, sharing a pale, round shape with high, ruddy cheeks and liquid blue eyes, one skin smooth and luminous, the other softly folded and powdered bright. As long shadows closed out the forest, the gypsy knelt, snatching a handful of dirt and raising it to the darkened sky. "*Oghma, Celtic God of Wisdom, tonight I beseech you: Silver my lips with your gift of words that I might persuade this young heart to hear and feel the story of her kin, upon whose great land we now sit.*"

Flinging open her hand, she slashed dirt into the fire, where it spit and snapped, doubling the flames' height. Startled, Celeste jumped in her seat, spontaneously clapping until Gamma gently squeezed her hands quiet. Turning their attention back to the gypsy, they saw her standing alongside the fire, her arms lifted high, pointing long bony fingers as she spoke. "*Is story of long ago, before the rise of Greece or fall of Rome. Before the birth of Mohammed, Buddha or Christ. Before words were written or candles lit the night. Of a time after the icy north's fingers withdrew their grip and left upon this land a magic dust.*"

With her lithe body in colorful garb, only gray streaks in the gypsy's raven hair gave any hint of her age. Prowling the campfire with pursed lips, she arched a bushy eyebrow at Celeste. "*And south from here, in the land between rivers, this icy dust made a valley fertile. A hearty loam with minerals that proffered many crops: wheat, barley, sesame and flax. When news of this abundance spread, to that basin many tribes flocked for the promise of fruit and bread. To Mesopotamia the masses flew, and among them a noble group: the people of your ancient heart – the Celtic tribe of Boii.*"

A flash of recognition crossed Celeste's face as she looked to Gamma, who nodded and closed her eyes.

Spinning around the fire, her bangles tinging furiously, the gypsy suddenly dropped onto the log beside her startled young visitor. "*Your people, the Boii, journeyed to find a home to live in harmony. To grow crops and raise families and honor the divine Goddess from whom all goodness flowed.*"

Standing in the shadowy edge of the campfire, a younger gypsy girl swayed, with a ruddy-faced baby on her hip. With narrowed eyes and pouting lips she scowled at her mother's embellished delivery of the old Bohemian tale.

"*Like many people of the time, the Boii were in need of new earth to call their own. Roaming south to east to north to west, with every sense awake, they watched for signs of what direction they should take.*"

"What kind of signs?" Celeste interrupted in a clear voice.

Gamma's eyes flew open as the gypsy replied.

"Oh, there are many kinds. Signs crawl below and fly above. A whispering breeze on the back of your knees. A fallen tree blocking your way. A prickle of skin when someone walks by, or a burning ear at the sound of a lie. Everywhere signs are waiting to be seen or heard or felt. Signs of change, signs of comfort, signs to snap alert. A tall, white bird standing in the creek told us of your birth long before your grandmother's letter reached our hearth."

The baby's sudden cry turned the older gypsy toward the girl, visible by the fire's glow, her eyes seething and defiant. With a flip of her hand, the older gypsy dismissed her daughter and fussing grandchild and returned her attention to their guests around the fire.

"Following the signs, the Boii were led; first to that Mesopotamian fertile basin between the Rivers Tigris and Euphrates. But instead of harmony and health, the Boii found a valley distressed. Crowded with camps and quickly sprouting cities, bloated with people shouting in strange tongues and with scheming kings, demanding their will be done. Under such confines, the Celtic spirit withers, so the Boii moved on. To the north, along mountains they climbed, then west across vast open steppes until at last they come to this grassy plain, flanked by rivers and mountain forests. Only then did they feel the 'Ahhh' in their breast, confirming the land where their hearts could rest."

Celeste interrupted once again. "Excuse me, but how could they know?"

"Know what?" The gypsy asked sharply.

"Their heart's call?" Celeste asked, her rounded eyes sincere.

With chin in hand, the gypsy looked over the girl's head into the eyes of Gamma, who smiled benignly, lifting her eyebrows in return. The gypsy shrugged, but felt a brief quiver in her chest. *"Is simple. In each heart lies the code for what your spirit seeks."*

Celeste sat up taller, slightly raising her hand. "But what does it sound like?"

The gypsy grunted as she rose from the log, crashing one bangled arm against the other. *"No single sound, but to all – it feel the same. In here –"* The gypsy tapped her chest as her voice trembled. *"Where you feel – the sound of Yes."*

Around the campfire, the other gypsies stomped in agreement as Celeste smiled weakly, glancing across the weathered faces.

With outstretched arms the gypsy whirled. *"And here is where the Boii heard 'Yes.' Among the seven hills of Prague and along the River Vltava, they made their home and found their truth and freedom to raise children and grow crops and work their crafts, sharing the secret of living from the heart – for two thousand years, or more."*

A distant howling in the woods sent a shiver up Celeste's back, but she would not unlock her eyes from the gypsy's.

"Artisans and honest traders, the Boii were known for vivid colored threads and joyous carvings in stone, bone and metal crafts of copper, iron, tin and bronze. But for one gift the Boii were most renowned: Masters of the Story Told.

All at the campfire was very still as the gypsy spoke, save the cackling flames and wandering smoke. *"A skill so great, their stories traveled well beyond these hills, on the lips of travelers to lands far away, and scribed on papyrus by ancient Greek scholars."*

Celeste's eyes followed the gypsy pacing around the campfire three times, then standing still, looking to the sky. In a loud whisper, Celeste dared to ask: "Then why did they leave?"

Without moving a hair, the gypsy replied: *"Jealousy. Envy. Greed. Man's worst enemies."* She glared at the girl for a moment before softening. *"Fifty years before the Christ was born, a sulking unrest crept across these lands with swords, battles and bloodshed by marauding barbarians, hired by Caesar to vacate the land. Feeling the discontented winds, the Boii built fortified walls for protection, but was not enough against a sudden assault by warriors who savagely killed every Boii they could find. Those who survived scattered west and south, toward France, Spain and Italy and perhaps farther still. But it is said, on this land, a handful remained, tucked safely away until quiet returned."*

Sitting taller, Gamma pushed back her shoulders and raised her head, eyes dancing with pride. Celeste looked at her and quietly mouthed: "Us?" Gamma nodded as the gypsy strutted around the campfire.

"As quickly as they came, the barbarians left, and save the pocket of Boii safe in these northern forests, the rest of the land lay fallow for many years until, from the east came the Slavic clans, who embraced the remaining Boii and lived peacefully alongside."

The gypsy slowed her pace, stopping in front of Gamma and Celeste. *"Through it all, the Bohemian spirit thrived, and in 600 A.D., when the Bohemian-Slavic mix rose to claim this land as their own, they named it Bohemia – Home of the Boii – and thus it remained, no matter what kingdom rose or fell, for thirteen hundred years, until … until …"*

"After war, was no more," Gamma spoke in an icy voice.

Roiling her hands in pained discomfort, the gypsy silently invoked the smoky fire and wind to wash from her heart the final, soothing words. *"Yes, is so. Our Bohemia is forever gone but not the Bohemian Heart. For in* these trees and soil the bohemian spirit still soars, passed by blood from grand-mother to son to daughter and further still to children soon begotten. And with its people flung across the world, the Bohemian spirit thrives in distant lands, through all those who seek truth in the wisdom of their heart." The gypsy abruptly turned to address her tribe, while pointing to Celeste. "And from the loins of this Vojen girl, a great Bohemian spirit will rise and travel forth, teaching many more the true wisdom that lies within each chest."

Suddenly exhausted, the gypsy twirled three times, clapped her hands and ended the story. Without another word, she clasped Gamma's and Celeste's hands and escorted them to the camp's edge, where she stroked Celeste's hair and kissed her forehead. Then gazing deeply into Gamma's eyes, she raised her arm and shook her many copper bracelets before selecting six and offered them to her. As the bracelets exchanged hands, the Gypsy murmured something to Gamma that Celeste could not hear, and with a final nod, she abruptly left, leaving her honored guests to be guided home under her brother's safe care.

The old gypsy slowly climbed her wagon's steps and pushed open the door, where she found her sullen daughter sprawled on the bed with her baby suckling her breast. Swiftly the gypsy grabbed the girl's arm and hissed. "Daughter, you are disgraced by your tantrum tonight. The campfire is now yours to tell the nightly tale, but this night was my destiny and right, prophesied by my mother two decades prior. To tell the Bohemian Tale you so despise because of the Bohemian man who gave you that child. Now, you too are forever tied to Bohemian blood and one day, mark my words, it is you who must do what I did tonight: to tell the tale to the last child of our young visitor. Yet you, so hateful of all things Boii, will likely detest her on sight. But caution what I say and be wiser than today, when that true Bohemian arrives – in forty years time."

4 Vojen Village

August 1930

As the early morning light crept through the small, leaded window-panes, Celeste awoke and bolted upright, startled and confused by the carved, wooden creatures rising from the ornate footboard. This was not her bed, nor did her room have rough-hewn beams overhead. As panic fingered her throat, she heard the smothered snore under the covers, the lullaby she'd slept to since birth, and slid back down, drawing the feather comforter to her chin, sighing. This was her grandmother's childhood home, one of a dozen thatch-roofed cottages clustered along a ridge in the Bohemian Forest, thousands of miles from her whitewashed Connecticut bedroom.

In the quiet, Celeste studied the thick veins of lead separating the small panes of wavy glass and the speckled plaster on the walls under the sloping eaves. She counted the dark, uneven beams across the ceiling and felt centuries of stories seeping from every crack and crevice. How many generations of her kin had slept beneath them? Did Gamma say the 14th Century, or was that something else? Everything she'd seen on this trip was so old she'd begun to lose track. But it didn't matter; the stories from all the years hugged her like soft, goatskin gloves.

Dozing off, her thoughts flashed to the gypsy fire, recalling the rolling, colorful skirts, clattering bracelets and clapping hands. She could still smell smoke lingering in her hair and hear the gypsy's lilting voice singing something about "the Vojen girl." *Who was that*, Celeste wondered? Her name was Howe.

Several snorts and sneezes erupted next to her. "Celeste?" Gamma muttered, emerging from the blankets. Clasping her grandmother's flailing hand, Celeste helped her sit up, fluffing the pillows behind her. "Good Morning Gamma! Sleep well?"

"Mmgh. Smoke in my nose. Water, please."

Celeste poured a glass from the pitcher on her side table and watched Gamma drink it down by small sips. "Good now." Gamma handed back the glass. "And you? How you sleep after such foretelling?"

Celeste shook her head, "Foretelling?"

"What gypsy say. Your fate."

"What do you mean? She talked of a Vojen girl, but I'm a Howe, like you."

Gamma shook her head. "Howe I marry, but still Vojen, as you, too." Pushing herself up to lean on the headboard, she saw Celeste's doubtful expression. "Biology? Remember what your father teach you of the chromosomes? Father gives the X or Y for the child's sex, but mother always X? So every child has mother memories. To your papa I give Vojen memories, and he to you. And to your children, you pass the same. Is how Vojens of Bohemia continue, no matter what name is last."

Celeste's eyes crinkled. "So the gypsy spoke of *my* children?"

Gamma touched the six copper bracelets on her arm. "All six."

"For certain?" Celeste asked, afraid to touch the bracelets.

Gamma shrugged. "Nothing certain. Gypsy see, but is yours to choose, or not."

Celeste fell silent, imagining six runny noses, twelve booted feet, and a dozen mittens for her to fetch and mend. It did not feel sweet.

As if reading her mind, Gamma patted her hand. "Is not just chores, *dítě*. Think of stories you have when old like me!"

"Is that why you love this place so much? The stories?" Celeste asked, looking at the carved wardrobes and burled bedding chest.

"Mmmm," Gamma patted the covers to draw her close. As Celeste snuggled, Gamma stroked her hair. "With grandparents, aunts, uncles, cousins … so many stories since time of Boii."

"Really, Gamma?" Celeste interrupted. "Before Christ?"

"Long before."

"But Gamma, why didn't they fight the warriors instead of running away?"

"They not live all together. There were many villages along Vltava River. But at river Danube, where Valtava joins, is biggest settlement; where warriors first strike. Then word come up river …"

"How did it come?"

"By running or on horse."

"To get help?"

"No, to warn. The Boii not fight. They hide or run, hoping to keep alive."

"But how did … you, the Vojens, end up staying here?"

"Maybe we just stubborn," Gamma said with a wink. "Or maybe someone sick or maybe the mama with child and could not run far. So they hide until birth, and by then, warriors gone. So we stay and build new home – far from river bank."

Celeste silently counted in her head. "Nineteen hundred years ago?"

Gamma nodded.

"But how can you *know* it's true? That Vojens are descendents of Boii Celts?"

"Ah. Story say my great, great, great grandfather dig in caves near here, high in hills, and find many things: fossils, pots, carved bones. But best thing he find make everyone believe: old silver coin. A Boii coin, with carved horse, made 75 years before Christ born."

Celeste shook her head "They had money?"

"Everything, Celeste. Everything to make life good: food, art, trade. Maybe is why warriors came. Maybe they not like Boii happiness. So they came and kill, but soon leave and we still here, on river and hill."

"Was it like that for you, Gamma? Growing up here?"

"Oh yah! Very happy. From everyone I learn good gifts." Gamma patted the comforter. "But enough talk now. Is time to see and do. Up! Up!"

Scrambling out of bed, Celeste reached for her clothes, neatly folded on a chair.

"No. Today we dress Bohemian," Gamma said, opening the chest at the foot of the bed and pulling out long skirts of many colored fabrics. "One for you and one for me and a kerchief for your hair, so it don't get full of hay from working farm."

"Working farm?"

"Yah, today your hands learn. Take these boots. City shoes can't muck stalls."

"Muck stalls?" Celeste hoped Gamma was kidding as she changed into a long, full skirt and white cotton top. By the time they entered the kitchen, everyone was gone, but a plate of hard-cooked eggs, toast and bacon waited for them, along with a pitcher of cool milk. Celeste poured herself a glass and took a big swig.

"Augh!" She gagged. "It's spoiled!"

"Ha-ha-ha-ha. Not spoiled. Is goat's milk!"

Celeste swished her mouth with water. "Awful."

"They don't care, so long you don't squeeze teats too hard."

"What?"

"When you milk them. Come, eat up, chores we have."

For the next five days, Celeste ran around the farm learning everything she could. Milking goats and cows, cleaning stalls, tossing pitchforks of hay from the top of the barn to the animals below, hiking to the pasture with the goats and learning the names of all the trees and flowers along the way. She practiced the Czech language with her cousins as best she could because they didn't understand her English, and they laughed at her bumbling pronunciation. Once, she spied the gypsy girl she'd seen at the campfire, on the far side of the pasture, and she ran to say hello, but the girl disappeared into the woods. Each afternoon, with trembling arms from carrying wood and pails of milk to the house, she rolled up her sleeves and cooked alongside Gamma for several hours, roasting chickens and lambs and potatoes and funny looking roots she'd never seen before.

"Kohlrabi and rutabaga," Gamma said, then sent her scuttling to collect watercress from the stream.

Celeste loved how all the food they needed grew under their feet, and she adored the warmth of a newly laid egg in her hand. She even came to like the taste of goat's milk, squirted directly into her mouth from a teat. One cousin showed her how to sling a stone and another how to stitch lace. She thought she might faint when they first set her on a horse without a saddle. "Hold with your legs" they shouted, slapping the horse's haunches as she instinctively grabbed its mane and held tight, yelping as it cantered across the field. And every night, before she fell into an exhausted sleep, unlike any she'd experienced at home, she'd listen to someone tell a story about life or dreams or history. Even though she couldn't understand what they were saying, she liked the way they told it, particularly the elders, who were animated in voice and body as they spoke the tale. But when she was asked to tell a story, she always declined, afraid she had nothing interesting to say.

"Tell them about our town" Gamma suggested one night.

Celeste's head dropped. "It's not nearly as lovely as this."

While it was too early to shear the sheep, one of the aunts taught her how to spin and card wool. An uncle showed her how to swing a scythe to cut the grass and told her she had such a good arm he'd gladly keep her on to cut the wheat. It made her more proud than any good grade she'd earned in school.

"Tinka's my favorite," Celeste confided to Gamma, snuggling in bed on their last night. "She's always so kind to me, and I like how she sings to the goats, throaty and sweet. Do you think we can come back here again next summer? There's so much more I want to learn."

No words could have been sweeter to Gamma as sleep kissed their eyelids.

The next morning, Celeste did not want to get up so fast. She wanted to savor every second, every image, and every sound her body could absorb. "Gamma, growing up here, what did you like best?"

Rolling over, Gamma looked at Celeste's face, tinged with sadness. "The same as you: learning new things."

"What were your favorites?"

Gamma didn't stop to think. "When my brother Yazi teach me slingshot."

"I know how to do that now, too!"

"Yah, and then bow and arrow, to keep goats safe."

Celeste's eyebrows shot up, remembering the pillow with the arrow and heart. She pushed herself up. "Gamma, on our first day, I saw a story pillow, one I'd never seen before, with a golden arrow piercing a crying green heart, and I've been wondering what it meant."

For an instant, Gamma froze, then drew her lower lip under her teeth. "Where you see this?" The sharpness in her voice surprised Celeste.

"On the window seat in the kitchen, with all your other pillows, on the first day. But when I looked for it again, it was gone. Did you make it?"

Gamma shuddered, feeling a chill in the warm room. "I'm ... I'm ... can't say." She continued haltingly. "Maybe some time ago, but ... unless I see, don't know." Her mind raced. How could it be? That pillow was to be destroyed 20 years ago. Her sister swore she'd burn it after they agreed both had cried enough and nothing more could be said to erase the sorrow and shame of the mistake. After her sister died, she'd thought no more about the pillow – yet now it comes again. For why? By who? Gamma wanted answers, but not to tell Celeste. The girl did not need to know about this. Not now, when everything was good and fresh. Not knowing what to do, Gamma changed the subject.

"Do you know Auntie Mae taught me sewing? She want I be a dress-maker in Prague and escape the farm she could not."

"But why would anyone want to leave?"

Gamma shrugged uncomfortably. "Farm not for everyone. Some like city life."

"Then why didn't she go to the city?"

"Because when young, she too afraid, and then she marry and babies come and was too late. But she help everyone with wild hearts and itchy feet to find contentment outside here, wherever it may be."

Celeste sighed, flopping on a pillow. "I wish I could stay here all my life."

"Yah? What you like so much?" Gamma asked, relieved by the diversion.

Looking around the room, Celeste lifted her arms, trying to embrace it all. "I don't know. It just seems there is so much more laughter here than in Gladdenbury." She giggled. "I never noticed that before: Glad-en-bury, where they bury all the gladness?" Rolling over, Celeste continued laughing as Gamma patted her back.

"A good, simple life, yah. Not so much want."

Celeste looked up. "How do you mean, not so much want?"

Gamma opened her mouth, then shut it. This was the crux of her discord with Myrtle, and the town, for that matter. She didn't wish to put Celeste at odds with her mother; but the girl was nearly grown and would have to make her own decisions soon. Plus she had vowed to answer any question asked. "In Bohemia, needs are few. Good food. Soft bed. Strong work. Good eyes and ears to hear our heart's call and path. But in Connecticut, and many places, seems not enough. So much want for things outside ourselves. Things for flattery and social ... how you say? Status? Things to put on show. Make me weary."

"But Gamma, what about all our nice things? The rugs and crystal and china and furniture Grandfather bought you? Those aren't bad, are they?"

"Not by themselves. My husband choose gifts to honor life's beauty. Treasures we share, filled with good memory. But not for showing off. Not for outside admiration. Understand?"

Before Celeste could reply, the door jolted open, revealing a stout young woman carrying a tray with coffee and toast. *"Dobré rano, teto Bertro a sestřěnice Celeste."*

"Good morning, Cousin Maya." Celeste replied.

"*Děkuji,*" Gamma thanked her great niece as she placed the tray on the blanket chest. "Very kind. Tell your mother we soon be down. Much to see in Prague before the night train."

Maya closed the door as Celeste poured the coffee, adding sugar and cream.

"I didn't know Maya understood English."

Gamma laughed. "She never let on, eh? Some girls hide smarts to not scare off marriage partner. But Maya is just quiet. She know several languages and has big dream for life."

With bright eyes Celeste nodded, chewing a corner of crusty bread slathered with butter and a tart, red jam she'd come to love, thinking how some old-country ways were still the same in her life, too.

In quick order they ate, bathed, dressed in their city clothes and rapidly packed their trunk and carpet bags. After three weeks of travel, it was their only day to enjoy Prague before catching the overnight train to Port Le Havre, where their ship departed tomorrow. With tears in her eyes Celeste bear-hugged and kissed her newfound relatives in their ancient village, then climbed into the rattling farm truck with cousin Maya at the wheel. Gamma spoke very little as they drove to the city's train depot, where they would store their luggage until departure. At the station, Celeste supervised the storage while Gamma said goodbye to Maya.

Holding Maya close, Gamma kissed her hair before pulling back to look hard in her eyes. "Maya," she said gravely. "Truth I must know. Did Lidia put crying pillow for Celeste to see?"

Maya's mouth dropped open as she slowly shook her head.

"So, not burned? As my sister promise?" Gamma pushed on Maya's knowledge even though she had been very young when the promise was made. But in their small village, secrets were hard to keep, and everyone knew the story. Lidia had seen to that.

Nodding, Maya answered haltingly. "Gramma Lidia kept the pillow. She promised to burn it as great grandmamma asked, but she did not. I … haven't seen it … in a long time. I give my word."

Gamma looked at her sharply, searching for truth in every expression on her face and body. Satisfied, she squeezed Maya's hands. "God willing, is gone for good. But if you see it, burn it and send me the ashes." She then slipped a small envelope into Maya's pocket. "For your help this week. Buy new dress, or books, whatever you like – and remember me."

Maya hugged Gamma, and the two clung to each other for a long time.

Having returned before they finished, Celeste stood at a respectful distance, examining the lace gloves Maya's mother had made for her. She'd never seen such delicate yet strong stitches. Maya called to Celeste as she climbed into the truck and saluted before turning the wheel and driving off. Gamma waved her hankie until she could no longer see any glimpse of the taillights. Patting her eyes dry, she pointed to the horse-and-buggy stand.

"Old Town Square via Wenceslas," Gamma ordered the horse squire.

"To the Astronomical Clock and Rathaus Town Hall," Celeste gleefully added. As the horse clopped along the wide avenue, Celeste consulted her map. "Charles Bridge is your favorite, right?" she asked.

"Yah," Gamma said, trying to brush aside her jumbled feelings and resume her role as travel guide. "King Charles the Fourth build it, in 14th Century."

"That's where you'd sneak off with Uncle Yazi on market days, right?" Celeste asked, but Gamma did not answer. The sway of the carriage overwhelmed her with memories; returning to the 1860's in the back of her father's wagon on their monthly trip to Prague market to sell their extra vegetables, goat cheese and woven goods. She was only eight on her first trip because most of her brothers and sisters were married and busy with their own households. Only brother Yazi, six years older, still lived at home with her. He was charged with teaching her the business of selling and buying, but he'd occasionally slip away to meet friends in other parts of the city and take her along. It was a heavenly time in her life, until she was ten and Yazi hopped a boat for Germany and all the world's ports. Even though he'd talked about becoming a sailor for as long as she could remember, it broke her heart when he actually left, and the very next market day, she ran off, finding her way to Charles Bridge, a massive structure lined with scary statues of saints and jammed with people strolling and selling wares. With blurred eyes she pushed her way through the crowd, past stalls and rank smells, to the middle of the bridge, where she leaned far over its rough, thick stone wall and wept into the river, calling Yazi's name.

"Gamma?" Worry tinged Celeste's voice.

Opening her eyes, Gamma smiled weakly. Some hurts never heal no matter how time passes. "Yah, to Charles Bridge. But enough; tell me, you remember Astronomical Clock?"

In perfect form, Celeste recited the mechanical marvel of the 15th Century. "Not only does it tell time but shows the position of the earth, sun, moon, signs of the zodiac, time of sunrise and sunset and the day, week and month of the year. Oh, and the twelve apostles come out each hour. What do they do? Just zip around the clock?"

"Run fast before reaper bangs bell and cock's wings flap and hour chimes." Gamma said, tapping the map on Celeste's lap. "Now look up. See my grand city with your own eyes."

How much different it was from London and Paris, Celeste noted. London was gray and dour compared to Paris' white-skirted style. But Prague was something much more. Like a fancy party dress with buildings washed in blues, pinks and tans, each donned with a red-tile hat. And singing a lovely, happy tune with wide avenues and curvy side streets and balconies dripping with pots of flowers and streaming ivy. Prague was a feast-ladened table compared to the butler's pantry of London and the dessert tray of Paris.

Arriving at Old Town Square, Celeste's head spun back and forth across the wide plaza thronged with sellers' stalls and townsfolk. Soon, her neck ached, craning up the block stone walls and spiky spires of Tyn Cathedral. But her greatest surprise was seeing herself in the faces of strangers walking by, mirroring her lips, eyes, cheekbones and chin. At home, her rounded features looked odd among her sharp-faced Connecticut neighbors, but in Prague she felt a cozy relationship with nearly everyone.

In one corner of the square, they found a man with deeply worn, cracked hands selling beautiful inlaid wood bracelets. Gamma bought three. Tucked in a doorway they found an old woman dressed in rags with a basket of ornate, batiked eggs. After a long conversation, Gamma bought the lot, basket included. The woman cried, patting Gamma's hand before tucking the money deep into her skirt pocket and scurrying across the plaza.

"Imagine," Gamma said, examining the eggs' intricate designs. "Four months to make these Pysanky eggs, to pay her grandson's schooling."

Wandering from cart to cart perusing the vegetables, breads, bedding and fineries, Celeste lingered over purses and crystal jewelry before selecting a few souvenirs. In the middle of the plaza, in front of the looming statue of national hero Jan Hus, a man stood on a box orating passionately to a small crowd. As hard as she tried to understand what he was shouting, Celeste caught only a word or two, unable to comprehend his passionate message.

As the sun rose higher, they climbed the Town Hall tower for a full view of Prague. Celeste laughed at the ant-sized people in the square below and marveled at the stretch of red roof tiles. "See the spires over there?" Gamma pointed across the Vltava River. "Is Prague Castle; where I most want to go as a child."

"Why didn't you?"

"We were farmers, Celeste. Only rich and powerful visit castles. But," she added wistfully, "once a year doors opened for a ball in Spanish Hall."

"So why didn't you go then?" Celeste asked simply.

Gamma sighed. How could she explain to a child who wanted for nothing? Who was embraced by everyone? Who had only to speak a wish to see it granted? It was the difference between the old world and new. "At sixteen I leave Bohemia. If not, maybe one day I dance in Spanish Hall, but … not likely for poor farm girl."

It was nearly noon when they climbed down the tower steps. Celeste's sundress floated as she ran to see the Astronomical Clock. Gamma caught up just as the cock flapped its wings and the noon bells chimed.

"Just as you said!" Celeste said. "Those twelve apostles whizzed by before the skeleton came out. But why a skeleton in a clock?"

"To remember life is fleeting. One day we also be skeletons, so enjoy what we can," Gamma answered, looking at the thinning crowd and scatter of people opening lunch pails. She decided they would go to the café Kavarna Slavia, across from the National Theater, by the river where her brother used to meet his friends. "The café not built until 1881, ten years after I leave, and became most important place for news and discussion among artists and intellectuals," Gamma explained as they wove through cobbled side streets and alleys toward the river.

Entering the café, Celeste was surprised by the triple-height ceiling and wall of windows flanking the L-shaped room. Like wide-opened eyes, the tall sheets of glass framed the river, the theater across the street and the never-ending procession of passersby. Already half-past noon, the café was crowded and buzzing as they waited for a table.

Gamma amused herself by looking at the seated people: some aristocrats, some laborers, some politicians. She could tell by their cut of clothes; a good mix of young and old with quite a few students and artists. Smoke twined up to the ceiling as everyone ate, drank and talked, waving their hands in the air, tossing their heads, shaking a fist now and again. She was glad to see her people's zest for conversation was still as invigorating and substantial as their stews.

While Gamma watched the diners, Celeste explored the waiting area, drawn to a large bulletin board boasting items for sale, apartments to rent and situations wanted. Among the wall of messages, she found a large, colorful poster, glinting with gold. On it was a sketch of Prague Castle, encircled by dancing couples. Chewing the inside of her lip, she concentrated on translating its message. Then she spun on her heel, rushed to Gamma and pulled her to the poster.

"I think there's going to be a ball! At the Castle! In just a few days. *Středa:* that's Wednesday, right? Five days from today?"

Still flustered by Celeste's sudden scurry, Gamma tried to focus on the poster, studying it carefully.

Celeste could not wait for her answer. "*Pražský Hrad:* that's the castle, right?" She pointed to another word. "And *Španělský Sál:* Spanish Hall?" Celeste's voice cracked with exuberance.

Gamma placed a hand on Celeste's shoulder to calm her while fighting her own rising excitement and fluttering stomach. Slowly reading the poster again so as not to make a mistake, she translated each word aloud. "The Citizens of Prague Are Invited to a Summer Solstice Ball 8 PM Wednesday, 13 August 1930, Spanish Hall, Prague Castle." Gamma froze, afraid to move for fear the poster would disappear, like a dream upon waking. Turning to Celeste, she felt like a child at a shop window full of every delectable she craved. What a surprise to feel this way again so late in life; emotions pitching between dreamy desire and unfettered abundance. The same flush of excitement she felt when seeing Charles Dickens in a London pub and her first glimpse of New York City from the harbor and the ruddy, sweet face of her firstborn. Barely breathing, she stood stock still while Celeste saw confirmation roll across her face.

With a whoop, Celeste swung up her arms and twirled, her skirt swinging high around her knees. The café hostess looked up, frowning, and several nearby diners glanced in surprise. Grabbing her grandmother's shoulders, Celeste shivered all over, tapping her feet. "It's true then, isn't it? There is going to be a ball at Spanish Hall! Just what you've always wanted to do, and here we are, only a few days away. Oh, can we go, Gamma? May we, please? Oh don't you see we must? The ball could change everything. It must be our fate! We could take a later ship, couldn't we? Oh Gamma, can we find a way? *Can We?* Please? Say yes, oh, *please-please-please say yes!*"

5 The Howes

August 9, 1930

At the shrilling ring of the doorbell, Myrtle's hands jerked out of the wash water and nearly dropped a plate. Who could be calling? She'd made no appointments this evening. Looking out the kitchen window, she yelled to her husband, kneeling in the vegetable garden. "Martin, the doorbell's ringing."

"Well, answer it," he yelled back, without getting up.

She sniffed, giving her shoulders a shake. Of course she'd answer it. All she wanted was his speculation, a bit of chitchat. Ever since Gamma and Celeste departed for Europe three weeks ago, the house had been deadly silent. Martin seemed perfectly content reading and gardening when he wasn't at the store. But after several weeks of his terse comments: "Good morning … nice meal … love some coffee … Good night," Myrtle would have welcomed even Gamma's silly prattle. Thank goodness her girl would be home in a week.

Wiping her hands on a striped linen towel, Myrtle removed her apron, laid it on the back of a chair and primped her hair as she walked to the front hallway. Taking a deep breath, she pushed back her shoulders and pulled open the door, ready to present her most chipper self – until she saw the telegram uniform. Her face dropped flat.

"What are you doing here?" She blurted, unable to conceal her upset. Telegrams were never good news. Telegrams were for deaths and tragedies. Her mind flew through a dozen ways her daughter could be in danger or harmed in a foreign land. Oh, why had she agreed to let her go? This must be a mistake. He's come to the wrong address.

"Telegram for Mr. and Mrs. Howe," the tall, clean-cut boy announced, holding out the yellow envelope and clipboard for her signature.

"No. You can't mean us. Just a minute." Myrtle halfway shut the door and called to the back of the house. "Martin, come this instant." Her cry carried out to the garden and beyond.

Dropping his trowel, Martin huffed up the back steps, roughly pulling off his garden boots at the porch door, and called back: "What's happened?"

She came to him, her eyes wide and cheeks white, looking ghostly through the screen. "It's a telegram," she whispered hoarsely.

Martin recognized his wife's distress but he was a practical man, a hardware merchant, anchored in the nuts and bolts of things; a man who dealt with facts as they came along. He softened his voice to calm her. "Where is it? What does it say?"

"I don't know. I'm scared."

"Awfff, Myrtle, I'm standing in my stocking feet and covered with dirt. Do you want me to track through the house?"

"No."

"Then go get the telegram and bring it to me."

The young man standing on the front porch listened to the Howe's exchange. His summer job with the Hartford Telegram office had involved all sorts of reactions to his deliveries. In the wealthy homes, telegrams were a matter of course. His own mother used them as a primary means of communication, especially with her eldest son, who traveled the world on company business. It was a matter of convenience. At the Hartford Playhouse on opening night, telegrams poured in, were torn open on the spot and read aloud with joyous abandon while he waited for a signature. These well wishing messages always gave him a happy jolt, and the theater people were big tippers. But among the regular folk he'd noticed the fear a telegram could engender. More often than not, the news was good: a baby born or the time of someone's arrival or word of an important discovery from far away. He'd seen all kinds of messages this summer. It was the most interesting job he'd ever had. But he didn't like delivering bad news and wasn't sure what was in the envelope he held.

Returning to the front door, Myrtle roughly pulled it open. She was not going to let Martin show her up silly. Snatching the yellow envelope, she slit it open with her fingernail and quickly scanned the page, steeled for a plunging knife to the heart.

"What?" She yelped. "They're not coming home?"

Having brushed off his pants, Martin entered the living room.

Leaving the boy standing in the doorway, Myrtle turned to her husband. "I can't believe this. What nerve your mother has!" She grasped the paper with both hands to read aloud. "All is well. Stop. Delayed return. Stop. Attending Castle Ball Wednesday. Stop. Sailing from Antwerp Aug 16. Stop. SS Belgenland. Stop. Arrive NYC Aug 22. Stop. Archduke Stephan Hotel Prague. Final stop." Looking at her husband with reddened cheeks and angry eyes, Myrtle yelled. "WHO does SHE think she IS?!?!"

The sudden shout caused the boy to jump. Peeking around the open door he saw Mrs. Howe snapping the telegram in the air as she paced across the room.

"I gave your mother permission to take Celeste to Europe for a month. A month! Right in the middle of the social season! She promised to be back in time for the Regatta. *The Regatta! The one event* where everyone who's anyone attends and a *must* to secure an invitation to the Cotillion." Myrtle stopped and turned to her husband, nostrils flaring. "But now Celeste is going to miss it for a *ball* at *Prague Castle?* What nonsense! And besides, if anyone should take Celeste to her first *ball*, it should be her own mother. Of all the nerve! I could just scream."

Shifting nervously by the door, the boy waited for his clipboard to be signed, but the news brightened his face. This was Celeste's home, the prettiest girl in town. Not that he knew her well. He'd only seen her once or twice since returning from boarding school. But they'd actually been introduced last June at the Presbyterian Tea. Recalling her shy smile and dancing eyes, he felt warmed. "Celeste is in Prague?" he asked, unable to stop himself and ignoring the rules of protocol. His boss had repeatedly warned him to remain detached, as telegrams can cause lethal reactions. But standing on Celeste's doorstep compelled him. "My older brother's in Prague right now, too!" he offered without thinking.

Myrtle was in such a stew she didn't realize who was speaking. "I don't care if the Pope is in Prague right now!" she addressed the air. "My daughter was supposed to be home next Friday and I …want …her … home …next …Friday! Martin? Do you hear me?"

The teakettle began whistling full blast from the kitchen, and Myrtle continued her tirade unabated as she stomped down the hall. Crossing to the front door, Martin silently reached for the clipboard and signed the confirmation line. Handing it back to the boy, he studied his face. "Are you a Meaden?" he asked. There were few people in town he didn't recognize. Over three decades since opening the hardware store, he'd come to know all the families in town and the surrounding area. The Meadens were among the most prominent and their features were distinctive: strong chins, high foreheads, narrow eyes, with thick locks of black hair. A family long established in the insurance trade and excellent customers of Howe Hardware and Goods.

"Yes sir," the boy stood straighter. "Ron Meaden, sir. Pleased to meet you."

They shook hands.

"I haven't seen you at school functions. How do you know Celeste?"

"Oh, no sir. I attend St. Andrews in New Hampshire, but I met your daughter at the church Social Tea last June. We were both servers."

Martin Howe nodded, reaching into his pocket. "Well, thank you for bringing the telegram. Sorry for the fuss." He handed Ron a folded dollar bill, and the boy's eyes widened. He started to protest.

"No," Martin interrupted "For all your trouble." He winked.

Ron slid the bill into his pants pocket, touched his cap and said goodnight.

Watching the boy stride down the walkway, Martin called after him. "Ah, by the way, which brother is in Prague?"

"James, sir. The eldest."

Martin nodded, waved and closed the door.

By the time Ron arrived home that evening, supper was finished, but his mother kept a plate warm for him. Joining her son at the dining table, Estelle smoothed the tablecloth and gracefully lowered herself onto her chair at the end. She did not believe in the custom of sitting to her husband's right. Born to wealth, she assumed an equal position on all matters of her household, taking the lead on most. Ron held the back of her chair as she rustled into place, adjusting her skirt and pearls. Then he sat to her right and began to eat.

A regal woman with gentle features, Estelle savored her youngest child's gusto. There were so few days left to enjoy the mundane routine with him before he was gone again to school. She knew his future was better served by attending boarding school, but she missed him terribly. Not one of her four other sons or her daughter had been as attentive to her. Or perhaps it was she who had not been as attentive to them.

But something about Ron tripped her heartstrings, like falling in love at first sight. "Not so fast, dear," she mentioned quietly. "You'll upset your stomach. Now," she tapped the tips of her fingers together, "what happened today? Anything exciting?"

Ron's eyes glowed as he finished chewing. "Celeste Howe is in Prague."

His mother's eyebrows rose slightly. "That pretty blond girl from tea?"

"That's the one." He could see Celeste's rosy cheeks in his mind's eye. "She's there with her grandmother. They were supposed to return on Saturday, but they're staying to attend a ball at Prague Castle."

Estelle's lips pursed as she nodded. "Of Howe Hardware, hmmm." How curious to have Celeste's name come up now, just when she'd been considering the list of potential debutantes for the coming season. She knew the Howes were excellent shopkeepers, but she had overlooked their young daughter. "How old is she now?"

"Must be seventeen, like me," he replied. "She'll be a senior this fall so, geez … I wish …" His mother waited for him to complete his sentence, but he chewed in silence, knowing his wish was ungrantable.

Estelle's eyes softened as she appraised her tall son, still a bit gangly with stringy limbs, though his face was filling out. She most loved the thick fringe of lashes curling around his green eyes. Most unusual for a boy and as a baby he'd often been mistaken for a girl. "I wish you could stay home, too," Estelle answered for her son. "I ache when you are away, wondering what you do each day." Reaching over, she petted his arm. "And I long to hear your adventures first hand. But …" she pulled back, folding her hands together on the table. "Your father and brothers were well-served by attending St. Andrew's, both for Yale and business."

Ron nodded, having heard the explanation repeatedly from his parents, uncles and grandparents.

"And with your squash abilities …" His mother added before her voice trailed off, thinking of the hundreds of spirited squash matches she'd watched over the years. All of her children, even Beatrice, were mad about the game, but none was as gifted as Ron. As a pipsqueak he'd demonstrated a natural grace and unswerving deftness in smashing an unreturnable ball. Beatrice was the first to teach him and when Ron was seven and big enough to play his brothers, he beat them handily. Soon he was the undisputed champ in local tournaments. St. Andrew's, which had spawned quite a few squash champions, was the very best place for boys who loved the game. As Estelle silently mused, she saw Ron looking down at his plate, chewing small bites of pot roast with slumped shoulders.

Normally, she would correct his posture, but tonight she wanted a bit of cheer. "Let's play the game," she offered. "If you didn't have to go away to school, what would you do instead?"

Ron sat up. "Make friends with Celeste Howe."

"You like her that much from just one meeting?"

Ron nodded. "Mother, I think she's the kindest girl I've ever met."

"And what is she doing in Prague?"

"I don't know. Her grandmother sent a telegram about attending a ball and taking a later ship." Ron repeated, purposefully leaving out Mrs. Howe's upset. "Isn't James there now?"

Estelle nodded. "Do you know the Grandmother's name?"

"No, but she's Mr. Howe's mother." Of that he was sure.

Estelle nodded again. It should be easy enough to find out.

Clearing his dishes to the kitchen, Ron washed his plate and cup, setting them in the drying rack. Although his mother repeatedly told him to leave it for the day maid, he didn't like adding to Maize's work. As the only child left in the house, he had made friends with the maids, and learned a lot from them about the town and life and housekeeping things. 'The muck gets stuck,' Maize chided him one morning about dishes in the sink. Had Estelle known about these talks she would have fired her instantly. Maids may be seen but not noticed.

As it was still light outside, Ron decided to head over to the park. Sometimes he'd join a ball game or find an old friend hanging around the tennis courts or swings. Since going away to prep school, he'd found it hard keeping up with town friends. But every now and again, he'd meet one who'd introduce him to someone new. That's what he always hoped for, the chance to make new friends.

Kissing Ron's forehead before he left, Estelle went to her writing desk in the parlor. She felt a tingle inside, but wasn't sure from what. All she knew was she wanted her eldest son to come home from his world travels and settle down. Perhaps tonight's news could help that wish come true. Picking up a pen and sliding a piece of creamy white paper from her desk drawer, she sat down to compose. Once satisfied with her choice of words, she picked up the telephone at the edge of her desk and waited for the operator.

"Yes, Mrs. Meaden?" A dry voice inquired on the other end of the line.

"Hello Gertrude? Yes, Hello. I was wondering, could you tell me the name of Mr. Howe's mother? Yes, of Howe Hardware. Bertra? Ahh, Bertra Howe. Lovely. Thank you. Now, would you kindly connect me with the telegraph office?" While waiting for the connection, Estelle lightly tapped her cheek with the end of her pearled pen. "Ahh yes, hello. This is Estelle Meaden. … Ron's mother, yes. … Very well, thank you. I'd like to send a telegram. Yes. To Hotel Archduke Stephan in Prague. Yes. To Mr. James Austin Meaden II. Yes. The message is: Neighbors Bertra Howe and granddaughter Celeste attending Prague Ball. Full Stop. No, that is all. He'll know what to do. Yes, thank you." Replacing the telephone receiver, Estelle tapped her fingertips on the polished burled wood, smiling as she stared off into the cooling evening air.

6 The Ball

August 9-13, 1930

By the time they finished lunch, Gamma had agreed to stay for the Ball. Promptly leaving the café, they walked directly to her favorite hotel. "The most elegant in Prague," she told Celeste. "Was your grandfather's choice for celebrating my forty years."

As they crossed the wide boulevard of Wenceslas Square, a trail of ivy geraniums fluttering against yellow stucco lifted Celeste's eyes. Raspberry petals and dark mossy leaves entwined the iron balconies of the Hotel Archduke Stephan. Pointing a gloved finger, Celeste declared: "Those balcony rooms must be the loveliest." As the uniformed doorman tipped his hat and swept open the enormous front door, she felt puffed full of helium, ready to float away, but quickly returned to earth as she stepped into a lobby more beautiful than she could have dreamed. "Like a church," she thought, circling the room with her eyes, trying to absorb everything at once. The tall columns and archways, the ornate iron staircase railing, the scatter of demure tables and chairs, the muffled hubbub from the café and a heavenly shaft of light pouring from the atrium in the middle of the lobby, washing every floor in hues of yellow-white.

Undistracted, Gamma walked to the reception desk and pulled off her gloves. The desk clerk was turned away, slotting mail into small cubbyholes.

"*Vezmu si u vás pokoj,*" Gamma politely requested a room.

The desk clerk turned with a smile, as she had for thirty years, first as a maid and now as manager, but upon seeing Gamma, she gasped. "Oh my goodness! Mrs. Howe? Were we expecting you?"

Tilting her head, Gamma studied the woman's features, then, slowly, a smile spread across her face. After her first stay at the Archduke with her husband shortly after it opened, she'd returned many times, booking a room at least one night whenever she came home. Twenty years had passed since her last visit, but she wondered: Could this be the girl who played in the lobby all those years ago?

"Little Greta?"

"*Ano!* Yes! But as you see, not so little anymore. Oh, I wish my parents were yet alive. How they loved you! Always retelling the stories you told them, but not so well. No one as good as you in that. In their honor, let me extend my best welcome."

Across the room, standing in the center of the atrium, transfixed by the warmth bathing her upturned face, Celeste heard Gamma laugh and turned toward the desk.

Seeing the girl, Greta instantly recognized the facial similarities and drew a quick breath. "Is she your ...?"

Gamma followed her gaze and nodded.

"Ooofff! Mama would never believe!" Greta gasped, remembering how, twenty years ago, Mrs. Howe told her mother the story of her husband's and grandchild's sudden death, their move to Connecticut, her daughter-in-law's barren years and the gypsy prophecy for a baby to come. For ten-year-old Greta, the prophecy was pure fascination. "The granddaughter the gypsy foretold?" Greta said in a hush, then stopped herself, not wanting to overstep her bounds.

The animated expression on the desk clerk's face drew Celeste out of the atrium's warmth to find out what was so exciting. Passing the small tables by the window, she deliberately paid no notice to the dark-haired man who had been watching her as she examined the upper floors from the atrium's center. As she passed, bathed in golden light, she heard him whisper: "Perfect innocence," as his fingertips made circles on the white linen.

"*Dobré odpoledne!*" Celeste did her best to greet the woman behind the desk.

Greta's face burst open at Celeste's attempt to speak Czech. She extended her broad, well-worn hand over the desktop. "*Dobré odpoledne!*" she said, pumping Celeste's hand vigorously.

"Greta, I am pleased for you to meet my granddaughter, Celeste." Gamma said, squeezing Celeste's shoulder. "Greta was just a baby when first I come here."

"With Grandfather?"

"Yah! In a cradle she was, behind the desk. Imagine?"

"Oh my, yes," Greta grinned. "My parents tell me your grandparents came the first year the hotel open and how much they love the Howes, always looking forward to their return." Greta turned back to Gamma. "Papa thought you indulge me too much, told me not to be pesty, but I couldn't help myself. For me, you are the most exciting person I ever met."

"Oooffff," Gamma brushed her hand across the desktop. "You meet kings and princes here, dignitaries from all Europe. How is peasant girl most exciting?

Greta nodded harder. "Just that! You came from peasant stock, same like me, and became a great lady. Gave me hope for the same, and look! Now I am first lady manager of hotel." She fanned her arms to the grand lobby. "How far we both come from country roots."

Gamma swallowed hard, instinctively reaching for Greta's hands. Clasping both, she blinked several times to clear her eyes as they smiled deeply, sharing a silent bond of admiration and love.

Clearing her throat, Greta returned to business, her voice still rough with emotion. "So, for how long will you be with us?"

Placing her purse on the polished wood, Gamma folded her hands on top. "Until Thursday; five nights."

Greta frowned as she scanned the reservation book. "To attend the Ball?"

"Yah! We go to London tonight, but then we see … Greta, can you tell me? Why is Ball in summer? Usually in fall, no?"

Greta grinned. "Is true, but this is special, the Poet's Ball."

"Poets?" Gamma was confused.

"Prague is hosting a Poets' Conference this week. It was President Masaryk's idea, to soften the depression. He invite poets from all over the country and Europe for a *Convergence of Creativity*. And the poets make a Ball for all of our citizens, to become a Moving Poem of Prague. Quite exciting, *ne?*"

Gamma laughed, turning to Celeste. "For all my dreaming, a Poet's Ball make it more worth the wait!" Then Gamma asked with a lilt. "Greta, have you a suite available? One with a balcony overlooking the square?"

Celeste's eyes brightened and she quickly kissed her grandmother's cheek.

Eager to please her favorite guest, Greta scoured the reservation book. It would not be easy, but she would find a way.

"And the name of a good seamstress?" Gamma added.

Across the lobby, the elegantly dressed man with a wave of dark hair finished his coffee and dabbed his lips with a small white napkin. He could not take his eyes off the girl at the desk. Who might she be, he wondered? The older woman spoke fluent Czech, but their dress was decidedly not Czechoslovakian, so perhaps a foreign poet's daughter? Tucking his napkin under the saucer, he rose; admiring the young girl's hushed but attentive demeanor as the two women spoke. *She's fresh, like a spring shower with the sun shining*, he thought, then shuttered his mind to such futile idleness. Crossing the lobby with a purposeful gait, he placed a large woven key tassel on the desktop, averting his eyes from the clerk.

"Thank you," Greta smiled, slipping the key into one of many small cubbies behind her, and called after him: "Enjoy your afternoon, Mr. Meaden."

Upon hearing the name, Gamma and Celeste both swiveled, but they only caught a glimpse of the tall man striding out the door.

After settling in their suite, they began making new arrangements. Before sending a telegram home, they met with the concierge to exchange their sailing passages. It was he who suggested the Red Star Line departure from Antwerp in Belgium instead of Le Havre in France. "A much shorter train ride to Brussels," he informed them, "and more time in Prague, should you wish. For the Saturday boarding, we could arrange a hotel in Brussels on Friday. However," with a trill in his throat, he added, "Should you wish to stay a little longer, Prague now has air service to Brussels." The pride in the concierge's voice matched Celeste's squeal at the possibility of an airplane ride, but Gamma said she would have to think about it.

With the shops closed on Sunday, they spent the day sorting out their clothes for possible Ball attire. Sprawling each item in their trunk across the room, they considered every possibility: Blouses, skirts, dresses, shoes, stockings, gloves, crinolines, scarves, shawls, jewelry and hair adornments. Gamma had packed several simple evening dresses for the sailing that would serve her quite well, spruced up with the hand-embroidered shawl she'd purchased in Paris. But all of Celeste's dresses were tea length, so they would have to find her a gown.

A knock on the door ushered in their afternoon tea.

"I'll set it up on the balcony," Celeste volunteered as Gamma lifted her carpet satchel to the bed.

"OK, I be right out." Gamma said, opening her carryall for the first time since leaving the farm. Immediately, she was puzzled by the square package of brown paper and string sitting on top. Feeling its light softness, her body flushed hot. Could it be? Untying the coarse string, she unfolded the paper and gasped. She had not looked upon the Crying Green Heart pillow for thirty years, not since she'd given it to her sister in recompense for the suffering her foolishness had caused. Who would have kept this heartbreak? Who would have saved it from being burned? Why had it been set out for Celeste to see? And for what purpose was it placed in her satchel if not to torment her? Only one name came to mind: Lidia, who had never forgotten or forgiven her tragic mistake.

"Gamma, the tea's getting cold," Celeste called from the balcony.

Snapping upright, Gamma swallowed the pillow with its wrapper as her eyes swept the room for a place to hide it. Under the bed? In the wardrobe? Behind the chair? Every spot could be easily found, if not by Celeste then certainly the maid. Nothing in the room was secure. The trash shoot, she thought, and reached for the door to the hallway when Celeste called again.

"Gamma, come quick. There's a parade! Schoolgirls carrying signs and chanting poems."

"Yah, yah," Gamma replied as she scanned the room once again before stuffing the wrapped pillow behind the armoire, safe enough from discovery until she could throw it away. Joining Celeste on the balcony overlooking the square, they watched the girls in their pinafores, waving signs and chanting down the street and around the corner. Once they were out of sight, Celeste sighed. Her mind had been full of questions about the Ball all day long, and she now felt panicked.

"Who will I dance with?" She blurted. "I don't know anyone!"

Still disturbed about the pillow, Gamma half heard her and shook her head. "Balls have a magic all their own. You'll see."

But the answer did not assuage Celeste, and she whispered into her cup, "But what if no one wants to dance with me?"

Looking at her beautiful granddaughter, face white with concern, Gamma could not help but laugh – long and loud enough for the doorman to hear and look up, from three floors below.

⟡

On Monday they rose early, heading directly to Soukenická Lane, where all the dressmaking and tailor shops were clustered.

"Is where Auntie Mae want to apprentice me," Gamma said as they began wandering in and out of the shops, eyeing fashions and fingering bolts of cloth. Modeling gown after gown, Celeste endured poking, prodding and checking for fit from both Gamma and the clerks until they found the perfect dress and a seamstress for alterations.

Although ready for a nap, Celeste dutifully followed Gamma as she briskly set off down the stone street toward Cobbler's Lane, in search of dancing shoes.

"Why are all the dress shops on one street and the cobblers on another?" Celeste asked, huffing to keep up. Gamma explained the expansion of Prague in 1348 by King Charles, who solved the cramped, noisy quarters of the old city boundaries by creating a 'new city' for the artisans and craftsmen outside the city walls.

"One street for butchers, another for rope makers, another for carpenters and blacksmith and foundries and tanneries and furriers and potters and cloth weavers and shoes. Easy way to find best item at best price, no?"

Celeste only nodded as she scurried to keep up with Gamma's stride.

On Tuesday, after no luck with the local cobblers and too late to have a custom pair made, Greta recommended they travel to a shoemaker in the countryside who specialized in dancing slippers. Fortunately, he had one pair in Celeste's size. They also procured two pairs of long gloves and a crystal necklace and earring set for Celeste from a shop near the cobblers before racing back to the city for a second dress fitting.

On Wednesday, the day of the Ball, the dress was delivered late morning and the hotel arranged for a hairdresser to come to their suite in the late afternoon. While Celeste was taking a bath to soothe her nerves, she heard a knock on the door. Bolting up from the water, she cried, "That can't be the hairdresser! I'm not ready!" Listening hard, she heard the heavy oak door of their suite open and Gamma murmur but no other voice or telltale rustle of anyone's arrival. Chewing her lower lip, Celeste waited for the thunk of the door closing before yelling, "Who was it, Gamma?" Her voice echoed off the marble and porcelain fixtures in the bath.

Opening the door, Gamma held out a nosegay of white violets. "An admirer you have," she said, with a lilt in her voice.

Celeste's eyes widened as she slipped her hand out of the bubbles to hold it. "Who?" she asked, smelling the violets.

"No card, but in flower language, white violet means youthful innocence. So, perhaps your father? He is good at petal messages, like your grandfather, who sent me white tulips, for forgiveness, after every spat, even when is my fault."

Celeste recalled when Gamma taught her the language of flowers a couple of summers past. She'd laughed so hard at Gamma's stories about the conversations she'd carry on with her husband using the flower code. Then Gamma gave her a book on the subject and she'd looked up all her favorites: white zinnias for goodness, yellow zinnias for daily remembrance, weeping willows for mourning, ranunculus for radiant charm, bachelor buttons for anticipation, azaleas for abundance, peonies for healing and lavender roses for love at first sight.

"So it was Papa?" Celeste asked.

"Who else knows we here?" Gamma countered.

The hairdresser arrived at the appointed hour and wove Celeste's long tresses into a crowning braid, decorated with a scatter of small white flowers and tiny crystals and soft curling tendrils edging her neck and face. She lightly blushed and powdered Celeste's already flushed face, leaving a tin of rouge for her lips. Gamma then insisted Celeste eat a proper meal, as the night would be long and who knew if there would be anything to nibble besides heady wine and sweets. Celeste took a long time eating her noodles and stew, but Gamma paid no mind to her dawdles. When she finally finished, it was time to dress.

Celeste walked into her room an excited girl and emerged as a radiant young woman, swathed in a pale yellow silk gown, dotted with small, periwinkle stars. She glowed. Her face perfectly framed by the portrait collar wrapping her shoulders and her youthful curves hugged by the slim bodice. With a periwinkle belt cinching her waist, the skirt fell into soft, luminous folds, dancing over a light crinoline. As Celeste slid on her long white gloves, Gamma caught a glimpse of the woman beneath her girlish face.

"I love how it feels against my legs," Celeste giggled. "The silk sashays like a train." Then she insisted on walking down the three flights of stairs, enjoying the weight of her dress as it dropped behind her, step to step.

As Gamma walked out of the lift in the lobby, looking regal in her Parisian embroidered shawl, she realized she was not the only witness to

Celeste's grand descent; gliding down the stairway, head held high, one hand glazing the banister as the other held her nosegay. On the last step, Celeste paused, surveyed the crowd, nodded to Gamma, then swished across the polished floor, commanding the eye of every man and woman in the lobby.

As Gamma laid their room key on the reception desk, Greta beamed.

"Did she like the nosegay?" she asked.

"*Ano, Ano,* but from who? I find no card."

"*Vím,* no card from the florist. I check. A secret admirer, perhaps?"

"Hmmgh," Gamma murmured, not liking such an idea, and turned to see Celeste standing serenely by the door, awaiting their carriage.

Riding through the cobblestone streets, traveling past the icons of Prague's past grandeur to the methodical clop of the horse's hooves, Gamma slipped into a reverie.

Up on the hill, surrounding the castle, she could see the aristocrats' palatial homes, constructed in the 1600s and continuously remodeled in a centuries-long game of one-upsmanship. Chuckling, she realized the nobles of old were not much different from her Connecticut neighbors. She also admired the many churches they passed, home to the hearts of rich and poor alike. What spirits live in the rocky bluffs upon which Prague was built that called all freedom seeking souls? It had always been so, long before it became the seat of the Holy Roman Empire in the Gothic and Renaissance eras, and well before Queen Libuse reigned in 900 AD. Something in this soil and air drew her ancient people and kept calling for her own return. A place even mavericks could call home, doing what they believed to be right and true, despite the mighty will of the ever-changing rulers who tried to control the land and people. Where else but Prague would a brotherhood of monks risk offending the church by offering Holy Communion to the common folk in 1414? And despite its history of warring monarchs and religious battles, it was a jewel still. Over the centuries, innovation and pride poured out of its people in the creation of clocks, bridges, towers and, most of all, art – the heart of Prague's bounty. Though the art was regularly stolen at the end of countless wars, the Bohemians would simply start again, creating and collecting. In Prague, there was no end to the enjoyment and value of art, the essence of her homeland's soul.

Gamma sighed aloud to stop the chatter in her head. It was the same conversation she had every time she came, a private travelogue. As they trotted along the Charles Bridge, a chill swept across her shoulders. Looking up the hill, Gamma's heart pounded. Every window glowed around the castle walls and in the surrounding houses. The whole city was on tiptoes tonight, and she felt a rippling in her chest.

What if I hadn't left Bohemia when I did? She silently wondered. *Would I have been lucky enough to apprentice at one of the shops on Cloth Makers Lane? And still be alive on this night, tailoring another woman's gown for the Ball? Or might I have been a chambermaid at a hotel even half as nice as the Archduke and worked my way up to front desk, as did Greta? Or would my fate have remained on the farm, caring for my parents and an early death, as did all my sisters?*

It was impossible, Gamma knew, to calculate the innumerable gems bestowed upon her for having taken a chance, leaping where others hesitated. On this night, yet another precious stone was being added to her life's crown. A Ball at Prague Castle seemed more than she deserved after having already enjoyed abundant servings of life's ice cream and cake. But to share this dream with her beloved granddaughter was a joy inexpressibly complete.

Passing Loreto Church just below the castle gates, the Bohemian Hymn to Mary chimed from the steeple's glockenspiel as it had since the 17th century. At the first note, Celeste's hands flew out of her lap. Try as she had to remain calm and mature, she could hold back no more.

"Oh, Gamma, I'm going to burst! What will we do first?" she implored.

Gamma turned with quiet eyes. "I have no idea. Is new for me, too."

As the carriage rolled to a stop a dozen feet before the castle steps, waiting for other carriages to empty, Celeste craned her neck out of the carriage.

"Just a few minutes more, Miss," the driver told her.

Celeste leaned out a little farther, then suddenly pulled back, turned to Gamma and whispered, aghast, "There are clowns up ahead!"

"Clowns?" Gamma laughed. "Clowns at the castle?"

"Well," Celeste peeked out again, "men with funny hats, helping the ladies up the steps."

With a lurch, their carriage moved forward, then stopped. They had arrived. A tall man with a beard and an enormous jester's hat boldly announced their arrival to his compatriots on the steps. "Ho, HO, my fairy gentlemen! Look at the beauty here!"

He spoke so quickly in Czech that Celeste could not understand. She rose as he opened the carriage door, swept off his hat and bowed.

Extending his hand, he helped her down the carriage step, passing her to another man wearing a tall, stovepipe hat who also loudly exclaimed, "Indeed, good sir, is truth you speak! Here be the original model for such famous beauties as Helena and Aphrodite." He offered the crook of his arm to guide her up the steps.

Celeste hesitated, turning to Gamma, who was speaking with the jester. "Gamma, what are they saying?" she implored.

Gamma laughed, shooing her forward. "An ode to your beauty! Now go. Go! Up the steps! Into the hall! The poets lead our way. You are their muse, so let the adoration pour."

Celeste blinked, then giggled and waved to Gamma before clasping the poet's waiting arm. Lifting her skirt high, she climbed the wide stone steps and entered Spanish Hall, where the glint of gold and white-diamond sparkle swept away her breath and set her soul afire.

7 Ede

August 13, 1930

"Yoo hoo! Mrs. Howe, Hello. Anybody home? Hello, it's Eee-Dee."

Standing on the front porch, the tall girl balanced a stack of oversized paper on one hand while knocking with the other. The screen door rattled under her sharp raps. She peered in. Only cool, damp air greeted her. She could smell remnants of tobacco and wood polish but nothing simmering on the stove, which was odd because Mrs. Howe always started supper by three or four. Turning quickly to check the backyard, her long skirt twisted and tangled in her gangly legs. Clasping the papers with both hands, she jumped off the stoop, freeing her legs, and dashed around the house, where she found Mrs. Howe standing in the middle of the vegetable garden, holding a half-filled basket of tomatoes.

"Hey, Mrs. Howe, want some help?" Without waiting for a reply, Ede scooted up the back steps, dropped her papers on a wicker table and then leapt off the porch, landing at the garden gate. Admiring the plump tomatoes on the vine, she picked a small one and bit it in half. "Wow. *Quel delicioso*," she said. "These tomatoes are *magnifico!*"

It was just the kind of comment that made Myrtle cringe. For the dozen years she'd known the girl, she tried very hard to like her because Ede was Celeste's best friend. But her mannerisms made Myrtle uneasy. Too much like the immigrants she'd gown up with in New York City. Too much a reminder of her shanty past, and she didn't want that influence on her daughter. So when the girls had a falling out last spring and stopped seeing each other, she was relieved. But Ede wouldn't let go. Indefatigable, she kept appearing at their door, like a penny bright, with energy to burn.

"Hello, Ede." Myrtle sighed. "Has a brush seen that head of yours today?"

Finishing the tomato with a slurp, Ede laughed. "You know it has, Mrs. Howe. But this mop gets tangled the minute I walk out the door." Grabbing a fistful of thick black hair off her back, Ede twisted it into a knot that hung on the back of her head. "I can't wait 'til Celeste gets home on Friday; I've got so much to tell her." She pointed to the stack of papers on the porch. "I made her a painting. A welcome home sign! Plus, it will be perfect for her needlepoint designs. She's been badgering me to paint it forever!"

Ede's blast of personality always startled Myrtle, and the intensity seemed to increase since she'd begun teaching an art class at the local club; a development that set all the tongues a-wagging. How could a sixteen-year-old girl know enough about art to teach anyone? And an immigrant at that! Never-the-less, everyone signed up to see if the girl's talent was as good as her father's, and the initial reviews were excellent.

"Temperance, Ede." Myrtle chided. "Too much enthusiasm by the artist can dampen the client's interest." Myrtle snapped handfuls of green beans off a vine. "But I'm sorry to say, Celeste won't be home this Friday."

Panic washed across Ede's chest, instantly summoning the fear she had felt as a three-year-old crossing the ocean from Italy with her father in 1917. The war had not yet ended, but Ede and her father were desperate to be reunited with her American-born mother, who had returned home before the war began to care for her own mother and then could not return. They had jumped at the first chance to reunite with her, regardless of the danger. Ede now felt that same desperation for Celeste's return. She had been counting each lonely day since Celeste left, especially as they'd just made up after a stupid fight, their only one since meeting in dance class as five-years-olds. Nothing had ever come between them, until Celeste insisted on taking Ede's art class, even though Ede had already shown her everything she knew. It had gone alright until the student exhibition. Ede was admiring Celeste's entry when a man approached and completely ignored Celeste's work while buttering-up Ede, telling her how much he admired her father's paintings and how she had an "obvious talent," too. The exchange stunned Celeste into a sullen silence, as if she had been slapped in the face, until the man moved on. Then she turned on Ede.

"You think you're so good, miss arty pants, but you're not so special," she hissed, surprising them both. "You're just stuck up, and I don't like stuck-up girls." Flouncing away, Celeste did not look back to see Ede's face turn ashen. And that was that. Celeste stopped walking to school with Ede and eating lunch with her and took up with another group of girls for the rest of the spring. It broke Ede's heart. Having no idea why Celeste was so upset, she'd cried for a week straight. Then she began stopping by Celeste's house after school, only to have Mrs. Howe repeatedly say Celeste was busy. She'd lost not only her best friend, but her only friend. Because while Celeste was cute and popular; Ede was a tall foreigner, and stuck out with her odd dress and odder artist parents in their upright Connecticut town.

Then, just when Ede thought it was hopeless, she chanced to meet Gamma at the park, and the old woman told her of their travel plans. "Come see her off," Gamma urged, letting Ede know when they were leaving. "She'd love it more than she knows." Early on the morning of the ship's departure, Ede skipped up the street to the Howe's' house, peace offering in hand: A hand-stapled pad of sketch paper tied with a ribbon and a freshly whittled drawing pencil she'd snitched from her father's drafting table. "Sketch what you see, and I'll paint it for you," Ede whispered, slipping the package into her friend's hands. Celeste's face, icy at first, melted in unfettered joy. Without another word, the girls clung to each other until Mr. Howe insisted it was time to go. Waving 'til the car was out of sight, Ede felt certain all would be right again, once Celeste returned.

Ede shook her head to clear it and looked at Mrs. Howe with scared eyes. "What happened? Did something go wrong?" her voice wobbled.

"Did something go wrong?" Myrtle sputtered. "Well, I certainly think so, but Mr. Howe disagrees." Myrtle brushed aside a few strands of hair that escaped her tight bun, looking at the sky. "What time is it? A bit after 3?"

Ede looked up, nodding.

"Well then, at this moment I suppose Celeste is dancing at Prague Castle. For some crazy reason her grandmother decided to extend their trip to attend a ball. So they won't even set sail until Saturday and won't be home until Friday next."

With exaggerated relief, Ede's arms swung to the sky as she twirled around and around until she plopped on the porch steps. "A ball?! Oh, wow!" she exclaimed, oblivious to Myrtle's frown. "At a castle in Prague? *Quel Magnifico!*" Her head filled with visions of bejeweled women and dashing gentlemen. She'd seen such spectacles at the club, peeking through the windows when she was young and in the ballroom itself when she was old enough to be a server. She had been transfixed by the gowns and glowing lights and white gloves and flying coattails as the men whirled their ladies around the room. "OK! Then I'll paint a picture of a ball for Celeste. That will make the time zoom by."

Wiping her hands on her apron, Myrtle stepped past Ede, heading for the kitchen. "Before you go off, what about these papers?" she asked.

Ede scrambled to the porch, scooped up her artwork and followed Myrtle into the house. "A surprise for Celeste. Can I put them up in her room?"

Myrtle set her basket next to the sink. "What is it?" She did not ask out of politeness; Ede's art was a topic of interest among her friends. She might procure a valuable bit of gossip for her tea chats.

Dropping the stack on the kitchen table, Ede carefully unfolded the top flap, revealing a large painting of flowers.

"A bed of flowers," Myrtle acknowledged dryly. "Not your usual style."

"No!" Ede said, happy Mrs. Howe noticed. "Because it's for Celeste." Ede picked up each page to reveal a dozen watercolors. "I made the flowers as real as possible because that's what she likes – even though I usually paint the essence, not the reality, as papa always advises."

"Mmmm." To Myrtle, each page looked too much like the others.

"I thought since Celeste loves flowers as much as needlepointing, I'd paint your garden so maybe she'd be inspired to needlepoint a pillow of it. That way, even in winter, she'd always have her garden near."

"Very nice," Myrtle murmured.

"So can I put them in her room?"

Myrtle moved to the sink. "Go on. Mind you, don't mar the wallpaper."

Snatching up her papers, Ede banged up the stairs.

Alone, Myrtle carefully washed each vegetable, enjoying the routine of food preparation. Unlike her friends with maids to avoid the daily drudgery, Myrtle found a medicinal tonic in cooking. A time to think on the day's events and consider what she'd like to accomplish next. But Ede's presence muddled her. The girl's energy and unflagging joy brought attention to how different her own youth had been, even though they were both of immigrant parents. Though Myrtle kept her past secret from her Gladdenbury friends, she could never fully escape the memory of her family's noisy, scruffy household with more cursing and cuffing than laughter. The horror of life in the filthy New York tenements, surrounded by the stench of glue factories and turpentine distilleries, still made her shudder. As did the visceral memory of her father's rough hands and body odor, redolent of factory sweat and beer. What she'd endured she never wanted anyone to know, especially her daughter. But today, watching the light on Ede's face as she spoke of her painting, she wondered what life might have become if she, too, had something special, something more than her body and sharp wits. If she had an obvious talent like Ede's art, how much different might she and her life have been?

A thumping down the steps interrupted Myrtle's reverie.

Stomping into the kitchen, Ede wore a wide grin. Myrtle blinked, having forgotten Ede was in the house.

"Where have you been?" she asked as Ede drew a glass of water from the faucet.

"Putting up Celeste's surprise," Ede answered simply. Noticing the platter of green beans, she asked, "Can I help?"

"May I," Myrtle corrected, pushing the platter across the table.

"Oh, sorry. *May I* – I always forget. Boy, do I love the snap of fresh beans."

Ede rapidly clipped off the bean top and bottom with her fingers. Myrtle said nothing, but Ede didn't mind. She was accustomed to no response from her father as they painted together. There she'd be, jabbering away while he was lost in the color and form taking shape on his canvas. Shuffling her feet under the table, Ede felt parched for conversation, even if it was only with Mrs. Howe.

"I met a boy last week," she began.

"Mmmm?" Myrtle's eyebrows rose but her tone remained even. Celeste never spoke on such matters, even when repeatedly asked.

"At the park last Saturday. He was so nice to me – which is unusual, because boys … I mean … generally, boys aren't very comfortable around me. I guess 'cause I'm so tall, but he was tall, too, so it was alright."

Myrtle smiled. She should have this child over more often. Maybe she'd get news about her daughter, as well. "Someone new in town?" she asked sweetly.

"Yes. I mean, no. New to me, but he's lived here all his life. He goes to boarding school in New Hampshire."

"A nice boy?"

Ede smiled. "The nicest." She recalled his eyes: big and green with flecks of brown and yellow and long curly lashes, like hers. The kind every girl wishes for but boys often got. "His eyes are kind," she said. "My father taught me about eyes on the ship from Italy."

"Oh?"

"For days and days there was nothing much to do except watch the sea or other people, so Papa showed me how eyes tell more about a person than you could ever think to ask. He said they speak in a blink." Ede giggled, flapping her eyelids like wings, as her father had.

"Oh my," Myrtle scowled at her silliness.

"And for the rest of the trip we studied eyes. He told me that mean people try to hide it, opening their eyes wide to make a good impression, to look sincere," Ede demonstrated. "But if you catch them when no one's looking, their eyes narrow and dart, protecting their territory." She again showed Mrs. Howe what she meant, squinting and shifting her eyes across the kitchen. "But he said the kind ones don't do anything at all. They just stay calm and observe and you can feel their warmth, like my Nonna's wide-open arms when I'd run up the path to see her."

"Your Nonna?"

"My grandmother in Italy. Geez, I cant' believe I haven't seen her for fourteen years." Ede handed the platter of finished beans to Mrs. Howe with a wistful stare. "I was hoping Celeste could meet him before he went back to school," she confided. "But next Friday will be too late."

"Who?" Myrtle asked, flicking a match to light the gas under a pot of water.

"Ron Meaden. He lives on Front Street."

Startled, Myrtle dropped the lit match, then scuttled to stomp it out on the floor.

Surprised by her reaction, Ede asked: "Do you know them?"

Myrtle quickly struck another match and lit the gas burner with a whoosh. "Of course. They go to our church." She brusquely waved out the match, suddenly remembering it was Ron Meaden who had delivered the telegram last Saturday and hadn't he said something about his older brother being in Prague?

"Oh, well, I guess I'd better be going," Ede said, wiping her hands on a towel. "Mama will be home from work soon, and I've got to get our supper on, too. So, a week from Friday?"

Myrtle barely heard Ede. "Mmm?"

Ede rocked on the sides of her shoes. "Mrs. Howe, would it be alright if I went with Mr. Howe to pick them up at the dock?"

Vaguely hearing Ede's question, Myrtle automatically replied, wanting to be alone with her own thoughts now. "Yes, yes, fine. Now scurry on, Mr. Howe will be home soon and I've got to get his supper ready."

Without a sound, Ede slipped out the back door and skipped all the way home.

Later that night, after serving supper, washing up and tending to some mending, Myrtle took several packages of new school clothes up to Celeste's room. Since Ede's mention of Ron Meaden, she couldn't stop thinking about the possibility of Celeste bumping into his older brother, James, in Prague. She'd asked Martin about it, but he said he didn't know. How odd and strange to have the very person she'd most hoped her daughter to meet be in the same city at the same time, thousands of miles away. Maybe it was a sign, she thought, and then shook her head, unwilling to agree with Gamma in any way.

With her mind still spinning possibilities, Myrtle opened Celeste's bedroom door and jumped back. "Sweet Jesus!" she yelped, dropping her packages to the floor as a huge, shadowy form billowed on the far side of the dim room. Shaking from tip to toe, she groped for the light switch on the inside wall, flipped it and held her breath as the overhead light revealed her monster. She blinked, not believing her eyes. Hung across the bay window was a giant mural. An enormous reproduction of a flower garden – *their* flower garden, to be exact – painted to perfection. A full, life-sized replica of Gamma's well-tended beds, draped from floor to ceiling and glowing from the soft light of the gas lanterns on the street below. "Well, I never," Myrtle muttered, picking up her packages as she recalled Ede's appearance that afternoon and simultaneously wondered what other unexpected surprises might come from Celeste's delayed return.

8 *Alchemy*

August 13, 1930

Spanish Hall was a creamy white fairy's world, dripping with gold trim and long chandeliers refracting halos of golden light in the tall windows and mirrors lining each side of the grand room. Transfixed, Celeste was sure she was dreaming, until Gamma whispered: "Close mouth or get in flies." She then whistled softly. "Such elegance I never see."

Celeste giggled, "This is what majesty means, I guess! Look at the windows!" She began to raise her arm but Gamma clamped it to her side.

"No point. Just nod in direction."

Celeste nodded to the wall of deep-set, arched windows lining one side of the long room, rising forty feet high and flanked by ornate candelabras that matched the chandeliers. "And look," she nodded to the opposite wall. "The mirrors are exact replicas of the windows."

Following her granddaughter's gaze, Gamma stared into the mirrors and the swirling colors of her city: burnt gold, midnight blue, brick red, sienna orange, burnished yellow, and henna browns. "True reflection of Prague," she murmured as satins swished alongside heavy damask and boiled cottons. Where bosoms glistened with sparkled powder and lips gleamed in every shade of rouge and men in tuxedos and tailcoats or rough-hewn suits proudly led their ladies in a whirl around the room.

At the far end of the hall, a woman slipped in through a door camouflaged by the mirrored wall. Dressed in heavy silk with a rope of bejeweled gold around her neck, she paused, searching the small clusters of aristocrats and special guests until she spied a man with dark wavy hair and a strong chin. Dressed in formal tails, he stood a head taller than the group of poets surrounding him, even with their hats on. Coming up beside them, she gently placed her hand on his arm, interrupting their conversation. "You were easy to find with such height, Mr. Meaden," she spoke quietly.

James Meaden turned, bowed and brushed a soft kiss on her extended, gloved hand. "Honeysuckle?" he asked. She nodded, and with a subtle turn of her chin, summoned him away. James gestured farewell to his poet companions, offered his arm to the elegant woman and crossed the hall with her at his side. As they slipped through the crowd, each cluster turned to watch them pass, their heads close together, whispering.

By a corner window, a white-bearded man in formal military dress stood on a platform, in front of two high-backed upholstered chairs. Surveying the room, he rocked on his heels, lips curved upwards, enjoying the evening's success. As the bejeweled woman approached, his smile widened, and she ascended the platform.

"Darling, there is someone I'd like you to meet," she said quietly, kissing each cheek, then turned to the dark-haired man. "This is Mr. James Austin Meaden the Second, from the United States. His family is in the insurance business. Mr. Meaden; President Tomáš Garrigue Masaryk."

The President's clipped mustache crinkled with his smile. "*Vítáme vás*, Mr. Meaden. Welcome to Czechoslovakia."

"It's a great honor to meet you, Mr. President," James said crisply, bowing from the waist and clicking his heels.

"I'm pleased my wife could share this fine evening with a countryman," the president said, extending his hand. "What brings you to our fair city?"

"I have long admired your dedication to your country, sir. During the war, I heard you speak at Yale. I was only fourteen, but I was quite inspired by your philosophy. Then, by chance, I met your lovely wife at a mutual friend's in Belgium. When she told me about the Poets' Conference, I felt compelled to come pay homage."

The President chuckled, shaking his head. "Don't be too smitten, young man. I've done nothing another man could not, if he pays attention." Gesturing to the behatted men in the crowd, he said, "Who you should thank are the poets: Karl Teige, Vitˇezslav Nezval, Jaroslav Seifert and

František Halas. They dreamed this up. They knew what Prague needed in difficult times, and I'd have been a fool not to listen."

"Another bit of wisdom I'm grateful to receive." James again made a slight bow.

The President rocked back on his heels. "Artists have a stronger sense about society and where it's going. They feel what's coming and what's needed, better and sooner than most. Like an Eskimo smelling snow, I suppose. A smart leader pays attention to what they see and say. In my cabinet, artists sit equal to the ministers of education, military and finance because they are all threads of the fabric with which we work." Pulling on his beard, he repeated "All threads of the fabric. Now tell me, what really brings you to our fine country?"

It took only one song for the young men of Prague to spy the beautiful, unattached women gathered near the hall entrance, especially the young, lithe one. In clockwork succession, they took turns dancing with Celeste, leaving her not a moment's rest as Gamma's eyes followed her granddaughter's whirling head. As the dancers glided in waltzing circles around the floor, Gamma tracked Celeste's progression up one side of the hall, where the dignitaries and aristocrats gathered, and back down the other, where the common folk stood. Only momentarily did Gamma dare take her eyes off Celeste, to admire the President and his wife talking with a tall, familiar looking man. She didn't know why, but something about him kept drawing her attention. After watching them longer than she intended, she turned back and was unable to find Celeste among the swaying heads. Panic seized her, and everything began to blur as her eyes switched across the room. But then she heard a scrap of Celeste's laughter from near the punch bowl, and relief flooded her body. Sighing, she watched Celeste closely, as the girl wound her way across the dancing hall with raised arms, holding her nosegay and two cups of punch above her head.

As James Meaden spoke with President Masaryk about his family's business and his mission to find suitable investments, he silently calculated the valuable introductions this brief meeting would produce. He could hear his grandfather repeating his mantra: "Get to know the top chief and see how fast doors open." Meeting Charlotte Masaryk in Belgium last week had been good fortune. In his early days on the international circuit such a coincidence would have surprised him, but now such happenings were practically routine. Five years of travel had made the world small, especially among the inner circle. Looking at the powdered, painted faces of the aging matrons he was required to entertain, he silently sighed. When first embarking as a scout for his family's company investments at twenty-three, he was cocksure how the world worked and imagined himself a tireless bon vivant, wrapping up business with time to spare for glittering dalliances in Paris, Lisbon, Barcelona, Berlin, Brussels and Prague. But that naiveté soon faded, replaced by ennui at the endless social fripperies of the landed gentry. There was no escaping the grand dames who controlled the means of entry with their codes of social behavior. But entertaining these women and their marriageable daughters was getting old for James, even as he soldiered on, viewing it a necessary drill for securing access to their husbands, the men who controlled the best investments.

Thanking the President and his wife, James departed their company, returning to a circle of ladies where he obligingly laughed at their jokes and commentaries, no matter how boring or banal. In the beginning, he rather enjoyed being their object of desire. The game had its perks. Many a rebellious debutante sought a few notches on her own belt before settling down. And Europeans, he had learned, were much more comfortable with sex than were girls at home. Stateside, he'd brag to his pals about the waves of physical pleasure he enjoyed with European women, without any concern of an emotional wake the next day. For the most part, those women were equal to men in desiring a no-strings tryst. But that, too, had begun to feel like a noose; un-tethered freedom also had its price.

Itching to politely slip away to a local beer hall where the women carried no pretense, he stared in a trance above the sea of dancing heads – when he caught sight of a bobbing nosegay. A round orb of white violets wrapped with a periwinkle ribbon that jolted his memory. "Please excuse me," he said abruptly to the women surrounding him. "I must attend a request of my mother's," knowing full well they could not object to his departure for maternal obligation. Slipping around the various groups stationed at the top of the hall, James worked his way along the mirrors, keeping the floating nosegay always in sight, arriving at the exact moment Celeste reached Gamma.

◦

Negotiating her way carefully through the jostling crowd, Celeste kept one eye locked on the cups of punch in her hands, willing them not to spill.

"I didn't think I could make it, but I did," she announced, handing a cup to Gamma. Looking up, her face flushed and haloed by tendrils of curls, she found herself staring straight into a pair of narrow, black eyes on a face she somehow recognized.

"Oh, hello," she said, remembering the man from the hotel, sitting at a small table by the lobby window, watching her. A flutter rippled through her belly. Her eyes grew wider. Her apple cheeks lifted and her lips spread into a smile that walloped James like a one-two-punch.

Well practiced in social smiles, James normally could adeptly stretch his lips to perfect warmth on command, no matter what he actually felt. But the sudden rise of heat in his chest prompted an uncharacteristic, open-mouthed, toothy grin.

Turning, Gamma realized it was the same man she'd seen speaking with the President and his wife.

James made a short bow. "Why, hello Mrs. Howe. What a great pleasure to meet you." Then he turned to Celeste. "And you must be Celeste. Wow. I see where you get your beauty." It was not at all what he intended to say. He knew perfectly well how to properly introduce himself, maintaining the requisite distance. Yet a glance from two sets of identical blue eyes evaporated his manners. Snapping his heels, he returned to protocol.

"Allow me to introduce myself. I am James Austin Meaden the Second of the Gladdenbury, Connecticut Meadens, and I believe our families are neighbors." He then briefly explained about his brother's delivery of their telegram and his mother's request to look out for them.

"So you sent the nosegay?" Gamma guessed.

"Yes." James was delighted his well-placed clue had worked; no one else at the Ball was carrying a white violet nosegay. He had checked with all the florists.

"Thank you, Mr. Meaden," Celeste said. "It's lovely." She found his angular face and courtly ways immensely exciting and felt a prickling on her palms and the bottoms of her feet.

As if on cue, the orchestra struck up the opening bars of a lilting waltz. Gamma sighed on the first note and looked up, softly singing along, as did many others, filling the room with a hushed choir.

"I dreamed I dwelt in Marble Halls, with vassals and serfs at my side.
And of all assembled within those walls, I was the hope and pride."

"The Bohemian Girl opera!" James sparked.

"You know?"

"Yes! In New York ... I saw a production ... oh, ten years ago."

"The same I saw. You like?"

"Yes, very much, and here we are – in Bohemia's marble hall!" Exuberance shone on his face as he extended his hand to Celeste. "I must have the honor of dancing this song with the most beautiful woman here!" Before she could answer or even look at Gamma, James swept her off into the circling crowd; her slippers barely touching the marble floor.

Sitting on a chair against the mirrored wall, Gamma watched them bob and weave in perfect waltz form around the hall for several dances. She did not like how close he held her, nor the moony haze overtaking Celeste's expression, but there was nothing to be done except wait – for their return.

Breathing in the sweet freshness of Celeste's hair, James couldn't stop smiling. How soft she seemed; nothing yet broken or tarnished. How lithe and surefooted, each step a lighthearted laugh. Gazing into her crushed-crystal-blue eyes, he felt laughter bubble up his throat. When had he ever felt this crazed? He was refreshed, rejuvenated even, by the simple pulse of her fingers in his palm. Not even as a boy had he felt such newness. Had he grown old before growing up? Too much sophistication and not enough dreaming? He couldn't say. All he could do was wonder why, with all his experience, had he never felt such promise in a woman's arms or the trembling hush that comes before the first kiss of someone he couldn't help but love?

As James pulled her closer, Celeste drew in his scent and held her breath. How was she following his lead? Or even standing upright? If not for his firm hold on her back and the brace of his arm, she would have melted into a puddle with each sumptuous whirl. One-two-three, one-two-three, she silently counted to quiet her mind, roiling with questions and feelings. Feelings she never dared dream! Forbidden feelings, pushing against her body, tip to toe. Turning in undulating circles across the floor, the sensations cascaded one to the next: jumping beans in her belly, ripples down her back, tickling up her legs and a small silver bell tinging inside her chest that sounded like Gamma's copper bracelets. And his gaze! The black, unswerving focus of a matinee idol's unfettered desire for his leading lady. As the third waltz came to an end, she nestled closer, longing to be deeper in his arms. She lifted her face, grazing her cheek on his chin, tilting up her lips just so, hoping he'd turn his head and ...

"Celeste," James breathed in her ear as the dance was ending. "I could dance with you all night, but we must respect your grandmother."

She froze for an instant, then dropped her heels to the floor, reluctantly releasing his hand, and walked dutifully before him, returning to where Gamma patiently sat.

For the rest of the evening James stayed by their side, enchanted by Celeste's face and youthful ways; her giggle and rapt attention contrasted sharply to the cynicism of his regular escorts. Though his friends would certainly chalk up his gusto to Celeste's tender age, he didn't care. Her adoring gaze was intoxicating. Why had he never felt it before? Was it the type of girls he'd chosen, or had he lost something inside? In between his turns dancing with Celeste, he sat with Gamma, seizing the opportunity to charm her, as well.

"What brings you to Prague?" he inquired, assuming they were on the Grand Tour of European Capitals.

"Here I was born," Gamma replied, "On a farm in Bohemian Forest, where my family live for centuries. So I bring Celeste – who is only sixteen – to know her roots."

James felt chagrined by her caution and his ignorance of their background. Knowing things, in the insurance business, was his family's stock and trade. "So you actually *are* the Bohemian girl. When did you immigrate to America?"

"1870," Gamma replied tersely, not sure how much she trusted this man with her past or her granddaughter's future. Who could not notice his enchantment or Celeste's unchecked adoration?

"As a child?"

"Young man, you try to guess my age?"

"No, no, Mrs. Howe, please forgive me. It's just I know nothing about you or your family beyond the hardware store, and for that you have my sincerest apologies."

Gamma listened to a few measures of music before answering. "Sixteen. I come to America at 16. My brother, who left Bohemia to be a sailor, return with a marriage proposal for Mr. Howe, in New York City. A decision I am very glad for. But he pass, twenty-six years ago, and my son move us to your town, where Celeste born. But Bohemia is her heritage, too. Much different from your English gentry."

James instantly understood Gamma's lines of distinction. Through his years of travel he'd experienced both sides of snobbery's sharp blade. "Mrs. Howe, would it surprise you to learn our family is not all English?

In fact, I've been told my great, great grandfather emigrated from this very region."

Gamma's eyebrows lifted. "But your face …"

"I know, I know," James laughed. "Our true heritage has been whittled away by too many marriages to, shall we say, a lesser race?"

Gamma laughed at his bluntness, and James saw a chink in her protective armor.

As the Ball began to wind down, James suggested they take a walk around the castle. "Has she seen Golden Lane?" he asked before turning to Celeste and adding, "Where alchemy was once pursued?"

Celeste's exuberance cemented his plan.

As they walked slowly up the narrow lane lined with tiny houses along an ancient castle wall, James explained the history to Celeste. "These little houses were built in the 16th century, when this wall was the outside fortress of the castle, as workshops for the king's craftsmen. But years later, chemists took up residence to discover the recipe, the alchemy, for turning base metal into gold."

Celeste tried to concentrate on every word James spoke, but his words paled to the jingling in her toes. Here she was, as far from home as she could be, yet walking alongside James Meaden! The eldest son of the family her mother most admired and spoke of with great deference. The very top of society, and not just in Connecticut! While she'd met his youngest brother, Ron, last June at the church social, dancing all night with James was more than her mother would even dare dream, and she couldn't wait to tell her. Oh, what good fortune! Gamma's Ball had wrought a knight of her own. Did that make her a princess? Peering through the small, leaded windows in one of the several dozen houses, she shouted to Gamma and James as they strolled up the lane. "There's a suit of armor in here!" And added to herself: that must be a sign of good luck.

Gamma, however, felt something altogether different. Coolness surrounded her heart, raising a flag of caution as she questioned the young man's objectives. Surely he'd fulfilled his mother's obligation hours ago. "What bring you to Prague this evening?" she asked.

James's smile deepened. He felt an odd calm and ease, more than he had in years. "Business," he answered matter-of-factly.

Gamma matched his tone. "What insurance business you have here?"

"I find investments for securing the company's profits. Logging forests and mines: copper, coal, tin. Some oil and gas. Irreproducible resources with growing demand.

"At a Poets' Ball?" Gamma inquired.

"Most certainly. All the city's prominent people attend, where we meet and make plans to talk business, later."

Sure she had him, Gamma swiftly served her sword. "Why then leave them to spend your time with us?"

With a jaunty step, James slipped his hands into his trouser pockets, wondering if he should burst out in song and dance like Fred Astaire: *Taking A Chance On Love...* on Golden Lane. Looking in Celeste's direction and then directly into Gamma's eyes, he answered with a surety that surprised himself.

"Why, seeking an alchemy of my own, of course."

9 Traveling Blood

August 14-17, 1930

The morning after the Ball, Celeste and Gamma sat on their balcony dressed in their robes, eating eggs and ham with famished gusto, when Gamma announced they would stay a few days more. Celeste could not believe her ears.

"And take the airplane to Brussels?"

"Why not!" Gamma declared, saluting with her teacup.

"And see Prague with James?"

"Yah. Let's see what he knows."

As it turned out, James Meaden knew a lot, particularly about art. Even Gamma was impressed as they toured the churches, museums, side streets and boulevards, where James constantly pointed out one artistic treasure after another in architecture, stained glass, sculpture and painting. He was especially knowledgeable of the art in the many cafes they visited, waxing especially long whenever they came across Art Nouveau. The curving, asymmetrical designs, the arches and floral embellishments enraptured him. By the end of their tour, Gamma had no doubt James was cultured and savvy, but she still wasn't convinced he had any business with Celeste. She didn't like how he coddled her, attending her every whim as if she were a new toy. For when the novelty of her beauty and innocence wore off, what would they have? They were too far apart in age and experience for Celeste to be anything more than a passing fancy, and for that reason alone, Gamma kept up her defenses.

Early Saturday morning, exhausted from two days of touring, Gamma and Celeste took a taxi to Kbely Airport, the military base northeast of Prague. The expanse of field was vast and lonely, with a cluster of massive airplane hangers, a single, masonry building with an aviation tower and several frightening-looking airplanes. The scariest one looked like a blunt-nosed trolley car, with two enormous prop engines on either side, all sandwiched between parallel wings above and below the fuselage and strung together by columns and a corset of wires, zig-zagging between the wings.

"How can that fly?" Celeste asked, her eyes as round as Gamma's.

A small man in a beige jumpsuit approached them. Hearing her comment, he chuckled. "Oh there are bigger and badder planes in the fleet, but don't worry, that bus is not for you. Mrs. Howe, I presume?"

Gamma nodded.

"You're our only passengers today," he continued, nodding to Celeste. "So I came to welcome you myself. I am Josef, Joe, your pilot to Brussels. Follow me and we'll get you set up." He plopped their carpet bags on top of their trunk and rolled it across the cement tarmac. Celeste and Gamma followed in reverent silence. Walking toward the monstrous trolley-plane, their fear swelled, as it towered twelve feet over their heads. But rounding its bi-wing, their calm returned as they spied the small, silver, single wing, center engine prop plane. This, they could manage.

Two men waited by the tail to load their luggage while Joe helped Gamma and Celeste up the small steps and duck into the tiny cabin with a tight cockpit for a pilot and co-pilot, and four seats behind.

As Joe took his seat and began flight preparations, Gamma and Celeste stared out the front window, at the long cement strip in front of them. So long they could not make out its end before the looming mountains. "How to get over?" Gamma was saying out loud when the engine exploded to life, causing them to yelp, jump in their seats and grab each other's hand as the plane began rolling down the runway, faster, faster, faster than any thing could ever, should ever go! As the mountain came closer and closer, their fingernails dug in, through their gloves, gouging each other's hand when, miraculously, off they lifted, swooping up and left, neatly sideswiping the mountain as everything dropped away, looking small, then tiny as they glided through the sky. Gamma and Celeste simultaneously took a deep breath and grinned, astonished. Who could believe it? Then Joe pointed out the Bohemian Mountains up ahead and they began shouting to him, pointing out their farm, the gypsies and everything they loved. The noise of the flight was deafening and the occasional bumpiness terrifying, but the spectacular views were beyond their imagination. Their senses stunned by the changing terrain of mountains to valleys, with hundreds of snaking rivers. They loved every second of flying, except for the landing, which scared the bejesus out of them. With wind gusts wobbling the wings, their stomachs flipped several times before the plane bounced onto the runway and rolled safely to a stop. Looking at each other, they grimaced in disbelief at what they'd just survived.

After collecting their bags and spontaneously hugging Joe good bye, they endured a careening taxi ride to the docks, arriving just in time for the last boarding call of the S.S. Belgenland.

Once they were finally in their stateroom, Celeste and Gamma collapsed on their beds, shuddering with relief. After a few moments, Celeste began to laugh, deep in her belly. As her laugh quickened, she rolled onto her stomach, clutching a pillow.

Gamma chuckled. "At what you laugh?"

"You! Throwing dollar bills at the taxi driver," Celeste's words choked out as she doubled over. "'Faster! Go faster!' you kept yelling, when our hair was already blowing straight off our heads!"

Gamma's small ha-ha-ha's sped up as Celeste added, "And the pilot! Tipping the wing back and forth over the Bohemian Forest, waving to the gypsies. And then you!" she could barely speak between outbursts. "Crossing yourself and praying: As-it-began-so-may-it-end. I thought we were going to die right then and there!"

Gasping for air, Gamma held up one hand. "Me too!"

Celeste rolled off the bed to the floor, nearly shouting: "And won't Mother be *out of her mind* when she hears James Austin Meaden the Second escorted us all over Prague for two days. *Two* days! She'll be wild! It's better than she could have planned. Ever!"

The comment instantly halted Gamma's laughter. Rising from the bed, she drew the trunk latchkey from her pocket. "Enough," she said sharply. "We unpack now."

Startled by Gamma's suddenly grimness, Celeste scrambled to her feet and for the rest of the afternoon dutifully sorted clothes for the voyage, sending out several items for pressing. Finally, they washed away the traces of their mad dash to the ship and dressed for dinner.

◦

The first supper on a transatlantic journey demanded extra spit and polish, as it was an introduction to a table of strangers. While Celeste begged to wear her ball gown again, Gamma suggested she save it for the mid-week dance, and Celeste relented. Descending the grand stairwell to the first-class dining room, Gamma and Celeste matched the elegance of their surroundings. Celeste portrayed understated sophistication in an evening skirt, pin-tucked blouse, satin sash and lace collar while Gamma looked resplendent and serene with her white, upswept hair that beautifully contrasted her dark, beaded jacket.

They dined with three couples. One was from Brussels, another from Stockholm, and the third from Chicago. For most of the meal, Celeste listened as the adults talked, but finally the Swedish woman drew her into the conversation.

"What did you enjoy most in Prague?" The woman asked.

Celeste wanted to say, "Meeting my neighbor at the Ball," but refrained, knowing Gamma would not approve. "The Slavin National Cemetery," she answered.

"A cemetery? How odd. Why is that?"

"Because of its history. So many poets, artists, musicians and sculptors are buried there, and all their gravestones are unique, some designed by the artist … before they died, I mean."

The adults smiled at her youthful fumbling and nodded for her to continue.

"When I was there, I felt something I'd not felt before," Celeste said, then paused, avoiding Gamma's eye. "Like I am part of something bigger than just myself. That in my blood runs the same possibility, if not as an artist, at least to live artistically, creatively."

Their dinner companions nodded thoughtfully, impressed by Celeste's mature perception, but Gamma held her face steady, revealing no expression, knowing Celeste's words were nearly identical to those spoken by James at the cemetery the day before.

The Brussels man turned to Gamma. "I can hear, in how you speak about it, you love your country very much. Why did you leave?"

Gamma's face flushed pink, suddenly remembering she'd left the green heart pillow stuffed behind the armoire in Prague. She waved her hand as if swatting away a fly. "Oh, I've a bit of traveling blood, I guess. When my brother come home with ticket to America for me, all I thought to say was yes."

Everyone laughed in agreement about the allure of travel and tasting the world's adventures. But later that night, as Celeste strolled the deck with Gamma, she sought more.

"Gamma, weren't you scared when you left the farm?"

Surprised by her sincere tone, Gamma pointed to the deck chairs. Settling in, they stretched their legs in the balmy air and rearranged their skirts. Gamma cleared her throat. "Not scared so much, right then. First I think only of adventure, and since I would be with my brother, what need I fear?"

"So America was always your dream?"

Gamma flinched. She was not ready to tell Celeste the full truth, but she did not want to lie. "My dream? How can farm girl dream so big? I dream of Prague back then, maybe because Aunt Mae. But our storytellers often talk of travel and from that, I get some thirst, too." Gamma traced her fingers along the braided crown of her hair, remembering the rich worlds woven around the campfires of her youth. Never did she imagine she'd actually see many of the places they described. She laughed softly and reached for Celeste's hand. "In truth, the boat ride to Dresden, train to Brussels and London freighter was enough for me. After that, I could go home, satisfied. But something niggle inside, to keep me going. Not just my promise. Was a feeling, the one I know mean truth, for me. So I go. In the end: was more adventure than ever I dream." Gamma paused, hearing the sea wash against the ship's hull, just as it had on her first transatlantic voyage. "But yes, I feel scared … in the steamer for New York …when Yazi leave me to work the ship.

"What scared you?"

"Everything. The ship's bottom, many strangers, odd smells, noises. But most I feel scared when I remember was not Yazi I would marry."

"You thought you were going to marry your brother?"

"No no. But, thinking of what come next, I feel … overwhelmed. Before then, I not think of marriage, not even in my village. I guess I knew someday I marry, but until Yazi come with your grandfather's proposal, was not in my thought. Sixteen is young for marriage, don't you think?" Gamma looked up, gauging Celeste's comprehension.

Celeste couldn't remember when she didn't know about Gamma's arranged marriage, but the enormity of her blind leap of faith never fully struck her until that moment. "How did you do it, Gamma? Travel all that way to marry a stranger?"

Gamma shrugged. "Is not so different from bumping into stranger on street or in shop, no? And since my brother think him good, I say OK."

"Or at a Ball, far from home," Celeste added with hopeful eyes.

Gamma looked down at her hands. "I lucky, because my husband did think about it. He knew he want old country woman, like his mother. When he meet Yazi and hear about me, your grandfather say: I think your sister would be good for me. Apples from same barrel often taste alike." Gamma chuckled.

Celeste didn't understand. "But you're not like Uncle Yazi."

"Why you say?"

"Because Uncle Yazi is wild. He never settled down, never took a wife or raised a family. You did all those things. Some twice," Celeste said, pointing to herself.

Gamma laughed, stroking the copper bracelets on her arm. "Yah, yah, and maybe I live long enough for third time more."

Celeste's eyebrows rose in surprise, then crumpled in worry. "Gamma, I don't think I want to have children, at least not until I've had some adventures of my own." She leaned forward, hugging her knees. "I sometimes wonder if Mama ever wanted to do or be something other than a wife and mother. You got to see some of the world before you settled down. And a lot more, after, too."

Her words were music to Gamma's ears. "What you like to see?"

"Oh, I don't know. There's so much. What did you love most?"

As the tea steward rolled his cart to their deck chairs, the image of the London pub came into Gamma's mind. "Two Earl Grey, please," she ordered, waiting for his service to complete before answering Celeste. Gazing into her steaming cup, she saw the short, dark-haired man sitting in the corner of the pub, the author of those wonderful stories. "Dickens," she said aloud, as if she'd been speaking all along.

"Dickens? Where's that?"

Gamma laughed. "London," she corrected. "Where I see the book writer: Charles Dickens." And with a gust, Gamma's mind returned to the dockside pub sixty years earlier. "Was my first day in London, cold and wet. Yazi march me for hours, showing every sight. So by suppertime, I long to sit," she began the story, remembering each detail as if it happened yesterday.

Six weeks of travel had swelled her limbs to an achy stiffness. She was so tired she barely noticed the rough surroundings as they walked through a dark alley, across a rickety plank and pushed open a heavy, wooden, windowless door. Crossing the room to the bar, she didn't smell the oily air from the lamps and cooking grease. Nor notice the stench or ogle of the seamen who turned to admire her smooth brow and long curves. But the bitter aroma from the pint of dark ale served by the barmaid caused her nose to flare. Sipping gingerly, its sharp sweetness surprised her. After a few more sips, the room's heat enveloped her with sleepiness. That's when Yazi pointed out Mr. Dickens.

"Bertra, look over there. The author of the stories I sent you." He nodded to the corner table where an oldish man sat wrapped in an enormous cloak, scribbling in a small tablet. Books were a rarity in her village, so the newspaper clippings Yazi sent home via a traveling friend were as prized as rare seeds for their field. Bertra easily recalled each chapter. "Great Expectations," she replied. Through those stories, she'd begun to learn English, with her uncle teaching her each word. And she re-read the chapters incessantly until she remembered every character as the author described them and how she'd come to imagine them. How they looked, what they wore and what they might like to eat if they came for supper. Not that she would invite all of them to her table, for some were scoundrels. But to find herself sitting in the same pub with the author of that story was beyond her imaginings.

"How odd," she said to Yazi. "His characters I know by heart, but never did I think of the writer; yet there he is," slouched at a small round table in the dank, smoky pub where she stole long glances at him. And odder still, all she could think about was the quality of his cloak, a thick weave of chocolaty gray. With an eye for the drape and weave of fine fabric, she knew his was as prized as any her aunt had shown her in the Prague markets. By the fabric she deduced he must be of good wealth. Why then would he choose to visit such a hovel, she wondered? They had little choice in their evening meal, but he would certainly be welcomed in any of the elegant restaurants her brother pointed out in their day's walkabout. Yet there he sat, writing away, too clean for the rough-hewn, salty wood surrounding him. She didn't realize she was staring until Yazi hoarsely whispered:

"Looks poorly, don't he?"

"More than just poorly," Bertra raised her voice to be heard over the tavern's clamor. "Quite sickly, I say." Even across the room she could see a yellow tinge on his face. Perhaps she'd spoken too loud, for Mr. Dickens raised his eyes, looking in her direction. She ducked, faced the bar and swallowed a mouthful of bitter brew in lieu of biting her tongue. Keeping her lips close together, she asked Yazi in halting English: "Think he often come here?"

The barmaid, a round, red-faced woman of stout weight and height, heard the question as she set down their bowls of sausage and potato mash. No other patron had ever given a fig of notice to Mr. Dickens, and she was protective of his privacy, for his tips were quite handsome. "Comes once or twice weekly, drinks a few pints and makes notes in that small pad he keeps in his vest pocket," she said curtly, proud of her eye for detail. Nothing in the bar escaped her notice. The scruffy woman looked sharply into Bertra's eyes. "Speaks to no one and no one speaks to him."

Bertra nodded politely, not understanding half the barmaid's brusquely spoken words but certainly the meaning of her sharp tone and shoulder waggle. After the barmaid returned to the kitchen, Bertra snuck another glance. Peeking around her brother's shoulder, she saw Mr. Dickens hunched over his ale, looking even older, now. He had stopped writing and was staring into the bottom of his glass, appearing quite tired and not at all approachable. Not that she would have considered speaking with him. She barely knew his language. Besides, what could she possibly say to such a learned man? Still, she felt very happy and special to have seen a famous author before boarding the steamer that would take her across the world.

"And only a few months after I come to America, I read in the paper Mr. Dickens pass away. Only 57. I cry hard, as if he were my own blood," Gamma said, patting her own leg.

At the story's finish, Celeste hugged her knees tighter. "Gee whiz, Gamma. I sure hope something like that happens to me someday."

"It will," Gamma predicted. "If you take time to listen for your right way. Come now. To bed we go."

The next day was sunny and hot. Dressed in loose ship trousers and a light blouse, Celeste spent the morning playing shuffleboard with the Brussels couple. By noon she was hungry for more than lunch. Finding Gamma stretched out on a shady deck chair toward the stern, Celeste plopped alongside her and immediately asked the question that had burned in her brain all morning.

"Gamma, how do you know what's right?"

"Hmm? What?" Gamma awoke from a doze, her needlepoint canvas dropping to the deck. Celeste automatically picked it up, set it on Gamma's lap and asked again.

"Last night, you talked about listening for my right way. But how will I know, for sure, what's right?"

Still half asleep, Gamma shifted in her chair, adjusting her jacket and patting her hair. "About what?"

Celeste swiveled back and forth, fidgeting her hands. "I think you and Mama see the world differently," she blurted. "For Mama, teas and cotillions are how I should prepare for my future. I like them just fine, but I also like the things we do together, like the shelter in Hartford. I love serving the meals and sorting the clothes. It makes me feel good, inside. And the people I've met there, even though they're poor, are all so nice. Nicer than some of Mama's friends and my schoolmates." Celeste paused, still trying to understand what she was asking. It was just a feeling, and Gamma always helped sort out her feelings when she wasn't clear.

"You mean, what's right for *you?*" Gamma guessed.

Celeste's eyes brightened. "Yes! It's confusing to know sometimes. When you left the farm, how did you know it would work out alright?"

Gamma's face clouded, recalling a searing memory which never went away, no matter how much time had passed. "Was not like that ..." she began, then quickly stopped. It was not yet right to tell why she could not stay at the farm. Still too close to sweet memories just made. "I not know it would work out right, but I knew was right time to leave. So I go. From one step we can't know what turns life will take, and we can only take one step at a time. So I step to what felt most right, right then." Gamma said with a soft shrug of her shoulders.

Celeste thought about her words, chewing her inner lip, then sighed. "It's so confusing. Papa says the store is my birthright. He said just because I'm a girl doesn't mean I can't run the store. He said he wants me to have it, when I'm ready. But Mama says it's not a woman's place. She said I'm best suited to marry well and tend to my husband and children. She said I can do the most good for the world, there." Celeste looked earnestly at her grandmother, hoping for a clue as to what she should think, but Gamma's face revealed nothing. Shaking her head, she continued: "I like that idea – children and all – just as much as I like the idea of taking over Papa's store. But then I think of Ede, who loves painting with her whole heart and I wonder why I don't have something like that."

"Like what?" Gamma asked, even though she knew.

"An obvious talent." Celeste said, quoting the man's praise of Ede at the art show. "Something you love so much it haunts you."

A smile crept along Gamma's lips. "You make my heart glad."

Celeste perked up, smiling. "Why?"

"Already you know most important, even if you don't yet understand."

Celeste leaned in to hear her grandmother's soft voice.

"Life is confusing, but not so mysterious. Each of us are given different talents, interests. Ede's art talent is good, and will lead to places she must go. You have different path, but just as special. You know what I say, to Ede, to you, to anyone who ask: *pay attention to what shows up, honor what beckons and listen to your heart voice.* Is all you need to find your path, what you want most, even when you don't know it; especially when you don't know it. This, I can promise."

It was a statement Celeste had heard Gamma say many times, but she still didn't understand what it meant. She had no idea what her life should be, could be or might become. "But shouldn't I have a notion about it already? Could I have missed the clues?"

"Dítě, you only sixteen …"

"Seventeen in two weeks."

Gamma took Celeste's hand. "Yah. Seventeen and so beautiful, already a man of twenty-eight want you to mother his babies."

Celeste blushed but did not pull away, staring into Gamma's eyes.

"Yah. I see how he look at you. I only wish, not so soon."

Celeste pulled back. "But you said pay attention to what shows up and he did."

"Is true! But what about the beckon? Tell me: how you feel?" Gamma patted the air in front of Celeste's chest. "In your heart? What truth is speaking?"

Celeste blinked several times, her face mixed with hope and confusion. Dancing with James and touring the city had been a dizzy whirl. He was so kind, so gentlemanly. He treated her as a lady, not a child: asking her opinion, holding her chair, ordering from the menu. In his presence, she felt more grown up than ever before, but now she wasn't sure it was all real. Something niggled inside, creating a gap she wasn't sure how to fill. Finally she answered. "I'm not sure."

Tapping Celeste's hand, Gamma leaned back in her chair, straightened her blanket and closed her eyes: "And how could you yet? Maybe he be right, but before that come, maybe you have a little travelin' blood to satisfy." She rolled her head to look directly into Celeste's eyes. "Being not sure is good for now, I think. Wait, and trust, until is more clear."

10 Society

August 18, 1930

The Meaden's parlor buzzed with chitchat and bobbing hats as the ladies waited for the Gladdenbury Womens Social Club meeting to begin. They adored their monthly visit to the home of Estelle Meaden, who chaired not only the local chapter but also served as vice president for the regional division. Along the eastern seaboard, it was considered a most advantageous group, ranking in the same social strata as the amateur squash clubs, which the Meadens had belonged to for decades.

Standing in the middle of the room, Estelle deepened her voice, calling the meeting to order. "Ladies. Let's come together, please. Ladies?"

Fine china cups clattered in unison across the long parlor as the chatter faded.

"Very nice. Good morning everyone, and welcome."

A high-pitched chorus warmly greeted Estelle.

"I hope everyone's summer holidays were lovely. Now, I officially call this meeting to order and ask our club secretary to read the minutes from our June meeting. Margarite, would you be so kind?"

Estelle sat down in a large wingback chair as a smallish woman rose from the couch. In a soft-spoken voice, Margarite recited the notes, causing everyone's ears to strain. Under her long skirt, Estelle's right foot tapped the air impatiently. Managing the local club was not nearly as satisfying as officiating at the regional level. The neighborhood ladies, bless their hearts, were well meaning, but not as adept in decision making or taking action as were her compatriots on the board. Thank goodness her mother knew all the right people when she was young, or the ladies of Gladdenbury might have been her only social companions.

"Thank you Margarite," Estelle said without standing. "May we have a vote to accept? All in favor?" Ayes rippled through the room. "Excellent. Now, new business." Estelle opened a leather folder on her lap. "Item one: Recommendations for the debutante cotillion." As expected, a titter rose. The cotillion was their most prestigious event, and the members' sixteen-year-old daughters were automatically included. "As decided in June, we are considering non-members for the November Cotillion, and I open the floor to suggestions."

Enduring another murmur as the ladies conferred with one another, Estelle saw her front door open and Ron walk into the vestibule, wearing his telegram uniform. He waved a yellow envelope in the air. Crossing the room, she kissed his cheek and took the envelope from his hand. "You all know my son Ron?" she politely introduced him to the club as she opened the flap and extracted the message. As the ladies clamored to greet the boy, Estelle slipped on her reading glasses and scanned the telegram. With a smile, she patted Ron's shoulder, dismissing him. "Thank you, Ron. You've brought good news." Returning to her chair, she announced: "Ladies, some news from my eldest son, James, perfectly timed for the matter at hand. James has been in Prague on business. Listen." Holding up the paper she read aloud. "Appreciate Howe intro at Ball. Stop. Gamma delightful. Stop. Celeste charming. Stop. Starry night on otherwise dreary trip. Final stop." Estelle's eyebrows rose, inviting comments.

"The Hardware Store Howes?"

Estelle nodded.

"With that gorgeous daughter?"

"Oh, yes, Celeste is a delicious confection."

Estelle smiled.

"How old is she now? Sixteen? Seventeen?"

"The same age as Ron," Estelle answered. "Our first candidate?"

"Ahhh," the ladies confirmed, understanding Estelle's objective.

"But," Estelle cautioned, "I'm afraid I don't know much about the Howes, other than owners of my husband's favorite shop. Who are they, exactly? What's their background? Anyone know?"

Without another word of encouragement, Estelle sat back and absorbed a cacophony of information.

"They came from New York …"

"After the death of a baby."

"Oh, that Mr. Howe is such a gentle man. Such a pleasure to know."

"But his wife, on the other hand, what's her name?"

"Myrtle."

"Yes, Myrtle. She can be pushy now and again."

"So different from Gamma. Have you met her?"

"Who hasn't? A lady of grand proportions."

"Kind, gracious, funny. You'd think she was born with a silver spoon."

"Wasn't she?"

"Nooo. She's an immigrant. But I forget where from."

"Bohemia, I heard."

"Where?"

"It's called Czechoslovakia now. Prague."

"Has anyone else heard her stories about Bohemia?"

"Oh, yes, fantastic stories. That's why I go to their store so often!"

Talking over one another, the ladies depicted the Howe household. When Estelle had her fill, she called the meeting to order. "Well, by your reports, may I assume Celeste Howe is our first candidate for a cotillion invitation?

Everyone agreed, and Estelle wrote down Celeste's name in her notebook and asked for additional suggestions. Several hours later, having completed club business and a light lunch, the ladies dispersed, finally allowing Estelle to sit at her writing desk and compose an invitation of her own.

It was late afternoon when Ron returned home from work. Tired from the heat, he was looking forward to a swim in the creek before supper.

"Ron," his mother called from the kitchen, where she'd been giving final meal instructions to Cook. As he entered, she held out an envelope. "Before you do another thing, would you kindly deliver this to the Howes?"

With an almost imperceptible sigh, Ron nodded, slipping the scented envelope in his uniform pocket but leaving his telegram hat on the vestibule table. Walking several blocks through the tree-lined streets, he whistled, hoping he might soon see Celeste again. Wasn't she due home this week? Standing outside the Howe's screen door, Ron rang the bell. He could smell something good cooking, even with the inner door closed. Without a sound, Myrtle Howe suddenly appeared on the other side of the screen, wearing an apron and carrying a wooden spoon. Upon seeing

Ron, she snapped, "Why are you here again? Away. Go away!" She was confused. The boy was in his official jacket, but no hat. Panic grabbed her throat as she jumped to horrific conclusions about the ship her daughter was traveling on that very moment.

"Sorry, Ma'am. I didn't mean to startle you," Ron answered, quickly drawing out the pale-green envelope. "My mother asked me to deliver this."

As quickly as she'd heated up, Myrtle cooled, cracking open the screen door to take the envelope. Curtly thanking the boy, she closed the inner door behind her. With shaking knees, she sank onto the hallway chair. Laying the spoon on her lap, she carefully wiped her hands on her apron before examining the envelope. She looked at her name, written in beautiful script, and smelled its tender scent. She fingered the embossed EMM on the back flap. The pleasure in her hand was so great; she was in no hurry to open it. How many years had she coveted an invitation from Estelle Meaden? It was the penultimate accomplishment. She'd tried everything to secure one: attending the same church, supporting the same charity events, volunteering for the same committees; she'd even persuaded Martin to purchase Meaden insurance. But Myrtle had never found the key to unlock the door to that social set. Not that her own friends were undesirable; many were suitably well off. But Estelle Meaden was the gatekeeper to Gladdenbury's social constitution that determined who was who and what was what. It was no different in New York, probably even worse, because one had to be born into that circle of elegance or be preposterously rich. In New York, Myrtle knew she had no hope of entrance, even after marrying into the merchant class. But when they moved to Connecticut, she hadn't anticipated any exclusion. She assumed their ability to afford a fine house in a well-tended community would be enough to open the desired doors. But her considerable efforts had not yielded the Golden Fleece she now held: a personal note from Estelle Meaden. Carefully lifting the lightly sealed flap, Myrtle drew out the matching notepaper.

Dear Mrs. Howe,

Would you please allow my husband and me the honor of hosting a supper for you and your family upon the return of Gamma and Celeste from their Prague journey? The pleasure of their company at the Ball so delighted my son James that we are eager to express our gratitude. As you know, when far from home, a familiar face is such a treasure, and James reveled in their company. We do hope you will accept our invitation so that we, too, may celebrate their trip and share in their stories.

Sincerely,
Estelle Meaden

At Myrtle's scream, Martin bounded from the kitchen, holding a small knife he'd been using to slice some cheese. "What is it Myrtle? What's wrong?" With a flushed face he glanced around but saw nothing out of order; only Myrtle sitting in the hallway, waving a piece of paper in the air.

"Finally, after all these years ... after *all these years* ... it's happened!"

"What?" Martin's knife circled the air.

"We've been invited to the Meaden's for supper."

Martin's arms dropped to his side. "And for that you scream like a Banshee? What the devil's the matter with you, woman?"

Myrtle barely noticed Martin's dismissal. "It's the ticket, Martin. The ticket I've been working hard to secure all these years. You think it's been nothing but foolishness, my parading around town, making myself available for every cause. But I've been working. Working myself to the bone, and now it's been worth it. Don't you see? Wait 'til the girls hear."

"What in blazes are you talking about?"

"Our daughter, Martin. She's coming to marriageable age. And this ..." Myrtle stood and danced a little jig as she fanned herself with the pale-green note. "This little invitation will secure her best offers."

Martin plucked the paper from Myrtle's uplifted hand and scanned the page. "How did they know Gamma and Celeste were in Prague?" he blustered.

"Perhaps Ron told them, after delivering the telegram. Oh, don't you see it's fate? Here I was so worried about their delay and missing the Regatta, but instead ... Celeste is introduced to the very best family, thousands of miles away! Oh, I never dreamed it could work out so well."

Martin had never appreciated his wife's preoccupation with social hierarchy. He had enough on his plate getting a business up and running without bothering about tea invitations. But Myrtle's social lust never ceased gnawing on who, what and where to be seen and heard.

"I don't know," he muttered.

"About what dear?"

"All this social frippery. It's not the way I was raised."

"Nor I, but our daughter has much more opportunity."

"Rubbish!" Martin countered, slashing the air with his paring knife. "She'll not be married off to the highest bidder. *If* and *when* she chooses to marry, it'll be to whomever she damn well pleases – high or low on your social chart." With a huff, he returned to the kitchen. His youth had been simple, grounded by wood planks and hardware, enfolded by the warm arms of family and friends, where swapping stories around the stove's belly was all they needed for a fine time.

Myrtle stiffened and could not help calling after him.

"What's wrong with wanting the best possible life for our child? What's so terrible about a secure future for her?" When he didn't stop, she ran after him. "You're a fine one to talk. What have you known of hunger or cold? Or the terribleness of being discarded in the world?"

By the kitchen table, Martin turned with a sharp look. "I believe we've covered all this before." His eyes swept the room, fitted with every modern convenience any woman could desire. "What worries have you now?"

"But Martin, look what's happened. The world's gone mad since the stock market crash. So many have lost everything." She added a tremble to her voice, "We have to be vigilant. We don't know what will come next. We have to watch out for our daughter's welfare." Contrary to her husband's strong family hand on the small of his back, she had only her wits and cunning to get what she needed, and she'd used them, however she could, to secure what she thought her daughter deserved.

Martin turned away. "Celeste will always be taken care of. I've seen to that."

"But how can you be sure? No one predicted the market crash. Who knows what this depression will do? And what if something more happens? What if we lose all we have? We never expected your father and the baby to die, all at once."

The gloom that Martin worked hard to keep at bay crept over his brow. He sat down with a heavy sigh, taking a long swig of water, wishing it were rye.

Wiping her hands on her apron, Myrtle picked up the green note he'd dropped on the table and carefully folded it back into its envelope. Turning to the stove, she stirred the stew she'd prepared for supper.

They didn't speak until she cleared the dishes. With her hands in warm sudsy water, she tried again.

"Martin, remember how distraught I was, how we all were, after the baby died?"

Martin looked at his wife's stiff back, standing at the kitchen sink. "Of course."

"You've been so good to me." She felt his eyes on her. "First saving me from the dirty streets, then bringing us here, leaving all the sadness behind. It was a miracle, such kindness coming to me, so I think it must have been my fate."

Martin remembered it very well; a bubbling cauldron of change. While the move almost instantly turned around Myrtle's attitude, he faced daily terror, rebuilding a business in new territory with a wife who seemed preoccupied only with buying new hats. "Hard work squeezes out sorrow," he said, repeating the phrase his mother often used as they built the Gladdenbury store and clientele.

"Yes," Myrtle agreed. "And such hard work it's been. Not only for the business, but for our family, as well. Who would have guessed that after 10 barren years we'd be blessed with such a beautiful child? And also how you gave me the chance to become more like you – and your mother. A wife worthy of your fine standing."

Martin frowned. He didn't brook false flattery and didn't like the way Myrtle equated the value of people with their money holdings. Many of his friends had barely two dimes to rub together, especially now, but they were still the best blokes he knew. "Myrtle, I never ..."

She cut him off. "I know," she said to her reflection in the window above the sink. "You never equate the goodness of a person with their financial standing, and I agree. But not everyone has your good heart. Most people judge others by their social footing. If you hadn't been so kind when we were young, when I had nothing to offer but my admiration, I'd never have met or done or seen all I have. Your kindness raised me up."

She pursed her lips, looking over her shoulder to gauge his reaction.

His head was tilted left, staring at his folded hands.

"Like being born again." Myrtle added quietly, building to her finish. "Since coming to Connecticut, you've put no strings on me, let me become what I like, and by and large, it's all gone well." Wiping her hands on a towel, Myrtle walked to the kitchen table, entwined her fingers and looked directly at her husband's down-turned head. "But our daughter has more choices than us. Better choices. Don't you want that for her? To become what she'd like? Not like me, whose only luck was meeting you. Celeste can be so much more because she has you and me ... and Gamma, too … and all the advantages of this town. I didn't want her to go abroad this summer, but look what it brought." Myrtle nodded to the invitation on the table. "Perhaps meeting James Meaden so far from home is an indication of her fate, as well. We should at least see where it might go."

Martin looked at his wife. He knew that expression: an unbending resolve despite cautionary words. He'd tried fighting it in the past, but it only led to prolonged, cold, wars, lasting weeks on end, filled with stiff shoulders and frozen silence. Had he not been so busy re-knitting the torn fabric of their lives, he might have taught his wife the ways of his heritage, the lessons and truths instilled by his mother and grandmother; honoring the truth of one's heart despite the outside pushes and pulls of society. But now Myrtle had no ears for his ideals, and he'd long ago come to terms with whom he married, three decades prior. He also knew holding his tongue was not abandoning his beliefs; a point his mother made after a particularly long battle before Celeste was born. "Myrtle can't be ruled," Gamma had counseled. "Since birth, she's been wily. You can't fight it, but you can stand your ground, quietly and alongside." It was advice Martin knew he'd best abide this time, as well.

"You'll let Celeste make her own choices?" he cautioned.

Myrtle's lips broke into a broad smile. "Isn't that why we moved here in the first place? To give our daughter the chance for a better life, better choices than the ones we've known?"

Martin did not agree. He had quite liked his life in New York and often wondered if Celeste would have been better off growing up among trusted family and friends, even in the noisy streets of his youth. He didn't like the pretense he saw among many who populated their quiet, well-off town, and he was tired of his wife's constant clamor for more. But all of it was water under the bridge, water he could never have contained.

"Alright, we'll go." He added solemnly, holding up one finger, "But you are not to get carried away. This is Celeste's life, not yours."

Myrtle's hands flew to her cheeks as she walked around the table and kissed her husband's forehead. "Yes. Yes. Yes," she agreed, bursting to call Estelle and accept the invitation, while imagining the dress she might wear as mother of the bride on the day Celeste married into the Meaden family fortune.

11 Homecoming

August 22, 1930

Searching the S.S. Belgenland's deck, Ede finally spied Celeste. "There she is!" she yelled, pointing, when the blast of the ship's horn toppled her into Mr. Howe.

"Waaaahhhhhgggnnnn, wahng, wahng."

"Holy cow, is that ever loud!" Ede cried, clamping her ears.

Martin laughed, glad Ede had come along. Her lighthearted chatter had made the long drive to the docks pass swiftly.

"Celeste! Celeste!" Ede waved madly.

Seeing Ede, and then her father, Celeste grabbed Gamma's arm and pointed to the dock where they stood.

Jumping up and down, Ede clapped her hands, then raised them in the air, index fingers extended. With a whoop, Celeste held out her own fingers and nodded. Gamma and Martin watched the girls tap their fingers together twice, flip them over, tap twice again, then draw a big X over their hearts and finish with two taps on their lips.

"What were you doing?" Martin asked.

"Our secret sign," Ede said, repeating the hand motions. "Best-friends, for-ever, cross my heart, seal with a kiss."

When it was finally her turn to disembark, Celeste skipped down the gangplank and tumbled into Ede's arms. The girls jumped and screeched with joy as Martin gave Gamma a bear hug.

"Good to have you safely home," he whispered in his mother's ear.

She tossed her head. "What? You thought to lose me? With precious cargo on my wing? Hah."

"Papa!" Leaping into her father's arms, Celeste nearly knocked him over. "Oh, Papa, it was the most wonderful trip in the whole wide world. We stayed at the hotel where Grandfather took Gamma, and we saw gypsies, and I danced with so many men at the Ball!"

Martin's raised eyebrows made Gamma laugh. Pointing to her eyes, she silently mouthed: "Never out of sight."

Squeezing through the crowded arrival area, they retrieved their trunk and Martin wheeled it to their sedan. Settling in the back seat, Celeste and Ede talked over each other most the way home.

"What was the Ball like?"

"Oh, Ede, I'll never forget a single moment ..."

"I have to tell you who I met ..."

"You won't believe who I met ..."

"Celeste, you know how tall I am and everything, well ..."

"The most handsome man in the ..."

"Well, he's tall too, so it didn't seem to matter ..."

"And we toured Prague with him ..."

"I was so lonely. I didn't think you were ever going to return ..."

"And we flew on an airplane ..."

"What?" Martin asked. Gamma stared straight ahead.

"A real airplane from Prague to Brussels ... and we almost crashed ..."

"What?!" Martin asked again, now glaring at Gamma, who shook her head.

"Flying around the mountains twice, dipping the wings for the gypsies we met."

"What!?" Martin said a third time to Gamma's waggling head.

She patted his thigh. "As Mr. Shakespeare say: All's well that ends well, no?"

"Real gypsies?" Ede asked.

"Yes! Swirling skirts, beads, horses, a wagon circle, a blazing fire. She gave Gamma six copper bracelets ... for my six children."

"What?!?!" Martin wasn't sure how much more he could take.

Gamma lifted her arm, showing the bracelets to Ede and her son.

"Wow Wow Wow! But not right away, right?" Ede asked.

Gamma confirmed with authority. "No. Definite not soon."

"Oh, Ede," Celeste gushed, "I have so much to tell you ..."

"And me, too ..."

"Stay over tonight so we can talk 'til our eyes fall out."

Ede squealed, but Martin cleared his throat. "Afraid not tonight, girls. We have a dinner to attend."

"What?" Gamma turned in surprise. "Tonight? Where?" She was far too tired for any further activity.

"At the Meadens, I'm afraid." Martin replied.

"The Meadens?" Celeste and Ede burst in unison.

Celeste grabbed Ede's arm. "That's who I met. James Meaden, at the Ball!"

Ede grabbed back. "That's who I met! Ron Meaden, in the park!"

Gamma looked at her son. His eyes were crinkled with worry. "How come?"

"Estelle sent an invitation." Martin sighed. "And Myrtle would not be denied."

Gamma leaned back her head. "For the Cotillion, I suppose."

Martin nodded. "I suppose."

Upon their arrival home, Myrtle swallowed Celeste with hugs and kisses. "I want every detail, especially how you liked James Meaden," she winked at her daughter.

"Mama, it was beyond the moon. The best trip ever! I had no idea about our Bohemian history."

Wincing, Myrtle glanced at Gamma, who stared back coldly. Feeling the unrest between his wife and mother, Martin called out as he struggled to remove the steamer trunk from the car. "Girls, come take the small bags upstairs."

"And wash your face, Celeste." Myrtle added. "All that smoke-stack soot."

As the girls vanished, Gamma approached Myrtle. "Why this very night?"

Myrtle feigned innocence. "Because we were invited." She held out the invitation to prove she wasn't making it up. Gamma opened the pale green envelope and read the note. "Has no date."

"No." Myrtle slipped the note back into her pocket. "But it was their only opening for months. The Meadens are very busy people."

Struggling to yank the trunk up the steps and into the house, Martin tried to defuse the tension. "Mother, I know it's inconvenient, but with a little lunch and a long nap, it might turn out all right. I hear they have the best cook in town, And you know Jack from the store; an excellent fellow."

Gamma looked to her son and blinked once, in tacit agreement and defeat.

A thundering down the stairs brought Celeste into the parlor. Ede followed but stopped on the last step, swaying nervously on the banister.

"Mama," Celeste began breathlessly. "I can't bear another day without Ede. Do you suppose it would be alright if Ede came with us to dinner?" Both girls crossed their fingers behind their backs.

Myrtle shook her head, imagining the tawdry note Ede's unfettered flamboyance would ring upon the evening. "Now Celeste, that's not polite. How might you feel if someone brought a last-minute guest to our table?"

"It'd be OK! There's always extra food. And we could bring something."

Myrtle shook her head again. "You forget table settings and placements. No. You'll see Ede tomorrow. Now, say good-bye and have some lunch so you can nap and be fresh this evening." Myrtle returned to the kitchen, leaving the girls to finish up their visit.

With sad eyes, Celeste joined Ede on the bottom step, their chins sunk in their hands, trying to think of something to change their luck.

"I was hoping to see Ron again, but I think he went back to school already," Ede sighed, a bit relieved he was gone so he couldn't be smitten by Celeste and forget all about her.

"I wish James was going to be there, but he's still in Europe," Celeste replied, not interested in a boy when she'd met a man. Sitting in gloomy silence for a few minutes, Celeste suddenly sat up. "Hey, let's meet in the park after dinner. We're going at five, so it can't finish late. I bet I could slip away after dessert."

Relieved, Ede smiled as she stood. "By the swings. I'll stay 'til dusk."

"Ede," Celeste grabbed her arm and hugged her. "I'm so glad we're friends again, and I love your mural. It's better than best."

Smiling from head to toe, Ede sashayed out the screen door.

Before the Howes arrived for supper, Estelle Meaden sought out her husband in his study, politely rapping on the open door before walking in. Jack looked up from his desk. "Hey there, ol' gal. What's on the docket tonight?"

She sat on the oversized leather hassock beside his desk, stretched her legs, crossed her ankles and leaned back on her hands. "I think the Howe girl might be a good match for James. They met in Prague, you know."

"Right. You mentioned the other night." Jack closed his newspaper. "But James ought to be able to figure that out for himself, don't you think?"

Estelle blinked, lowering her eyes. "At twenty-eight, it's not a matter of if but when. You said yourself you'd like him to buckle down and learn the rest of the business so you can retire. It's time. He's sown enough wild oats."

"Right. So what are we looking for?" Jack rarely argued with his wife.

"Character. Intelligence. Grace. Breeding. What kind of children they might have. Influences her family might bring. We don't know much about them."

Jack nodded. "Just from the hardware store, but what I've seen of Martin Howe, I like. Clear-eyed. Sound judgment. Looks straight at me when we talk. Seems family minded. The grandmother's always there, sitting by the stove, talking with someone."

"More details of their background would be good, before anything unexpected pops up. I hear his mother emigrated from Bohemia, but nothing about the wife."

"Right." Jack winked and saluted, having received his marching orders.

The Meaden home was the grandest in Gladdenbury. An oversized Victorian, it boasted bulging turrets and deep, wraparound porches lined with fretwork brackets and spandrels between the turned posts, sheltered by striped awnings and pitched slate roofs and surrounded by green lawns, ever-blooming hydrangea bushes, and more gardens and orchards in the back.

Approaching the curved front walk, Myrtle welled up inside, fingering her many ropes of paste pearls. Glancing back at her husband, daughter and mother-in-law, she worried about their attire.

"What did she say?" Gamma had asked when they were dressing.

"A simple summer supper," Myrtle admitted, but she believed the occasion called for her best finery, which included a white dress, satin sash, lace collar, gloves and hat. She thought Gamma's skirt and blouse and Celeste's tea dress were too plain, but neither one of them listened to her suggestions.

As they approached the porch step, Jack Meaden opened the front door with a flourish, his voice booming. "Welcome, welcome, and a very good return to our weary travelers." Striding across the porch with Estelle right behind him, he extended his hand, helping Myrtle up the steps.

Myrtle flushed when she saw their simple dress; Jack in blue seer-sucker vest and trousers and Estelle in a beige linen skirt, white blouse and neck broach. As the ladies followed Estelle into the vestibule, Myrtle stepped into the cloakroom to remove her hat and left behind her gloves, lace collar, sash and all but one strand of fat pearls.

On the porch, Martin extended his hand. "This is very kind of you, Jack." His voice was soft but clear.

"Not at all, not at all," Jack crowed, then dropped his voice. "To tell the truth, I didn't even know until this afternoon. You know how the ladies are. In social matters, Estelle's the boss. It's the only time I happily sit back and follow. Come, let's get a drink."

Martin followed Jack around the porch to the back of the house.

"Fine looking family you have, Martin," Jack said as they walked. "When Estelle told me James met your daughter in Prague, I was shocked. Is that the same little girl who ran around the store with pigtails, showing off her dolly?"

Martin shook his head. "Astonishing, isn't it?"

"Indeed it is."

Estelle waited in the vestibule for the ladies to stow their hats. "We're having drinks on the back porch," she explained, leading them down a long hallway, passing the half-opened pocket doors to the parlor, study and dining room. Myrtle craned her neck to see their furnishings, catching glimpses of mahogany, heavy brocade, plush rugs and large urns of lush ferns. "How lovely your home is," she called to Estelle, hinting for a tour, but Estelle bee-lined to the wide, covered veranda overlooking a long expanse of lawn and orchards. Everyone settled into cushioned wicker chairs, and Jack dispensed glasses of lemonade to the ladies before taking charge of the conversation.

"Now," he said, looking directly at Celeste. "You certainly have grown up to be a beautiful young woman, already traveling the continent and attending a ball! Quite impressive. Tell us about your trip. Any surprises?"

Celeste opened her mouth, but quickly shut it, having no idea where to start.

"Go on," Gamma urged. "What you like most?"

As Celeste hesitated, Estelle interrupted. "James said he had a splendid time with the belles of the ball."

Celeste grinned. "He was so nice to us."

Gamma nodded, adding. "Very kind. But we must be boring company after talking with President Masaryk and his wife."

"Oh, really? He met Masaryk?" Jack sat up in his chair. "That old son of a gun. You know I met him, too, briefly, at Yale after the war. He had some interesting ideas."

A maid came from the house with a tray of appetizers: small baked circles of cheesy pastry with a dollop of apricot jam.

"James said you danced beautifully," Estelle said to Celeste. "Did you learn from your father? I've heard he's a fine dancer, too."

Myrtle swallowed the pastry quickly. "She had proper lessons at the dancing school since she was five."

"And Papa, too," Celeste smiled at her father. "We practice at night sometimes, after supper. He shows me steps they didn't teach."

"And Gamma taught me," Martin completed the circle.

Estelle turned to Gamma. "Bertra, might I ask about the name Gamma? Is that grandmother in Czech?"

Gamma smiled. "No no. In Czech, grandmother is Babička. My late husband name me Gamma, a sort-of joke, when Martin in college." She paused, looking to her son, who nodded. "I like to help him study, because I learn, too. One night, we were all together in the parlor, me quizzing Martin on definition of gamma …"

"The third letter of the Greek alphabet?" Jack interrupted.

"No, for physics. Gamma is measure of strong magnetic force. My husband, he look up from reading and make joke. He says I am 'human gamma.'"

"What did he mean? You're like a magnet?" Jack asked.

Martin cleared his throat. "More like a force field. The gamma ray is the most energetic form of light, and my father, who always was impressed by my mother's abundant energy, began calling her Gamma. Soon, so did everyone else in the neighborhood."

Everyone laughed except Myrtle, who was staring at her black, lace-up shoes, wishing she had a pair of pale kid buttoned pumps like Estelle was wearing.

Noting her distraction, Estelle asked Myrtle, "Did you grow up in New York, as well?"

Suddenly realizing Estelle was speaking to her, Myrtle blurted, "Oh, no. I mean, not in their neighborhood. I grew up across the city." She couldn't talk fast enough.

"Where is your family from?"

Myrtle swallowed hard. "From the isles," repeating the well-practiced answer she had carefully cultivated since coming to Connecticut.

"England?"

"N-no. I-Ireland. My relations come …came … to Manhattan during the famine." Myrtle's eyes switched to Martin, then to Gamma, who kept their faces still, holding fast to their promise never to speak of her past.

"Oh, yes, the potato famine," Estelle said. "Devastating. What courage to leave one's country, even in such circumstances." She rose, passing the tray of canapés. "Celeste, James mentioned you met a gypsy in your travels. That must have been very exciting,"

Celeste's face brightened, then clouded when she caught her mother's glare.

Seeing the silent exchange, Gamma answered. "We met a daughter of my childhood friend. We stop by their camp, pay respect."

"I didn't know gypsies lived in Bohemia."

"Only for summer. For winter they go to Portugal or Spain."

Jack rose to refresh the drinks. "What an interesting life you've led, Gamma."

"Not so much," she blushed. "Different food in different places, but same eating and sleeping."

"Heck of a lot more than I've done," Jack replied, refilling each glass.

Celeste could not hold back. "Their roofs are made of grass."

"There you go," Jack replied, slapping his thigh as he sat down. "I never would have known that. And there's something else I'd like to know." He turned to Gamma. "How did you make your way here from Prague? How old were you?"

Gamma laughed. "Oh, you Meaden men! Your son want to know the same."

"Don't mean to pry, just curious about, well, did someone bring you or did you come on your own? Not many of us get to have such an adventure."

"I came with my brother, in 1870, when almost seventeen."

"As Celeste will soon be," Myrtle said, trying to deflect attention off Gamma.

At that moment, Ron Meaden walked onto the porch from the house, his damp hair slicked back. "Hello Mother, Father. Sorry to be late. The game went a bit long, and I had to shower."

Estelle rose. "You're just in time. May I introduce our youngest son, Ron? Mr. and Mrs. Howe, Gamma Howe and Celeste." As everyone murmured hello, the maid arrived on the porch, nodding to Estelle. "And supper is ready. Shall we proceed to the dining room?"

As the adults followed Estelle, Celeste lagged behind. Something in her throat quickly pulsed as she studied Ron from across the porch. She had forgotten how different he looked from his brother. Taller? Thinner? Were his eyes green? She tried to see, but the waning light obscured them. As she stepped into the house, she was surprised to find Ron waiting for her, by the French doors, leading to the dining room.

"Hello." His smile overtook his face as he offered the crook of his arm.

"Hello." She smiled just as wide. Her throat tightened when she took his arm, her body warmed by his close presence. As he held her chair, she could feel his energy on her back. Then she watched him walk around the table and take his seat across from her, between Gamma and her mother, a perfect placement to observe him.

The maid presented a soup tureen to Estelle, who ladled gazpacho into bowls, handing them to Myrtle to pass. The maid re-entered with platters of cold, boiled lobsters garnished with watercress and lemon wedges, and bowls of potato salad, coleslaw and celery sticks stuffed with cheese and ham, along with a basket of rye rolls slathered with mustard butter.

"Simple summer supper, indeed," Gamma laughed. "Is fit for queen!"

"That's another thing I've heard about you." Jack responded from the table's end.

"Pardon?" Gamma looked surprised.

"You know how the ladies get to talking? Well, they say some surprising things. Some believe you were a queen in Bohemia. Or was it one of your ancestors? Either way, it's downright fascinating. So what's the truth? Are we really sitting with a queen?"

Gamma mused on his question with a small, teasing smile. Having told more stories than she could recount, it would be impossible to track the source. Deciding to play along, she shrugged insouciantly. "Not queen, but royal stock, I am told, in very ancient past."

"Slavic royalty in Gladdenbury!" Jack boomed, tapping his spoon on his glass.

"Ne, not Slavic. Celtic," Gamma countered. "Bohemians are Boii *Celts*."

Jack looked quizzical. "Bohemians? I thought those were the arty types who lived unconventionally in France? Like the … oh, what are their names, Estelle? The painter and his wife here in town?"

Estelle thought as she passed a bowl of soup to Myrtle. "The Encinos."

Celeste sat up. "That's Ede's parents. She's my best friend."

Looking at his soup, Ron recalled the Ede he'd met last week.

Gamma nodded. "Yah, Bohemians are artistic and free thinkers … but is not all."

Jack raised his glass. "All right then. Set us straight. We're here to learn."

Estelle coughed slightly. Jack flashed a look to his wife, then nodded to Gamma who explained about the Boii's travel to find a new territory around 3,000 B.C.

"Wait, wait, wait," Jack interrupted. "Three thousand years before Christ?"

Myrtle twitched. "Gamma, we shouldn't bore them with this folklore …"

"No, no, no, I love history." Jack would not be deterred. "Gamma, have you any idea where they came from before they settled Bohemia?"

"Is said they live among other tribes near Caspian Sea. But when it get too crowded, many leave to find new homes. Most go south – some to Middle East, some to India, some to Asia. But Celts go north, around the mountains and settle across the Europe we know today. But with each group go the roots of a common language they all spoke."

"But how do you know it was 3,000 B.C.?"

"Our old stories tell of that journey … through the land of milk and honey when first kingdoms were rising …"

Ron snapped to attention. "The land of milk and honey: that's Mesopotamia, the cradle of civilization! We learned that in history last year. It's where group agriculture first began, and led to the rise of the first kingdoms – around 3,000 B.C.!"

"Is that right?" Jack asked. "But if it was so rich, why wouldn't your people have stayed there?"

"Because was too much people," Gamma replied. "And too much ruling. Many little tribes with big kings – trying to take each other's territory. The Boii cannot live under another's rule. We value freedom, above all."

"Well, I'd have to agree with that," Jack laughed, finishing his soup. "That's what this country is all about. Heck, they should have come here!" After setting his spoon in his empty bowl, the maid quietly replaced it with a clean plate. "So the prevailing definition of Bohemian as artistic, free thinkers is essentially true?"

"Yah, but not only. They also great merchants, traders along the Vltava."

"The Vltava?" Jack asked.

"A river running through Prague, down to Alps."

Myrtle could not stop her hands from twitching in her lap. "Gamma," she interrupted. "Perhaps we might talk about something more modern, so we all could participate?"

The table was silent for a few moments, punctuated by the slight tap of silver spoons on china. Myrtle glanced at Estelle, who smiled benignly. She wasn't sure how to read her expression. Then she looked to Martin, but his eyes were cast down.

Gamma turned to Jack. "Myrtle's right. Is just old woman stories."

"No, Gamma," Jack countered. "I consider myself a learning man, and there's something to be learned from every story. You say these Celts were successful merchants, but for how long? I don't know much about ancient history."

"Some say Boii live there several thousand years, growing bigger from small beginning. But for certain, by 400 B.C., they settle all over Bohemia and were well known for skills and art."

"Several thousand years? Yo-ho-ho and a bottle of rum! Estelle, can you imagine? That outstrips any continuous civilization I know. What was their secret?"

"Jack," Estelle's eyes cautioned him to go no further.

"What? There's many a soul who'd pay a pretty penny to know such a thing."

Gamma laughed to diffuse the building tension. "Your son say the same."

"Did he?" Estelle was surprised.

"He did?" Myrtle was surprised.

Celeste sat up in her chair. "Oh yes, he was very interested in Gamma's stories. All through Prague he kept asking her about what happened to the Boii and telling Gamma she should go on the speaking circuit."

Ron snorted. "James interested in history?"

Celeste nodded. "And philosophy!"

Jack jumped in. "What philosophy are you talking about? Socrates? Plato? Aristotle? I know a bit about those."

"The Bohemian philosophy," Gamma stated quietly. "For true happiness."

Traveling the world as a young woman, Estelle had run across many Bohemian types, and while she found their approach to life too lax for her tastes, she could not deny being drawn to their spirited style. "What do you mean?" she asked.

"Happiness. Inside. Maybe better say: contentment," Gamma said.

"Inside what?" Ron asked.

Gamma turned to him, patting her chest. "Inside your heart."

Ron smiled shyly, glancing around and stopping on Celeste. Her blue, clear eyes emboldened him. "That's where I always feel strongest," he said quietly. "When I'm playing my best, I turn off my mind and just feel the other player, how they'll move and where the ball will fall. That's when I win, when I play from my heart."

"But that's just an expression!" Myrtle blurted.

Martin looked up sharply, but she shook her head, holding her ground.

"It's poppycock Martin, her idea of a heart code. It's not how you, or the Meadens for that matter, built a solid business, family or community."

Jack seized on Myrtle's comment. "Heart code? What the devil is that?"

Shaking her head, Myrtle muttered, "Oh dear, this is dreadful."

Estelle stroked Myrtle's arm, as if soothing an agitated child. "Myrtle, I'd like to hear about it, too."

Gamma, whose eyes were lowered during Myrtle's outburst, raised her head regally, looking straight at Jack and answered in a low, sonorous tone.

"Boii Celts believe each heart has code; a unique map to our contentment on earth. We are taught, as small children, how to hear our heart voice: the feeling inside," she said, tapping her chest. "Telling what's right for us, no matter what's right for other."

"What do you mean, right for us?" Jack asked.

"What *you* seek in this life. How to use *your* gifts. What *you* are here to create. Each one is different. Sometimes big ways, sometimes small. We are taught to dream but to listen to our heart wisdom for specific direction. Because sometimes what we think is our dream, is not meant for us. Not for our contentment. For that, each heart knows its own way best."

"And you were taught this by your parents?" Estelle asked.

"Parents, grandparents, great grandparents; passed down from one to next to next. Is why, I believe, they survive as a people so long. From small group, they grow big and strong, by honoring the gift each person offer. If everyone were same, no one survive very long. Nor would we want it so. For when each person follows their own heart code, new things come to tribe, good things, and honor for all. This is our way. The Heart Code is the Bohemian Way for contentment." Gamma leaned back as she finished, feeling her heart pound, applauding her courage.

Myrtle felt mortified, unable to look up.

Martin sat higher in his chair, eyeing his mother proudly.

Celeste glanced at Ron, who smiled directly at her.

Estelle folded her hands under her chin as she watched her husband slowly finish chewing then dab his mouth with his napkin and begin to laugh, deep and loud and long from the pit of his belly.

"Ha, Ha, HO, HA, Ho, Ho HA! Estelle! Who would have guessed? After all these years? I find out I'm more Bohemian than anything else?!"

The Heart Code

Part Two

12 Ron

August 22, 1930

Jack's declaration set everyone laughing. Even Myrtle couldn't help herself, relieved that Gamma wasn't a complete embarrassment. Then, when Estelle suggested Gamma give a talk about old Bohemia to the Social Club, Myrtle felt her destiny taking shape. Gamma wouldn't be invited without including her.

By the time the maid placed a bowl of ice cream in front of Celeste, she suddenly remembered her promise to meet Ede. "Thank you," she said, politely eating a few spoonfuls as her legs jiggled under the table. Dusk wasn't far off. As she tried to figure out how she could excuse herself, Ron caught her eye with a wink.

"Mother," he said, "May I show Celeste the garden?"

Estelle nodded.

Walking around the table, Ron pulled out Celeste's chair, sending another shiver of energy down her back, and they demurely walked through the French doors to the back porch. But once they turned the corner and were out of view, they spontaneously broke into a run. Leaping off the back porch, Ron spun in midair, then reached back for Celeste's hand. She jumped to him, and together they loped toward the hillcrest, hand-in-hand.

At the top, they stood for a few moments, catching their breath while still holding hands. Ron didn't know what to do. The heat of their pressed palms made his hand sweat and sent pulses up his arm. He didn't want to let go but was unsure whether Celeste felt the same.

With a twittering in her heart, Celeste felt elated and confused. Her hand hadn't sweated with James, nor had she felt this kind of quiver. She suddenly felt a compulsion to tumble down the hill, rolling around and around, yelping at each turn. Something about Ron made her giddy. She squeezed his hand hard and let go.

"Race you to the creek," she yelled, diving to the ground and rolling down the hill, faster and faster until all the blues, browns and greens merged into a dizzy whirl. Slowing to a halt on the creek flat, her heartbeat filled her ears as her chest heaved. Lying with her arms crossed over her chest, she began laughing and couldn't stop. Until she glanced up at the sky and saw Ron standing over her, his shoes and socks dangling from one hand.

"What took you so long?" he asked, squatting to roll up his pants.

She sat up. "No fair! You didn't roll!"

"You didn't say anything about rolling. You said, "Race ya to the creek." So I did and won, fair and square. Come on now, take off your shoes and socks."

Jumping into the water, he waded through the shallows and climbed onto the boulder in the middle. "You have to try my new swing," he called, grabbing the thick rope hanging from a tree limb with a round wooden seat at the bottom. Wrapping one leg around the rope, he leapt, sailing across the water, yelling: "Iiiiieeeee! King of the Jungle!"

"Oh my gosh, the swings." Celeste scrambled up. "Ron ... I'll be right back ... my friend ... I'll be right back ... wait for us?"

"Sure," Ron replied, not understanding where she was going or the deflated feeling in his chest as she disappeared out of sight.

Cutting through a yard to Front Street, Celeste ran to the large expanse of park and fields called Town Green. She could see Ede standing on one of the swings, facing away, toward the playing fields. "Ede! Ede!" she called as she got close. Ede turned around just as she arrived. "I'm sooo sorry. Dinner went longer than I thought. But ... ," she paused for a breath. "We finally got away. Come on. Ron's waiting for us at the creek."

Excitement surged up Ede's spine. "Ron's there? Really?"

"Yeah. Come *on!*" Celeste grabbed Ede's hand and they ran back to the creek.

Standing on the boulder, Ron saw them coming, and his chest swelled. "Oh hey! It's you, Ede! Nice to see you again. I didn't know you and Celeste were friends."

Ede could only grin as she plopped on the bank to pull off her shoes and socks.

"Oh yes you did," Celeste corrected. "We talked about it at supper."

Ron looked confused and Ede surprised.

"Remember? When your father asked about the Bohemian couple in town and your mother said 'the Encinos,' and I said they were my best friend Ede's parents!"

Ede shivered. It felt good to be included in the conversation, even if she couldn't be there. She waded into the creek, holding her skirt high. "They called my parents Bohemian? But we're from Italy ... at least my father and I are."

"No," Celeste explained, "Gamma said they think and act like true Bohemians ... 'cause they live from inside to out. Now Mr. Meaden thinks he's one, too."

"Me too," Ron added, helping Ede up the rock and handing her the rope swing.

The touch of his hand felt electric.

"Wrap your legs around the rope and ... jump!"

Following instructions, Ede let out a holler as she sliced through the air and back, where Ron caught her, pulling her onto the rock. As she came to a stop, their legs whisper close, she looked into his eyes. The same warm pool of green she'd seen on their first meeting. Stepping off the swing, she bumped into him and relished his grip on her arms to steady her. "I guess that means I'm a Bohemian, too!" She giggled.

"Oh most certainly you, Ede," Celeste said, reaching for Ron's hand to help her up the rock. "Even more than me."

Taking turns, they spun on the swing, yelping and nearly knocking each other off the boulder. As twilight approached, they waded back and sat on the cool, soft bank of grass. Ede plucked a wide blade, held it between her thumbs and blew hard, making it hum. Celeste did the same, and together they made a croaking melody. When Ron tried, they couldn't stop laughing at his futile attempts. Finally, Ede suggested they play a game she'd learned from her father.

"It's called 'What I love best in the world,' and you fill in the blank."

"What's yours?" Ron asked, well trained for polite society.

"Painting, of course," Ede replied, assuming everyone knew.

"What kind?" Ron asked, having been dragged to more museums than he liked.

"Wiggly and wild," Celeste asserted, "but sometimes she'll paint perfect flowers for me because she knows they're my favorite."

Ede could have hugged her for that. "OK, now you," she said to Ron.

"Oh no, ladies first." He gestured to Celeste.

Demurely, Celeste wondered what she should say, having now seen more of the world than ever before. "Well, it's not the only thing, but right now what I love best in all the world are ball gowns."

Ede looked at her askew. "Ball gowns? I thought it was needlepoint."

"Well yes, but this is a new thing to add. Can't I do that?"

"Well, heck, sure, I guess." She hadn't thought about that possibility before. Her father always answered the same, no matter how many times he played. She turned her attention to Ron. "OK, now you. What do you love best in the world?"

"That's easy. Squash."

"The vegetable?" Ede asked.

"No, the game of squash."

"Is that what you play with the funny racquet you had when we met?"

"Yes, but you don't play on a tennis court. I was just fooling around, showing my friend some strokes. A squash court has walls around it for the ball to bounce off."

"Like those little courts at the club?" Celeste asked. "With a long-handled racquet, like badminton?"

"Precisely. Have you played?"

"Oh no, we're not members, but I saw some people playing when Ede was teaching her art class last spring."

Both girls tensed at Celeste's comment, not wanting to revisit that unhappy past.

"You teach art?" Ron was impressed.

Ede smiled, unable to douse her pride. "Yep. It's the second-best thing I love."

"Wow." Ron nodded with esteem.

As twilight fell to dusk, the three sat by the creek listening as the peepers' call, and the slow scratch of cicadas filled the air. Celeste felt uncomfortable, bothered at not having anything as special as art or a sport in her life. All she had was her beauty, which her mother said would get her anything she wanted. What did she want, she silently wondered? What about Ron? Leaning back on her arms, she watched him sitting close to Ede as she taught him how to weave dandelions into a crown, her hands deliberately touching his. He was very cute, sweetly shy and fun, and she was thrilled when he took her hand. But compared to his older brother's sophistication? Not the same. Besides, she thought as she sat up and straightened her skirt, she could see how much Ede really liked him, rolling her big goofy eyes and whirling her head in a spin every time he wasn't looking.

"Tell us about squash," Ede suddenly demanded, placing the crown of dandelions on his head and fluffing his curls around it.

"Yes," Celeste agreed, sweeping her hand over her hair. "How good are you?"

Ron shrugged. "I seem to be fairly good."

Though initially reluctant, he gave in to the girls urging and told them how he came to be the regional champion. "The game has been a longstanding tradition in my family, all the way back to great grandfather. Even my sister Bea loves it. She played on the women's squash team at Trinity College and still plays in regional tournaments."

"Women play squash?" Celeste was not at all sure she'd enjoy getting sweaty.

"Yep, lots of women play. They have their own tournaments all over the east coast and sometimes in Europe. It was actually Bea who taught me how to play, when I was three or four. She's good. So good that when I first played my older brother …"

"James?" Celeste interrupted in a high-pitched voice.

Ron looked at her oddly before continuing. "No. I first beat Fischer, who's only two years older than me. But when I was eight or ten, I beat them all, including James. After that I just kept winning all the local matches and then the regional finals."

"Wow, a real champion," Ede enthused. "Have your brothers *ever* beaten you?"

Ron smiled shyly. "Only when I let them."

Both girls laughed, wondering what it would be like to have a sister or brother.

"But I don't take the game so seriously," Ron explained. "For me, it's fun, like ice skating." He couldn't help but see himself on the boxy court returning the small, soft ball to a corner drop, just out of his opponent's reach. "It's a lot of geometry, too," he explained, "hitting the ball so it bounces at just the right angles." But he could not tell them that beyond his athletic prowess, it was his genuine good nature that most infuriated his foes and impressed his fans. His easy laugh when losing a point, his genuine caring for opponents when they did not do well, and his always calling "good shot," even when it cost him the match. He liked the game for the playing of it. "That's why I go to school in New Hampshire," he said. "St. Andrew's has been famous for squash since 1883."

"Do they teach you to play better?" Ede asked, wishing for a painting school.

"Not really," Ron admitted. "There isn't a coach, and we mostly just fool around on the outdoor courts when the ice ponds aren't frozen enough for hockey. But since so many squash champions have attended the school, my parents insisted I go. It's a pain sometimes, but I get to hear a lot of stories about squash from the boys at school."

"Like what?" Celeste asked.

As dusk turned to dark, Ron told them stories he'd heard at the Academy as well as from his relatives around their Sunday dinner table, recounting antics and memorable matches over cigars and snifters of port and cognac. He talked about his favorite squash hero, Tom Pettitt, a poor, 16 year-old English chap who arrived in Boston in 1876 to apprentice a squash champion. After only six months of instruction, he trounced his mentor and became champion himself. "Pettitt was world champion for five years, and then he retired to coach at the Newport Rhode Island Casino. He would put on crazy shows for his patrons. He was famous for his antics, like using a chair leg or champagne bottle for a racquet. Sometimes he even played on roller skates!"

"Why would he be such a clown?" Ede asked.

"To amuse them, I guess. They paid his wage. But he was also a serious teacher of stratagems and techniques. He taught the psychology of coaching to Harry Coles!"

The blank look on both girls' faces made Ron flush. "Harry Coles? The famous Harvard squash coach?"

Ede and Celeste nodded vaguely. At least they'd heard of Harvard.

Ron looked down, muttering, "Harvard's the best for squash, and I'd really like to go there, but everyone in my family has gone to Yale, so I guess I'm out of luck ..." He finished with a sigh, not knowing what else to say. Besides, he'd already talked enough about himself. "So what's school like in Gladdenbury?"

Ede released her loud, happy trill. "Nothing like your school, I can tell you that! We just have the normal stuff: English, science, math."

"Don't they teach any art?"

"Heck no," Ede replied. "I bet they think it's frivolous, but I've learned more geometry working on modern art with my father than I have in any math class."

They all fell silent once again. Celeste wished she had something she could talk about with the same passion. Everything she liked seemed silly and small by comparison.

"Well, when do you leave for school?" Ede asked, hoping it would not be soon.

"Tomorrow, actually," he said, feeling a twinge of gloom.

"Tomorrow? Oh phooey," Ede said. "I was hoping to show you my paintings. But maybe ...." she brightened, "I could write to you ... and *send* you a painting!"

Though shrouded by the near dark, both girls saw Ron's face lift at Ede's suggestion.

"Would you? That would be great. New Hampshire gets really cold and boring. I swear I'll write back!"

A long, low whistle pierced the air, and Celeste jumped up. "That's my father," she said, grabbing her shoes and socks. "I've got to go." She dashed off before Ede or Ron could say good-bye.

Alone with Ron in the dark, Ede closed her eyes and listened to the creek's babble, the crickets' call ... and she imagined the rustle of Ron moving to her, wrapping his arms around her, kissing her skin with firm, soft lips and gently murmuring her name. A thrill spiked through her belly.

"She's really nice," Ron said, puncturing Ede's dream.

Her eyes flew open to see him gazing across the creek to the spot where Celeste had disappeared, flipping his thumb against a thick blade of grass.

"Mmm," she murmured, forcing a smile. "Everyone feels that way about Celeste."

"And so are you," Ron quickly added, turning to her. "I've never met anyone who had something they loved doing so much."

"No different from yours," Ede countered. She didn't want to feel like the outsider any more. Not with Ron, the first boy who seemed to like her despite her being tall and foreign born, despite her grubby hands, shadowed with paint and linseed oil.

"I suppose, but it's not quite the same. When your painting's done, you can look at it, study it, show it. You create things that last. When I win a match, it's just that, with maybe a trophy and some bragging rights. But by next tournament, it's all past."

Ede kept silent. Beyond her own pleasure of painting, she didn't know what art would bring to her. Most likely she'd become a schoolteacher or a nurse and paint on the side, like her mother. But at that very moment what she wanted most of all was to find out if she was likeable … to boys … for romance. She was already seventeen and had never been kissed, and Ron seemed a good place to start.

"Would you really write to me?" Ron asked, his green eyes sincerely wide.

Ede's heart jumped. "Oh, yes. Every week!" She blurted, not meaning to sound so eager.

13 *Dancing*

Fall 1930

Cotillion, Cotillion, Cotillion. It was all Myrtle could talk about once the invitation arrived in September. After Gamma's silly prattle at the Meadens', she wasn't positive they'd be included. But when a Social Club member delivered the beige linen envelope, her aspirations were revived and she boasted to anyone who would listen. To be among Gladdenbury's finest and present Celeste at the town's social event of the year filled Myrtle's mouth with sweet madness. "What more could you want?" her closest friends asked, and although Myrtle contentedly shrugged, she knew exactly what more there was to have.

Though not as intrigued as her mother, Celeste enjoyed the attention. What girl wouldn't? Shopping for dresses, trying new hairstyles, experimenting with makeup was fun, particularly after her introduction to fine couture in Paris and Prague. And the other debutantes seemed nice enough. But she felt a niggling in her belly for things she didn't like. Such as the way some of the girls acted snooty when the adults weren't looking, and having to be so preoccupied with her appearance all the time, and the drills her mother forced on her daily – etiquette and posture and walk – which left no time to see Ede. It seemed forever since she'd had time to splash in the creek or walk in the nearby hills, scuffling her feet along the roadside. Always being dressed up, at her mother's insistence, conjured an empty feeling inside. Sometimes she felt like an orchid under glass: to be admired but not touched. Her mother's constant fussing so stifled Celeste, she sometimes could not catch her breath. So when the Cotillion finally arrived, she felt a great relief. Awaking on that bright November morning, she made a wish that once it was over, everything would return to normal, despite a feeling it might not be possible.

⌒

Late afternoon, as Ede helped Celeste dress, both girls giggled at the multi-tiered white gown, billowing like a cumulus cloud.

"Wouldn't this be fun to wear on the creek swing?" Celeste chirped, pulling on her long white gloves.

Ede's laugh spilled into the hallway.

Hearing it, Myrtle shouted from her room, "Celeste, take care not to muss your ringlets."

Preening into the mirror, Celeste switched her head back and forth, making the hairdo bob, and both girls laugh even harder.

"Tell Ron hello for me?" Ede asked as they walked to the front door. Her voice was smudged with sadness even though her face was brave. As promised, she and Ron had written each other throughout the semester, growing closer with each letter. When Ron wrote that his mother insisted he be an escort at the Cotillion, even though it was in the middle of the intercollegiate squash tournaments, Ede hoped they'd be able to see each other, until he said he would be home only for the evening and had to return Sunday morning. Ede squeezed Celeste's hand. "Just thinking of him gives my belly tingles," she whispered.

Celeste didn't say anything, remembering how she'd felt the same about James at the Ball, but somehow, when she came home, the feeling faded away.

"And be sure to ask if he'll be home in time for the holiday dance."

Celeste wrinkled up her nose. "You mean like a date?"

"No, no, no, I'm going with you," Ede protested. "I just want him to know it would be nice to see him there."

"OK," Celeste promised, but almost forgot with all the night's surprises.

⌒

Peering down the line of twenty young women, each dressed in a flowing white gown with elbow-length gloves, Celeste wiggled her toes inside her new, silvery, satin T-strap dancing shoes and giggled. They looked like a host of misplaced angels waiting to get back into heaven. Then the first girl stepped forward and turned, standing at the top of the staircase, head raised, gazing above the crowd, waiting for her name to be announced before sliding her hand on the banister and bobbing out of view, gracefully descending, step-by-step, to her escort at the bottom. Celeste had practiced diligently and was ready, but when a burst of applause carried up the stairs, she suddenly felt nervous, her hands fluttering by her side. Seeing Celeste's distress, the girl behind grabbed her hand and squeezed it tightly. They smiled at each other but said not a word, glancing at the stern eyes of the cotillion matrons, keeping an orderly watch. "Step-turn-gaze-hold-descend," Celeste repeated to herself as she watched each girl began her presentation walk. Imagining herself in each debutante's shoes, making the descent in her mind's eye, she anticipated Ron's arm and warm smile when she got to the bottom.

Finally, she was next. Stepping into place, she turned, facing the crowd, but kept her gaze high, letting them admire her, as she had at the Hotel Stephan in Prague on the night of the Ball. As her name was announced, her blood pumped faster. Reaching for the banister, she held it tight, shifting her gaze to the bottom step, to shoot Ron a special smile – but found James standing there, instead.

She froze.

"Celeste, go!" the cotillion matron hissed.

The girl behind her peeked down the staircase and gasped. She turned to the few who followed, "It's *James* Meaden – not Ron!"

Celeste flushed head to toe, surprised by James but twinged with disappointment. She really wanted to see Ron again, had even imagined dancing with him. Then she heard the girls behind her twittering, making her even more conflicted. How did it get so complicated all of a sudden?

Noticing Celeste's hesitation, James gave an encouraging nod.

She forced a smile, squeezed the banister and slowly stepped toward him. By the time she reached the bottom, she'd regained her composure and held on to the crook of his arm as they promenaded around the room, passing every guest, who each smiled and cooed to their faces. Then James began whispering funny comments about the people they had passed, setting Celeste into giggles she couldn't suppress. By the time they joined the line of debutantes and escorts, waiting patiently for the presentations to complete before entering the ballroom for dinner and dancing, Celeste and James were outright laughing.

Letting go of James' arm, Celeste was adjusting her dress when the next name was announced. Glancing at the top of the staircase, she saw the girl who'd been behind her, staring down the steps, wearing the widest, toothiest grin she'd ever seen. Then she saw Ron at the bottom and lost her breath. A jealous heat shot up her neck. She couldn't keep her eyes off him as he began the promenade around the room.

Turning away, Celeste tossed her ringlets and grabbed James' arm, bombarding him with questions to catch up on three months of news, while silently hoping Ron would at least be seated at her table.

As it turned out, Ron was across the room. With only eight place settings per table and the inclusion of Gamma Howe along with her parent's and Mr. and Mrs. Meaden, Celeste was the only debutante in her group, so she danced only with James, Mr. Meaden and her father. But she looked for Ron whenever she could, and occasionally caught his eye and smiled.

To make matters worse, Celeste might as well have been a mute that evening, with her mother dominating the conversation, interrogating James with one question after another. Myrtle was so excited her head bobbled continually, threatening to spin off her neck. Amusing herself, Celeste imagined her mother's head bobbing on the ceiling, still talking a mile a minute. But she had to admit that James was very gracious, politely indulging her mother's nattering and telling everyone how lucky Celeste had been for his business endeavors, from which he'd only recently returned. "Like a charm she was," He said several times, recounting the many good feelings engendered from their brief time in Prague.

As he danced Celeste across the Club's polished wood floor, James told her, "Meeting you revived me." Celeste laughed demurely, keeping her face animated, but something in his voice didn't ring true. Not that she knew him well enough to be sure, but his tone felt flat and false, with none of the lightness it carried in Prague. And why couldn't she stop thinking about swinging at the creek with Ron?

Sitting at the table while James danced with her mother, and the rest of the adults conversed, Celeste noticed Ron was not at his table or on the dance floor. Slipping off to powder her nose, she found him in the hallway, looking out the glass doors to the courtyard, his hands fidgeting behind his back.

"Oh, Ron." She rushed up with ringlets bouncing. "I thought I'd never see you."

Turning, Ron's face flooded with delight.

Out of the corner of her eye, Celeste saw her mother on James' arm, returning from their dance and waving for her to join them. "I have to get back, but I wanted to ask: Will you be home from school in time for the holiday dance?"

Ron's smile widened. "On the 20th? Yes. Will you be there?"

Without hesitation Celeste squeezed his arm. "Of course. Ede and I will meet you there. Good luck in school and all 'til then." Consumed by her own agenda, she didn't notice his eyes cloud as she quickly turned away and sallied back to the ballroom, feeling happier than she had all evening.

⌒

"He'll be at the dance!" Celeste triumphantly reported to Ede the next day.

Ede jumped up and down before her face went pale. "But what will I wear? I don't have fancy dresses like you."

Celeste didn't blink. "We'll make a dress. Gamma can help. She has piles of fabric in her chest. We'll find something perfect, I'm sure."

But Gamma had a better idea, instructing them to open the long, low chest at the end of her bed. Carefully, they removed folded garments, fabric and a handcrafted quilt until she pointed to a white cardboard box. Setting it on the bed, Gamma opened it gingerly and lifted out a magnificent dress. A flowing sheath of blue-green silk with thin shoulder straps and a short, buttoned jacket, edged with woven ribbons in a deeper hue. Both girls sucked in their breaths. It was obviously too big for Celeste, and Ede couldn't believe she'd fit into something so elegant.

"Where did you get this?" Celeste asked, wondering how it could look so modern yet be at the bottom of Gamma's storage chest.

"At our stopover in Paris, last August."

Celeste looked confused. "But it's too big for me," she blurted.

Gamma grinned. "It shout 'Ede' in the shop window, so I buy for Christmas. Now, here you are, a little bit early."

Ede nearly cried as she modeled the dress while Celeste did her best to keep up a smile. It was spectacular on Ede's tall figure, the color glowing against her olive skin and black hair.

"Ahh, won't you be the belle," Gamma said, sending Ede home in a happy spin.

⌒

For the next month, all Ede could talk about was Ron and the dance. What should she do with her hair? What shoes could she use? Maybe her mother would let her buy one good pair? Would she need a different lipstick to suit the dress? Isn't blue-green just the dreamiest color?

Celeste struggled to be a good friend, but her jaw tensed as Ede blabbed on. She wanted to lash out and felt horrid at her own thoughts. But it was just a dance, not a date, and Ron was just a boy. To calm herself, Celeste tried to think about James and how handsome he'd been at the Cotillion and the envious eyes that followed them around the room. There was no dispute; James was the night's prize, studied equally by the young ladies, their mothers and society matrons. It all should have been enough to make Celeste feel better, but somehow it did not. So, as she always did with bound-up feelings, she sought out Gamma for a talk.

⌒

Fixing the afternoon tea, Celeste brought it to the parlor, where Gamma was knitting. Gamma held up her stitching as Celeste walked into the room.

"Look! These large needles make it lace-like," she said.

Celeste nodded and poured the tea, setting a cup and saucer on the table in front of Gamma. Thanking her, Gamma noticed the strain and pucker on Celeste's face.

Picking up her own teacup and sipping, Celeste gazed around their parlor. Unsure of how to begin, she distracted herself by studying how the heavy drapes framing the window and the brocade couch both had similar muted-gold patterns. Placing her cup on the mahogany table, she fingered the carved edges, appreciating the wood's pinkish brown hue against the bone white china. Colors and textures flooded her eyes without even trying. Celeste wished her feelings were as clear. Sighing, she slumped in her seat.

"How do you know if you're in love?" she finally asked.

Gamma glanced at her granddaughter, listing to the side, one shoulder cocked and the other drooping, looking very defeated.

"Not like you, shaggy-girl."

"Why do you say that?" Celeste was surprised.

"Look at you, all slouched and sad. For certain, not feeling love."

Straightening up, Celeste smoothed out her dress. "How can you tell?"

"No matter what say your mouth, the body speaks truth."

Feeling even more self-conscious, Celeste's legs and arms were suddenly too long and her hands too large for her lap. She shook her head to start again. "What I mean is, I'm all mixed up about what I'm feeling, or should be feeling and … well … it's just that Ede is making me all jumpy inside and I don't know why."

"What she doing?"

"Going on and on about Ron and the dance, and it's driving me crazy."

"Not like you and Prague Ball I suppose?"

"What?"

A small smile crept onto Gamma's lips as she let the click of her needles reply.

"Gamma, I wasn't like that!" Celeste's nostrils flared.

Gamma raised and dropped one shoulder.

"And anyway, that was Europe, for gosh sake. This is just a silly town dance."

Knit, purl, knit, purl, knit, purl, Gamma's needles sang, to which she added: "I like very much pattern the needles make."

"Gamma? Was I really like that?"

Laying the yarn in her lap, Gamma chuckled. "Child, you know so. Why begrudge Ede's fancy? Must you always be center stage?"

Celeste chewed her lower lip. "But she's acting goofy."

"What's that to do with you?"

"Because I think I have feelings for Ron, too."

There it was. She'd said it. The tension between her shoulders drained away as her face softened and her eyes opened with a tender look. "And I feel bad because he's the first boy who's ever liked Ede back."

Gamma looked at her granddaughter, letting the words sink in. "Hmm. Well, what you want from me?"

"Tell me what to do."

Gamma lifted her tea cup, sipped, replaced it in the saucer and resumed knitting before replying. "What can I say? All I hear is Ede likes a boy you *think* you like, too. And now I feel rather foolish, because it seem I teach you nothing about your heart's way. Tell me, in all these years, do I ever say *thinking* was how you know love?"

Celeste's face scrunched for a moment. "No?" she ventured.

Sighing, Gamma echoed her back. "No? ... Another question? Since I hold you in my palm, I whisper all I know true, and this is what you learn? At best, I am very poor teacher."

"Gamma, don't do that. I'm trying to understand what I'm feeling."

"And fine job you're doing." Gamma's voice became serious. "The Belle of the Cotillion, with two – two! – Meaden boys on a string. Yet still you don't know how you feel. So I ask: What say your heart? For either one, does it spark true?"

"That's what I'm trying to figure out, Gamma." On the verge of tears, Celeste's cheeks were taut and her brow furrowed.

"Yah, I see. Still summing with your head. Is wrong tool for job."

Blinking, Celeste's face slightly relaxed. "What's the right tool?"

Gamma flushed pink, wanting to burst out laughing, but she held her amusement in check. "You want to know what real love feel like? Is question for the gods, some say. But I say, you already know love is many different feelings. Sometimes like quiet snowing, sometimes like trumpets blaring … but always – all-ways – in your heart, is a whoosh that cannot be forced by practice or prayer. Are you working arithmetic or sensing truth in there?"

Celeste's head drooped. She knew the truth but wished it otherwise.

Gamma picked up her cup and saucer.

Celeste shook her head, sighing. "What's wrong with me?"

The wistful look on her face undid Gamma's resolve. She burst out laughing so hard her cup rattled dangerously on the saucer before she pushed it on the table for safekeeping. "Oh my child. Whatever will become of you?" She coaxed Celeste into her arms, where the girl began to cry.

"Now, now." Gamma stroked her hair. "No worry, dítě. Nothing is wrong. Love is not a game for winning. What is meant will come, when time is right. But not by will. Love does not deceive. It come only with true intent."

Celeste's tears slowed. "Was it like snow or trumpets for grandfather?"

"Augh, more like squawking geese running from the reaper." Gamma's chest heaved a sigh. "So embarrassed was I … soot-covered and grimed from travel. I want to hide, but he stood there, beside Yazi outside customs house. There was no escape."

"But you felt love right away?"

"No, not right away. I come to marry, not for love. Mostly I want to see the world. Now look how far I come!" Gamma wiggled her eyebrows to make Celeste laugh.

"But you did love grandfather, didn't you?"

"Who could not? It took some time, to know each other, but once I did, augh, my heart would not stop. And from him I learn more love than I knew possible." Gamma shifted Celeste to look into her eyes. "But I knew right from first glance it would be good, even if not love, for his eyes were kind. For poor farm girl, was enough. And he let me find my way to him. And soon, he be my dearest one."

Celeste never tired of this story. It made her feel safe and hopeful that one day she, too, would find her dearest one.

Gamma tapped Celeste's arm. "So let Ede have her fun. Enjoy her spark. And what is to be yours will come. Promise. Now, let's go help your Mama with supper." Tucking her knitting into her bag, Gamma slid to the edge of the sofa and pushed herself up as Celeste gathered the tea service.

After her talk with Gamma, Celeste stopped brooding and her happy, singing self returned to the household and her friendship. The next week, she engaged Ede in every aspect of the upcoming dance. Together they found the perfect shoes, and she loaned her friend the crystal earrings and necklace she'd worn to the Ball, and they dressed together at Celeste's before skipping to the dance with anticipatory delight.

How then, she would later wonder, did it end up so wrong?

The annual holiday dance was held in the large activities room at the back of town hall, framed by an outdoor garden, and every inch of it was decorated for the event. The garden glowed with torches, and red ribbons were wrapped around the tree trunks. Inside the hall, dozens of small candles illuminated tables dressed with green linens and boughs of holly. Every doorframe was draped with plumy red fabric and sprigs of mistletoe. Celeste and Ede had painted a hundred silvery stars that hung from the ceiling. Even the cloakroom was decorated with fabric and greens, which so excited Celeste that she wrapped a red ribbon around each pair of galoshes lining the floor under the coats, just so their owners would be delighted at the evening's end.

"There he is," Ede said, spying Ron standing behind the refreshments table. She rubbed her suddenly moist palms together to dry them, not wanting to spoil her dress.

Celeste elbowed Ede in front of her. "Go on."

Shaking out her long, black, freshly curled locks, Ede cleared her throat and gingerly stepped to the table. "Hello, Ron," her voice wobbled as Celeste jabbed her in the back. Swallowing hard she said: "I ... we're ... sure glad you could be here. I ... we ... wondered if the snow would delay you."

Celeste smiled, tilting her head down and to the side, so her eyes twinkled.

Ron's eyes popped and heart pounded as his gaze alternated between the two girls. The glass in his hand nearly slipped. "No! ... The snow was no problem. Trains go, no matter what the weather ... Would you like some punch?"

"You bet," Ede exhaled, glad the beginning was over. Where it would go from there she had no idea, but at least she'd gotten through the hello without stumbling too much.

As Ron ladled punch into their cups, Celeste swished her skirt, looking around the room, as Ede watched Ron. Within the first sips of the rosy punch, a boy came up to ask Celeste for a dance. With a giggle, she set down her cup, waved goodbye to Ron and Ede, and it was the last they saw of her for a while, which suited Ede just fine.

"Do you mind if I keep you company?" she asked Ron, her voice solid and clear.

"No, I'd be honored," Ron said as he filled a few more cups. An awkward silence rose between them for a few moments until Ron said, "Your eyes look extra big tonight. Is it the color of the dress?"

Ede's grin hurt her cheeks. "I think so." Then they began talking non-stop.

He had questions, lots of questions, about her painting. How she picked a subject and her choice of colors and the inspiration behind the small canvas she'd sent. "It's so alive and vibrant, I keep it on my desk to motivate my studies," he said.

She wanted to hear all about his squash tournaments. Where they were and how he did and what he learned from the last round of games. She also wanted more stories about his schoolmates. "The way you wrote about them was so funny, it kept me laughing for weeks," she said.

When he was relieved from serving punch, they stood at the edge of the dance floor still sharing stories while Ede tried to figure out how to get him to ask her to dance. She kept pointing out Celeste, dancing by them with one boy after another. Then she described the latest dance steps she'd learned. Then she asked him which dances he liked best, but before he could answer a Ladies Choice was called and the band began to play the Connecticut Waltz.

Eureka! Ede thought, her hands instantly sweaty again. Pressing her palms together, she turned away to discretely rub them dry when Celeste swooped in, grabbing Ron by the arm.

"Come dance with me!" she sang, slipping her hand into his and pulling him to the floor without a glance back.

As Celeste sashayed away with Ron, a slow-motion tunnel enveloped Ede. She felt like a spy, peering down a long tube into a distant world as they whirled by, each of Celeste's ringlets slowly unfurling and bouncing on her shoulders as she winked and giggled and flipped her skirt. Then the band's music collapsed into a tinny horn as Ede felt her chest tear apart. How long could she stand there, willing herself not to cry, frozen in place, cheeks burning from a plastered smile? For two more songs she stood as they circled past, until something inside finally broke and she shook herself free.

Marching across the hall, she ducked into the cloakroom and grabbed her coat, roughly pulling it on as anger clutched her chest and welled up so fast she wanted to kick something. Spotting Celeste's coat, its fur collar still damp with droplets of melted snow, she yanked it off the hanger, throwing it to the floor, stomping and grinding it, then kicking it as hard as she could, knocking down a row of neatly beribboned boots. The wreckage felt good, cleanly good, until her anger seethed again and she ran, bursting out of town hall into the sharp, cold air, trudging through the crunchy snow, across the Green toward home, alone, head down, arms folded across her chest, tears stinging her cheeks, wishing the music trailing behind her would disappear and Celeste would fall down in front of everyone and smash her perfect face.

The next morning was crisp and clear. The late-night sprinkle of rough snow crackled under Ede's boots as she tramped to Celeste's house. At 8 a.m., no lights were on, so Ede went round back and scraped together a snowball to smash against Celeste's bedroom window. As the curtain parted, Ede saw a sleepy-eyed Celeste waving to her. Taking a breath, she yelled in a friendly voice, "Come out here and see something."

Celeste waved again and left the window.

Waiting by the back porch, Ede stood tall, her hands behind her back.

Coming out the door, Celeste shivered in her bathrobe and slippers. "Get in here, it's freezing," she called, not seeing either snowball coming her way. The first one split her lip. The second smashed her chin with crusty, stinging snow.

"What? What? Augh! Ede? What are you doing?" Celeste screamed.

"Thank you very much for giving me a chance with one boy!" Ede yelled back. "*One boy*, Celeste! You have *all the rest* at your fingertips, but you have to have the ONE BOY I like, too!"

Wiping the crystals off her face and tasting blood, Celeste retorted in a flash of anger. "Oh, yeah, well, what do you care? You have your painting. I can't help who likes me, and anyway, it's the one thing I can do best. It's *my* art!"

Celeste couldn't believe Ede had hit her with snowballs.

Ede couldn't believe what Celeste just said.

Both girls stared hard at the other, their faces twisted with emotion. Anger. Hurt. Rage. Then Ede shook back her head, swiveled and strutted away, not caring – for the first time in her life – if she ever saw Celeste Howe again.

14 *Estelle*

December 21, 1930

Oozing vitality, Jack Meaden swung into the dining room, still clad in his squash attire. "Well, well, my sweet bride Estelle. You must be on top of the world after last night."

With a half smile, Estelle placed her thumb where she left off reading the newspaper articles on New York society, the parties, the luncheons, the dances for debutantes and society's juniors, before offering her cheek to Jack, who gently bussed it, then slipped around her chair to survey the sideboard buffet. Cream cheese, smoked salmon, scrambled eggs, bacon, sausage, fruit cocktail, toast and apple Danish. "Standard fare," he noted as he poured a cup of coffee from the silver service and devoured a Danish in two bites.

Estelle sniffed but held her tongue, having learned when to sidestep criticism. In Estelle's younger, feistier days, her mother often counseled: "Pick your battles wisely, dear, and don't needle unnecessarily." Estelle now repeated that axiom to her own married children. Though Jack's manners were sometimes a bit gauche, it was not enough to shift her focus, not today.

"I honestly didn't think he was going to come," Estelle replied, fingering the filigreed pin at her neck. "Wasn't his arrival a delight?"

"At 11 p.m.?" Jack set out his newspapers at the end of the table. "Hardly seemed worth the trip from New York."

"He said he had a function. It's ghastly this time of year, with one social event on top of another. But he promised to try, and it turned out well worth the effort," Estelle countered. "They looked captivating together." Having watched Ron and Celeste dance together most of the night, she'd begun to wonder if theirs was the potential match. But when James arrived, she dismissed the idea. Ron was only 17, while James was approaching 30.

Jack didn't reply, scanning the headlines of the New York Times, Hartford Courant and the New London Gazette.

UNITED STATES BANK GOES UNDER

FINANCIAL SCHEMER PONZI TO BE DEPORTED TO ITALY

NOBEL PRIZE FOR LITERATURE TO SINCLAIR LEWIS

CAPONE AIDE FOUND GUILTY IN TAX CASE

REAL ESTATE FINANCING DECLINES FOR 1930

SWISS ALPINE GLACIERS IN FULL RETREAT

Jack shook his head. The world was going to hell in a hand basket while the band played on. Without looking up from his papers he asked casually: "Why now, Estelle?"

She barely blinked. "Have you forgotten last summer? James complaining the travel being too tiresome. And didn't you say you were ready to pass the baton?"

Jack did not reply or look up.

Estelle continued, "I can see he's had his fill. Six years is ample exposure to the intercontinental life. We're very similar."

"Hmm, a biting wit, a short temper and quick to laugh." Jack smiled charmingly.

Estelle did not smile back. "I meant our need for adventure. I'm glad he's had a chance to scuff his shoes a bit before settling down. Had he not, I don't know where he'd be today. But I know all too well the toll it can take. The frivolity gets a bit much over time. Lucky for me, you came along at just the right moment."

"Right. I've been meaning to ask about that," Jack winked. "Was I *your* decision or your *mother's* pick?"

Lowering her chin, Estelle's eyes sparked. "Not even on her list. But then, she had no idea how to corral me. She thought you far too young and I'd be quickly bored."

Jack looked surprised. "By a scant three years?"

Estelle shrugged lightly. "With irresistible, winsome ways. Anyone less spirited could never have tamed me."

Their eyes locked across the table and he blew her a kiss. Smiling, she picked up her napkin and dabbed the corners of her mouth. "But James is a completely different matter. We've discussed the kind of wife he'd like, and he specifically said someone young and not so worldly wise. So when Ron brought the news of Celeste Howe in Prague at the same time as James ... well, it seemed a bit of fate. Did you see Celeste's reaction last night? She lit up like a firecracker when James appeared behind Ron. All in all, I think it's going rather well." She looked at the door leading to the porch. "What's taking the boys?"

"They'll be along," Jack replied, still reading the paper. "James was bent on beating his brother, once and for all."

"Again? No one's beaten Ron since he was ten."

"Something to do with a girl, I'd say." Jack looked up with doleful eyes. Estelle blinked and shook her head.

He shrugged, calling into the butler's pantry, "Any soft boilers in there, Kitty?"

"We have a bell." Estelle lifted the small sterling hand bell.

Jack grinned, waving her off as the maid swept through the door carrying a tray with his regular breakfast: two soft-boiled eggs, an empty bowl and a small dish of saltine crackers.

"Thanks, Kitty." Jack grinned at her averted face. "You're terrific!"

The young maid blushed as she left the room.

With two sharp cracks of his knife, Jack opened the eggs, poured them into his bowl and crushed the saltines on top. "Where in blazes are the S&P?" his eyes switching across the table.

"Above your knife, dear." Estelle nodded to the small sterling shakers.

"Ahh, that katydid thinks of everything."

After his first bite, Jack spoke, in between discrete chews. "Estelle, I think that Howe girl is terrific. If she's anything like her grandmother, James would have one heck of a woman."

Estelle sipped her coffee. "That's my concern."

"Mmm? What?" Jack asked, sopping a slice of toast in his bowl, wondering what he'd just missed. Since meeting Gamma Howe he'd become very fond of her, regularly dropping by Howe Hardware on the pretense of needing specialty nails or sandpaper or a cleaning solvent in order to spend an hour leaning on the counter, goading Gamma for more stories about her Bohemian youth and New York in the late 1800's.

He genuinely thought Gamma was the reason Estelle had zeroed in on Celeste. In the business of selling insurance, he'd learned a lot about people, and one thing he knew for sure: apples don't fall far from the tree.

"I wonder about Gamma's influence," Estelle answered simply. She made no bones about sharing her opinions with her husband. From their very first date, she'd spoken her mind without demur. The only child of a wealthy family, she was accustomed to getting her way and didn't seek anyone's approval on anything.

For the most part, Jack didn't object. While her superior attitude was occasionally irritating, he'd learned plenty about life, women and business from his wife, and he was quick to admit his decent education paled compared to Estelle's savvy. She had a knack for navigating society's strange underpinnings with aplomb, and after their wedding, business soared for Meaden Insurance from Estelle's finesse and extensive network of contacts. But what possible objection could she have about Gamma?

"What about Gamma's influence?" he asked.

Estelle was about to reply when the porch doors banged open.

"You tricked me," James declared, entering the dining room.

"You ran out of gas, as usual," Ron said, pushing past his brother.

As their bodies steamed on the tapestry rug amid the polished rosewood furniture, James and Ron looked as if they'd taken a sauna in their white shorts and ribbed-neck sweaters, while snowy crystals still clung to their canvas shoes.

"Nice of you to join us ... fresh from the shower," Estelle teased as each son kissed her cheek. "Thank goodness the coffee overpowers your ... aroma."

Before she could ring, the maid entered with a tray of cinnamon toast.

"Cinnamon toast! My god, Kitty, you've been holding out on me!" Jack declared, snatching a slice before she set it on the table.

"Oh, Mr. Meaden, I'm sorry. I didn't know," Kitty replied in a soft voice. "I make them special for Mr. Ron."

"The boy wonder," James said dryly, standing by the sideboard sipping coffee. "Is there anyone who doesn't fall under his spell?"

Estelle felt a flinty tension pass between her sons across the table.

Ron's eyes were hard. He hadn't meant to dance so long with Celeste last night. He didn't even know James was coming to the party; his brother was always too busy for townie events, but suddenly, there he was, tapping Ron's shoulder to cut in. "Thanks for keeping her occupied," James had quipped in Ron's ear as he relinquished Celeste's soft fingertips to his brother and walked away.

"Learned it all from you, big brother," Ron said, snatching two pieces of cinnamon toast. "Think I'll grab a shower," he said, leaving the room with shoulders squared and head high.

Still scanning the papers, Jack hadn't seemed to notice the exchange. Looking around, he asked, "Hey, where did Ron go?"

"The showers," James said, helping himself to some eggs and taking Ron's seat next to his mother. Jack closed his papers and shuffled them into a loose stack.

"Me too," Jack said, standing up. "James, when are you heading back?"

"After breakfast."

"Not going to see the Howe girl before you leave?"

"No, I ... ah ... have an appointment this afternoon, in the city."

"Well, let's talk before you go. Get our ducks in a row. Meet me in the study in an hour," Jack ended with a nod to his son and wife as he left the room.

Estelle and James sat in silence for a few moments until James cleared his throat.

"Mother, I'm not sure this was such a good idea."

"What?" Estelle asked brightly. "Breakfast? Or trying to beat your brother at squash?"

With stony eyes James drank his coffee until Estelle relented.

"All right, all right, but tell me, what's not to like about the girl?"

"Well ... she's a girl," James said, tilting his head forward. "Still in high school. Isn't that enough, for gosh sakes?"

"But she'll graduate in six months."

"Along with my baby brother."

"But girls are different." Estelle launched into her practiced reasoning. She'd convinced her three other sons on her choice for their mates, and she would do the same for James. Men didn't understand the nuances necessary for a good marriage. A raised eyebrow or narrow ankle or any one of a woman's many charms too easily snared them. "Girls mature faster than boys. With five sons, I should know. And most girls marry straight out of school. We've discussed this already. Didn't you say you wanted someone simple? Uncomplicated? The Howe girl is a perfect confection. Charming, beautiful, properly educated, a good temperament, a respectable family and brought up right here in town, where she'd still be close to her parents. Honestly, James. What have I missed? I thought we agreed it was time for you to settle down."

James pursed his lips at his mother, purposely rattling his cup in the saucer. "We did, Mother, but I've rethought that decision. Not quite yet."

Estelle smoothed the tablecloth in front of her and examined her hands. "Oh. I see. Which is it now? Dancer? Singer? Actress? Is there no end to your thirst for ... entertainment?"

Her clipped voice did not stop the upturned corners of James' mouth. "I never said you'd like her," he smirked.

His insouciance ran up Estelle's neck. Pulling her hands to her lap, she leaned back hard on the chair, her shoulders pressing against its carvings.

His mother's obvious distaste was one of the features James liked best about her. She never hid behind illusion. She looked straight, talked straight and dished it out straight.

"Actress," James admitted, brushing his fingertips across his lips, the scent of their date last night still lingering, before he had to leave for the hometown dance. "Terrific legs and, well, the whole package, as you might imagine," James laughed. "Just met her last week, so who knows. It'll probably be done by June, when they run away to summer stock."

Estelle looked sharply at her son, appraising his high cheekbones, bony nose and pointed chin. Without that thick wave of hair to soften his rigid features, he'd have a harsh, English look, she thought: all points and no curves. However, she had to admire his debonair flair, and she understood his desire to play as long as possible. Besides, regardless of what she wanted, he would not return home until he was good and ready. In that way, he was most like her. His brothers were easy, never straying far, quickly acquiescing into husbands and fathers. She'd even managed to marry off Beatrice, whose awkward looks threatened to destine her to old-maid status, tromping around the world in size ten shoes and explorer hat, promoting women's squash.

But James was different. From too young an age he'd shouldered too many family burdens, and it was a relief when he shucked it all off at Yale, becoming a ringleader in his group, for all sorts of she-nanigans. She adored his gang of friends, who made the house sing all weekend with pranks and laughter and nonstop record playing and spontaneous bouts of dancing. He was so like her she sometimes found it unbearable to be without him, even though his world travel had been her idea. Seeing how he chafed under the routine of office work, she'd helped craft a plan for researching investment opportunities throughout the world, sold it to Jack, and off James flew: to Brazil for Carnival, California for surfing and golf, Austria for waltzing in Fashing Season, Italy for the grape harvest, Germany for Oktoberfest, and Paris and London anytime, except August. She kept abreast of his activities through his religiously sent telegrams, and she relished the details he delivered on his intervals home. But when he decided to take an apartment in New York, his returns to Gladdenbury became more infrequent; which is why Celeste Howe was so enticing. She was a perfect fit as her son's mate. Someone content with being a good wife and mother who could also look smashing on his arm while providing the quiet, ordered home every successful man needs. Estelle had no doubts she could teach Celeste anything she didn't already know. But she also knew, despite her best persuasion, she could not force James to agree. He would yield to her will only when he was ready.

"So you are no longer bored with the falderal?" Estelle asked curtly.

"I did indeed say that, but I guess it was a passing concern."

Estelle rose, snapping her napkin before dropping it on the table, then stepped behind James' chair, reached around his broad shoulders and pinned her cheek to his.

"James, I cannot fault your enjoyment. I certainly had my fill, long after my mother gave up any hope of my marrying. When I met your father, at your same age, I felt very much the same. I adored him at first sight, but it still took two more years before I agreed to walk the aisle. I guess we're just that type of people, who have to tear up the hills when we're young. So I do understand. But tell me, is there any possibility you'd be interested in this girl in the future? When you're ready?" As she finished speaking, she released him, stepping to the side with her hand on the back of his chair.

Wiping the corners of his mouth with his napkin, James smiled with self-satisfaction. "Mother, I can sincerely say yes. She is a fine girl who will likely become a great lady, once she matures. But I can't promise our timing will match."

Estelle swung her head in a circle as she considered her next question. She wanted to secure some sort of measure to keep James on track. "Alright then. What might you suggest to ensure her proper maturation?"

James paused, thinking about Celeste. What could he complain about? She was kind, with an angelic face. Her eyes sparkled, her lips naturally turned upward, she even had small dimples when she smiled deeply. Her figure was exquisite, she made excellent small talk, and her laugh was warm. Might he like her to be a little more knowledgeable about the world? It certainly helps conversation along, but it was a double-edged sword that could so easily get out of hand, and then what do you have? A debutante taking a stand! James nearly laughed at the thought.

"I don't know, Mother ... except ..." he hesitated, unsure Estelle would agree. "Except I don't think her grandmother has too much regard for me. I felt that in Prague and at the Cotillion and even last night's dance. She gives me a cold fish eye. Perhaps if Gamma had a little less influence on Celeste, it might turn out right ... *if* it is to be."

Estelle's eyes narrowed as she smiled at her son. She completely agreed. Gamma Howe's spirited ways had already captured her husband's attention to the point where he was beginning to spout off bits of Gamma wisdom. He even said he wanted to travel to her birthplace, this Bohemia. Not Prague, he insisted, but to the woods and rivers where the Boii Celts first lived. He wanted to feel their spirit in the soil and water. Whatever was going on, Estelle knew it had to stop. Or at least shrivel a bit. And Celeste's attentiveness to her grandmother's every word bordered on dangerous, at least for Estelle's objectives. Uncertain as to how she might curtail Gamma's imprint upon Celeste, Estelle kissed her son's cheek, silently agreeing to the challenge, and exited the dining room, heading for her study.

15 Legacy
December 21, 1930

When Jack left the dining room he did not follow his Sunday routine. He did not shower and dress for the day, nor circle pertinent articles in the newspapers, nor read and prepare for the business week ahead. Instead, he sought the quiet of his study to think about the questions Gamma Howe had raised the night before; questions that churned his mind and disrupted his slumber.

At the dance, Jack had corralled Gamma for more stories. His thirst refused to be quenched. Using every skill, he had kept Gamma talking until she turned the tables on him, asking about his heart's desires, and Jack hadn't known how to answer. So much of his life had been built around duty. Then James arrived at the dance and Gamma grew distracted. They parted company, but he could not forget her questions: What had he chosen? What did he let pass? To what was he now being drawn?

It placed Jack in an unusual situation. He considered himself a practical man who rolled up his sleeves and got things done, never wasting much time on analysis. He believed success was achieved by action, not contemplation, particularly not the past. Yet Gamma's questions would not leave his mind.

Slapping the newspapers on the oversized partners' desk, Jack stood in the middle of his study scratching his head. It was her last question he found most haunting. "Has it turned out as you dreamed?" she'd asked, squeezing his hand. The question baffled Jack because he didn't think about life in terms of dreams. He'd been too busy building the business and a family. Throughout the night he had tried to remember his boyhood notions about life before joining the family business, built by his father and grandfather. But his mind had remained blank as he tipped into a frustrated sleep. Yet by the morning's early light, he had dreamed of his favorite childhood pastime: a game called Adventure that he began playing at seven or eight with neighborhood friends.

They were explorers, charting undiscovered lands and seeking treasure. They began by choosing a location; a wet jungle or high mountain or vast desert or one of the seven seas. Then they'd select a leader, usually Jack because he loved being a fearless captain, leading his mates across rough terrain. Through the backyards, up the trees and around the creek they rambled, capturing every treasure in their path. The bounty generally consisted of rocks and bent sticks, but they occasionally found a dropped comb, hankie, broken teacup or button. Sometimes they'd split up to evade approaching warriors and reconvene at the boys-only clubhouse underneath the Meadens' back porch. Every day, Jack played the game with his friends or by himself, happily swinging over the creek, escaping fast approaching pirates.

Standing in his squash shorts, Jack wondered what that dream had to do with his life. Walking around his desk, he was drawn to the wall of photos lining the study; pictures of people, places and things, framing three generations of Meaden success. Staring at the captured accomplishments of his father and grandfather, Jack suddenly realized he had not been living his dream at all. He'd been following theirs.

As first son of the first son of an immigrant, Jack was preordained to inherit the business they had built, and along with the clients, staff and management came this memorabilia-filled study, a testament to his family's first 100 years in the United States. Everywhere he looked, the past whispered to him. It was in the selection of fine books lining the barrister shelves behind the desk and the thick memory journals documenting important family events and the stuffed moose head, twelve-point antler rack, opalescent pheasant hide and full standing grizzly bear, commemorating Meaden hunting trips. Every tabletop and corner contained a tribute, a remembrance, of their lives. Even the leather-topped partners desk, where father and grandfather worked, facing each other, from the earliest days of the business. But of all these ornaments, it was the photographs that most reminded Jack of the sacrifices made for his sake.

The first frame enclosed the immigration papers of his great grand-parents, German peasants who'd arrived in 1836 with Jarden, their two-year-old toddler in tow. Their names were barely legible now, but Jack could still read them. Jarden Meaderheim, his grandfather's original name before he became an insurance agent and changed it to James Meaden.

The next frame featured Grandfather Meaden as a young man, his face stern, holding a rolled, beribboned diploma. Flanked by a man and woman, they stood next to a sign for The Free Academy. Jack shook his head, still confounded as to how his grandfather managed to attend the school that became City College of New York. He knew the Academy had been created for poor young men in his grandfather's time, but that didn't explain how he got in. His great-grandparents barely spoke English, so how had they even found out about it? In search of an explanation, Jack flipped over the photo and found a scrawled inscription:

1853. Jarden Meaderheim's Graduation. The Free Academy.
T. Harris, K. Howe

"Jumping jehosaphat. Who in blazes were T. Harris and K. Howe?" Jack whispered under his breath. He'd always assumed the photo was of his great-grandparents, who died around that time in a factory explosion. "Harris, Harris … he had something to do with the school's creation … but who's K. Howe, and why is she with my grandfather?"

Jack rehung the photo as his eyes bounced to the next one, and smiled at the youthful faces of his father and grandfather, shaking hands in front of a door with a small, freshly painted sign: *Meaden Insurance Company*. On the bottom of the photo his grandfather had scribbled:

1875. Hardware for the Future.

Those words had puzzled Jack until Grandfather Meaden told him about working in a hardware store as a young man and how much he liked the feel of nuts and bolts and selling useful things. Jack glanced back at the graduation picture with K. Howe and briefly wondered whose hardware store grandfather had worked at and how he came to be offered the sales job at Connecticut Life Insurance, taking him in a different direction. He also remembered grandfather talking about how insurance helped people in times of disaster, cobbling back a life, one nail at a time. And how he told his clients and prospects that insurance was just like hardware: nuts and bolts for securing the future. On that motto alone he sold many insurance policies and became a success.

Fifty-five years after Meaden Insurance's opening day, Jack was still impressed by his grandfather's guts to leave behind a secure career with an established company and strike out on his own, still with a houseful of children to support. When asked about taking such a big risk, Grandfather Meaden would only laugh and repeat the prayer his parents had recited daily for their own children: "Sum-ting betta than we come from, and perhaps a bit of sum-ting more."

The last photo of grandfather was taken at his 70th birthday and retirement celebration in 1905. Jack was 29, with two children at the time. The extended family had gathered underneath a banner made especially for the day. Jack remembered the photographer's call to look at the camera, but at the last moment, before the shutter clicked, Grandfather Meaden had turned, pointing to the banner, imprinted with his favorite slogan: "Always Victorious, Never Vainglorious." It was as if Grandfather knew he'd be dead within six months and used that celluloid moment to send one last message to his heirs: Persevere, no matter how tough the battle, but always with humility.

Jack's belly began to rumble. Victorious at what? Business? Marriage? Family? Squash? He'd done it all, exceeding everyone's expectations, but in light of Gamma Howe's question, "Has it turned out as you dreamed?" it all seemed shortsighted.

At 20, he'd graduated Yale and joined the company. By 25, he'd wooed and won the richest, most independent woman in the county. By 35, he'd turned a decent fortune into impressive wealth. By 37, he'd sired six children who grew up with privileges far beyond those of his own youth, and he still continued to deliver on his duty: *make something better and something more*. At 45, he inherited the Meaden Insurance Company, and the following year his own first son, James, graduated from Yale and joined the firm. The Meaden legacy was on track, from first son to first son. But at 54, Jack now wondered what had happened to his youthful dreams of exploring the world. Standing in his study, he realized how he'd tried to quell them by being the life of the party, the man with big laughs, good cigars and better stories. It had worked for a long time, but he now recognized that being the affable, dutiful chap had not extinguished the fire in his belly. He still hungered for adventures of his own making. Where were *his* dreams on the wall? Hadn't he earned the right to pursue a few of his own by now?

By Meaden family standards, it was too early for Jack to retire, but he'd already drafted succession plans. He did not want to turn over the reins as an old, spent man and drop dead six months later, as had both men before him. Exploring the world was still possible, by himself and with Estelle, once Ron was launched at Yale. There was no reason not to

– except for James. From first son to first son the legacy stipulated. So until James settled down and learned the less glamorous side of the business, Jack was stuck. But with Estelle's selection of Celeste Howe as a bride for their fastidious son, Jack saw his way out. She was from a solid family. Martin Howe was a first-rate merchant and good community man. And if the girl had half the spunk of Gamma Howe, his son's life could be very well inspired. Feeling suddenly optimistic, Jack slapped his hands together as he strode to the bookcase, slipped out a slim volume, leaned against his desk and perused the well-worn book with excited eyes.

After finishing breakfast, James Meaden showered and dressed in gray flannel trousers, a crisp white shirt and dark blue blazer. Inspecting his appearance in the mirror, he admired his slicked hair, feeling himself again and eager to return to New York after meeting with his father. Dropping his bag by the front door, James approached the study where he saw his father perched on the desktop, bent over a book. Leaning against the doorframe, James glanced around the room. Everything was in exactly the same place since his youth. In younger days, he loved to look at the wall of pictures, studying the grainy, black-and-white images of his father, grandfather and great grandfather on their quail hunting trips, traveling on steamships, breaking ground for a new building and proudly showing off their first-born sons. Turning his head, James' eye was drawn across the room to the bay window, where the bear stood, its claws outstretched with a ferocious, snarling face that had always scared the younger children. None of the family's matriarchs wanted it in the house, but as it was a gift from an important client, a big-game hunter and family friend, so it remained.

Feeling a bit snarlish after the late-night festivities and early morning squash game, James cleared his throat. "Ready, Father?"

Jack looked up, snapped shut the book and waved his son into the room. "Yes. Come in, come in. Take a seat," he replied, pointing to the chair at the side of the desk while sitting in his own high-backed chair, the old leather squeaking against his bare legs. He held the book up. "The Alaskan Gold Rush," he said. "1896, the year I joined the company, a major gold strike was discovered on the Klondike River and some friends decided to go out. They invited me along, and I desperately wanted to go, but father insisted I honor my duty. So I stayed."

James had heard the duty story many times before, but never the ending. "So you've said, Father, but how did they fare?" he asked sincerely, hiking his pants as he sat down.

"What? Oh, I don't know," Jack replied, swiveling his chair to slip the book into the barrister case. "Never heard from them again."

James nodded, hoping for a swift meeting. He had a date with his new girl, Kate, in New York and didn't want to be late.

Jack sat pensively for a moment. "Now that's not exactly true. I did get a letter from one of them, outlining their trip out. Sounded like a first-rate adventure and I was damn jealous. Held on to that letter for years but never got another. Maybe they struck it rich and they're sitting pretty somewhere out west, or maybe they slipped into the Klondike's icy waters and died trying. Either way, I've always admired their get-up-and-go."

James nodded, stroking his chin. His father's voice sounded odd, almost emotional.

"And that's why I wanted us to talk today," Jack said, smacking both hands on the desktop. He leaned forward, looking James in the eye. "Did you know I met Gamma Howe before you returned?"

"Mother had a dinner," James dryly confirmed. He was still under the assumption he was there to discuss business, and he found his father's behavior rather strange. It was already Sunday afternoon, yet the old man was still dressed in his squash whites, when he'd normally be preparing for next week's meetings, either here or at the office.

"Yes, your mother had a dinner," Jack laughed. "Only this dinner turned into something I didn't expect."

"What did you expect, Father?" James asked. Not that he cared. He asked questions as a matter of rote. A little trick he'd learned for making the other person feel important, an essential for successful business deals.

"What did I expect?" Jack's voice was robust. "Why, the normal social drudgery. Old Mrs. So-n-so monopolizing the table with drivel until the men are mercifully released to smoke and drink in the study. But this dinner, by God, was downright invigorating."

"Because of Gamma Howe?" James looked a bit incredulous. Gamma seemed to bristle in his presence, and besides, what did she have to do with their business?

"One and the same," Jack confirmed. "That woman is a marvel. Leaving everything behind to find something better, as a young girl! Like the Klondike boys. Tip top! That's verve and guts, which you expect in men, but not a girl. Did she tell you about seeing Dickens?"

James shook his head. What in blazes was going on? Was his father going mad?

"Hell," Jack continued, ignoring the blank look on his son's face. "On her way here, she saw the man in a lousy London pub just months before the old chap died. And that big gray cape she wears? She made it in homage to the one she saw him wearing that night! Spunk. That's what she's got, and that's why I wanted to talk with you today."

"About Gamma Howe?" James tried to mask his sarcasm.

"Yes," Jack replied, rubbing his hands as he stood and paced behind the desk. "Son, you know your mother wants you home and married. She's been looking for the right girl for years, and she thinks Celeste Howe is the one. As far as your mother's concerned, the wedding should be next week." Jack stopped, leaned on the desk and stared at James. "That's all well and good for your mother's objectives, but quite frankly it suits mine, as well. The sooner you settle down and learn the back end of the business, the sooner I can turn over the reins and have a bit of adventure myself. What I want to know is, straight out, what do you think of the girl?"

James smirked at his father's direct-approach style. Just like his squash game: Set up the point and demand an answer. It was so brusque it often worked, startling a client to action. While Jack closed many a deal with this technique, James preferred a more subtle, noncommittal approach. He twirled his hand. "Straight out? Well, Father, I'd have to say when the time is right, I suppose she'll do as good as any."

The twinkle in Jack's eyes vanished. He stepped back and asked in a flat, measured voice, "What do you mean, as good as any?"

James returned his shot. "I meant that when I'm ready, Celeste will probably do just fine for the things I need in a wife."

Sucking in a sharp breath, Jack looked around the room for something to focus on to keep his temper in check. He dropped in his chair and leaned back, straining the old leather. "What does that actually mean? The things you'll need in a wife?"

James finally heard the change in his father's temperament and sat up. "Nothing, Father. I'm just answering honestly, as you've always requested."

Jack nodded, confirming the code he'd taught his children. He repeated his question. "Alright then, tell me honestly. What things will you need in a wife?"

Recognizing a taunt, James clenched his jaw. At 28, he could damn well make up his own mind on what he wanted, and his answer was clipped. "A lovely girl to tend the home and children without being too much trouble."

Trouble. The word reverberated as the men stared at each other. For a long moment, neither moved, the air thick with tension. Then Jack swiveled his chair, rose and walked to the bay window overlooking the garden, standing in front of the bear. Hands in his pockets and legs twitching, he quietly replied, "Well then, you just go ahead and forget about Celeste Howe, because I won't allow you to do that to her."

"Do what to her?" James challenged back, his tone edgy.

"Ruin her," Jack rumbled.

James burst into a spitting laugh. With narrow eyes he stood up, matching his father's height. "Ruin her? What in blazes are you talking about?"

"That girl ..." Jack began in a slow, measured pace while staring out the window. "That girl ... she's more like me than I am anymore. Young, vital, on the verge of finding out who she is and what she wants, with a wide-open field in front of her. She looks like a lot of girls in this county, with rich parents and the right connections, but *that* girl has something different from all of them. *That* girl has Gamma Howe, who's so chock full of adventure it sputters out. *That* girl shares her blood and spirit, and I'll be damned to see it squandered on being *your* wife."

A hot-triggered flash rose in James's chest. "That's rather insulting, Father. Especially from someone who married up, and rather well, I might add." The words rushed out before he'd thought them through, and as soon as he finished, James knew he'd gone too far.

Jack stood very still by the window, hands in his pockets, legs still, chest barely rising – his mind on fire. He'd felt a punch in the gut and knew a kick to the groin, but never, in all his days, had the wind been snatched out of him until that very moment, by his own son, in his own home, with two simple words.

"Married up?" Jack spoke quietly, staring out the window. "Well, I suppose a big shot world traveler would see it that way. Especially one who's done it on his ancestors' sweat."

"Father," James relented, "I didn't mean ..."

Jack's hand flashed in the air, cutting him off. "No doubt. I did just that. Your mother was upper crust to a plebeian Meaden, but that's not my problem. What I find most insulting," Jack said, his anger percolating, "is your idea of a wife. As you describe it, she's equivalent to a servant. Not a partner or mate. Not an equal who brings gifts and talents you couldn't possibly replicate. Not a friend and trusted confidante, but little more than hired help. Tell me, is that how you see your own mother?" Turning his head, Jack's eyes switched over his son's face and body, looking for signs of weakness.

James stared back, not daring to blink. "Of course not," he replied with disdain. "Mother and I are much the same."

Crossing his arms over his chest, Jack leered at his son. "Now that's a bit of truth coming from your soggy mouth. Your mother makes mincemeat of anyone who tries to box her in, shredding them before they even consider a defense. I've seen her do it many times, and you as well. So that raises the question: was your definition of a wife actually a description of me?"

James twitched, hoisted by his own petard, not knowing what to say.

Jack asked again. "Do tell, son. If you are like your mother, what does that make me? The whipping boy? The lucky SOB who can provide good service without being – what was it you said? – too much trouble?" Jack stared down his son, and then looked away, shaking his head. "By God, I wish I'd gone to the Klondike when I had the chance and be spared the *hell* of finding out what my son *really* thinks of me, after sacrificing *my dreams* for his."

Stiff with discomfort, his legs aching, James stepped toward Jack. "Father, I didn't mean to imply ..."

Jack interrupted him again. "Oh, but you did." He turned sharply, hands punctuating the air. "At least be man enough to own up. Just as you meant to imply that Celeste Howe was really not up to snuff." He stepped forward, causing James to pull back. "But mark my words: No one else will ever be, either. Because along with your good looks and debonair charm, you've inherited your mother's self-possession." His voice tightened and pitched, his pointed finger underscoring his words. "You both have an uncanny way of turning everything into self-reflection. *Her* saving grace is that she's put it to some good use, helping those less fortunate, *but not less worthy. What*, in God's good name, can *you* claim to offer the world?"

His fury no longer containable, Jack pulled back his arm with a guttural growl, pivoted and plunged his fist deep into the belly of the bear, ripping through the old flesh and exploding the dry, dusty hide, peppering both men with a cloud of hair and stuffing. It happened in an instant, but rolled on in slow motion as dust powdered the room and a dazed James staggered backward, dropping into a chair.

Pulling his hand from the belly of the beast, Jack faced James, arm still raised, ready to slug again. Slowly stalking toward his son, Jack spoke through gritted teeth, "I love my wife, and I've treasured my children, and

I've worked hard to deliver a good life. But suddenly I realize the legacies I've been upholding are the wants of my father and grandfather, not mine. Without question, I believed their beliefs and tacitly agreed to pass them onto you, so you would pass them onto your heirs. But it's not what I really wanted, and look at the return: a son who doesn't understand one wit of what matters in life and a business that will never release me from its grip. So I'm going to do for you what I should have done for myself years ago. James Austin Meaden the Second, I formally release you. This company will not shackle you as it has me. I won't be party to robbing anyone of their dreams or subjecting them to a marriage of convenience. I didn't marry your mother for money or possession. She was a wild mare when I met her, full of fire and spit. What I love most about her is she won't back away. She holds her point of view. She gives me a knock on the head when I'm too foolhardy or stupid. I chased her for two years before she was convinced I meant it, before she trusted me not to own her, only to love her. That's why we married, young man. That's the only reason we married."

Drawing a deep breath, Jack towered over James, cowering in the chair. Realizing his arm was still cocked in the air; he slowly lowered it, then circled it to loosen the muscles as he walked to the far side of the desk. Leaning on its edge, he flipped open the humidor, extracting a cigar. Deliberately, he clipped the end, struck a wooden match and slowly drew the flame into the blunt end. After a few long puffs, his nerves calmed and his thoughts collected. All the while, James sat mute, his mouth too dry to speak, even if he had an inkling of what to say.

"I mean it, son." Jack finally spoke. "From this day forward, I remove the yoke of your birth. From first son to first son has been the family legacy, but no more. You haven't shown any interest in the nuts and bolts of the business, and you've liked the role you've played. I'll grant you've done a fine job at it, too. No reason to swap out the horse when he's winning the race, just for the sake of legacy."

James's face twisted in confusion as Jack continued.

"So from now on, do as you like. Take a wife or not. Live in New York or Europe or Asia, for all I care. Do as you see fit. There's no law requiring you to inherit the Meaden mantle. One of your brothers will jump at the chance to take the reins, and I'll get on with my retirement. But there is one condition: You're to stay away from that Howe girl. She's too much filly for you. Hell, if I were a young man again, I'd marry the girl myself."

Jack pushed off the desk and stood by James' chair. "So off you go." He started to offer his hand, and then dropped it with a shrug. "We'll catch up on business in the office next week. Glad we cleared this up. Good you came by. Your mother especially appreciates your visits." With a few swift steps and both arms swinging, Jack Meaden left the room and thumped up the center-hall stairs, taking them two at a time, trailing smoke like a locomotive.

16 Graduation
June 1931

For some Gladdenbury citizens, the winter of 1931 was riddled with angst.

Ede set her chin after the dance debacle, resolved to show Celeste she didn't need her anymore, and she made several new friends so quickly she even surprised herself.

Celeste dug in her heels in spite of knowing she'd made a selfish mistake, ignoring Gamma's urging to apologize, and pretended not to care what Ede said or did.

Ron moped his way through the semester up in frigid New Hampshire, with an empty mailbox and a hole in his heart. Without Ede's letters, he realized how much he liked her, but he didn't know how to set things right, especially after the confusing feelings Celeste had stirred up at the dance.

James left Gladdenbury in a huff after the confrontation with his father and returned only for an obligatory appearance at their traditional Christmas Day open house, where he attended select friends and clients but steered clear of his parents and the Howes, and he subsequently turned down every invitation his mother extended thereafter.

Estelle harangued Jack for an explanation about James' sudden departure and the punched-out stuffed bear in the study to no avail. When Jack also refused to have the ragged tear repaired, insisting he liked the bear better that way, she did her best to disguise the gaping hole, draping

Christmas greens across the outstretched paws, but had no notion of how to fix the underlying rip between father and son.

Myrtle didn't understand why Estelle became distant and James remained absent from all community events, and became increasingly depressed at the sudden crash of her dream for a June wedding. Unable to express her consternation, she became snappishly moody, angered by the swings of her wretched fate.

And Martin, baffled by the sudden chill in his household, hibernated his way through the cold months, working extra hours at the store, and in his small home study tucked underneath the stairs.

Only Jack and Gamma carried good spirits throughout the winter snows into spring. Spotted regularly with their heads together, they looked like spies conspiring on a secret mission, often bursting out in hearty laughter. And no one understood why Gamma stayed up late every night, working at her desk.

But all of winter's murky, sluggish feelings finally melted away in June at the Gladdenbury High School graduation.

On the Town Green, with rows of yellow flags fluttering alongside the pink dogwood trees, everyone who could attend did so, dressed in their best finery. With collective pride, the town gathered to send off its next generation. Even the shops closed for several hours to free employees for the annual social ritual.

Jack Meaden, school board president for the past dozen years, considered presiding over the graduation to be his favorite civic duty. For months he'd work on his speech, researching and honing a fresh message for each class. No cookie-cutter talk for him. To find the right tone, he'd prowl among the teachers, storeowners and parents, seeking unique bits about the students. Many attended the festivities just to hear Jack's speech.

In the middle of the Green, a platform and trellis were erected, draped in white sailcloth and ropes of ivy. Seven rows of chairs faced the stage, with hundreds more lining the sides for family and friends. Par for the second Saturday in June, the air was warm and scented with fragrant blossoms. At the far end, the graduates milled about, twirling in their caps and gowns and waving to the gathering townspeople. The Howes arrived early, with Myrtle marching ahead, across the lawn, claiming front-row seats near where Celeste would be sitting.

Looking up from checking arrangements on the dais, Jack hailed the Howes and hopped off the stage. Heartily shaking Martin's hand and complimenting Myrtle's fluttering green dress and matching cloche, he then slid into the chair alongside Gamma, tucked under a wide brim hat, cooling herself with a faded silk fan.

"And how do you feel today, Gamma?" Jack patted her hand.

"Proud," she winked.

Jack puffed up his chest, slipping his thumbs under his vest. "As you should be. That's quite a girl you've raised."

Myrtle, who was scanning the arriving audience, wheeled about with furrowed brow, ready to contend it was she who raised Celeste, when Jack jumped up.

"And a great day for the Meadens, as well," he said, pointing across the Green. "Look, the whole clan came out to hear the old man's speech."

Whirling back, Myrtle's heart leapt as she saw Estelle gliding across the lawn, escorted by James. Impeccably dressed in a Chanel, belted, off-white summer sweater and navy pleated skirt with a long strand of pearls and a navy style beret set low on her forehead, Estelle was closely followed by a cluster of her four other grown children, spouses and grand-children. Several paces behind them, Ron scuffled along, his hands stuffed in his pockets.

"Why, Myrtle Howe," Estelle released James' arm to embrace her. "How long has it been? And how happy you must be for your daughter's success."

Before Myrtle could open her mouth, Estelle swept back her arm, presenting her brood. "Of course you know James and Ron, but I don't believe you've met my other children."

The hubbub of introductions bemused Gamma as she watched all the men shake hands and the women nod politely and the grandchildren stare blankly down the Green, looking for their friends. A trumpeter strutted onto the stage and blew a few flourishes, summoning the crowd to their seats. Martin sat next to Gamma, with Myrtle on his other side. Estelle sat next to Myrtle, and the rest of the Meaden family filled in around the Howes. Ron sat behind Gamma and gave her shoulders a squeeze hello. But when James sat down by her side, Gamma wondered what other surprises the day might bring. Looking around, Myrtle couldn't believe this good fortune. A gentle thrill rose in her throat and light footsteps of hope returned to her heart.

With another trumpet flourish, the dignitaries filed onto the platform, and everyone stood as the high school band played the processional march.

Spontaneous cheers burst forth as graduates passed their families. Ranked in height order, the fifty-two young men and women filed into their rows and stood waiting for the band to finish, their gowns quivering in the gentle breeze and high excitement.

Celeste stood in the fourth row, third seat from the end, her legs twitching under her gown as she looked to her family. But first she spied James, then Ron, a head taller behind him. Both were waving to her. Mustering a smile, she waved back.

Several rows behind Celeste and diagonally across, the taller Ede saw the Meaden brothers and Celeste waving. Bile crept up her throat until Ron moved his head and began waving in her direction. Looking down at her feet, Ede's cheeks burned hot and her heart thumped wildly in her chest. She wasn't sure she wanted to forgive him, but her heart's pounding confirmed she felt the same as when they'd met. Lifting her head, she sloughed off her upset and smiled. After all, it was her graduation day, and soon the whole world would be brand new. Her broad grin caused Ron to tip his straw hat.

Tracing the direction of Ron's attention, Celeste smiled weakly at her lost friend, but Ede didn't see. Reluctantly turning back to face the stage, Celeste was mighty sorry her last school function was beginning without her best friend in her corner. The late morning sun hovered behind a grove of trees on the east side of the Green, dappling shade across the lawn as the band finished playing, and Jack Meaden, standing at the lectern with his arms outstretched, welcomed the graduates to their long-awaited day. Following ceremonial routine, he invited the minister's blessing, acknowledged the principal and staff, received the class gift and introduced the mayor and then the valedictorian, who made their predictable speeches, before returning to the lectern to make his address to the graduates. The audience rustled in their seats, anticipating another good speech.

"As you all know," he began, "I've never been one to turn down an opportunity to have my say."

Everyone laughed. Ever since he was a kid in knickers, Jack had been a town fixture, voicing his opinion on matters large and small. He was also the first in line to lend a helping hand, no matter what the trouble, and he could just as easily sit in a fancy parlor as around an oilcloth-covered kitchen table. Bridging the divide between wealthy and worker, he was the glue that kept the town together, and people regularly sought him out for big belly laughs, howls at the moon and the good thoughts he always had time to share.

"Graduates … you are my favorite treat of the year. I love sending you off with an earful of ideas to begin your adult life. But this year I've found someone I think can do a better job."

A murmur danced through the crowd, and Jack waited for it to pass, smiling at the confused faces among his neighbors, friends and clients. "Now, this is not something I'd do lightly, anymore than I'd throw a squash match. But we have a very special person among us who has a few things to share. The kind of things we like to talk about at graduations, when one stage of life is ending and another beginning."

A rustle of leaves and shifting clothing drifted across the Green as the graduates and attendees turned to each other, trying to guess whom Jack meant. Even the dignitaries sat up, craning their necks to the sides of the stage, looking for a person out of place. Biding his time, Jack let them wait.

"Would you like a hint?" He finally asked, with raised eyebrows.

"Yessssss."

"Well, it's not a he."

Jack waited for the ohhhs and ahhhs to pass. "And let me tell you a bit more before I invite her up. First, she isn't famous in the conventional sense. At a cursory glance, she's lived a typical, ordinary life. Nothing more than a good daughter, wife, mother, and grandmother which might lead you to ask: What could she possibly offer our youth as they prepare to make their mark on this world? And perhaps you also wonder if old Jack Meaden hasn't dropped a marble or two."

He grinned at the soft chuckling from the crowd. "Well, I'm here to tell you that in her ordinary way, she's lived an extraordinary life. Not by the external standards of modern success, but by having the courage to live her own life fully, on her own terms, which is not an easy thing to do, by anyone's measure."

Jack nodded along with the concurring whispers throughout the audience. "Easy though it may sound, it's hard to live your own life, especially with so much well-intentioned advice coming from everyone, whether you ask or not. And harder still when the world is changing so fast. Just think about what's happened in our own town! We began as a small farming village in the 1600s, living alongside the Indians. Then ship-building came along, followed by factories and farm markets and ultimately fruit, each one changing our way of life. Imagine the courage it took for the people behind each of those businesses to follow their ideas and make them happen. I think it's fair to say that no one but old man

Hale believed peaches could grow in Connecticut! But, by dang, he was right, and now … we're famous for them!"

Someone whooped in the audience and Jack whooped back. "And our speaker has lived through equally interesting times. Think on this: The year she was born, the contemporary writers were Bronte, Browning, Dickens, Tennyson, Whitman and Longfellow, and the living composers were Berlioz, Verdi, Wagner, Liszt and Schumann. It was also the beginning of the great wheels of industry, with such inventions as tungsten steel, the telegraph printer and the electric light bulb. As she was growing up, our Civil War freed the slaves, Levi Strauss made the first pair of jeans, and the products we now use daily were just being created: the telephone, phonograph, fountain pen, dishwasher, zipper and paperclip. And when she was just your age," Jack pointed to the graduates, "she took a brave step, the first of many, traveling a great distance to marry, bear children, make friends and face heartbreak: burying a child, a grandchild and a husband. Now you'd think that would be enough to fill one lifetime, but at 50 years old, she picked up and started all over again, moving to our fair town. And through all these revolutions, she's carried with her a notion bigger than any scientific discovery I've ever known." Scanning the lawn, catching every eye he could, Jack saw Martin Howe staring at his mother, with her eyes downcast, locked on the purse in her lap.

"Ladies and gentlemen, young graduates, family and friends, there is only one word that sums up what makes this simple woman positively extraordinary, and that is: philosophy. From her, I've learned things I wish I'd known as a young man. And many times, as I've prepared for this day, I've wished it were me beginning again, with the chance to retackle the world. She has some important ideas to share about what matters in life and what courage and gumption really mean, and best of all, it's something we all can do, no matter how old or young. So I thought you should hear directly from a woman whose verve belies her 77 years. By now, I'm sure you've guessed of whom I speak. So please welcome Gladdenbury's most beloved citizen, Mrs. Bertra 'Gamma' Howe."

In the burst of applause, Martin squeezed his mother's arm as they both rose. Friends from every pocket of town called Gamma's name as Martin walked her to the stage.

Myrtle sat motionless in her chair, her mind shocked blank.

Estelle tried to catch James' eye, but he was watching Gamma.

Instinctively, Celeste popped around to find Ede, and they grinned like monkeys at each other, vanquishing their winter anger.

Taking Gamma's hand from Martin, Jack ushered her to the lectern as the crowd clapped even harder for the petite, robust woman, standing center stage, smiling shyly.

Gamma held up her hands. "Please, please, is too much," she said.

As the audience settled, she removed a few note cards from her purse and handed the bag to Jack, who took his seat behind her and held the purse as if it were fragile treasure.

Drinking in the picture of all her neighbors and friends in one place, Gamma felt her heart swell; similar to what she felt on her Bohemian farm, surrounded by family. Though this was not her homeland, it had become her home, and while these were not her people, somehow she'd become one with them. Shaking her head, she began.

"Never could I imagine such honor, since I not graduate from any school. We have many good schools in my homeland, but our farm was far away. So, I learn from some books as a child, and more from my son's school books. You know, of course, my son, Martin, who is everyday at the hardware store."

Gamma nodded to where he sat as quiet applause breezed through the rows.

As the crowd looked her way, Myrtle forced her pinched expression into a weak smile.

"Of him, I am very proud ... but you should have met his father!" Gamma quipped, rolling her eyes with a saucy smile. "Lucky was I, to marry such a smart, handsome man. But I offer something, too. Something I share today." Glancing over her shoulder at Jack, Gamma waggled her finger in the air. "Something Mr. Meaden thinks interesting, and for your sake, I hope he's right."

Bursting with pride, Celeste squeezed her whole body tight.

Gamma paused, letting the laughter settle. "This journey you begin now, has many questions, yah? Questions of ... who you might love ... and what you might do ... and where you might live ... and how you might like to try something new. Good questions, yah? Good questions for creating a life we love. Is important, these questions, for discovering what suits you best, and for some, you already know what that is."

Gamma nodded to a boy in the front row. "Like you, Johnny Hale."

Surprised, Johnny rolled back his shoulders, nudging his seatmates.

"For long time, Johnny, I see joy on your face when you talk about peaches."

Johnny immediately swiveled to the row behind, winking at his giggling sweetheart.

Following his glance, Gamma blushed, blurting a laugh. "Oh, no, Johnny! I mean the peaches on your family farm … I see how you love their growing."

As the audience and classmates burst out laughing, Johnny ducked his head, ginning sheepishly, showing his dimples.

Gamma sent him a warm smile in return, then switched her gaze.

"And then there is our best artist, Ede!"

Popping up tall, Ede sucked in her cheeks, restraining her toothy grin.

"What a colorful life you live already, Ede, and kindly share with us, too. And for certain, will be much more color coming to you as you follow your love of painting."

Ede's mouth broke into an open-mouthed grin and her father yelled from the sidelines: "That's my girl!"

Celeste wanted to look at Ede but held herself very still, barely breathing, hoping Gamma would mention her, too. But after speaking to three other students, Gamma's eyes switched over the entire class.

"What each of you will become I cannot know. Some will go to college, some to work, some to make a family. And for each of you, I know will be some happiness, some sadness and some hard times, too. Is true for us all, and in this way our lives seem very much the same. But I want you to know is not true. Every one of you will live a very different life. Because even though we come from same town or church or even family, no life is exactly like any other. Every person must walk different path, with different questions to be answered, and this difference, I think, is very best part of life. Because when you find your own answers to your own questions, you also find your own unique happiness. You find contentment, from inside to out, in your heart. This is my very best wish for each of you, to find your contentment. But I must tell you true: Is not so easy to do."

Gamma looked straight at the graduates, who stared directly back. A few licked their lips, but nothing else stirred.

"In my old country, Bohemia, our history is long and ancient, told by stories around the fire, about life, wisdom, contentment, passed from generation to generation. Today, I like to share three stories I learn at just your age. Stories that help, when facing big questions, such as choosing a life of my own."

Gamma let out a deep breath. "Is wonderful to see before me such beautiful faces. Excited for what is next and a bit scared, too, no? I know, because I feel same … many years ago … at my own graduation … standing on a ship in New York harbor, in a smoky dawn with fog so thick the shore is barely visible. After three weeks of travel on that ship, I wait for ferryboat to take us to the city. Imagine, after so much ocean, the relief and thrill I feel for what comes next, maybe just like you, today, yah? But suddenly, my whole body is washed in worry and my mind fill with questions. Would I even like America? How could I live with so little English? Could I ever see my family and homeland again? And what would happen when my brother, who brought me here, sailed away, leaving me alone with strangers? Suddenly I feel dizzy and began to cry, big fat tears down my dirty cheeks, frozen in place, too scared to go forward but no place to return. Others push past me, but I stood like a stone, not knowing what to do, afraid to move, for long, long time. Until I hear a whisper in my head. The voice of my Auntie, repeating what she say the day I leave. "Listen, my little Bertra," she say, close to my ear, "Don't be afraid. Remember the ancient teaching: Your Path Will Open to You."

Nothing stirred as the words echoed across the lawn and graduates' eyes opened wide.

"Your Path Will Open to You is something the elders tell me many times. *Pay Attention,* they say, *to what attracts your attention! For is sign to your path.* Nice words, yah?" Gamma nodded her head, then vigorously shook it. "No. Not so easy – to believe or do! Especially when standing on a deck, frozen in my shoes, crying as people push past, carrying bundles of nothing. I cry harder, thinking: What kind of sign could be on a ship for me? Thousands of miles from everything and everyone I love? But then … it happen."

Most of the audience leaned forward.

"Suddenly, I hear a sound that lifts my head and stop my tears. A sound so clear, so familiar it make my heart leap. "Baaah," I hear. The bleat of a small goat. The exact same sound *my* goats make in my home village, as I follow them up the mountain where we play in the same stream and eat the same berries. And even though we come home late some nights, my mother never worry, because she know the goats always lead me home safe. All this I remember in a flash, and again I hear the bleat. "Baah," closer now, and around the corner comes a small girl in a long dirndl dress with a tiny goat tucked under her arm, looking just like me when I was her age. Clutching her goat, she comes up close, staring hard at my wet eyes as she passes to board the ferry. Watching her go, I feel a laughing in my belly. "Of what am I scared?" I say to myself. "Look, even in America, a goat leads me home safe. All I need do is follow." So I wipe my face with the back of my hand, pick up my bundle of nothing and follow the goat onto the ferry, to find my path in this new land."

A hushed murmur moved through the rows of chairs. To Celeste it sounded like "yes." To Jack it sounded like "wow." To Martin it sounded like the sea. But to Gamma it sounded like laughter, so she began to laugh, too.

"OK, is first one. Now for second ancient teaching of my people: Honor What Beckons You." Glancing at the parents and friends, Gamma noticed a few worried faces. "Honor What Beckons You," she repeated. "What that mean? When I tell my son, Martin, when he was seven or eight, he ask: What means beckon? And I say: After your studies and chores, what you like best to do? And quick like frog, he jump on a stool, wave his arms in the air and say: I like to be pirate, sailing the seas for booty and gold bullion."

A big laugh erupted from the crowd. Many turned toward Martin, who was now beet red, but smiling, as he slowly shook his head at his mother.

"Forgive me, Martin, but now everyone knows what means beckon."

Then she pointed to the graduates. "I'm sure every one of you knows exactly what beckoned you at six and eight and ten because that age is very special time. An age when you don't question what you like. You just know it and do it, no matter who else approves. Be it sewing or sports or music or building forts with sticks and stones. You know, and you do, without question. Yah?"

The graduates immediately nodded and some of the audience, as well.

"But funny thing happen as we grow older. At 11 or 12 or 13, something change and we start to question what we like. We wonder: Is good enough? Or, will other people like it, too? We look outside ourselves for others to confirm what we like. Is crazy, no? But is something most do. Then, life becomes even more confusing, with more questions and, of course, many more people suggesting answers for you. Everyone is caring with advice, but makes it easy to forget what *you* like, what *you* dream and what feels right for *you, in your heart.* But for this, I offer clue."

Gamma leaned into the lectern, as if sharing a deep secret. "As you grow, you will change, and so will what beckons you. But one thing remain same. No matter what your age or circumstance, what stay the same is how you *feel* when you are beckoned." Gamma patted her chest. "In here, I mean, in your heart, that special feeling when you find something you really want to do or see or learn or be. The feeling of yes, I call it, is something only you can know. A humming maybe? A tingle? A burst of horns or quiet hush? Whatever is for you, is always there, waiting for your listening. So, if ever you get confused, remember the feeling, at seven or eight, when playing pirates or learning to paint. That feeling is *your* special clue, for discovering what is meant for you."

Gamma stood up straight, raising one hand above her head.

"Now tell me, who here knows this feeling?"

Over half of the graduates shot their hands in the air, some coming off their chairs in excitement. The rest quickly followed, turning to each other, bursting to talk.

"Yah, is good. Now you know the sound of your own heart's voice." Looking down at her note cards on the lectern, Gamma squeezed her hands together. "OK, so one more thing I like to say … if you not too bored with me."

In perfect unison the graduates yelled "Nooooo," as they clapped and yelped.

"Attagirl Gamma," Jack said above the fracas. "Bring it home now."

Although she was laughing, Gamma felt a bit uneasy, seeing a few veiled scowls peppered among the crowd, so she spoke a little faster.

"This voice of my heart I hear many times, but one special time I will share. Was when first we come to Gladdenbury, after our losses. A most sad time. I miss my husband so much I want to die, too. Is true. Everyday I pray to leave this earth, but instead, I feel my heart speak. It say: Wait; more is coming for you. I not want to hear this. I try to ignore. But what could I do? So finally I trust my heart voice and wait, patiently, ten long years, until great surprise finally come … the birth of my granddaughter, Celeste." Gamma let out a big poof of air. "Oooof. Suddenly all those years of sadness disappear, and I most glad I trust my heart and wait. For to miss my granddaughter's life would be a loss too great.

The girls on either side of Celeste wiggled closer to her, giggling under their breath. But Celeste looked only at Gamma, who smiled deeply at her, with sparkling, silvery blue eyes.

After a long moment, Gamma released Celeste's gaze and looked over the crowd, ready to finish and leave the stage.

"So these are my ancient gifts to you: Your Path Will Open to You, Honor What Beckons, and Listen to Your Heart Voice. And trust that even when life offers frustrations or disappointments, is also a gift that will lead to contentment, if you keep true to your heart. This is The Bohemian Way."

An audible gasp rushed through the Green.

Gamma raised her voice and spoke faster. "I wish for each of you, courage, to live your own life, fully and true. And I thank you, for your most kind attention."

Turning to Jack with misted eyes, Gamma reached for her purse. She did not see the graduates standing en masse, clapping with their arms above their heads, nor the audience members following suit. Lost in a mix of feelings, Gamma walked to the edge of the stage until Jack gently turned her to witness the joy coming from the crowd. Her hand came up to her mouth, hardly believing she had the chance to speak the words she'd carried all these years. With a short laugh, she squeezed Jack's hand, and he guided her down the steps into the welcoming arms of her son.

As Gamma walked back to her seat to ever increasing cheers, Jack stepped to the lectern and picked up the three note cards she'd left behind. Turning them over to see what she had written, he found one word on each card: Open, Beckon, Yes.

17 Dreams

June 1931

Exuberance rushed through the crowd at the conclusion of Gamma's speech, and lasted throughout the awarding of the diplomas, the final blessing and the recessional march. At the ceremony's end, everyone rose with a joyous whoop and followed the graduates to the end of the Green for some punch and convivial banter, with oversized picnic hampers lining the walkways, waiting to be opened and spread across the lawn for the Graduates' Luncheon with family and friends.

Diploma in hand, Celeste burst from the processional line and raced to Ede, falling into her outstretched arms. Clasping shoulders, they jumped in a circle, laughing and talking over each other, unsure of what to say about their winter anger but knowing their rift was mended.

At first James was flabbergasted by his father's choice of speaker, but by the end of Gamma's speech he was flummoxed. How had he missed this side of her? Was his ego singed because she had not instantly succumbed to his charms? But he now saw what Gamma offered, and it was the air he longed to breathe. She epitomized how he liked to think and desired to be, and he suddenly felt an odd tenderness toward her, patting her arm when she returned to her seat. Her proximity gave him a sense of relief that he didn't have to pretend anymore and could just be himself.

His reaction proved short lived, however. By the end of graduation, he'd snapped the notion right out of his head. "Straighten up," he scolded himself as they followed the graduates across the lawn. His achievements weren't gained by happenstance or foolishly following signs. No, he'd made judicious plans, and although his life was not exactly the imaginings of his youth, it was nearly so. He lived as close to his dreams as anyone could, given the constraints of reality. "So why do I feel defensive?" he silently brooded, while smiling benignly at the young Miss offering him a cup of punch.

As everyone floated down the lawn, Jack stood at the lectern, watching. It was the loveliest sight to his eyes, the gathering of family and townsfolk; all the people who gave his life ballast and depth. Drawing a breath, he savored the feeling in his chest, knowing he would not be the center of their worlds much longer. His plan for greater freedom would soon be in motion, and he was eager to come and go as he pleased, to find a Klondike adventure of his own, wherever it might be.

Not knowing what else to do, Myrtle stayed close to Martin, who was tending Gamma at the end of the Green, his hand close by her elbow in case she got dizzy in the swarm of well-wishers.

"I'm perfectly fine." Gamma tisked at his hovering.

"Would you please get Mama some punch?" Martin directed Myrtle, who now felt unstrung by the turn of events. As she retrieved a cup of punch, Myrtle's thoughts festered on how Gamma had upstaged her again. Contrary to Jack's comment, it was *she* who raised the beautiful Celeste. *She* was the mother of the graduate and honor was due *her*. Jack didn't realize how his words stung, like a glove slapped across her face. She felt dismissed and diminished, and what's more, Gamma was accruing even more attention, stealing the graduate's limelight. That's what Myrtle would have argued if anyone had asked, but no one paid her any mind; certainly not Martin, nor her own friends, who were swept up by Gamma's malarkey. Standing alone on the periphery of the milling crowd, Myrtle was greatly surprised when Estelle approached and broached the very subject.

"What a terrible mix of feelings you must have," Estelle prompted, steering Myrtle to an empty bench, away from the crush of curious ears.

Myrtle glanced at Estelle, wondering: friend or foe? "My-my only concern is for Celeste's future … and if …" she broke off, uncertain if she should share her concern about Gamma.

Estelle replied instantly. "Are you wondering if Gamma's philosophy might quash Celeste's social standing?"

Myrtle smiled, involuntarily. "Is that terrible of me?"

Estelle pursed her lips. "*Au contraire.* A mother's concern for her daughter's welfare is the most natural thing in the world." Leaning close to Myrtle's ear she added: "As is the desire to be mother of the bride."

Myrtle's hand flew to her cheek. "But I didn't mean …"

"Ah-ah, don't be coy with me," Estelle waggled her finger. "I've already suffered the betrothal drama of four children, one fussier than the last. But James, by far, has been my most recalcitrant groom. I honestly thought we were finally home free with Celeste. They seemed to get on so well until … well, I'm not really sure what happened last Christmas. James had a sudden change of heart, and frankly, I was embarrassed. Simply didn't know what to say to you. And for that, I do apologize."

As Myrtle listened, her hand drifted down to her lap. She felt as if bathed in warm water. Finally, someone was on her side. "So James went away by himself?"

"And would not return home for any reason, no matter how I pleaded."

For a moment, the two women silently appraised each other.

"So you weren't mad at me?" Myrtle asked quietly.

"Oh, heavens no! Myrtle Howe, if I am ever cross with you, you will certainly know when, what and why."

They both chuckled and fell silent again, glancing around the Green.

They spied James in the crowd, laughing with a client's family and pumping the hand of their newly graduated son. Then Ron, talking with Ede and Celeste, his stance a bit awkward, probably from nerves, but each of them was smiling, Ede most widely.

Estelle nodded toward Ron and murmured, "He's like a bird, light boned for flight. What a marvel he's been to watch on the squash court, and Jack adores having a champion in the family."

Myrtle made no reply, ignorant of the sport.

Estelle continued. "How different Ron is from his prowling panther brother. Do you think she could accept either one of them?"

Myrtle hiccupped. Estelle Meaden speaking so frankly, to her! Fidgeting a handkerchief out from her sleeve, Myrtle looked down as she replied. "Goodness Lord, Estelle. I never thought of Ron that way, but I see your point. They're being the same age and certainly how well they get along. But … I don't suppose he'll be ready for marriage for a little while yet, given school and … well, all those things expected of Meaden men. And Celeste … well, she's rather special and I don't suppose she'll have to wait long before an appropriate suitor sweeps her off her feet." Myrtle looked up slyly as she finished, patting the perspiration on her throat with her handkerchief.

Estelle's face remained placid, neither upset nor impressed. It was as she suspected. Myrtle Howe was going to marry off her daughter one way or another. But why the rush, Estelle wondered? She'd quite enjoyed her independence throughout her own twenties. Her years of solo adventures had delivered the best asset she could offer as wife and mother: inventive curiosity. Having seen so much of the world before settling down, she never felt bored or unstrung by the unavoidable minutia of home life. She never understood why the very women who'd never spread their wings were usually the first to condemn those who had. For such narrow minds, Estelle had little tolerance. But this she would not reveal to Myrtle, for she had an agenda of her own, as well. Besides the obvious beauty of Celeste, Estelle liked what she saw in the girl; especially her natural curiosity and impetuous spirit. It was exactly what James could use a bit more of in his life.

"That's a fair observation, Myrtle," Estelle replied. "Ron is still quite young and at the precipice of an excellent sports career. But James … he's slated to inherit the company, which requires he settle down and step up to his duty. Jack is eager to pass along the reins soon, while he still has energy for other things. So I had hoped …" Estelle trailed off, letting her message sink in. She did not want to reveal just how restless Jack had become, demanding she get James in order so he could be released from the day-to-day grind. If Celeste had been her own daughter, Estelle would have sent her off to see the world before settling down, as she'd done with Beatrice, who only recently married in her mid-twenties and subsequently delivered her first child. Although Estelle believed Celeste would be better off pursuing her own interests before settling down, she was very well suited for James. So, with a willing accomplice in Myrtle; Estelle imagined they could both achieve their objectives, before too much more time had passed.

Watching the crowd, Estelle and Myrtle saw other families setting out their picnics. Large blankets were spread across the lawn with plenty of room for strolling in between. The Meadens' maid had already marked their spot with three oversized quilts. Estelle pointed to it as she rose to gather her flock. "Myrtle, why don't you tuck your picnic alongside ours, so we can enjoy the afternoon together."

With a toothy grin, Myrtle scurried off to retrieve her basket and blankets.

◦~

After a delicious lunch of finger sandwiches, lobster-stuffed avocados, shrimp, apple and potato salads, cookies, fruit, soda pop and lemonade,

Jack Meaden settled back on a stack of pillows, his broad hands cradling his head, and called out: "Now tell me, Son ..."

Without a blink, every Meaden knew which of the five sons he meant. The term was reserved for the first son, as it had been for Jack.

"What did you think of that speech, eh?" Jack asked, winking at Gamma, who sat nearby. "Hear anything new and exciting?"

James cocked his elbow over a pillow and sanguinely faced both his father and Gamma. "Positively brilliant!" he began. "I'd love to borrow a few of your points, Gamma. They'd go over smashingly in Europe. Imagine prompting a client with: Your path will open to you." He snickered. "What better way to get my prospects to sign? Of course I'd have to fudge an appropriate story to bring home the point, but I think I could muster a good yarn. Would you mind?"

Gamma's eyes brimmed with water as she choked a guffaw in her throat. The boy was cheekier than she'd guessed. "I would, unless the story's true. Now I must ask: Your path, how did it open for you?"

Hearing the question, Estelle hushed Myrtle mid-sentence to observe.

Jack whooped, his eyes dancing. He hadn't discussed this part with Gamma: The unmasking. "By golly, that's right. It wasn't just the graduates you were addressing. We'd all do well to reflect on the questions," Jack expounded. "Do tell, Son, how was your path revealed?"

James scanned the faces turned toward him, not quite knowing how to sidestep the inquiry, but fortunately Beatrice shot her arm up, snatching the opportunity.

"I can tell how mine was," she asserted. At a young age, Bea had learned how to jump in with both feet in order to be heard among six boisterous men and an outspoken mother. A well-endowed woman, with her father's broad shoulders, Beatrice looked very comfortable in her tailored jacket with the matching A-line skirt fanned across her crossed-legged knees.

"My path opened when I was trying to decide which college to attend," she began. "It was between Vassar, Wellesley and Smith, but then, by chance, I heard that Trinity College ..." Beatrice looked at the Howes to explain. "That's in Hartford ... I heard they had squash courts that the women could play on. Not as an official team or anything, but us girls could use them! None of the other colleges even had courts." She leaned toward Gamma and Myrtle. "For so many years I've had to scrap for court time with my brothers ... the boys always came first, ya know. So to play regularly, with other women, put me over the moon. I'd never heard of Trinity until I met a gal at the club who went there. I'd call that a path opening, wouldn't you?"

Gamma laughed as she patted Bea's leg in agreement, enjoying her forthrightness. Looking over at the baby and nanny on the adjacent blanket, Gamma asked, "Still do you play?"

"Heck yes! Every chance I get!" she said, slapping a knee. "Got me right back in shape after Anne's birth. Plus I have to keep up with my USWSA responsibilities."

Gamma shook her head, not understanding.

"Oh, sorry" Beatrice laughed. "I'm so nuts on this sport, I forget everyone doesn't know. The United States *Women's* Squash Association: USWSA. It was formed just last year. I'm on the Board … well, the Junior Board. We organize the women's national squash tournaments and keep records for the regionals. I work with Eleo Sears and Margaret Howe – *Oh!* Howe! Look at that! Any relation?"

Gamma laughed. "I think no."

"Well, anyway, they're great gals. Mother introduced me because they love the sport as much as I do, and *oh*, the marvelous things they do for it. We call them the Squash Suffragettes!"

Groaning, James laid back on his pillow, flinging his arms over his eyes.

"Go ahead and moan, big brother," Beatrice jeered, throwing a pillow at him. "But mark my words, some day women will have equal court time, and we'll be as good … if not better … than any male champion!"

James waved his hands in the air. "Not even among my grandchildren will that be true."

Beatrice hoisted 9-month-old Anne onto her lap, nuzzling her neck. "And what's the likelihood of that, Mr. Batch-a-lor? How are you going to have children, much less grandchildren, without a wife?"

Jack saluted Beatrice. "Hey, she's got you there, Son!"

James shook his head. "Augh, the insufferable rectitude of the newly converted. A spouse and children is not the *only* holy path in life!"

A gaggle of Meaden grandchildren rapidly approached the blankets, followed by their parents, thirsty after playing. Jack doled out drinks and told everyone to settle down. "Now that you're all here … I've an announcement."

Estelle watched Jack face his family, elbow resting on his crooked knee, looking relaxed, refreshed, alive.

"Martin, Myrtle, Gamma, please excuse the exclusion, but if you don't mind listening, I've something to say that your very company inspired."

All three nodded politely as Jack surveyed the faces of his brood. Everyone, but James, was looking at him. "I want to be above board here so there are no misunderstandings. I'm 55, and while my father worked until 65 and grandfather 'til 70, I'm doing things differently. I'd like to retire as soon as possible. The business is in fine shape, thanks to all of you, and especially James, whose very smart investments saved our tukus in the market collapse. So I feel reasonably comfortable handing over the reins. Now, as you know, by Meaden law the leadership passes ..." Lifting his hands, Jack prompted his children to finish the sentence.

"From first son to first son whether he wants it or not," they replied in droning unison.

The grandchildren laughed at their parents as Jack nodded.

"Right, but I've decided to change that, too. Not that James is excluded. I just don't want to make it *a fait accompli*, because each of you should have the opportunity to do what you prefer. I say this because I now realize that if I'd had the option so many years ago, I might not have taken the job in the first place."

Jack's children automatically looked at James, who continued to keep his head down.

Jack slapped his hands together. "So here's my point: I want each of you to think about what you're doing and what you might like to do. Consider what beckons you ... as Gamma reminded us today ... and let's talk about it. Discuss it robustly, as we would a down-to-the-balls squash match. Because taking over the business has serious responsibilities attached. You've got to know the nuts and bolts as square as Ollie, and how to recognize a good investment as well as James, and dedicate your time to people far beyond the scope of your family and community as Austin and Fischer well know. The leader has all the risk on his shoulders, with hundreds of people relying on your dedication and good judgment ... employees and clients alike. I've already discussed some of this with James and offered him the option to continue doing what he already does so well. There's no reason for a man to change his life to suit another's whims. That's the difference I'm bringing to the table. So I want you each to think about it, and let's talk it out over the next few months, to find a mutually satisfying solution."

Silence reverberated after Jack finished. His boys were speechless at the sudden turnabout in family protocol. Their father had just upended their prescribed fates. Only Beatrice, who had been staring at James throughout her father's announcement, began to smile wickedly.

"Father," she asked, with a slight sneer in her voice. "Does the top position require living here in Gladdenbury?"

Fiddling with his glass of lemonade, Jack looked at James as he answered. "The head of the company needs to live close to headquarters."

James sat up, ignoring Beatrice's taunt. "Since everything else is being tossed in the air," he suggested. "Why not move headquarters closer to our most important clients ... say, New York?" Before anyone could snipe at his implied superiority, James asserted: "By the way, where's Ron in this? Is he included in this bidding war?"

"No," Jack answered, glancing at Ron, sitting at the back of the blankets. "I'll be transferring the responsibilities before he graduates college, so he won't be eligible for the position. Besides, I don't think it's how he wants to spend his time." Jack raised his eyebrows to Ron, seeking confirmation. But the boy only shrugged amiably, not sure if he agreed or disagreed.

With surprise, James looked back at his father. "That soon? Why, old man, you certainly have gotten a new religion." Glancing at his mother, whose face remained placid, James abruptly stood up, dusting off his pants and jacket. He felt a pressure in his head and a jumble of feelings. Anger, pride, relief, distrust, and he didn't know what he could say without sounding caustic, so he decided to leave before he said, or did, something regrettable.

"Mother, Father, thank you for the fine afternoon, but please excuse me. I have an appointment in New York." With a curt nod, he strode off across the lawn at a furious pace, not even noticing Celeste or Ede as he swept past the swings.

They caught sight of him passing.

"There's James," Ede whispered as he crossed the street.

Celeste looked on silently.

"Do you think you could like him? Enough to marry, I mean?" Ede asked.

Celeste shook her head. She'd thought about it all winter long, worrying what she'd done when he no longer came home, and at the same time wondered why she felt more free dancing with Ron than she had with James. But no one was asking her about Ron. All of her girlfriends and their mothers talked only about James and how lucky she was to attract his eye. But since he no longer seemed to care about her, she no longer cared back.

"He's too old for me," she whispered back. "And cold," she added, remembering how stiffly he held her at the dance and how rarely he laughed. Not like Ron, who was full of fun and spring with a bouncy sense of humor. Shaking her head, she changed the subject. "How was your talk with Ron?"

Ede's wide and wondrous smile returned. "He explained how shy he felt at the dance and how he never would have danced at all if you hadn't grabbed him, and then he didn't even realize what had happened until James arrived and how sorry he was to have hurt my feelings." Planting her feet on the ground, Ede pushed her swing back and forth.

"What does that mean?" Celeste asked gingerly. "Are you going to date?"

Ede shrugged. "I don't know. He said he was going to be awfully busy with the squash tournaments all summer, teaching and playing. Then his family goes to Maine for most of August, and then he's off to Yale. But he said he really liked talking with me and that I am the smartest girl he's ever met."

Celeste's shoulders rose with defensiveness, but she quickly quieted herself. She'd made her decision never to hurt her friend again, no matter what she felt about Ron or any other boy. There were plenty of likable ones who were eager to fill her time. But Ron was Ede's first crush, and she wasn't going to get in their way, ever again.

"OK – smart girl!" Celeste pumped her legs to lift her swing. "Then let's talk about us. Let's do what Gamma said and imagine how our lives will be! Let's get out of these fancy clothes and go to the creek, where we can think freely. Oh, Ede, I'm beginning to believe I don't have to get married, not yet, not so soon, not before I've found my heart's desire. You're so lucky; you've always had your art! But you have to help me so I can live from my heart's calling, too!" Celeste jumped off the swing and began running toward home, via the creek, with Ede close behind.

As the girls' squeals carried across the Green, Ron looked up and was sorry he wasn't with them.

Collecting the picnic remnants, Estelle and Myrtle stopped to watch the girls' lithe, running bodies.

"Well," Estelle said to Myrtle as the girls disappeared around the block. "I guess we'll just have to wait and see if the fates bring them together." Leaning close, she whispered, "With a little nudge now and then, from their devoted mothers."

꩜

18 Choices

January – March 1932

After the graduation ceremony, summer began with a lovely feeling of promise. Celeste and Ede were inseparable, yammering incessantly about their future. By August, their declarations were brazen. Ede would be a brilliant artist, a darling of the critics and public alike, and Celeste would be equally celebrated, although they were not yet sure what she'd actually do. But what mattered most was a passion for their endeavors, and both swore to marry only for love; the unabashed kind they saw in movies, with fits of swooning, perspiring palms and flights to the moon. Flinging her arms wide, Ede pantomimed the sentiment with twirling spins, which always sent Celeste into fits of laughter. They didn't see much of Ron, but neither cared because they had so much catching up to do after their lost winter.

But as fall elbowed in, summer's thrill began to fade for Celeste. She often found herself alone, as Ede was always busy with her own college classes, her waitress job and painting commissions. And to top it all off, Ede had fallen in … like.

"Just a partial swoon," Ede confided, "on my art professor."

"Isn't he old?" Celeste wrinkled her nose for emphasis.

Ede's shoulders popped up. "Forty-ish," she guessed, positioning her new red beret in a jaunty tilt. "Celeste, it's not like I'm having an affair or anything. We just have coffee … and talk … in Italian."

Celeste's chin lowered and eyebrows rose. "Eye-taliano?"

Ede slapped her shoulder. "Stop it. He just likes to practice the language with me. That's how it all got started. He asked the class to name their favorite style of painting or painter. I don't know what possessed me, but I answered in Italian."

"Mmmmmm." Celeste wanted to believe Ede's innocence, but her glow and sassy new gait raised suspicion, coupled with the fact she had not a minute to spare.

Not that Celeste was idle. Between the boys she met at college parties and her mother's continual arrangements, she had more dates than she wanted. By the time autumn began to fade, she declined more invitations than she accepted. Working at the hardware store and taking three college courses was more exhausting than anticipated, and she preferred spending her evenings curled up with a good book, doodling needlepoint designs in the margins. It was far more fulfilling than chatting nonsense with boys whose only objective was to fondle her breasts, which most of them tried to do as they kissed her good night, drawing their hand around her back to the side, just about to cup her when she'd push them away and flounce into the house.

But what troubled Celeste most was her lack of zeal, for any one thing. Although constantly busy, nothing beckoned her, as Gamma had counseled at graduation. She didn't share her father's enthusiasm for the business, even though she'd been doing so well at the shop he'd begun transferring more day-to-day responsibilities to her. While it felt gratifying to be appreciated, it didn't offer the satisfaction she sought, one with the bite of passion and an unmistakable call.

With summer's exuberance long gone and Ede's continued preoccupation, Celeste felt constrained by an invisible boundary and an unnamed, lingering fog that muddled her brain. After the Christmas holidays, in the mucky dankness of mid-January, Celeste could stand no more of it and sought out Gamma for a talk.

She found her outside the conservatory, standing on a stool, filling the bird feeders, draped in her chocolate gray cape. Celeste dropped the package that had arrived for Gamma on the loveseat, wrapped her shawl over her head and stepped outside to help.

"Whoa, bitter!" she gasped, tucking her hands under her armpits as her nose flared in the cold, scrubbed air.

"Hel-lo," Gamma cheerfully chirped. "How be things today?"

"Boring," Celeste replied without a thought.

Gamma glanced at Celeste as she sprinkled sunflower seeds on the feeder platform.

"Yah, can be so," Gamma replied. "But to see them, I must do."

"I didn't mean the birds, Gamma. I meant my life. Do you need help?"

"Yah," Gamma smiled, pointing to the seed bucket. "Bring that for me, please."

As the sun receded in a fiery glow, Gamma picked up her stool and led Celeste back into the conservatory. "Leave by the door," she said, slipping off the hood of her voluminous cape. "With such cold, I refill in morning."

Firmly shutting the glass door behind her, Celeste shivered all over, then scooped under Gamma's cape, hugging her as they stood silently by the windows, watching the flocks of species return to feed, darkening the wall of glass. The tufted titmouse, blue jay, sparrow, wren, nuthatch and red-bellied woodpecker swooped in for a bit of grain and gossip.

Celeste pointed to a cluster of small, gray-cloaked birds with white bellies eating the ground seeds. "Look at those," she said. "They look like you in your gray cape."

Gamma laughed. "Yah, yah, my little juncos. Only in winter they come."

"Where do they go?"

"North for summer cool."

"I think I'm the other way around," Celeste sighed, slipping from the cape. She shuffled across the slate floor and plopped onto the garden chair. Gamma shrugged her cape onto another chair and moved to the loveseat, where she saw the opened box.

"What this?" she asked.

"Oh, Mama said it arrived today and she opened it before realizing it was for you. It was addressed only to "Howe," but then she saw the card inside."

Opening the top, Gamma touched the rough brown paper package tied with string and picked up the envelope with her full name written in a beautiful, old-style script. Glancing at the return address, her stomach flipped, and she dropped the envelope into the box and set it aside, on the floor.

"Aren't you going to open it?" Celeste asked. "Isn't it from Prague?"

Gamma sat down stiffly, knowing exactly what had been sent from the Archduke Stephan Hotel. It could only be the pillow she'd hidden. Someone had finally moved the armoire and brought it to Greta, who would have instantly recognized her handiwork and sent it along, post haste. "Yah, yah, just some yarn I order," she replied, waving the subject away. "Now tell me ... how is girl with so much gifts and talents so bored?"

"Gifts? Talents? What talents?" Celeste folded her arms. "Those birds have more fun than me. Look at them. They only have to wait their turn at the feeder, but every day I wait and wait and wait … yet nothing ever changes."

"Ahh," Gamma said, fingering her knitting needles. "And for what you wait?"

"That's exactly what I'd like to know, Gamma. What *am* I waiting for? Why is my life so … blasé? School, work, study, an occasional stupid date … but nothing of importance. Nothing to make my blood bubble. Geez, Gamma, you were already married at my age … with a baby even!"

Gamma's eyes flicked "Not so wise for one with much ahead."

"Much of what?" Celeste whined, sliding her bottom to the edge of the chair, her arms folded across her chest. "Where's *my* grand adventures? Papa says the store is my inheritance. But I don't think hardware's much fun. And you know what Mama says." She pitched her voice and waggled her head, imitating her mother. "Marriage and children, marriage and children … like a broken record she is. But why would I want to have children when I still feel like a child myself? And you say: Pay attention to what shows up, but nothing has. My whole life is bor-bor-bor-ing. If I could have just a little of what you had at my age, I wouldn't be complaining. The farm you grew up on … Prague … travel through Europe and across the ocean … a whole new country and people … all that before you got married, with lots more adventures after. What have I got? Work with no meaning."

An amused smile crept onto Gamma's lips and she let out a slow, whistling breath. "My, my, my, you poor, poor girl. Work with no meaning, hmm? Is surprise to hear. I guess you not see the faces who would like a small crumb of your life. You know who I speak? Along the trolley tracks to Hartford? Scruffies, your mother calls them, staring while you pass for school, with no food on their stomach or place to sleep. Has that pretty dress blinded you to what is all around?

Celeste flushed, looking down at her custom made navy wool jumper with hand-embroidered flowers lining the neckline, waistband and full-skirted hem. It was her only Christmas gift that year, due to the depression, her father said. She sat up but kept her arms folded. "I don't mean to sound ungrateful, Gamma, but I'm not a scruffie, and what you said at graduation made me and Ede so happy. All summer long we dreamed how our lives could be. But she's off and running and I feel stuck in the mud," Celeste sighed. "What am I to do?"

Without missing a beat, Gamma nodded to the orchids and amaryllis lining the stone floor. "Since you have nothing else, why not water plants?"

Celeste's expression soured.

Gamma raised an eyebrow. "Dítě, did I say it would all be fun?"

Celeste chewed her bottom lip. "Did you?"

Gamma's piercing blue eyes narrowed. "No. And forget you the clue, too?"

"What clue?"

"The clue to what is meant for you: your laughter."

Celeste's eyes remained blank.

"The laughter that comes when doing what you love."

"I don't have any laughter."

"No? Hmm. Is odd, because I think I hear you laughing with customers at the store. And with the children at skating party. And at night, is not you giggling at the designs sketched in the margins of your art books?"

Celeste furrowed her brows. She hadn't thought about it that way. "Those are just things I like to do. Isn't my path supposed to be something grand?" she asked, leaning over and grabbing her ankles to stretch.

"What you mean, grand?"

"I don't know. School and the store seem so small. I'm hungry for something big ... like Ede's talent. It's so clear for her. If I had something like that, I swear I'd follow it to the ends of the earth. But nothing like that beckons me. Could I have missed it?" She wiggled her toes inside her shoes, aching for Gamma to soothe away her anxiety.

Eyeing Celeste doubled over, her head nearly to the floor, Gamma saw the young woman trying hard to sprout from the little girl. Her long tresses were now wrapped in a chignon. Her clothes sedate in color and cut. Her face powdered, nails trimmed and buffed, hands softly creamed. She even protected them with thin cotton gloves as she filled customer orders. Her mother's insistence on being a lady at all times had clearly worked its way into Celeste's seams, even if it cinched more tightly every day. Gamma wondered what might spark her granddaughter when her attention was caught by a beating of wings around a feeder as a cluster of birds snatched up the last of the seed before the sun's rays disappeared.

"OK. Is difficult to know sometimes what is for you and what is for others. And is easy to think theirs should be yours. Makes me wonder if a grackle ever wished to be a wren. Or a woodpecker a blue jay. What you think? Do they envy of each other, too?"

Celeste twisted her head to look out the window. "What?"

"But would be sad if they all the same, no?" Gamma asked, then dropped her voice to a conspiratorial whisper. "Dítˇe, have I ever told you ... after I die ... I like to be a bird?"

"What?" Celeste sat up, her face puckered. "Like reincarnation?" It was something they'd talked about when she was younger, but she hadn't considered it since.

"Yah. See? Their life so easy compared to ours." Gamma returned her attention to her yarn and needles even though she could knit a sweater blindfolded.

"Gamma, don't be silly."

"No, is true. Why you think I keep so many feeders? Even with your father complaining on seed costs. Everyday I must see them." Her needles clicked faster while her voice stayed low and even. "Dítě…you know why old people like to watch birds? Cupping our eyes to find the hammering woodpecker? Or the white-throated sparrow singing a bittersweet song? *Do dee dada, dee dada.* You know why we like so much the birds?"

Celeste slowly shook her head, baffled by her grandmother's conversation.

"Because their life is simple and free. No worries. Eating, mating, flying on the breeze. Seems nice, no? After such a busy, human life?"

Celeste's mouth went slack. She'd heard her mother whispering among her friends, wondering if Gamma's mind would go as she approached eighty. "Gamma, are you alright?"

Gamma grinned. "Yah, yah, better than fine. But I mean it. A bird lives … not so long … the small ones two, three years; the bluebird four or five. Would be sweet, I think, to have a few years of flight, after a long life of choosing. A bit of peace after so much doing."

"Gamma, you're scaring me."

Gamma patted Celeste's hand. "Yah? And for you I feel the same. Because I think you know what you like but are scared to do."

"You do?" Celeste's eyes opened wide.

Gamma set aside her knitting and walked to the tall glass windows, gazing out. The birds did not scatter upon her approach. "Celeste, life does not follow rules we think it should. We think only good things have meaning. So when our path is slow or not so happy, we think something wrong. But slow times and wrong times is life working, too. Because, if we could see how it ends, we would not hesitate to do. That's life magic. Not knowing where it goes, but trusting your inside truth and doing – blind, sometimes – but with the feeling it is right for you." Without looking at Celeste, Gamma stared through the glass, beyond the birds, tapping her chest three times. "Bohemians say: Your truth takes path you most want to go, even if you don't know where that is."

"But Gamma, why is mine so boring?"

Gamma turned, her eyes sparking. "Boring? Only because you choose nothing. So far, you enjoy a pretty life and home and friends, but nothing you create."

Celeste opened her mouth to speak but was silenced by Gamma's raised hand. "Here you wait … for some passion you cannot name … ignoring what's in your face. I must say, Celeste, you waste my time. Life is not a waiting place. Is a gift, for doing. And you, who have everything at your feet and fingertips, choose nothing. Create nothing from all those ideas in your head. From nothing, what can you expect life to give?"

Celeste blinked, not at all sure what Gamma just said to her. "I just want to be happy," she said weakly.

Gamma turned back to the blue-gray twilight outside the windows and the now empty feeders. "Pfff. Everyone want happy. But from where you think it come? Look at those feeders. My birds are off, collecting other food or washing or nesting. But they come back for my seed, and with them, my happiness return. Is how life is. You receive from what you do, what you choose, what you create. Is give and take, not a shopping list."

Celeste felt a small flame stir inside her, but an unnamed fear quickly doused it. "But what if I choose wrong?" she barely whispered.

"You will. We all do," Gamma said, still looking out the windows. "Some of us again and again. Is why we here: To learn who we are from what beckons us. You want perfect choice for perfect happiness? Cannot be."

Gamma faced Celeste. "No matter how perfect you think you choose, life will slap you with thing you don't want, don't expect. To wake you up, which is also a gift. You want to be happy? Happy not found in perfect choices. Happy comes from what you do with what shows up. Is the game life plays. It say: Can you make something new from old? Can you change sour to sweet? Do you see the gifts already in hand? And when you do, you have what every wise man seeks: contentment, from deep beneath." Gamma cupped her hands, one on top of the other by her belly, then raised them to her chest, where she pressed them together, like praying and swayed them side to side, like a swimming fish. "Is then you know happy is not a big far-away river to reach, but already here, under our feet, in many creeks and streams."

Celeste swallowed hard, not comprehending what Gamma said. "But Gamma, I just want a little adventure, like you had when Uncle Yazi brought you to America."

Gamma's expression sharpened. "Child, what you know of my past is less than little. I keep it so, for my path is not yours. But is time, I think, you know why really I come to America."

Startled by her grandmother's hard tone, Celeste solemnly watched Gamma walk to the cardboard box by the love seat and hold it out. "Look. See what inside," she instructed, brusquely.

Celeste blinked, unable to move.

"Go on. Here is why I leave the country I love so much."

Celeste reluctantly slid off her chair, took the box from Gamma and pulled out the soft, wrapped package. "Feels like yarn."

"Is yarn, of sorts. Unwrap and see."

Untying the string, Celeste tore open the paper's seam and gasped at a glimpse of a green needlepointed heart.

"Yah," Gamma nodded. "The Crying Heart Pillow, you see on the farm. Was placed there, for you to see, and made to follow me here, so I tell you the truth that yarn holds."

Celeste let the paper drop to the floor, exposing the entire pillow. It was just as she remembered: a large green heart, pierced by a golden arrow, with fat strings of tears gushing from its puncture wound.

Gamma sat down across from her. "What you think is true. I did long for adventure … but coming to America was to escape … my mistake." Closing her eyes, Gamma slipped back in time to the fields behind her village where she saw herself crouching in the tall grass, feeling the sturdy blades cut against her bare legs, as her taut arms pulled back the bowstring.

Opening her eyes, she stared at Celeste. "I make that pillow to honor a great hurt I cause when just a girl. A bad mistake, which make much pain for too many people: Lidia, My mother and father, my sister and, most of all, her little girl."

Celeste sat up. "Someone I met at the village?"

Gamma shook her head. "She no longer live. But you met her older sister, Lidia, who never forgive me and want you to know my mistake."

"What mistake?"

Gamma sighed, fatigued by the memory of guilt, but she knew this day would come and had promised to face it. "I was small when Yazi taught me to use the sling, so I could protect myself in woods. But when older, nearly six, before he left for sailing, he taught me bow and arrow. He want I hunt rabbits and keep goats safe from fox. I learn quick and shoot good. With big pride I bring home supper often. But I not so good heeding Yazi's warning. "Only hunt in mountains," he say, "far from village." Too easy

I forget and one day, when eleven, I hunt for a rabbit, a big one I see in mountains, a good one for whole family stew. Tracking him, I follow into the fields, not thinking how close to the houses I get. I sit, in tall grass, waiting for rabbit rustle, to aim my arrow. I forget Yazi warning: "always see the ears before releasing." I so want the rabbit, I see only the grass quiver, and *pfft!* – my arrow fly. A good shot, I feel right away, whistling straight through the grass and into my prey, I am sure, already proud, when I hear the scream. But not a rabbit scream. Horror I feel deep in my belly as my bow drops and I run to the screaming, pushing back the grass to find my three-year-old niece lying on the ground, writhing in pain, my arrow deep in her knee."

Celeste gasped. "You killed her?"

Gamma dropped her head. "No. Might have been better for her though. Maybe she come to wish it so. She live, but a deep wound fester inside, where we could not see, until too late and she lose it, her leg and never run and play again, because of me."

"Oh, Gamma." Celeste shuddered.

For a long while they sat in silence until Gamma looked at Celeste. "Was not only my niece I hurt. My foolishness cause Lidia to lose her dream, too. Of Prague, because she must now stay home and care for crippled sister, until she die, ten years before you born."

"But you didn't mean to hurt her."

"Of course not. But if I listen to my heart, maybe I not make mistake."

"What do you mean? What could your heart have said?"

"What it always say to me from time to time: Wait and see, just as Yazi try to teach. Wait and see the prey before release. But rush, I do, for prize and praise, ignoring that voice … and make my shame forever to carry."

Celeste cringed at the thought of such a burden, wishing she could erase the sadness in her grandmother's eyes. "But how did that bring you to America?"

Gamma sighed heavily. "Five years later, Yazi return with offer for marriage. I say yes to escape bad memories."

"That's why you came here? Otherwise you would have stayed in Bohemia?"

Gamma nodded. "My farm, my country, I love. But could no more stay. The hurt would never go away. But also know this: While my mistake bring me here, is here I find love, make family, and see you. From that bad, I make good. Never could I guess it would lead me here. The route was strange, but led to where I most want to be." Gamma finished, pointing to Celeste.

Celeste looked down at the pillow, tracing the spurting tears from the heart's wound, then looked up, offering Gamma a weak smile.

"See now?" Gamma continued softly. "Of course you make mistakes, to learn and make other choice, creating a journey from the truth of you. Is life's best gift, I am most sure."

With the pillow pressed to her chest, Celeste crossed to Gamma's side and hugged her, tightly, swaying together and not letting go until Myrtle called them to supper.

⌒

The next morning, as blue-gray fingers of light crept across her bedroom windows, Celeste found herself listening to the birds; hundreds of chirps, gwacks and querpels invading her sleepy mind with an erratic, compelling melody. Squirming under the covers, she thought about their uncomplicated life: rising with the sun, ruled by circumstance and instinct, lifted by the wind. *One day I'd like to feel that freedom*, she thought, *but not just yet.* A bird's limitations were not her own. She could fly in any direction, but she had been waiting for the boom of clarity to drop on her doorstep, tied in a big satin bow.

Then she saw the green heart pillow at the end of her bed and remembered Gamma's story. "What a fool I've been," she muttered. She hated being told what to do. She despised her mother's constant direction and cautioning. She barely tolerated her father's polite suggestions. And when playing with Ede, it was she who always directed the game. What Gamma always said was true: No one else can better know your truth.

"If it's really as simple as following my likes, that's the least I can do." Celeste said out loud, yanking open the side table drawer for a notebook and pencil.

"What I like," she announced to her room, looking around for inspiration.

A silvery cast of cool winter light painted her walls, like moonlight on ice, instantly transporting her to the frozen lake under a full moon, skating with the children from the shelter. She hadn't wanted to go, but after Gamma wrangled a donation of skates from a local manufacturer and Celeste began lacing up those small ankles, she was floating, forgetting her worries and laughing with those children, all afternoon and deep into the night.

"Working with Children," Celeste wrote down as she spoke, feeling a tickle trickle through her body, down to her toes, when a blue jay lighted on her windowsill. His feathers reminded her of a customer at the store who always wore something bright blue and whose laugh was like the jay's screech. Which got her thinking about all the different people she'd come to know through the hardware shop. "She's right again," Celeste mumbled. She did smile all the time at the store, not from obligation but because she genuinely liked helping. It felt good to be useful and respected. While she'd rather be selling needlepoint tools and new stitchery designs, Papa had promised she could expand the store's offerings in a year or so, once her feet got wet. Feeling a tingle of promise in her chest, Celeste wrote: "Stitchery and The Store." Though not exactly sure what she'd do with that, she felt her heart waggle with excitement.

What was that third thing Gamma mentioned? "Reading," Celeste said aloud, agreeing how much she loved it but unsure how history and art books could factor into her path. Papa described books as armchair adventures, to comfort wanderlust. *But I'd still like to travel,* Celeste thought, *especially to every ocean.* She relished the memories of their annual trip to Rhode Island, staying at the big yellow hotel on top of Watch Hill, where she rode the merry-go-round and slurped ice cream sodas at the Tea Room. With a bellyful of good feelings, Celeste wrote "See all the oceans," as a giggle trembled in her throat, one she'd felt many times before but gave no heed until that moment. "The tremble of recognition," Gamma called it. As warmth crept up her chest and down her arms, she felt alive; a definite confirmation that the clues were in the right direction. *But which,* she wondered, *was her one true track?*

While the Howes ate most of their suppers in the kitchen, reserving the dining room for company and special occasions, Myrtle changed the routine upon Celeste's graduation. In an effort to sharpen her daughter's home skills, she required Celeste to fully dress the dining room table every night from their extensive china, linen and crystal collections.

Martin abhorred the idea. He hated the isolation of sitting at one end of the oversized, fruitwood table. He preferred the kitchen's coziness, with his mother to his left, daughter on his right and wife across from him, with the cooking pots behind her on the stove; everything good at arms' reach, just as he'd known as a child. In the dining room, he couldn't give Celeste's soft cheek a pinch or pat Gamma's hand. He wouldn't have minded it once or twice a week but didn't see it necessary every night.

"To prepare her for married life," Myrtle insisted.

"What's the rush? She hasn't a steady beau," Martin retorted.

Myrtle teared-up, twisting her handkerchief, and Martin quickly relented to bring back her calm.

Every afternoon when Celeste came home, Myrtle would ask: "What are you considering today?" Then they'd look over the abundance of Gamma's tableware; a collection built by Grandfather Howe, who presented a special set of something for every anniversary and birthday. It didn't take long before Gamma's cabinets were bulging with crystal stemware from Prague and fine china dishes, tea sets, serving vessels and specialty items from around the world. The collection was a brilliant testimony to his dedication for the artistic and unique.

For Celeste, the challenge of making a cohesive presentation, balancing color and texture through the linens, flowers, candles, china, crystal and silver, became rather easy after the first few weeks. Every night, once the family had gathered at the table, she'd wait for her mother's evaluation of her creation, sometimes making a game of it by including something too bright or sparkly or disjointed to see if her mother would notice, which she always did.

Several months after Celeste had made her list of what she most liked, she was particularly inspired for the family dinner gathering and selected the bold, rose-colored china, which she softened with blush linens and pale pink stemware. Having tired of the amaryllis centerpiece, she replaced it with a cluster of protea she had dried last summer, relishing the strength of the flower's thick head surrounded by a flutter of pink and taupe petals.

"I thought its lush texture would stand up well to the table's arrangement," she said to everyone at the table.

"What do you think, Martin?" Myrtle asked.

Looking up from carving the brisket, Martin tapped the bone-handled cutlery together. "Nicely done," he said. In spite of begrudging the formality, he'd come to appreciate his daughter's handiwork. "Celeste, tell your mother about your proposal for the store. About the knittery."

"Needlery," Celeste laughed.

His broad smile revealed his tease. "Right, right. Needlery. Anyway, tell her."

"Well," Celeste wrapped her fingers around the napkin in her lap. "I was thinking about what beckoned me … like Gamma said …"

"As …" Myrtle said, passing the plate of boiled potatoes and cabbage to Celeste.

"As Gamma said," Celeste repeated, more annoyed at her own mistake than her mother's correction. "It's only an idea but, well, you know I love to needlepoint, as do many of the ladies in the area. And since so many of them stop by for some sort of notion at least once a week, I was thinking it might be convenient if we carried some needlery supplies."

Martin passed the meat platter to Gamma with a knowing nod.

Myrtle frowned. "But the Sew Shoppe is one town over."

"Yes I know, Mother." Celeste concentrated on keeping composed, as her father had counseled. "But I was thinking of something more than the normal supplies. And father said I could use a corner of the store to try out my idea."

"Like my baby clothes? That we sold in our New York shop?" Gamma asked, passing the meat platter to Myrtle.

"Exactly," Martin nodded.

"At the Sew Shoppe," Celeste continued, "You can buy only blank canvas or ones with patterns everyone carries and I find boring. They're fine for learning stitches, but not very exciting. I thought the ladies might prefer something they were familiar with, a local scene, like the old stagecoach house on Main Street or the creek or the river harbor. And we could even customize patterns of their homes or gardens. Ede can paint anything on the canvas, and I'll match up the thread." Celeste looked around the table, feeling excitement rise as she explained, but then she noticed how rapidly her mother was chewing.

Gamma rested her silverware on the side of her plate and gave Celeste a smile of encouragement.

"Like the one Ede designed of your garden, Gamma," Celeste said softly, hoping to calm her mother's obvious agitation. "She showed me how to paint the canvas, using all sorts of colors and shadows. It's the shadows that make the finished needlepoint so exciting, just like in a real painting. Shadows make a picture pop on a painter's canvas, so why not for needlepoint patterns? Mama, don't you think the town ladies would love to stitch their own gardens or houses or pets on a custom pillow or seat cushion?"

Looking up from her plate, Myrtle found Celeste's wide, hopeful eyes staring at her.

Martin also stared, at his wife, only his eyes were filled with warning: Do not squash our daughter's enthusiasm.

But Myrtle would not be quelled. She'd never been adept at keeping still when she found something out of place. It was her job, as a mother and wife, to point out what was missed. "What has this to do with your future?" She asked sharply.

Celeste tried to hold her face steady and not let her disappointment show, but her shoulders slumped under the blunt blow. Picking up her knife and fork, she pushed the food around her plate, making a guise of eating.

Myrtle maintained her defiance while Martin and Gamma looked at her with disgust.

"It's all well and good for you two to fill her head with notions of grandeur, but in the end it will be me who has to suffer and cajole her, when she is lost and lonely, with no prospect of marriage."

Martin's eyes shifted onto his plate, but Gamma held her gaze.

"Myrtle," she asked, "is that all you see for Celeste? Marriage and children?"

Arching her brow, Myrtle leaned back, wiping each fingertip with her napkin. "All? What do you mean, all? What's more important for a woman than attending a husband and raising her family? It was enough for you and me. Why not your granddaughter?" Surefooted in her argument, Myrtle restrained her victorious grin.

Gamma's lips parted then closed. She looked to her son, who stared into his plate, as was Celeste, winding her fingers in her lap. But Martin finally raised his head and spoke in a firm and measured voice.

"Myrtle, Gamma did far more than attend her husband and raise children. She learned every bit of the business from Grandmother Katrine, and it was they who ran the stores, in addition to tending their husbands and children. And quite well, I might remind you."

Myrtle raised her chin to reply but Martin continued. "And you seem to have forgotten your own mother, as well. How hard she worked to raise a large family. I'm surprised to hear you speak in such a manner when your background offers a very different truth."

Celeste glanced up. They never spoke of her mother's childhood.

Myrtle stiffened. "I've worked hard to make sure Celeste had more than I ever did, and she can do far better than any of us. Why, she's as good as Beatrice Meaden and could live the same life … which we cannot provide."

Gamma looked puzzled. "Beatrice Meaden? What life you think she live? Full of spitfire, she is, coming to talk all the time about what to do, besides wife and mother. Why you think she likes her squash game so much? Is her spirit. No different from her mother's charities. Work is good. No one is happy in gilded tower."

Myrtle's lips puckered. "I wasn't advocating for Celeste to do nothing. But I don't think her future should be so focused at the store. How could she ever manage it once Martin retires? She can't run a store with a household of children."

Chills ran up Celeste's back as she glanced at the six bracelets on Gamma's arm. Someday she wanted children, but not yet. Not now, when she'd finally found something she was aching to do.

Gamma saw her granddaughter cringe. "We not agree. But as Celeste is the one to have the children you think she must, is question for her to answer."

As the family turned toward her, Celeste closed her eyes, clenching her fists in her lap as she silently vowed not to give up and back away. This time, she would clearly claim what she truly desired. This time, she would speak her mind, her heart, her truth. This time, she would stand up for herself and let the cards fall, whichever way they may.

19 James

October 1932

As red and yellow maple leaves floated to the ground, Estelle raked her rock garden, preparing to add a host of bulbs for a bold bloom at the Spring Garden Tour. Although a full-time gardener maintained the rest of the property, Estelle cultivated the rock garden framing the back porch. It was her first garden, inspired by one she'd seen in the English countryside on her honeymoon and lovingly built over the years, one rock and plant at a time. Providing an immeasurable precious quietude, it was her respite from the noisy demands of running a household and administering charities, if only in all too brief interludes.

Across the yard, Jack sought his own escape from the endless stifle of papers and business meetings by vigorously tilling the spent pole beans and squash leaves in the vegetable garden. He relished the tangibility of growing food for his family and the good-to-the-bone feeling it delivered as he sorted out his thoughts along with the soil. By the end of his task, with a damp brow and warmth between his shoulders, he'd stand tall, clasp the head of his hoe, proudly survey his accomplishment and tamp the hoe's handle on the ground while declaring: "Done."

Under the hot October sun, Jack's mind churned along with the dirt. Despite his declaration to retire 16 months ago, he was no closer to his goal and knew it was his own damn fault. Setting up a competition among his sons hadn't worked. Although James was still quite productive in the business, he maintained a silent, social distance, indicating no interest in leading the company. That didn't bother Jack as much as the impact it had on his second son, Oliver, whom Jack thought would make a good leader, and, in the very least, a more astute administrator. With a strict work ethic, Ollie seemed to enjoy keeping an eye on the mundane. Jack would have happily passed the reins to him, except Oliver seemed uninterested. Three months after presenting his succession proposal, Jack asked Ollie if he wanted the job.

"What has James said?" Ollie inquired.

Jack shrugged. "Nothing, yet."

"Well, when he decides, so shall I."

Jack could never fault Ollie's loyalty to his older brother. After all, James had literally saved Ollie's life as a toddler, on a bristling-hot summer day, when the very pregnant Estelle had brought her three young children to the harbor beach for a splash in the cool, shallow water. James was six, Beatrice four and Ollie had just turned two. Oddly, no other families were at the beach. After instructing the children not to venture into the water beyond their knees, Estelle lowered her swollen hips into a small beach chair and stretched out in the mid-afternoon haze, watching her brood play. But the heat compounded her pregnant weariness and she nodded off. Just as her head bobbed to her chest, Ollie slipped on a stone and disappeared under the water. It happened so fast he barely made a sound. Just a last sucked slurp of surprise. James, who'd been fashioning a boat out of sticks on the shore, looked up just as Ollie was vanishing. Dropping his sticks, he sprinted to where his baby brother had been standing, slapping through the water, churning the sand and frantically grasping until he felt Ollie's hair and yanked him up, his mouth frozen in a breathless O. Beatrice's cry awoke their mother as James walloped Ollie's back. In sudden panic, Estelle struggled up and trundled half into the water with the chair still clinging to her ample bottom. By the time she reached her sons, Ollie had coughed out the water and was breathing, holding his throat with both hands. Dazed, Ollie didn't quite know what had happened until he saw his mother's terrified face, and burst into tears. Since that day, Ollie would do nothing against his older brother, as unswerving in his love and devotion as dog to master. Therefore, however long James remained mute regarding the company presidency, so would Ollie.

Jack also considered his third son a good candidate. Of all his children, Austin was most like him; a natural glad-hander with a wealth of kindness that fairly seeped from his pores. People were drawn to Austin without any effort on his part. But he didn't want the position, either. An avid sportsman, Austin loved to shoot, hunt and fish. He would never relinquish his search for the prize pheasant, moose, wolf or salmon for more money or prestige. Already the top salesman, he had ample time to pursue his passions, along with a spunky wife, who enjoyed the same pleasures.

That left Fischer and Ron, neither of whom were considerations. Ron was only a sophomore in college, and Fischer was incapable. Tall and wiry with a thick wave of red hair, Fisher had a young man's zest for life and although Jack admired that, he knew Fischer's temperament could not deliver balanced leadership. Fischer had neither the detail orientation of Ollie nor the people skills of Austin. Plus, he had a lazy streak, chiefly because Jack had chosen to forego the proper discipline and direction for Fischer that he'd provided his other sons. When Fischer was turning ten, Jack had been distracted, having recently inherited the full mantle of the company, and he found it easier to give in to the boy's whims and whines than to take the time to correct him. Thus, Fischer never outgrew his childhood antics. Fortunately, his swagger was well suited for overseeing the southern satellite offices. He liked telling yarns with his boots on a porch railing as much as mingling with the well-heeled mint julep set.

Having finished her gardening, Estelle removed her canvas jacket and long gloves to pour two glasses of iced tea. Approaching the vegetable garden, she noticed the furrows in Jack's brow seemed almost as deep as the rows of turned soil.

"All sorted out yet?" she called, holding out the glass.

Turning his hoe to clasp it by the head, Jack gratefully accepted the tea, drank it in one, long gulp, then rolled the cool glass across his forehead. "Well, I know the problem well enough, but …" He returned the glass to Estelle's outstretched hand. They didn't discuss business regularly, but after decades of marriage, a kind of telepathy had formed between them.

She guessed. "Still waiting to hear from James?"

Jack wiped his forehead with his sleeve. "Can't get Ollie to commit until James declines … and he's not talking. Has he said anything to you?"

Estelle shook her head. "But his friend Michael said some interesting things last week."

Leaning on the hoe, Jack gave Estelle his full attention. She was a wonder at extracting pertinent information from unsuspecting parties. In brief tête-à-têtes, she could piece together a situation like a jigsaw puzzle.

"Michael said that none of their friends understand James's choice in girlfriends; especially now, when they'd passed the tart stage – that's how he put it – and married respectable girls. He complained that the showgirls James flaunts brought down the tone of their gatherings."

Jack raised and lowered his eyebrows. "Has anyone said anything to him?"

Estelle nodded. "Michael said everyone has, and some of the wives even asked James if they could set him up with the right sort of girl. But James only laughs and leaves their parties early to head downtown for a jazz club or art opening or something of that nature." Estelle paused, sipping her tea. "Honestly, Jack, how do we get our boy back?"

Not a man inclined to wait, Jack decided it was time to see James face-to-face. Leaning his hoe on the fence, Jack strode across the lawn, declaring: "If Mohammed won't come to the mountain, the mountain will go to Mohammed."

Quickly composing a reasonable pretense to be in Manhattan the next weekend, Jack dialed James' number and was surprised when he picked up so quickly. "Hello, son. It's your father. Glad I reached you."

"Oh … hello Father. Anything wrong?" James felt the hair on his neck rise.

"No, no, not a thing. Not a thing." Jack shook his head. "I was calling to see if you were available next weekend …"

"Ah, awfully sorry, but that's shaping up to be a bear of a weekend for me," James interrupted, launching into a litany of commitments he'd made: Saturday cocktails at a client's town home, followed by clubbing with another client, probably 'til dawn. Then up for a Sunday brunch with the gang to celebrate yet another engagement and with luck, he'd fit in an afternoon squash game or two. "So, you see, I haven't a moment to spare." James finished, sure he'd adequately justified his absence from whatever Gladdenbury event they wanted his presence.

"Well, that sounds grand." Jack counted his luck. "Because I called to invite myself for the weekend. Your mother has some sort of regional club meeting and I have an early squash game in the city next Sunday, so I thought it would be a good time to come and see the new apartment. Maybe I could tag along? Double-team the clients? What-do-ya-say?"

A heavy silence hung on the line for a few moments until Jack sealed the deal.

"Black tie, I presume?"

Staring into his phone receiver, James felt ambushed and dumbfounded. Although he had found and secured the apartment, it was company funded and his father could not be denied access. "I can't imagine you'd find it very entertaining, Father."

"What? Spending a weekend with my son? I'd be delighted. I'll catch the Saturday midday train and take a taxi. Fifth Avenue and ... what cross street?"

"Seventy-Fourth." James replied tersely, recognizing the immutable resolve in his father's voice. Replacing the black receiver on its cradle, James' heart felt sodden. They had not spoken since Christmas, so he had no idea how they'd get through an evening, much less a weekend. The rest of the day he felt agitated, restless and snappish. However, as the week progressed, he had a surprising change of heart. He began to feel the cool distance with his father was a ridiculous matter. After 30 years of being a dutiful son, he no longer had to feel an obligation to satisfy his parents' expectations. He was free to live however he pleased, and rather liked the New York life he'd crafted for himself and intended to keep, no matter what his father's reaction. "So let him come," James said out loud, proudly surveying his well-appointed apartment; "Let him see the life I love," with a devil-may-care attitude about the outcome.

Pulling open his apartment door, James stepped back as Jack entered with a flourish. Quickly setting down his carryall and hooking his hanging bag on the foyer wall lamp, he glanced through the arched doorway, whistling. "My oh my oh my. Quite the bachelor's lair."

James slowly blinked as Jack strode into the living room, turning in a circle. "The address alone was a coup, but I didn't anticipate *this* stately interior. And the terrace! Holy smokes, it's a far cry from your first apartment ... where was that?"

"Upper East Side."

"Right. A postage stamp by comparison. How did you find this one?"

"After the market crash, I watched for someone's misfortune and snagged it for a song."

Jack nodded continuously as he looked about. "Right. Poor bloke. Lucky us."

James crossed to the fireplace, leaning one arm on the marble mantle, watching his father's examination of their investment with surprised amusement. "I got a tip before it hit the open market."

"Fully furnished?" Jack did not recognize the furniture.

"A few pieces, but most of it came from my travels."

Still nodding, Jack glanced up the long hallway. "Three bedrooms?"

James sucked a breath through his teeth. "Our overseas contacts seem to like it. Besides, mother and Bea's shopping junkets more than justify the extra bedrooms."

"No! No! Don't get me wrong." Jack asserted, saluting his son as he glanced into the large, well-equipped kitchen. "It's tip top. Everything. Why, your mother's eyes are going to pop when she sees what you've done. Not her style, but she'll recognize the quality, straight off." Pointing to the open terrace doors he added, "The view alone is worth the cost of admission. Brilliant coup!"

Walking across the stone-lined patio, Jack mentally measured its square footage, noting it paralleled the width and depth of the living, dining and study areas. A grand space, furnished for outdoor entertaining with several seating areas, a large, round, glass table and potted evergreens interspersed along the ironwork fence. Standing in the middle, Jack looked directly out, over Central Park, then turned south toward the Plaza Hotel, 15 blocks away, then north toward the Metropolitan Museum at 82nd street. A twinge of envy washed over him, wishing he'd done more of the same when he had the chance. Jack whistled again, with pride, calling to James. "What a gem. In the middle of the best clubs, dining and dancing. Very impressive. Well done, sir. Well done! You should be mighty proud."

Walking onto the terrace, James carried a tray with two martini glasses and a frosted cocktail shaker. His lips turned up for a moment at his father's compliment. Placing the tray on the table, he held up the shaker and quipped. "Too early for you, old man? I know the sun's not quite over the yardarm but …"

Out of habit, Jack glanced at his watch. It was nearly four. "No-no," he automatically replied. "It's five o'clock somewhere."

Neatly filling two long-stemmed glasses, James handed one to his father and lifted the other. "To this evening's adventures. May you find them … enlivening."

"That sounds jolly." Jack clinked his son's glass. "So which client is hosting cocktails?"

"Chuck and Joan Huber. The family owns a big swath of Maine – timber – and some mining concerns. They travel a lot but like to get the gang together when in town. I think you'll find them entertaining. Chuck can be a bit brash sometimes, but he's quite likeable. I'm sure you've met his father."

Jack squinted his eyes. "Huber, Huber, I know the name of course but can't say I've worked with them directly. One of Grandfather's big clients." He wasn't one to forget a face, but his own father managed that account until it passed directly to James. Looking around for a place to sit, Jack selected the hooded chaise lounge by the corner, to get his feet up before the long night ahead. "One of the gang. That has a nice ring to it. Good friends?"

Pulling up a chair, James shrugged. "More like good mates. Although they're far easier to be around than some of my pals from home."

Jack noted the shift in tone, a drop in formality. "How's that?"

Taking a sip of gin, James leaned back, elegantly folding one leg over the other. "Chuck and Joan have traveled extensively, seen a few things beyond this tidy world of the States, so they easily welcome all sorts of people, not just their own set."

Raising his eyebrows, Jack invited more explanation.

Lightly drumming his fingers on his bent knee, James clenched his teeth to mimic a British upper-crust accent. "As Oscar Wilde once said: 'The well-bred contradict other people.' That sums up my old chums. Contradicting anyone who isn't like them, which can be rather a bore."

Somewhat confused, Jack turned his head. "Who are we talking about? The Hubers?"

"No. They are very much to the manner born, but, unlike my childhood chums, they don't take it seriously. The Huber's first line of inquiry isn't breeding. They don't snub someone from a different economic class. They welcome anyone with decent manners, a sharp wit and sense of humor; and if they can sing and dance, all the better."

"So they fancy artistic types?" Jack attempted to be chummy.

James balked. His shoulders rose sharply. "What's wrong with artistic types?"

"What? Nothing. Not a damn thing." Jack retreated, opening the tin he'd brought from home. "Hey, your mother sent along some cheese biscuits."

Cooling down just as quickly, James selected and carefully ate his favorite cracker. Chewing slowly, he reprimanded himself: Don't lose your objective, keep focused, try again.

"What I meant to convey is that the Hubers, unlike others in our set, don't waste time finding fault. They enjoy unearthing what's interesting about someone, artistic or otherwise."

"Nice. Very nice," Jack replied. "Sounds like you're all on to something good." Jack could see his response lightened James' demeanor but he didn't want to push the subject any further. Popping a biscuit in his mouth, he rubbed his hands together. "So who's the other client for tonight's festivities and what clubs have you lined up? I fancy a bit of a twirl."

James cleared his throat. "Well, to be frank, Father, that wasn't quite the truth."

"No?"

"No. It isn't a client." James rose to stretch his legs, glancing down the avenue as he said in a rush: "The plans I've made for the evening are with my girl."

"Ah. Someone new?" He could not hide the false note in his voice.

"Actually, I've been seeing her for some time now."

"Anyone we know?" Jack tried again to sound genuinely interested, but he was not as adept as his wife in the art of social niceties.

James grunted. "Hardly! Mother appreciates actresses only on stage."

It was exactly as Estelle had warned: James' predilection for glad girls – singers, dancers and actresses – which fed Estelle's worry of one becoming pregnant and forcing James into marriage. Not knowing what else to do, Jack devoured three cheese biscuits in quick succession before wiping his fingers and mouth with his handkerchief. "Son, I'm no good at cat-and-mouse games. Please just tell me about her."

Standing by the terrace fence, James held on to an iron post for ballast as he delivered his practiced speech. "Her name is Kate. She was raised in the Midwest, and her father's working class. She came to New York straight out of high school and has been working for five years; mostly in the chorus, but she did understudy the lead in a Broadway production. She's cute, funny and smart. Daresay if you met her apart from me you'd very much like her."

"I daresay you're right," Jack replied carefully. "Is it serious?"

James winced. This was a question he'd asked himself many times. "She's seriously fun," he quipped, but quickly dropped his glibness. "I suppose it should be. I'm sure she expects it; it's been nearly two years. But I don't suppose anyone in my set would take her seriously if we were to marry, including Mother." As he finished speaking, the left side of his lip pulled upward, as it always did when he was uncomfortable.

Jack responded quickly. "Or perhaps *until* you do."

"What?"

Shrugging, Jack rattled the shaker for remnants. "Oh hell James, you know how it goes. No one takes anything seriously until there's definitive action. Until your mother finally agreed to marry me, there were running bets on how long she'd keep me on a string. Do you love her?"

James drew his lips together in a thin line. For all his worldliness, his escapades, the numerous women he'd romanced, somehow the notion of love had escaped him. He wasn't even sure he knew how to recognize it. Turning to his father, he half-held his breath and asked: "How do you know if you do?"

Jack polished off his martini and stood up, shaker in hand. "Another round?"

"Ducky," James replied, immediately regretting his question.

At the living room bar, Jack refilled the canister with ice, gin and a hint of vermouth before shaking it vigorously until his fingertips were ice-cold red. Returning to the terrace, he held out his splayed hand. "James" he called, "your fingertips run cold. Your heart burns hot. You cannot imagine a day without her, and – most important – you never run out of things to talk about. That's how you know."

As Jack refilled the glasses, James' demeanor lightened and his heart pulsated as he thought about Kate's warmth and laughter, her excitement over small things, the waggle of her hips. They regularly talked for hours. She was never dull, always kind, beautiful, and madly independent, which made her all the more desirable to James. He was sure she loved him but wasn't sure if he was capable of returning love, to one person, as his father described. James held his glass close to his lips but did not sip. "At the risk of sounding like a complete dilettante, I can say I do love what she's brought to my life."

Jack looked quizzical. What could the girl offer – beyond the obvious?

Pushing off the fence, James looked at his father with a quiet, resolved face. "Father, from where you're sitting, can you see the painting above the fireplace?"

Jack sat up. It was one of the first things he'd noticed upon his arrival, finding the angles and lines of the painting rather odd, unlike anything hanging on his own walls. "What about it?"

"It's by a young artist named Stuart Davis who lives in the city. I met him through Kate at a party downtown. She's introduced me to lots of artists and writers. So did the other girls I've dated. It's what I like most about them."

"That they know artists?" Jack's voice rose, unable to hide his surprise.

James instantly set his jaw but then saw his father's open, curious expression and released his breath. "To be blunt, yes. I rather like the life they lead. It's more vibrant than anything I've known."

"What in the dickens are you talking about?" Jack was bemused. Was this a joke?

James waved his father toward the living room. "Come look and tell me what you see."

The two men stood staring at the lines and swirls of color on the canvas until Jack blustered. "Heck, I don't know. Some buildings in some city?"

"Two cities actually, New York and Paris in one painting. Do you see?" James queried, enjoying being in a knowledgeable position, and in the art world he was becoming very knowledgeable. "This is part of a series Davis has been working on. I saw the next one in his studio and it's even more fantastic. Look at the shapes and colors. Can you see – and feel – the difference between the two sets of buildings?"

Jack moved closer. It looked a bit cartoonish to him, a few lines, a few strokes of color, somewhat unfinished, yet he felt a vague familiarity with the lower set of buildings. They reminded him of Paris, which he saw with Estelle on an anniversary trip several years ago. Modest structures compared to New York and representing what he most liked about Paris: its human scale.

"Father, I don't expect you to like the painting any more than you would my furniture," James added in a gust. "But I want you to know this painter and his work because he's pushing the boundaries of art, bringing something new to the table to expand our vision and ignite our imagination. He's going to be big and would make a terrific investment for the company; more so than some of our other long term investments."

The sudden intensity in James' voice caught Jack off guard. It was like water bursting from a cannon. He couldn't recall a time he'd heard such energy from his son; a cocktail of conviction laced with verve.

"Come." James abruptly walked to the foyer. "I think you'll like this other one."

As soon as Jack saw the canvas depicting a Lucky Strike tobacco tin and a newspaper, he agreed. "Yep, now this one I can recognize. Still odd for a picture, but kind of nice, too."

"Right. One of his earlier pieces. 1924. When he painted more realistic. But he's now moving toward the abstract and that's what makes it distinctive – and potentially quite lucrative. There's a lot more I want you to know about him and this investment strategy but it's getting late. We've got to change."

James walked away to gather the martini tray from the terrace when Jack noticed a series of enlarged photographs lining the hallway. Stately prints of Indians in traditional garb: on horses, in a canoe among the rushes, gathering mussels on the shore, weaving on a loom under a tree.

"Who photographed these Indians?" Jack called to James in the kitchen.

"Edward S. Curtis. Remember the 1911 exhibition mother took us to?"

"Was I there?"

James laughed lightly, joining his father in the hallway. "Probably not. Mother was always dragging us to shows but this one I never forgot. They created an opera at Carnegie Hall called 'The Story of the Vanishing Race,' and the pictures of the Indians awed me. In college I learned it was part of an enormous project Curtis led at the turn of the century, documenting Indian culture before it disappeared. J.P. Morgan was a major benefactor."

Jack's ears perked. "You don't say."

"Twenty volumes. An immeasurable effort. Wish we'd invested in a set."

"Can we still?" Jack was always eager to deliver his children's wishes.

"Only 500 printed, mostly for libraries and the Rockefeller set. So when I found these prints ..."

Jack was dumbfounded. All these years he never knew James loved art.

"When did you come to appreciate all this?" he asked, his hands gesturing to the prints in the hallway and the art in the living room.

James retrieved his father's bags, carrying them to the guest room. "That's what I've been trying to tell you: through the girls in New York. I'll admit when I first met their artist friends I thought them odd and vulgar, but I couldn't get them out of my mind. I found myself wondering how they spent their days and what gave them permission to be so free. I mean, to make your living, meager though it may be, painting pictures all day long? It seems reckless, yet they do it because they have to. Imagine me saying that about the insurance business? It wasn't long before I found their company wholly more satisfying than my cocktail set, even if they weren't candidates for insurance."

James set the small suitcase on a low chest at the end of the bed and hung the bag in the closet before turning and addressing his father in a clear, decisive voice. "I want you to seriously consider their work as part of our investment portfolio. It has enormous upside potential. Davis, Braque, Picasso and Georgia O'Keefe – have you heard of her?"

Jack rubbed his chin. "When fine art comes up in a policy, I leave it to the appraisers."

"She's a real maverick – paintings of skulls and bones in the desert and overtly opposing the painting schools of Regionalism and Social

Realism," James explained, bringing the towels the housekeeper had placed on the bed into the guest bathroom. "Snubs her nose at Benton and Wood and Curry and has single-handedly set a new course in the painting world. She makes a good point against them but you can't just dismiss the whole lot of them. Each group influences the next." Seeing his father's confused expression, James pointed to the picture over the bureau. "That painting is by John Steuart Curry, entitled: 'Tornado Over Kansas.' He is one of the painters in the Regionalism group of the Midwest. In his time, he was a maverick, breaking away from those preceding him. He wanted to bring life to the canvas – to bring feeling!" James moved closer to the painting. "Look how he captured the wind … whipping back the family's clothes and hair as they watch the approaching tornado funnel. The terror is palpable. Can't you smell it? Feel it? Even touch it? Yet it's just paint and canvas! Completely unlike the stiff portraiture of Early American Art and the flat landscapes of the Hudson Valley group." James stopped short, suddenly realizing those were the very paintings lining his parents' walls. "Sorry, no offence intended."

"None taken," Jack said, appraising the tornado painting. He was beginning to see what James was speaking about. There was a life in it, a vibration absent in the formal portraits and landscapes of his family's collection. "What makes it so different?"

"Less function, more form. Their use of color, lines and shadows capture and convey the energy of the scene, the jazz of the moment, and that's where painting is headed, away from replication and toward feeling. That's what Davis is doing: painting that jazz feeling, which I find damned exciting."

Jack nodded, only half understanding what his son had said but appreciating his passion. Without another word, he walked back to the living room, taking another look at the odd collection of furniture. Like the paintings, the chairs and tables were a mix of curving lines and colors, some with imbedded shapes, as well. Unusual angles to catch and hold the eye. Sleek. Cool. Refined. So different from the carved mahogany and over-stuffed upholstery he'd lived with since childhood. How had he missed his own son's enthusiasms all these years? Had the distractions of business and the children who followed robbed his eldest of his childhood dreams? It was confounding that he could not remember what James was like as a child, other than being prompt and courteous and compliant to his parents' wishes. If Gamma were here, she'd ask what he pursued on his own. Jack felt a bit of shame that he didn't know and suddenly realized he'd done to his eldest son what had been done to him: swept him along to be useful to the family's objectives, with no regard for his own heart's desires.

James stood in the bedroom doorway, unbuttoning his shirt and called to his father in a chipper voice. "Better get dressed, ol' man. We've got to be on time. Joan likes her parties to start with a bang."

Turning toward his son, Jack saw what he had missed for years: laughter and light dancing in his son's eyes. Until that moment, he'd only witnessed James' serious side, dutiful but removed. Yet somehow his true nature had survived ... perhaps because it had been kept under wraps all this time, safe from being stomped out by those who might disapprove.

"Just a minute, James. I have a question for you."

"Shoot." James unbuttoned his cuffs.

"This is hypothetical of course, but indulge me."

James shrugged easily.

"If you hadn't grown up in the insurance business ... no, better yet: If you didn't have to uphold all the trappings of your upbringing and could do anything you like – anything at all – what would you do today?"

Without a second's hesitation, James saw himself at a table of artists, scruffy and grimy from their day's work with oils, clay and iron, warmed by a round of drinks and conversation. Being with them had become his favorite pastime, but he didn't know how to explain it in a way his father would understand. He liked how they lived with pluck, regardless of financial station. Measuring their lives only by passion and follow-through; jousting constantly as to who had the bigger idea and the balls to get it done. And talk, constant talk, egging each other on as to who was wrong or right and the direction of art and the embrace of one style while breaking from another. Round and round they'd go, arguing about whether art should reflect the world as it is or what it could be? Was it to admonish, instruct, or inspire? Dressed in grimy overalls, they didn't give a fig for the accoutrements of the Noel Coward set, yet they didn't seem to mind that James was a card-carrying member. Far from the refined salons of society, James felt at home with them, and nothing about it bored him. As the bon vivant who sang and quipped and danced with all the cultured ladies, James had begun to feel like a fraud ... because the women he most liked were the ones who lived the Boho life. Who smiled when they meant it and spoke what they liked. Who loved from their very souls, not just their fingertips. He could no longer deny his truth. He liked being with them, not as an artist himself, but among them, helping them succeed while enjoying their company. Looking back at his father, James lifted his chin as if making a challenge on the squash court.

"Come downtown with Kate and me tonight and see for yourself."

Jack's heart leapt as he broadly grinned. Lifting his arm, clenching an imaginary hoe, he tamped the floor with his foot, loudly declaring: "Done."

20 Truth

October1932 – April 1933

"You did what with whom?" Estelle gagged, nearly spilling her coffee.

Having arrived home very late on Sunday night, Jack hadn't had the chance to speak with Estelle about his New York visit until Monday morning breakfast. Standing by the sideboard, he drained his coffee cup and refilled it to the brim.

"Met a whole gang of artists at McSorley's Pub."

Estelle blinked, slightly shaking her head.

"An old ale house near Union Square. 'Old' is actually too kind; it's dingy and grimy with sawdust on the floor – no women allowed, naturally – but we all just sallied on in with top hats and capes – James' girl included – and drank 'til the old man kicked us out. Then James took us someplace near the Bowery 'til five or so. Hell of a night. Hell of a night! I have to say, Stelly, James has got himself quite a girl. Quite-a-girl! Like you: spirited, with gumption. Stuffed her hair under a fedora to get into McSorley's. Talked in a gruff voice all night. They must have noticed, but didn't say a thing. You'll like her! Bet your best gem on it."

"Why on earth did you spend the night with … artists?"

"Because your son adores them. Sculptors, painters, writers, all of 'em. My god, they were a raucous bunch but I haven't had more fun in years."

"Friends of his?"

"Don't know I'd call 'em friends, but they sure brought out a side of James I hadn't seen. Completely banished his stuffiness! He wore a glint of a smile all night long, even laughed out loud a few times. Big and hearty, like mine. You should have seen him." Jack sat down, relishing the memories of his night with James as he crushed a few crackers in his bowl, un-shelled his soft boilers and mashed them together.

Picking up her pen, Estelle jotted a note on her ever-present pad. "Mmm. Seems to me just one more step on the road to hell."

"No, no, Stelly! I'm telling you, he was magnificent. Released! It was really something to see how he talked with them, matching idea for idea. I don't know where he got all his knowledge, but I was proud to be his father. Do you know when James' interest in art began?"

"Besides his extensive education?"

Chewing, Jack smiled benignly at his wife and rolled his hand for her to continue. He refused to allow her sarcasm to dim his good mood.

She dismissively shook her head. "He had the normal childhood interest in art. When he was four or five he'd spend hours gluing sticks into odd shapes and painting them, making a big mess, but ... as I recall ... his shapes were ... unusual ... and bright. But that all stopped around seven, when he became a serious young man."

"After Ollie's accident ...?"

Estelle cleared her throat. "I suppose. But really, where could it have led?"

"To right where we are today. He wants us to invest in the Modernists."

"Picasso?"

"And Braque and all those chaps. But what really has him jazzed is this new school of painters. Artists who paint energy, not just objects. Abstractionists, he called them. Bit of a stretch for me, but he's convinced they're the next wave. He saw it emerging in Europe. All I know is ... it lights the boy on fire."

"What about the girl?"

Jack took another bite, chewed and swallowed. "Good looker, spunky, smart. You may hate to hear this, my love, but they seem well suited. We should have her to dinner, meet the family."

Estelle snapped her fingers. "Just like that?"

"No no. When you're ready. But he's been going with her for two years already. Just thought it might go a long way to mending the rift."

"A rift I did not create."

Wiping his egg bowl with a small piece of toast, Jack popped it in his mouth. "Nope, you didn't. But it sure sounds like you're heading for a rift of your own, now."

To keep peace with her husband, Estelle invited James and Kate to dinner in early December, but not with the whole family; just the four of them, on a cold Saturday night before the holiday rush.

Watching from behind the window sheers as James opened the car door for Kate, Estelle immediately approved of her appearance: a dark cloth coat with a touch of fur at the collar and cuff, a matching fur hat and low-heeled ankle boots with sheer stockings. Not a touch of tawdry, Estelle conceded. She also admired her posture and walk. Demur but upright and stately, gently clasping James' arm as they walked to the house. As they shed their coats in the vestibule, Estelle listened from the parlor and found the girl's clear, light voice devoid of any distinct accent. But she was not prepared for Kate's deep, luminous smile as James presented her to them. Nor did Estelle appreciate Jack's jumping up to welcome the girl with a hug. It made her handshake seem emotionally stingy. No doubt this young woman could illuminate any stage with that smile, and a body to match, draped in a shapely, but not clingy, russet, *crepe de chine* calf-length dress. Not a trace of trollop, Estelle admitted to herself, fingering her neck pin. But she could not forget the girl was an actress and appearances can be deceiving.

Over cocktails and supper, Estelle was hard pressed to find a flaw. Kate's elocution was excellent, conversational skills attentive and engaging, interest in her host and their surroundings impeccable. Everything about her seemed genuine, just like her mahogany tinged hair, unsullied by the bleach so many girls were using to blonde their hair these days. She seemed completely unflappable – until they broached the subject of her family.

"What prompted you to leave your family so young?" Estelle asked with a chipper cadence, rhythmically tapping her fingertips together.

James shifted uncomfortably and slipped his hand around Kate's, giving it a squeeze. She looked to him and blinked. Having warned her of his mother's predilection to get to the bottom of things, he was prepared to change the subject, abruptly if need be. But Kate's blink was her sign to let it go, see where it ran.

"I could have stayed," Kate answered softly but directly to Estelle. "It wasn't that I'd gotten into any kind of trouble or anything. My family never wanted me to leave. We were very close ... despite some difficulties."

"Oh? Such as?"

James squeezed Kate's hand again and interrupted. "Mother ..."

Kate laughed lightly. "No James, I don't mind. I'd do the same in her shoes."

James kissed her palm and held it, looking directly at his mother.

"I'm from a small town in Kansas, Mrs. Meaden. My father is a mechanic, a good one, mostly for farmers, tractor repair and such. We lived out in the country where there wasn't much to do. So after high school I would normally have gotten married to start my own family, as most girls do, but honestly I wanted to see a bit of the world before settling down. We didn't have anything like you do here, but my father bought us a set of encyclopedia Britannica when I was around 5 and most every night, for as long as I can remember, I'd study a volume until I fell asleep. By the time I was 18, I'd read every one, cover to cover, and it made me hungry to know about life beyond the wheat fields. Someday, with children of my own, I'd like to be a mother who knows a bit of life, too. I don't see why we women should have to live our lives only through our children. That's what prompted me to set off, try something new, find out what suited me – in the big blue yonder." Her eyes widened as she lightly laughed at herself.

"So you came to New York?" Estelle took no notice at Kate's self-effacing laugh.

"Chicago first, for a couple years." Kate stepped into her question without hesitation. "Then a friend, another dancer, told me there was a lot more work in New York. But that was before the Crash." Dropping her head, her shoulder-length hair obscured her face. She shook it back. "That's when it also stopped raining in Kansas and the wind began to blow away the topsoil and the farmers stopped planting and my father's work almost ceased. It's been going on for years now, and no one knows what to do."

Jack shifted in his chair. "Why don't they move?"

"I've asked the same, but they would have to walk away from everything they've built, and mother's a bit sickly now ..."

For a few moments everyone was silent until Kate sighed, shaking her head, her hair cascading like silk. "It's horrible what they're going through, and I'm a bit ashamed to say I'm glad I didn't stay or I'd be trapped there, too. So I send what money I can and pray they'll pack up and leave, but so far they won't. They keep saying it can't last much longer, the rain has to come soon." Kate's lower lip trembled and she pressed her lips together.

James squeezed her hand, and she gave him a thin smile.

"Do you think they're in danger?" Jack asked.

"They say no. But what I've seen in the papers …"

Estelle shook her head. "But he's a good mechanic. He can work anywhere."

Tears instantly filled Kate's eyes, and James jumped in.

"Mother, what would it take for you to leave your home? Leave everything behind?"

Estelle was about to toss back a snappy reply, but Jack's glare reined her in. She cleared her throat. "It's a terrible situation, and I'm so sorry for your family's hardship, my dear. But I deeply admire your strength and will pray your family comes out of this trial in good stead." She then rang the small table bell. "Let's have coffee and dessert in the parlor. I believe Cook made apple crisp."

All in all, Estelle couldn't complain about the girl. Her story could very easily be true. The plains had become such a wasteland the newspapers were calling it the Dust Bowl, blowing great clouds of airborne dirt south and east, wreaking havoc in Chicago and even the East Coast. But even if Kate's story were a calculated ploy for sympathy, it didn't mesh with the rest of her demeanor; particularly how Kate admired her son. Not adoration, Estelle would later clarify to one of the ladies at church. It was not as simplistic as that. The girl held her own in every exchange, neither fawning attention nor withholding her own opinion. And there was energy between them anyone could see; both passionate and respectful, reminding Estelle of herself and Jack. Right down to the lingering trace of Kate's fingertips on the back of James' hand as they sat side by side on the divan, their shoulders brushing from time to time. Estelle had to admit Kate presented herself as well cultured and self-assured, even though it confounded her as to how she became so with only a farming-class breeding and none of wealth's advantages.

After church service the next morning, as James and Kate walked toward the Green, Estelle confided in Suzette, an old friend who was not known for her discretion. "I'm a bit ashamed to say I misjudged her," she said. "She was rather charming: polite, well mannered, an excellent conversationalist without being overbearing, and dressed to perfection. I'm sure James paid for the ensemble, but it was well chosen; sumptuous without being showy. Really, you'd never think …" Estelle broke off when she saw Suzette's smile turn into an I-told-you-so. "Now don't look at me like that. Of course I know no matter how well brought up she may appear to be, she's still an actress." Estelle's slight sneer on the word actress rever-berated for a moment before she turned to leave, sure it would only be a matter of minutes before her comments flitted through the ranks of church ladies and land, as intended, in the ears of Myrtle Howe, banishing any wrong assumptions if she happened to see James and Kate strolling around town that morning – which, of course, she did.

❧

"I couldn't believe my eyes, Martin," Myrtle blustered as she bustled around the kitchen making breakfast after returning from church. "I haven't seen James Meaden since … I don't even know when. But there he was, sitting pretty in church and then promenading around the Green with a tall, willowy thing! And the two of them laughing together in such an intimate way. It was embarrassing. Someone said she's a Broadway actress. Well, you can just imagine what that means."

Entering from the back door, Celeste overheard her mother's comment and called up the steps with a smile in her voice. "What does that mean, Mother?"

Myrtle whirled around, surprised. "I thought you went to church with Gamma."

"I did, but I didn't stay for coffee. I have a bunch of orders to finish for Christmas. Mrs. Quince is bringing Gamma home from Hartford. What did you mean about the actress with James?" Celeste asked, removing her gloves and hat, setting them on the shelf by the back door and hanging her coat on a peg underneath.

Martin randomly flipped his newspaper pages, keeping an eye on his wife's reaction.

"Nothing, really." Myrtle surged with vigor. "It's just that *the theater* can be a difficult life and, well, not very refined. It's just so surprising! Can't imagine what James sees in her."

Martin cleared his throat to squelch a chuckle, but Celeste laughed out loud.

"Oh, Mother, I'm sure you have *some* sort of idea. You're not blind. Anyway, I hear they make a charming couple. Did you actually see them on the Green? They say she's gorgeous. Everyone's talking about it. I'm surprised you aren't hiding out behind a tree, spying on them." She paused, and then quickly added: "Maybe we should invite them for lunch and see what all the fuss is about." She blew a kiss to her mother and ruffled her father's hair as she passed by on her way upstairs to change out of her church clothes.

Myrtle stood stock still in the middle of the kitchen.

"Are you alright?" Martin asked.

"Did you hear that?" Myrtle asked, spatula clenched in her fist.

"What?"

"What came out of our little girl's mouth?"

"She's not so little anymore," Martin replied. "Why does it bother you, this girl with James? Celeste hasn't seen him for years now."

"I don't know. I just always hoped one day they'd find each other again."

"Well, I think it's safe to say that ship has sailed," Martin said.

But Myrtle wanted to be sure.

❧

Although Myrtle saw Estelle around town over the holidays, they didn't get a chance to speak privately until the end of the January at the Women's Social Club meeting.

After the luncheon, Estelle signaled Myrtle into her study, and before she could shut the door Myrtle asked: "Is it true James wants to marry her?"

Estelle laughed softly. "We haven't discussed that directly, but I think there's something James wants more. All I'm at liberty to say right now is I'm working on a plan. But you answer me: Is Celeste seeing anyone seriously?"

"Oh, no! She's completely consumed with her Needlery and school and charity work. I barely see her myself. At this rate, I don't see how she'll ever …"

"Well, let's not worry about that right now. It's good she has something to keep her occupied. And I must say the ladies are agog about her little business. I purchased a few designs for gifts, and they're lovely. You should be very proud of her industriousness."

Myrtle glowed in the compliment and left reassured.

❧

In April, as spring teased itself awake, Jack ran up the steps of Howe Hardware, burst through the swinging door and tapped the bell. "Ho ho!" He chimed, seeing Gamma sitting behind the counter. "Aren't you as beautiful as the day!"

His booming voice caused Celeste to look up from her consultation with a customer across the room. She paused, watching Mr. Meaden pat Gamma's hand and lean across the counter to kiss her cheek. Her customer, Mrs. Adler, looked up from examining the painted cross-stitch canvas and nudged Celeste with her elbow.

"I hear James isn't seeing that actress anymore" she said with a wink.

Celeste blushed, quickly pointing to the canvas. "Do you like the picture?"

"Oh my, yes. Ede's done a fine job capturing our home. Even sweet kitty in the window. I think my daughter might like one of her home, too."

Celeste smiled. Since launching The Needlery in a corner of the store six months ago, her clientele had built steadily, keeping Ede very busy drawing new designs. "We'd love to do that, but first let's look at your thread," she said, redirecting Mrs. Adler's attention to her selection of colors.

Gamma clasped Jack's hand and held on to it. "You flatter this old woman. How can a whole winter pass since last I see you? In such a small town?"

"I've been busy … very busy … spending lots of time in New York, now that James and I have worked out our differences."

Slipping off her stool, Gamma raised the hinged countertop. "Come, sit," she said and led Jack to the chairs by the front window, encircling the pot-bellied stove.

Shrugging off his jacket, Jack slipped his thumbs under his vest. "I still can't believe James is on board."

"To run the company?"

"Better, actually." Jack slapped his thigh. "Don't know why I didn't think of it myself, but Estelle came up with a brilliant solution."

Gamma poured two cups of tea from the warm pot on the stove.

Jack took a big slurp. "Ollie and James are going to share the top spot, each according to his strength. Co-Presidents! Now isn't that the cat's meow?"

Before Gamma could reply, a customer came through the door and greeted her before turning toward The Needlery, where Celeste was gathering up Mrs. Adler's materials.

Jack looked over, seeing Celeste for the first time. "Jumping Jehoshaphat! Who's that gorgeous woman over there?"

Gamma smiled, tapping her ear as she pointed to Celeste, suggesting they observe her.

"Hello Mrs. Steadwell," they heard her say. "I'm just ringing up Mrs. Adler, but your design is ready, too. I've got it behind the counter, packaged with all the threads. Please, come with me."

As Celeste led both women to the cash register, Jack turned to Gamma. "What's going on there?"

"Celeste's business. She and Ede make custom needlepoint designs."

"Well I'll be a monkey's uncle. I think Estelle said something about that but … when did she become so … mature? I wouldn't recognize her on the street."

"Quite a transformation, yah? Finally she make some choice and begin a life for herself. College courses: economics and accounting; teaching art to the children at Hartford Center; and at night, elocution classes. Can you imagine? Such a good time to be a woman."

"That's what my Beatrice keeps saying. You been talking to her, too?"

Gamma shrugged, with a soft smile.

Having finished her accounts, Celeste came to greet Jack.

"So nice to see you, Mr. Meaden. You look well. How is Mrs. Meaden?"

Jack rose and made a slight bow, admiring her beauty. Celeste's pale green sateen sheath accentuated her blue eyes, framed by tendrils of curls loosened from her chignon.

"All's well, all's well. Don't you look terrific! All grown up! And I've been hearing great things about your business. How do you like it so far?"

Celeste blushed. "Well, at this point it's more a hobby than a business, but I love it. It started off slow, but bit by bit the word spread, and now Ede's so busy she's had to teach me to do a bit of the painting."

"Forgive me, but what are you painting?" Jack inquired.

"Oh, we make custom needlepoint designs for pillows, chair covers, wall hangings. We paint the design right on the canvas, ready for stitching. We'll even have it stitched, too."

Jack crinkled his eyes. "Is it true the ladies are putting their dogs and birds on pillows?"

Celeste laughed at his expression. "Dogs, Cockatoos, houses, gardens, cats, favorite flowers, pretty much whatever they like. Ede can paint anything, and I match up the yarn colors. Voila! Custom needlery."

"So you're an artist, too!" Jack declared. "By god, I'm surrounded by them. Overnight I went from being a business man to an art philanthropist."

Celeste and Gamma looked confused.

"Oh, sorry, I haven't told you. Seems that James has a bent for the arts, too. Spends a lot of time with painters in New York and has quite a collection of their work. And he wants to do more. A lot more. It's rather interesting, even for an old dog like me. Never thought I'd be one to understand the difference between the Regionalists, the Ashcan Group and the Abstractionists."

The bell above the door rang as a customer entered, and Celeste excused herself.

Jack watched her walk away. "Such an elegant young woman."

"Yah. She blossom since she choose to follow her truth. Sounds like James is doing same. Is he painting now?"

"Yes … No … I mean … *He's* not painting, but I think he's following his truth. For the longest time I saw James only as I wished him to be. It took a fight for us – for me, at least – to see who he really is. It's a hell of a thing to have missed all these years!"

Gamma shook her head. "What you miss?"

"How much James loves art. Not making it but supporting it, buying it, investing in it. He thinks – no, he believes – it should be part of our long-term portfolio … a substantial part."

Gamma laughed. "How many times they plunder Prague for her art? If only we had one of the paintings, for good old-age security!"

Jack smacked his hands together, rubbing them vigorously. "That's pretty much what James has been saying. We've been talking about how to integrate his love of art into the operation. I really can't afford to lose him. He knows everyone in our business, and he'd be impossible to replace. But with co-presidents – Ollie at headquarters handling day-to-day administration and James in New York focused on investments – both angles are covered. The boys like working together, and the art could be a boon to our portfolio. James said the right art can be purchased for a song and potentially return a thousand-fold, say 50 years down the road. He showed me the numbers from current art sales. Said he'd like to start a gallery to house the collection and attract the up-and-comers before anyone else snags them."

With a sigh, Jack let his shoulders drop. "It's been a hell of a fight to solve this problem, but Gamma, I think we've got it heading in the right direction, at least on the business side. Estelle still isn't too happy with James' lady friend, but I told her one step at a time, right? You can't change everything at once. She still wishes …" Jack's eyes flashed over to Celeste. "Well, what can you do? There's no accounting for chemistry."

Gamma did not want to encourage his hopes for Celeste. The girl had just found the joy of her own wings, and Gamma did not want them clipped for any reason. Rising, she excused herself. "I must relieve Celeste. She now go to Hartford shelter. The children depend on her. But how happy I am to hear your news, Jack. Is so long since you so easy smile. Finally you can plan for time free!"

Laughing, Jack squeezed Gamma's extended hand as they walked back to the counter. "Now that's a problem I like having." He called over to Celeste, "You have my deep admiration for your business gumption. We'll have to celebrate with a dinner at the house sometime soon."

Grinning, Celeste nodded and waited until Jack strode out the door before turning to Gamma with expectant eyes. "So? What's news? I overheard a little. Tell me what's been happening with James!"

"Nothing for your worry. Best skedaddle now or miss the trolley. Sister Katharine needs you on time. She's terrible with those children. She say only you they listen to."

Celeste giggled. "And wouldn't you, with this?" Reaching under the counter, she pulled out a covered glass container, tipping open the lid for Gamma to sniff.

"Ahhhh, you pixie. I dream chocolate last night."

"I was baking late. Will you be all right? Papa's on a delivery."

Gamma scoffed. "What? I can run shop with closed eyes."

Celeste collected her book satchel, art supplies and sweater. "After the shelter, I have elocution lessons, so I won't be home for supper."

"OK. I save some."

"And if anyone comes in for a design, tell them I'll be back tomorrow morning or make an appointment for any evening this week. I'll come to their house if they like."

Gamma nodded, shooing her out the door.

At supper that night, Myrtle was chipper, humming as she served each plate from the pots on the stove. When Celeste wasn't home, they ate in the kitchen.

Martin looked up from the evening paper. "Something happen today, Myrtle?"

"Nothing special, just a pleasant day."

Filling the water glasses at the sink, Gamma said, "I hear something nice. Jack Meaden came by to say his two sons will run the business together."

Wiping her hands on a dishtowel, Myrtle brought two plates to the table. "That was *part* of the deal," she said, turning back to the stove to make her own plate.

"Part of what deal?" Martin asked, reaching for the salt shaker.

Gamma took her seat and waited for Myrtle to join them.

"Estelle's deal with James." Myrtle almost sang the words as she sat down. "He's agreed to let her go in exchange for the art gallery."

"Let who go for what gallery?"

"The actress. Estelle told James if he let her go, she'd make sure Jack funded the art gallery he wants."

Martin looked at Gamma, who looked at Myrtle, who hummed into her plate as she cut up her meat.

"And Estelle told you this, directly?" Martin asked.

"Near enough."

Martin dropped his fist on the table. "Damn it to hell, Myrtle, I'll not have you gossip. It's not Christian, it's not ladylike, and it's not good for the shop."

Martin's coarse words caused Gamma to flinch and Myrtle to drop her utensils, clattering on her plate. But she stared straight back at Martin.

"It's not gossip. I saw Estelle myself, later on, and she confirmed it. She was never going to let that girl into her family."

"The actress?" Gamma asked, peppering her meat and potatoes.

Myrtle sniffed. "No telling where her kind comes from."

Martin growled. "Any worse than where you came from, Myrtle?"

Both women looked up in surprise.

Myrtle's face crumpled. "What?" Her voice was breathy.

"What?" Martin's eyes were wide and dark. "Have you thought about what Estelle might think about *your* past?"

Myrtle blanched. "You promised never … "

"And you promised to obey me. But somehow you keep forgetting. I won't have you slandering some innocent girl for a cockamamie notion in your head."

Myrtle shook her head, her husband's anger feeding her strength to counter. "It's not cockamamie. I'm no different from you, teaching her the business of the hardware store, wanting the best for our girl."

"How is our girl any better for James than this actress you disdain? How can you sit in judgment over someone you don't even know? Especially when you … "

Gamma rapped the table. "Caution, Martin!"

Myrtle's face was raw and vulnerable, her chin began to tremble.

Martin took a breath and let it out slowly. "Yes, caution." Martin said to his mother, his voice still upset. "But how else do I end this foolishness?

This constant clamor for more when our life is already better than most?" He looked at his wife. "We have enough, Myrtle, more than enough. I won't have Celeste sold off to the highest bidder."

Myrtle clenched her teeth to stop her chin quivering. She knew she had pushed too far. Martin had provided all the safety and security her childhood lacked. But something deep within would not stop gnawing at her, trying to satisfy her hunger for respect, for status; to be above the sidelong glances and raised chins of disdain, beyond reproach, and equal to the likes of Estelle. Toward that goal, she felt possessed … but she must convince her husband otherwise.

"What can I do?" she asked in a quiet voice. "I just want to be a good wife and mother."

"Then stop. Now. Have nothing more to do with any plans by Estelle or anyone else regarding James and Celeste. I don't know why you insist on their match. We know at least a dozen young men her age – when she decides she's ready. But right now she needs time to know and like herself *before* she marries. Damn it, I won't have her railroaded into responsibilities so young. I know the toll that takes. Celeste is not the puppet for your dreams. You leave her be. Let her discover and create her own life. Do you understand me?"

As the words echoed away, the tea water bubbled over on the stove, punctuating the silence. No one moved for a long moment, each looking at the other until Myrtle lowered her eyes and nodded. "All right, Martin. As you wish," she whispered, keeping her eyes on her plate – but her fingers crossed underneath the table.

21 Feelings

June 1933

Leaning against the hunt table in the Great Hall of Trinity College, Ron Meaden crossed his legs at the ankles and casually twirled his squash racquet, flipping it around and around in his hand as he looked about for his sister. Dressed in squash whites with his signature peacock blue stripe, he stood out among the college students dashing up and down the wide marble staircase to classrooms and offices. Glancing at his watch, he wondered what direction Beatrice would arrive. She'd asked him to test out one of her squash protégés, and he thought they'd agreed to meet at the school's main building.

Watching the summer student's bustle past, he was happy to be done with school and back on the court full time. Then, out of the corner of his eye, he caught sight of a familiar figure descending the steps, a tall, elegant, coiffed young woman with an upright carriage and a slight sashay to her walk. Clutching an oversized folder, she was talking with another girl as they bounced down the stairs. Then he heard the laugh that gave her away.

"Why Celeste Howe!" He boomed to capture her attention, twirling his racquet faster as he stood erect, his eyes bright and shining. "This must be my lucky day!" He hadn't seen Celeste for nearly a year, and she'd never looked better.

Surprised, Celeste instantly recognized the smooth, silvery voice, but she could not quite place it to the muscular arms and legs clad in crisp white. The last time she'd seen Ron he was skinny and just a bit over her height. But this was a much taller man, who filled the curves of his shirt and shorts rather well. As they reached the bottom step, Celeste's friend nudged her, flashing a wicked grin while whispering: "Yum-yum, the gods are with you today! Details! I want them all. Call ya later."

With an odd, fluttering commotion in her chest, Celeste took a deep breath and crossed the hall. "Ron Meaden, is that really you?" she asked, a trill in her voice and her eyes on his face.

"In the flesh." He beamed, loving her surprise.

Looking him up and down with practiced assurance, she cooed. "Well, aren't you just grand," and squeezed his right biceps. "Muscles galore and ... everything." It wasn't her usual style with men. She more often played coy and shy, but this was Ron, her creek pal, her buddy, who brought out her ease and sass. "What in heaven are you doing here?"

"I could ask you the same!"

"I'm a student! I take a few classes each semester." Celeste tapped her folder. "Just picked up my advertising project from last semester."

"Advertising what?"

"My new business at the store." She paused, delighting in the confusion in his eyes. "The Needlery. Bet you didn't know your mother was my first customer!"

"No kidding? Well I'll be ... Sorry! I hadn't heard. Don't get home much, and when I do, no one tells me anything. Between the squash circuit and school, I've been out of the family loop. But this is great news! Imagine that! Celeste Howe a business woman! Top drawer. Top drawer indeed! What's the biz about?"

Celeste glowed. "Ede and I make custom needlework canvases. Your mother ordered a pillow canvas of her rock garden. Papa gave me a small corner in the hardware store where I show samples, take orders and match up the yarn to the colors Ede paints on the canvas. She works whenever she can, in-between jobs and school. You wouldn't believe how quick she is."

"I'll bet I would. How is ol' Ede?" Ron grinned. It didn't seem possible his two creek mates were actually building a business together.

Celeste paused for a moment, wondering how much she wanted to tell him about Ede, but then caught herself. "Oh, she's fine. Very busy but fine, I think. She's going to teacher's college full time, working at the diner on weekends and paints whenever she can. But now with the needlepoint business, we barely see each other except when I bring over new design orders."

"Tip Top, really, impressive," Ron said, appraising this new Celeste. No longer the timid, giggly girl he'd known. Now she conveyed a confidence, a grace he hadn't noticed before – along with long, curvy lines lingering beneath her dress. Ron pointed to the folder. "Show me?"

"Oh, well, it's my first attempt at an advertisement." Celeste shuffled her folder, placing it on the hunt table, and opened the flap. "My professor liked it, but I'm not sure."

"So you're advertising the business now, too?"

"Well, I'm considering it. This was just a project for class. Economics of Small Business, where we learn a little bit of everything." Celeste pulled out a large piece of cardboard with a drawing of a woman sitting at a writing desk, a dreamy look in her eye, her chin resting on her clasped hands, and above her head a thought balloon with sketches of a dog, a cat, a patch of garden and a house exterior. A headline was scripted across the top.

Transform Your Dearest Treasures into Custom Furnishings

And along the bottom:

Pillows. Chair Covers. Table Runners. Framed Gifts.
Custom Needlepoint Canvas – Capturing Your Special World.

THE NEEDLERY
Located in Howe Hardware, Gladdenbury, Connecticut.

"WOWZA!" Ron whistled. "This looks professional. You did all this?"

Celeste's head snapped up. "Well, it was my concept, but Ede sketched it. And anyway, sir, it's not polite to sound so surprised."

Ron laughed nervously. "No, I meant to sound impressed. This is really good. *You're* really good. I just haven't seen you in so long, I didn't know … any of this."

"Well, now you do," Celeste laughed, letting him off the hook as she repackaged her artwork. When she first saw him, standing like a Greek god at the bottom of the stairwell, she wanted to shriek with delight and run to hug him. But now she was glad she'd resisted. She wasn't the 17 year-old who rolled down hills and swung over the creek. She'd worked hard to become a worldly young woman who knew her way around social circumstance. Meeting him today felt like a final exam, one she planned to ace with flying colors. "So, what brings you to Trinity? Yale kick you off their courts?"

Her sly smile and twinkling eyes shot a thrill up Ron's spine.

Seeing his eyes widen, she relaxed. She liked teasing men and was good at it.

Recomposing himself, Ron swept his racquet in an arc, taking a squash stance. "Heck no! I kicked them off mine."

"Whatever do you mean?" she asked, a spike of heat shooting through her belly. Instinctively, she picked up her folder and held it to her chest as a shield.

"I'm not going back next year. I quit, to play full time on the amateur circuit."

"Squash?"

"Yep. Didn't think Father would go for it. Thought he'd put up a fuss, insist I finish University. But he thought it was a grand idea. Said it would be jolly good to have a champion to brag about, and he even found sponsors to cover the year's expenses. So the rest is up to me now. Pretty crazy, huh?"

Celeste didn't know what to say. She'd been idly jesting. She had no idea Ron would leave college before graduating, to play squash, no less! The bizarre idea caused her to giggle.

"Hey, what's the big idea? Don't you think I can do it?"

His umbrage made her giggle even more. Covering her mouth, Celeste tried to calm herself enough to speak. "Of course I do. I think you can do anything you set your mind to. I'm only laughing because it feels so good … your decision, I mean. It's such a surprise, but of course it's just right. You've been the best … all your life! This is wonderful, Ron. I was laughing because, well, the best things do make us laugh, don't they? When they're really right, don't you think?" She dropped her folder on the table and swung her arms around Ron's broad shoulders, hugging his neck. "Oh Ron, I'm really, truly happy for you! Over the moon happy!"

Surprised by her embrace, Ron immediately wrapped his free arm around her, encircling the curve of her waist. Smelling her clean scent, he buried his nose in the nape of her neck, enraptured and never wanting to let go.

Suddenly neither did Celeste. Feeling the strength of his arm across her back, pressing her into his chest, she squeezed him even tighter. Of all the boys who'd ever hugged her, no one made her feel so secure and warm. She melted into his curves, the world around them disappearing as tingling shot through her body, from tip to toe. *This* was the feeling she'd been waiting for, hoping for, longing for. *This* was the feeling she'd read about in books she wasn't supposed to read. *This* was the feeling she'd imagined and dreamed. Just like Ede described … oh my god, she gasped, her vow to Ede. Dropping her arms suddenly, Celeste pulled away and glanced around the busy hallway, trying to recompose herself, wiping her hands down the front of her skirt before looking to Ron's face, hoping to see a sign that he'd felt the tingling too, but his head was down, staring at his feet. Stepping back, her hand flew up to check her chignon before picking up her folder and clutching it tightly, licking her suddenly dry lips. She looked at Ron, his arms by his side, eyes still to the floor. *Oh god, she asked herself, what have I just done?*

Ron slowly raised his head, his face crumpled. "I'm sorry."

"No, no," she whispered, shaking her head while her mind raced. *Was she just being a school girl? Remembering an old crush? Should she say something, or would that look even more foolish? How could she explain her promise to leave him alone, for Ede?* "I'm sorry. I didn't mean to cause …. I was just …" She shook her head to clear it. "So, when do you start?"

Ron's eyebrows pinched. "Start?"

"Your squash season! You must be so excited." Her face was falsely animated.

Ron withdrew his expression to neutral and let out a sigh. "This summer. Up in Rhode Island." He shrugged his shoulders, to loosen them, and picked up his racquet, squeezing the handle. "The Amateur Squash Circuit begins in the fall and runs through spring. Mostly on the East Coast, but a few tournaments are in Canada and other parts of the country."

"But you'll be based from home? Maybe we can get together? With Ede? Like old times?" Her eyes twitched across his face. How could she find out what he really meant? Did he feel what she felt? Was there anything in his heart for Ede? Did Ede even still carry a torch for him? She didn't know, but she couldn't risk breaking Ede's heart again.

"Thing is, I really won't be around much at all," Ron said dully, hating each word as it left his mouth, knowing it sealed his fate. A fate he'd chosen before he knew Celeste had grown up into a woman he desired, deeper than when they were children. But now he would have no time to see her, court her, woo her. Nor could he ask her to wait for him, particularly when he didn't know how it would all turn out. It could take years before he made a name for himself. Looking at her bright, eager eyes and lusting for her sinuous body, all he could do was hope she might still be available after he'd established a secure future in the sport.

Celeste nodded politely as her heart sank. So that was that. Why had they waited so long? From the very first evening on his back porch, they couldn't keep their eyes off each other; before Ede joined them at the creek and James returned from Europe and everything got so complicated.

"Oh. Gee, I'm sorry. It would have been fun to … well … anyway … it's great about the squash and all. You'll do top notch, I'm sure," Celeste said, stuffing away her desire. Shifting her weight from one foot to the other, uncertain what to do next, she found herself casually asking: "So how's your brother?"

A cloud swept over Ron's face. So this is what she's about, he thought. He should have guessed. Why would he expect her to be any different from all the other girls? He replied in a rush. "James? Pretty well, I'm told. Pops made a deal: He and Ollie will run the company together, and in exchange, James is opening an art gallery in New York."

"I heard something about that." Celeste tried to keep her voice bright.

Ron shrugged. "Don't know all the details, except Father went to see him and met all these artists in some hovel in Greenwich Village, and six months later, James is buying art and planning a gallery to showcase it."

"What kind of art?" Celeste asked, thinking again of Ede and how grand it would be to have her work shown in New York.

Ron shrugged again. "Heck if I know. He's not around much, either. But from what Father said … it's not the kind we have at the house."

Celeste nodded slowly, recalling the snatches of conversation she'd overheard between Gamma and Jack.

Seeing her preoccupation, Ron thought it was about his brother. Most every girl he'd ever known swooned when they met James, and he was sick of it. "Well, I guess I missed my sister. Better go check the courts."

The stiffness in Ron's voice jarred Celeste out of her reverie. She didn't want him to leave but could think of no logical reason to stay on. Besides, she was expected at the shelter 10 minutes ago. "Jeepers, I've got to go, too! But Ron, it was wonderful seeing you, and I hope … well … I wish you the best luck on the circuit and hope to see you, soon. Please give my best to your mother, too." She turned to leave then stopped, her heart pounding. Without thinking, she swiveled back, lightly dropped her hand on his shoulder and leaned in, kissing his cheek, gently yet firmly, as ribbons of feelings coursed through her body, swelling her heart, hoping he would feel her … love. Yes, she realized, this was the feeling of love. And she felt it … for the first time … with Ron. Lingering as long as she dared, she lifted her lips and whispered in his ear: "It was more than wonderful to see you again … much, much more than I dare say." Then off she slipped, down the hall, away, before she could make herself any more the fool.

Watching her glide away and out the oversized oak doors, Ron felt he was watching a rare, beautiful butterfly floating beyond his reach, going places he could not follow … an image that would haunt his dreams for years to come.

22 Hollywood
July 1933

At the shrill of the telephone, Celeste jumped up from the kitchen table. "Hello?"

"I've got the most amazing news!" Ede gushed. "Meet me at the swings!"

The phone went dead and Celeste's stomach dropped. Staring at the handset before replacing it on the cradle, she believed it could mean only one thing.

"Who was that, Celeste?" her mother asked.

"Ede," she said in a monotone, crossing to the table, flipping her books closed and stacking them in the corner. "Something's happened. I've got to meet her." That much excitement in Ede's voice could only mean one thing: Ron.

"But you're making dessert," Myrtle insisted, wiping her hands on a dish towel.

"Mother, I'll be back soon, but right now I have to go." Looking down at her clothes, crumpled and dusty from working all day at the store, Celeste shrugged. Even though she was afraid of what she'd hear, she had to know what happened.

Approaching the Green, she saw Ede standing on a swing, waving, her long black hair flowing in the breeze. Dropping onto the adjacent swing, Celeste watched her friend glide through the air, with an aura of lightness and promise.

"Just when you think it's all going to be one big bore," Ede chanted, rolling her hips to push the swing higher, "in drops a surprise." Letting go of the chains, she vaulted off, tucking her body into a somersault and rolled onto the grass.

"Ede!" Celeste bolted to help her, but she was already on her feet, twirling around and grabbing Celeste's hands. "You'll never, ever guess."

"Ron asked you out."

"What?" Ede dropped Celeste's hands as her buoyant spirit instantly deflated. "Gawd, no! Why did you say that?" she demanded, angered by an old hurt stealing her thunder.

Celeste's face twitched then flooded with relief. "Oh! Well I – I saw him several weeks ago, and it was the only thing I could never-ever-guess."

"What? Darn it! That stinks. Here I have great news – the best I've ever had – but now I feel all jumbled. When did you see him? And why didn't you tell me before?"

"I'm sorry, Ede. Let's forget it. I didn't mean to jumble you. It was weeks ago, at the college. He was meeting his sister. We talked … a couple minutes. He even asked about you. But he's going away for the summer and practically the whole next year on the squash circuit … so, honestly, what does it matter? Tell me *your* news?"

Ede studied her friend with jaded eyes. She couldn't help feel old pangs of envy whenever Ron's name was mentioned, instantly recalling that cold December night when she realized Celeste had turned Ron's head. Even though Ron had offered her nothing but friendship, Ede still felt he was hers, or should be, because he thrilled her heart silly.

Celeste stepped back, sitting down on the swing. "I'm really, really sorry … But please, tell me your news. I'm dying to hear." Her elocution lessons had given her a fine vocal command, able to project any inflection to convey her intended meaning, regardless how she felt.

Reluctantly, Ede reclaimed her swing as her smile slowly returned. "Do you remember me saying Papa had a friend from Italy coming to visit? An artist friend?"

Celeste nodded.

"Well, he's here. Mr. Moltano. He and Papa grew up in the same village, so he's practically my uncle. But he moved away before I was born, so we never met. Anyway, he and Papa always kept in contact through letters and common friends."

Celeste nodded continuously, hoping Ede would speed up the story.

"Mr. Moltano," Ede's voice was full and round as she swayed side to side on the swing, "has worked in Rome all these years and is well known for his set designs for the theater and cinema."

"For what?"

"The backgrounds in movies. They're mostly painted sets, not a real desert or forest or castle. Anyway, Mr. Moltano is on his way to Hollywood to become the director of set design for a big movie company. I forget which one."

Celeste felt a rising agitation. She had work to do, dessert to make. "Ede, I thought *you* had big news. What does Mr. Moltano have to do with it?"

Ede twisted a lock of hair around her finger. She wasn't going to let Celeste rush her. "If you'll be patient, Miss Smarty Pants ..."

Both girls swiveled away from each other then swung back together.

"OK, tell me." Celeste spoke calmly, with a practiced smile.

"Well, Mr. Moltano heard I was an artist, too, and when he saw my work, he liked it, very much. But he spoke so fast in Italian I couldn't understand him. He and Papa were talking over each other, pointing to my paintings. At first I thought they were fighting, but then they started laughing and clapping. So I laughed, too, not knowing why."

Celeste nodded, beginning to feel excited. No matter what transpired between them, Celeste always held Ede's art in high regard, wishing her the success she'd always dreamed. "So he liked your art?"

"He *loved* my art. Said I had the talent to be a successful designer – and then said something that stopped my father smiling. I could only catch a few words, but I suddenly realized Mr. Moltano was saying I should go with him – to Hollywood!" Ede stopped and sucked in a breath. There, she'd said it, out loud, to her best friend, so it had to be true.

Celeste sat motionless on the swing.

"Did you hear me?" Ede prodded. "Mr. Moltano wants me in Hollywood!"

Celeste opened her mouth, but no words came out. Since they'd graduated, Ede had secretly dated two older men. First her professor and then a fellow artist she'd met. She'd told Celeste all about them, and while her romances made Celeste a bit uneasy, she'd kept her friend's confidence, sure the right sort of man their own age would eventually come along for Ede. But now she was moving to Hollywood ... with her father's friend?

"Ede, what do you mean?" Celeste asked slowly. "Are you going to Hollywood *with* Mr. Moltano?" She left the question open-ended, hoping not to have to explain further.

Ede blinked. "NO! No, no, no! Mr. Moltano offered me an apprenticeship with his studio. I'll be working as his secretary and translator, because he doesn't speak English very well, but he promised I would learn about set painting and could help out now and again. I'll be right there in the studio, all the time, seeing how it's done, what materials they use. It's more opportunity than I ever dreamed. Isn't it the most grand and glorious thing you've ever heard?"

This was the moment for Celeste to rise up and embrace her friend with a shower of enthusiasm. To hold her up to the sun, already shining in her face, and dance on the field of dreams reflected in her eyes. But Celeste could not bring herself to do so. Her heart felt heavy with caution. Not for Ede, but for herself. No matter how hard she'd been working to find her own dreams, her friend, once again, eclipsed her ... and worse, was now leaving, taking Celeste's dream with her. How would the Needlery survive without Ede? All she could think to say was: "What did your father say?"

A cloud crossed Ede's face. "Oh. Well, at first he was having none of it. He walked away in a huff and then spoke with my mother, and they started yelling at each other while Mr. Moltano spoke with me, more slowly now, pointing out what he liked in my paintings and telling me about Hollywood and how he could use a smart girl like me to help him understand the crazy Americano ways. And all about California, where the sun shines constantly, and the pacific ocean and the unusual people. Many many artists, he said."

"But where would you live?" Celeste asked cautiously.

"With Mr. Moltano and his wife. She's coming over from Italy next month."

"Ohhhh," Celeste sighed, leaning back with relief. "He's married! Good! I thought ..."

Ede slapped her friend's arm. "*You* thought wrong, missy. It's not like that. This is a job, a real job, with a salary! A small one, but I won't need much, living with the Moltanos. Oh, Celeste, can you believe it?"

As the full picture emerged, Celeste tried to stifle the chill creeping up her chest. "What about school and your degree?"

"The apprenticeship is only until next May, so I can take a leave of absence and finish when I return. I could probably do a lot of the course work next summer and get my degree by December."

"But what about the Needlery?"

Ede's face dropped flat. She'd forgotten about the Needlery and suddenly realized how dependent the business was on her. Celeste could rough sketch an image, but Ede was the one who painted the canvas, making adjustments as she saw fit. "Oh Celeste, I'm sorry, I didn't realize. In all the excitement I completely forgot ..."

Celeste stared into the sky, unable to shake off the panic seizing her body.

Ede rose and stood in front of Celeste, connecting with her eyes. "I'll fix this. I will. Maybe my father can take my place while I'm away. Yes, I'm sure he'd do that for me. Or better yet, my mother. She hasn't been practicing much lately, but she's just as good, even better than me in matters like this. She's got an excellent eye for color and detail. Don't worry, Celeste. I won't leave you high and dry. We can work this out. Promise."

Swallowing to moisten her throat, Celeste nodded stiffly. "So when do you leave?" she asked, sure they'd have the summer to sort it all out.

"In three days. I'm taking the train with Mr. Moltano."

❧

After calling up the stairs several times for Celeste to come to dinner, Gamma found her in her bedroom, eyes red-rimmed, sitting cross-legged on her bed, scribbling hard in a notebook. "What happen?" Gamma asked softly.

Celeste shook her head, fear closing her throat.

Gamma slid onto the bed, hugged Celeste and gently rocked her, cooing away her distress. Folding into Gamma's embrace, Celeste calmed enough to be lulled into a tenuous sleep when Myrtle burst through the door. Wiping her hands on her apron, Myrtle opened her mouth to insist Celeste come downstairs, but before she could utter a sound, Gamma's hand swept up, pointing to the door, banishing her from the room. Whatever had happened to upset Celeste could wait a day.

❧

The next morning, Celeste awoke still dressed in yesterday's frock, covered by a light blanket. She felt a bit dizzy as she sat up, and then remembered rushing upstairs after seeing Ede, without any supper. On the bedside table sat a buttered roll and glass of water, which she immediately devoured.

Pulling off her clothes, she dropped them in a heap and donned a robe before quietly opening her door, hoping to avoid her mother or father. But she was relieved to see Gamma's door partially opened and her small feet, tapping to band music playing on the radio.

Celeste poked her head around the door and Gamma smiled, waving her in. "Your mother is out and Martin's at store. He say stay home if you want, he can manage. Hungry?"

Celeste shook her head, her chin trembling and eyes welling up again. Hadn't she cried enough last night?

Gamma patted the chair in her cozy nook by the bay window, and Celeste slid onto its smooth blue chintz, tucking her feet under. Then she noticed the breakfast tray on the window seat and reached for a slice of apple. Gamma poured her some chamomile tea, stirring in a bit of honey, which Celeste consumed with zest, along with toast, a hard-boiled egg, a bacon slice and sausage link before she felt ready to tell Gamma her story. Letting all her feelings pour out, she finished with her shoulders and eyes drooping. "And now I feel abandoned."

"Why?" Gamma was surprised by her reaction. "Ede promise her mother's help."

"But what if she can't?

Gamma blew into the air. "Then you hire another artist with Ede's profit shares."

Celeste blinked. She hadn't thought of that. "But what if they're not as good?"

"Ede is not only good artist. Lots, there are … hungry for work. You see. With not much looking, you find what you need. Good work for good pay today is hard to find."

Mulling Gamma's words, Celeste felt a bit less fragmented. After a few moments, she added: "But Gamma, it's not just the business. Ron and Ede are both off on big adventures, bigger than any of us dreamed, and it just came to them, with no effort. How come nothing like that comes to me?"

Gamma looked deeply at Celeste, curious at the blank expression on her face. "What you mean, no effort? How old Ede when she start to paint? And Ron first play squash?" She paused, waiting for the light of comprehension to return to Celeste's eyes. "Yah. You know. For long time your friends do what they love. For very long time. And now something come of their effort. Is not surprise. And for you is same. Look what you do so far! With just needlepoint canvas and paint!"

"But it's not the same. They're into the world, and I'm stuck here."

"Oh?" Gamma let a few seconds pass then snapped her fingers. "Then go with them."

Celeste's eyes jumped. "What?"

"Go with one of them. Share their adventure. Why not? You young yet."

"Are you making a joke?"

"No joke." Gamma's face was deadpan. "What you want? To be old, wishing for what you not do? When chance come – grab hold, before it pass. The price tag of regret is too high."

Celeste's eyes narrowed.

"Look," Gamma said, setting aside her needlework. "Now I have story to tell, as you are old enough to understand … about your Papa."

Celeste shifted, hugging her knees. She wasn't sure she wanted to hear another story that might change her feelings about Papa.

"What you know of your Papa?" Gamma began. "Is no more than any child of their parents, right? You never think of what his dreams might be, right?"

Celeste slowly nodded.

"So think now: What were you father's young dreams? You think to be hardware man?"

Celeste looked surprised, ready to nod.

"Oh, no! Most definite not. Your father have only one dream since very small: to be sailor. Is all he talk about, day and night: to be sailor, like big Uncle Yazi, and see the world."

"My Papa?"

"Your Papa. My son. How different he was then! Not the quiet man you see today. Such a feisty child! Playing pirate all the time with grandmother Katerine. Up and down the aisle in the store they run, making racket, eyes big and shining, laughing, like hyena sometime. I think, is just a little boy's dream. But, when he turn fourteen, he come with paper to sign. Permission to apprentice a boat, to go to sea."

"At fourteen?"

Gamma nodded, waggling her finger. "Of course I say no. Not 'til he finish his study. And he obey, saying no more until he graduate, with honors, mind you, but then he ask again, for permission to become a captain's apprentice." Gamma blew the air. "Oh, this struck terror in my heart. To lose my son to the sea; the wicked sea that swallows men younger than he. But what can I say? He make his bargain true. He complete his study. So I cannot say no. But, instead, I make his father keep him busy in the store, so he can't go. Because I afraid to lose him. Afraid to never see him again – and this was my big mistake."

Celeste couldn't believe her ears; her mild-mannered father? "Papa a sailor?"

"Not just sailor, a Captain! Every minute, between jobs, he go to docks or talk to Yazi about where he go and what he see. At supper every night he report what ship arrive and what one leave and where it headed, all the time searching for new apprenticeship. Even after he marry Myrtle he still plan to go. And she agree, as soon as first baby born. So while she pregnant, he found his replacement for the store and train him, himself. All ready he was, after baby born, to begin his life at sea." Gamma took a breath as old, hard-worn grief passed over her face. "But then – his son die, and soon next his father." Gamma let out her breath slowly, reliving the sad time. "So what could he do? Leave his grieving wife and widowed mother? Put the business in stranger's hands? Was not Martin's way. No matter how much he want to sail, no longer could he go." Gamma sighed, one foot unconsciously tapping. "I have been long sorry to get in his way. I should have let him run to the sea as he want to, before circumstance took his choice away."

Celeste stared at Gamma, who stared back, both pairs of eyes wide open, one sage with experience, the other seeking more.

Gamma squeezed Celeste's arm. "So for you, I not want same. You must honor what beckons you, no matter what anyone think. We are born alone, to find our way home, however that may be. And for this, your heart knows best. So if you want to go with Ede or Ron or somewhere else on your own, listen to your heart's call and go, before is too late. Before circumstance take your choice away, too."

Celeste was stunned. It had never occurred to her she could go. Just pick up and leave all she'd known. It was an enticing feeling, but for what? What did she want to do? Where did she want to go? No answers came to mind, so she shook her head. "No, Gamma," she whispered. "I don't want to go with Ede or anyone. I'm happy her dream is coming to her. It only makes me wish I had something as clear, something as strong as she has, and Ron, too. I just wish I knew what my dream is so … I'll recognize it … if it ever comes."

Gamma's hands dropped to her lap as she turned to the windows, gazing far beyond the leaded panes. "And what if no dream comes?"

"Huh?"

"Tell me, if Ede no longer can paint, who you think she be? Without brush, does her life mean nothing? Or Ron. If he no longer play squash? Is that all there is of him? And your father? He lose his sailing dream but gain something else, no? Otherwise, you not be with us today. And surely as I know myself, he would not trade you for one inch of sail. More than any dream he could dream, you are his heart's content."

Celeste's shoulders rose, not understanding her grandmother's meaning.

Gamma looked to her. "To make dream is good, is part of life. Is how we know ourselves, test ourselves … but maybe is only small part of journey. More important, maybe, is what happen along the way. The people we meet. The laughter we find. The trouble we work through. Things we cannot know or imagine. Things we cannot dream. Things that come out of following our dream. This, I think, is what life is really for. To find out who we are from what we face, with courage, with creativity, with truth. This is why we have life, I think. Dreams are just something to do while we learn how to live."

Celeste blinked. "Just something to do?"

Gamma shrugged. "Is good to follow what we love. Sometimes big dreams come true. But in end, not matter much. Many people, most people, do good things, great things even, and no one remembers. But what you experience, what you see, what you feel, how you live along the way – this is what matters most. This is what shapes your heart's code. We are here, all together, yet also alone, each on a journey, with no measure better than how we learn … how we grow … from the gift of life, itself."

As Gamma patted Celeste's knee, her six copper bracelets rattled down her arm, tinging brightly. Celeste's eyes widened as she reached for her grandmother's arm and gently stroked the bracelets, silently remembering the old Gypsy's prophecy.

The Heart Code
Part Three

23 Blue Moon

September – December 1933

"Why Myrtle, how lovely you look."

Holding out both hands, Estelle welcomed Myrtle at the Social Club's September meeting. Brushing cheeks, Myrtle beamed, grateful for Estelle's very public acknowledgement. Before letting her pass, Estelle leaned in, whispering in her ear, "We must catch up."

After the formal meeting, Myrtle anxiously mingled during tea, fingering her sandwich. The first meeting of the season was always kinetic, the ladies hobnobbing about summer news and fall plans. And although Myrtle was usually in the thick of it, she found herself standing alone in the middle of the parlor observing the buzz when Estelle tapped her shoulder.

"How is your darling daughter?" she asked. "I've been hearing great whispers."

Myrtle blanched. "What whispers?"

"Of her pluck: finding several backup artists since Ede left town. And do tell, what do you know of *that* situation?"

With relief, Myrtle confirmed Celeste's recent business actions, explaining how she thought they were in for a rough patch when Celeste came home crying, but by the very next day she had bounced back. "As to Ede's sudden trip to Hollywood," Myrtle spoke in a low, breathy voice, "I don't know what to think. Celeste said it's an apprenticeship, but the man is so much older, and Italian, so what can one believe?"

Estelle listened, smiling softly. She didn't give a fig for Ede's endeavors. She was merely testing if Myrtle's gossipy ways had abated any, which, sadly, they had not.

"Well, Celeste has blossomed into quite an accomplished young lady," Estelle said. "She must have dozens of serious suitors waiting in the wings."

Myrtle's glow dimmed. "No, I'm sorry to say. Sometimes I wonder if she has a secret crush, because I often catch her staring into space with a dreamy look on her face. But as for dates, she sees them once and not again. Maybe her standards are too high? Or her business endeavors put off potential romances? Who wants a career woman for a wife?"

Estelle winked, squeezing Myrtle's elbow. "Let's have a private word," she said, guiding her through the terrace doors. "High standards are never a hindrance. Better choosey and alone than cozy with an unequal chap. I've been eager to tell you about an opportunity that has re-emerged." Estelle's eyes glittered.

"Is James in town?" Myrtle guessed.

"Not today, but soon. Are you attending the church picnic on Sunday?"

"Of course. Oh, but Gamma's brother is joining us."

"Mmmm, Yazi?"

"Yes, that old goat. Nearly 90 but spry as ever. He's so boisterous and loud, but he makes us all belly laugh." As soon as Myrtle finished, she blushed, not meaning to sound so vulgar.

"Lovely. Then we shall see what transpires Sunday next." Estelle patted Myrtle's arm and left her on the terrace.

Myrtle sank down onto the stone wall as her mind began to spin. *Is it fate or fool's gold? Either way, she'd done nothing to prompt it, as she'd promised Martin. But if Estelle wanted James to reconsider Celeste, that was her business. And with Ede gone, Celeste might be more inclined to consider a proper gentleman's pursuit.* Myrtle looked around the terrace, patting her cheeks so as not to burst out with a whoop of excitement.

The annual picnic for the First Episcopalian Church of Gladdenbury is held on the first Sunday in September to welcome back its congregation, many of whom have summered in Maine or the Adirondacks or farther afield. After the eleven o'clock service, dozens of families gather on the rolling lawn behind the church with picnic baskets, hearty appetites for the latest news, and the sweeping desire to show off their newest finery.

James Meaden dutifully followed his mother across the grass, carrying a basket not previously delivered by their maid, becoming more and more annoyed with each step.

"Mother," he spoke sharply as Estelle strode ahead, her eyes searching the grounds. "When you called to say it was urgent, I immediately came home despite a terrific hangover. What in blazes are we doing at the church picnic?"

Sailing across the grass, nodding and waving to neighbors and friends, Estelle briefly glanced back at James, catching his eye. "I believe we have an agreement – an art gallery you so desire?"

"That's what this is about?"

"Possibly."

"How?"

"Wait and see, my doubting Thomas."

Trudging behind her, he resigned to endure the afternoon and then be done with his mother's meddling. Yes, he had agreed to drop Kate and marry a proper girl in exchange for Estelle's help in securing the art gallery, but he'd never agreed she'd pick his spouse. Nor did he believe she would deny him his dream if he did not select her choice. But he couldn't help musing as to who his mother thought could attract his attention at the church picnic. Yet no further explanation was necessary when Estelle finally stopped and subtly nodded in the direction of a lovely young woman; a vibrant beauty, worthy of at least his investigation, if not his educated affection.

Seated on a large fan of orange cloth, she was cutting a slice of lemony yellow cake while speaking to her picnic mate, a scruffy, older-looking man James did not recognize. Soft wisps of hair curled around her face, having fallen loose from an antique silver clip. From where James stood, he could see her eyes opening wide and her eyebrows fluttering as she mimicked some character in an obviously amusing story. Her round cheeks and chin glowed with the rouge of happiness, and her lithe body floated in a pale yellow dress, speckled with blue and pink, with a bright coral sash cinching her waist. James could see the outline of the long, slender legs tucked beneath her skirt, where elegant sandals peeked out. Although he was too far away to hear her words, he could not take his eyes off her animated elegance. With pursed lips, he forgot all his manners and stared across the lawn for a better look, drinking in every detail of her aura.

Still holding the cake knife, the young woman waved it in the air, demonstrating the size and shape of something when her lean arms swiftly swept up and over her head with such exuberance that a spatter of icing flew off the knife and onto the old man's head.

James let loose a boisterous laugh that carried across the crowd, causing the young woman to look in James' direction. But just as quickly, she turned back, leaping up to wipe the sticky crumbs off the man's cheek, both of them laughing. As Celeste swiped his face clean, the man grabbed her wrist, pulling it toward his open mouth, teeth bared to chomp her hand but then delicately licked the crumbs off her fingertips. Her laughter rang across the yard in a ripple of bird-song tones, and James suddenly felt something he hadn't felt in a very long time: a heart flutter.

"Who is she?" he demanded of his mother.

"You don't recognize her?" Estelle asked, reveling in the game.

"Should I?"

"I suppose after all these years she looks more mature. I think she's developed rather nicely. Did I mention she owns her own business?"

"Not possible," James retorted, turning back to the girl.

"Au contraire. Beauty, brains, a fine upbringing and a vivacious spirit. Might be a handful now and again, not unlike myself, but then, when did that ever frighten *you*, city cowboy."

His guess began to form. "I've met her before?"

"Indeed, and danced with her …"

"At a Ball in Prague! Celeste Howe! Are you kidding?"

"Never, on such matters. Shall we?" With a jaunty step, Estelle approached the Howe's picnic blanket. "Hello, hello, so wonderful to see you again," she sang, then introduced James to Gamma's brother, Yazi. "But of course you already know Celeste. How lovely you look today, dear. How are things at The Needlery? I was just telling James about your business success."

"Yes, she has," James chimed in, stepping beyond his mother. "And I'd love to hear all about it." Setting down the picnic basket, he squatted by Celeste. "Mind if I join you for a spell?"

"Of course not." Celeste smiled, then slid her eyes up to Estelle, who gave her a wink and wagged her finger.

"Now, Celeste, don't let him be a pest, and make sure he shares what's in that basket." Turning, Estelle slowly walked away as James flipped open the basket. They all peered in at two bottles of champagne, five glasses and a tray of large, brightly colored cookies. As she ambled off, Estelle smiled at Yazi's gruff exclamation.

"By God, them are some fancy cookies … is that a Picasso?"

James lifted out the tray and set it on the cloth where they all examined the cookies with astonished expressions. Each one had been intricately iced to replicate a modern master painting. "Picasso, Braque, Davis, O'Keefe – oh my goodness, where did she find a Kupka? And look, a Modigliani!" James held up one cookie. "She looks like you!" he added, holding it to Celeste's face. They all laughed.

"What is this for?" Celeste asked, "These must have cost a fortune!"

"A little joke between Mother and me, I'd say," James replied, spotting his mother's retreating sashay across the lawn. "A reminder of the art gallery I hope to open one day."

For the rest of the afternoon, James remained with Celeste, soon joined by Myrtle and Martin, popping the champagne corks, catching up on their lives, and by the evening's light, he strolled Celeste around the Town Green.

"I can't get over your transformation since we last met!" he said, drawing her hand through the crook of his elbow.

Laughing, she pulled it back out, swinging her arms freely. "I don't suppose I can say the same for you."

"Now why do you cut me to the quick?"

"Oh, let's see, wasn't it you, just a few months back, making this same stroll with … who was it now? Oh, yes, the actress – Kate?"

James sharply tugged his waistcoat. "Well, that's over now."

"At least for her, but who will be next, I wonder?"

Had he looked up, he would have seen the twinkle in her eyes. But he kept his head bent down, hiding the flush in his cheeks. Then he asked in a low tone, "Is my reputation that scorched?"

"Scorched? No. Smoldering might be a better term, at least among the town ladies."

He looked up sharply, shoulders tensed, until he saw her giggling. "You're not serious?"

"Oh, I'm very serious," Celeste said, ruffling her skirt. "I just don't happen to care. If I were a man with the world at my feet, I'd most likely do the same."

"Do what?"

"Grab every chance that came my way, just as you have. Bravo to you, I say!"

She flitted past him, crossing to the swings. "Why did you come today?" She asked gravely. "A church picnic doesn't seem your style."

Leaning against the swing post, he flicked his thumbnail against his pinky. "Definitely not … until today." He playfully smirked at her.

"Hah! I knew this wasn't your idea. Your mother's handiwork is all over it, starting with that picnic basket and those cookies! My god, they were spectacular! I felt guilty eating one. What was that all about?"

"You have no idea?"

"A plot for you and me?"

James nodded. "And don't think it's just *my* mother."

Celeste's laugh rippled. "I suppose … we could give them a show for their money," she said, patting the swing beside her. "Pull up a swing. Make us the talk of the town – at least for tonight."

As they conversed late into the evening about anything and everything, James became more and more entranced by Celeste. He was impressed by her range of topics, her style and grace, her jousting wit, and most of all, her independence. With a lighthearted, indifferent spirit, she was similar to his New York glad-gals, but from the right side of the tracks; the complete package, quite suitable for expanding his family tree.

❧

After the picnic, James found innumerable reasons to be in Gladdenbury at least once during the week and most every weekend. A month later, as he parked in front of his parents' house on a Saturday morning, Jack called to Estelle, "What's James doing here again?"

"Something about an apple festival with the church group," Estelle replied.

"Church group?" Jack stepped onto the porch, newspaper in hand.

"Hey, old man." James greeted his father with a wave as he got out of his car and headed down the street. "See you later tonight. I'll bring some apples."

Jack re-entered the house. "What's bewitched that boy?"

Tapping her chin, Estelle smiled. "Not what, who. Any objections?"

❧

Celeste made it a rule to spend time with James only at social events and informal group suppers, surrounded by well meaning friends and observers. While she enjoyed his attention far more than any other boy she'd dated, she didn't know if she could trust him. He was acting very differently from when they first met, less stiff, more jovial and even funny at times, but it had transpired so suddenly she decided it was wise to take her time.

From her bedroom window, Myrtle watched Celeste walk down the street with James, their apple basket swinging in between. She nudged Martin, sitting on the bed, pulling on his socks. "They make a handsome couple, don't they?"

Martin grunted as he pulled a sweater over his head.

"I want you to know," Myrtle added, rocking back on her heels. "I've honored my promise. This is all their own doing."

Snapping his head free, Martin shoved his arms into the sweater and muttered under his breath, "In a pig's eye."

By Halloween, Estelle decided it was time to plan a formal affair and invited the Howes to their annual Halloween Dinner Dance; a tradition established for the children when they were young and continued because it was such fun. Estelle provided a buffet meal in the dining room and pushed back the parlor furniture to host a dozen or so families. While the adults did not customarily wear costumes, Estelle set out a basket of moderately lavish masks so everyone could partake in the evening's frivolities.

After due consideration, Celeste announced to her mother: "I'm going as Harpo Marx. I've already got the wig and loose-fitting, striped pants and this horn." Honking it a few times, she waddled around the room. "So I won't have to speak all evening."

But Myrtle wouldn't hear of it. "You'd be far more elegant as an Arabian princess to his sheik," she insisted, having been informed of James's plans.

"Oh no, mother, I know what you're trying to do," Celeste objected. But Myrtle was persistent, and Celeste eventually consented.

Blithely playing her veiled role throughout the evening, she had fun flirting with James and displaying her well-honed social skills at every opportunity. Finding Estelle at the far end of the parlor, surrounded by glowing candles in the dozen carved pumpkins, Celeste complimented the menu. "The piquant kumquats set off the smoky flesh of the duck so beautifully, Mrs. Meaden, and the apple sauce with horseradish is a brilliant combination: hot yet refreshing."

Estelle smiled and winked. "Two of James's favorite recipes."

On the other side of the room, family and friends danced to the latest songs playing on the Victrola, and the evening imbued everyone with a feeling of promise.

Near midnight, as the party waned, James slipped his hand into Celeste's and led her through the parlor's French doors to the terrace for a walk along the garden path. The silvery shadows of the full, autumn moon mixed with the spiked pumpkin punch as James drew her closer. Swaying to a tune he'd recently heard at a New York party, he sang to her in a warm baritone.

"Blue Moon, you saw me standing alone,
Without a dream in my heart, without a love of my own

Without a thought, Celeste returned the song's second verse in a lovely treble soprano.

Blue Moon, you know just what I was there for.
You heard me saying a prayer for, someone I really could care for."

"How do you know that?" James was astounded. "It's never been recorded."

Celeste grinned slyly. "Ede's in Hollywood; she heard the composers trying it out with Jean Harlow. She wrote down the lyrics and mailed them to me, and when I called her, she sang it. Who could forget that croon? How did *you* hear it?"

"Richard Rodgers played it at a swanky party in the city …"

"Oooh, name dropping again?"

James laughed, twirled Celeste around, swept off her veil and kissed her upturned mouth. His warm, firm lips pressed deeply into her softness, and he quickly slid his cool tongue across them before releasing her into another twirl.

Giggling, Celeste slipped out of his grasp and dropped to the grass. "I feel dizzy."

"So do I," James said, squatting beside her. "And I'm not used to that."

"You? The bachelor's bachelor?" Celeste poked his ribs.

"The same name," he snatched her hand and kissed her palm, "but not the same person, anymore than you are. We've both changed – a lot." He sat beside her and stretched out his legs.

"True enough." Celeste lay back on the grass, throwing her arms above her head to gaze at the moon. "It's hard to imagine … after meeting in Prague when I wasn't even seventeen … and now, three years later, here we are … who would have thought it possible?"

"Our mothers, that's who. They're untiring conspirators, you know."

"Is that why you're here?"

"Initially, but not now. I find you intoxicatingly extraordinary, Celeste."

"Bet you say that to all the girls."

James chuckled, lying alongside her. "Only the ones who are."

"And how many would that be? Dare you keep count?"

"Internationally or domestic?"

She slapped his arm. "Oh, forget it," and rolled onto her stomach.

He rolled next to her. "Internationally, then: two." She propped on her elbows. "Oh go on. I'm not that naïve."

"No, it's true. Of my many women ... only two are extraordinary."

"Who's the other one?"

James turned on his back, his hands cradling his head. "Mother didn't approve."

"Ohhhhh, so I'm the consolation prize?" She mock whined, quickly rolling to him, pressing her plump, soft lips onto his and flicking the tip of her tongue.

Surprised, his arm instinctively encircled her waist and his long leg folded around her thighs, hinging them together: chest to chest, groin to groin, lip to lip, kissing her eyes, cheeks, ears, throat, chest and arms until she giggled, pushing herself off him.

Sitting up, she straightened her costume. "Well?"

"Definitely *not* the consolation prize," he declared, rolling onto his side, looking at her profile in the moon light. The air between them vibrated as they stared at each other, catching their breath, their feelings, their thoughts until James broke the reverie.

"Celeste, what do you want? Out of life, I mean. Are you one of those suffragettes?"

She laughed, hugging her knees. "Why? Are you afraid of suffragettes?"

"Hardly. But tell me, are you a career woman or do you want marriage and children?"

Celeste's shoulders rose. There it was: the dividing line, the either/or. It made her so mad. "Why do I have to make that choice? You certainly don't. Why can't I have a career, a husband and children, too?"

The upset in her voice bolted James upright. "What? I didn't mean ..."

"No; men never do mean to insult us, but it happens all the time. My grandmother and great grandmother were married, ran the store, managed their homes and raised children, to boot. So has your mother – look at all her charity work. For gosh sake, we can do so much more than just being a wife and mother!" She gulped a breath to continue when James grasped her hands, not letting her pull away.

"Stop now. I didn't mean it like that. I've met women, lots of them, who really don't want to have children at all – which is their right, and I respect that. If I were in their shoes I'd probably do the same. I ask because I want to know what's important to you – if you do or don't want children; not tomorrow, but someday – before we go too far. It's not an either/or but a question. I don't know you, Celeste, or what you want in life, beyond what you already have. How could I?"

Celeste's umbrage and arms went slack. "I'm sorry," she said. "It's just so frustrating … what people assume. Not just men, but my mother, too. It's as if she can't even see me and my desires. Doesn't understand why I love my little business, and working at the Hardware store, which I really do. Where I'm out in the world, not just stuck in the house, behind a stove. Yet I do want children, too … someday." Then she thought of Gamma's copper bracelets. "Six, I think."

"Six?" James smirked. "My my. Well then, Miss, don't you think you should get busy?"

Blushing, Celeste dropped her head, laughing at herself. "What about you? What's in your future?"

James got up, stretched his legs and reached for her hand, helping her up. "I've got several dreams in the hopper. I want to study and invest in modern art, open a gallery and have a family – not necessarily in that order. While I don't have a specific number of children in mind, I assure you I can certainly support six. More, if you like." He pulled her close, tilting up her chin, penetrating her eyes. "If you'd like that, too, I mean."

He drew his finger along her cheek and chin. "Miss Howe, I propose we approach this like adults and take a good gander at each other. I ask you: Look hard to see if I might be suitable for your plans, and I'll do the same. I don't mean to be clinical about this, but marriage is a contract that requires a clear head. So be thorough in your examination and take your time. No need to rush such an important decision, although I have to tell you I very much like what I've seen thus far." With a quick peck on her mouth to seal the deal, he turned, leading her back to the party, hand in hand.

Following a step behind him, Celeste wondered why a chill swept up her spine.

☙

The next morning over breakfast, James answered Estelle's unspoken questions.

"Well, you were right all along, Mother. She's delightful. Refined, yet with an irresistible Bohemian spirit. I think we shall all get what we want from this match."

At the same time, several blocks away, James' invitation arrived for a mother-daughter trip to New York, and Myrtle shrieked with glee. "A weekend for shopping and shows. My, my, my, that young man knows how to court a girl."

"I'm not a girl, mother, and why do you have to go? I can take care of myself."

"Propriety, dear. It wouldn't look right, you being alone in his apartment. But don't worry, I'll make myself scarce."

The next weekend, Myrtle gave James and Celeste a wide berth throughout their visit. Lingering well behind them while shopping on Fifth Avenue, she pretended to be studying the window display, while using the reflection to spy on them. And she wandered away among the couture racks at Bergdorf Goodman department store, keeping out of sight, but within earshot. That evening, at the Broadway show "Music in the Air," she sat quietly in her seat before the performance, studying her playbill, appearing intent upon learning all about Oscar Hammerstein and Jerome Kern, yet never missing a word or nudge between the budding sweethearts. At intermission, she lost herself in the crowd, observing from a distance. And she kept herself busy at James' apartment, in the kitchen or the guest room, to encourage the young love to blossom.

Celeste honestly wished she were smitten. It would have made life so much easier. Nevertheless, she couldn't help but find James' lavish attention a bit intoxicating. Strolling down Fifth Avenue, he repeatedly pointed out the latest fashions, asking what she fancied. Every time she showed a smidgen of interest, he'd immediately want to buy it for her, so she stopped answering his questions, until her mother urged her to be a sport, indulge him, and try on a few dresses. "What's the harm?" Myrtle asked so sweetly that Celeste agreed to play the model at Bergdorf's, making a show with several dresses for James and her mother. With each one, she became more bold: sashaying across the floor, flipping the skirt, poofing her hair, kicking up a heel to get them laughing, until she emerged in a column of flowing, pale pink silk with a high neck in front and a plunging, open back that gathered and fluttered into soft folds, from the base of her spine to the floor, edged with a deep red velvet ribbon that tied in a drooping bow. Sleeveless, sumptuous, demure in the front, daring in back, it silenced Celeste's antics. She shimmered.

"That's it!" James jumped up, waving to the clerk. "That's the one! You must wear it to the show tonight. By god, Oscar and Jerome will be bowled over when they see you! They'll positively lust after this costume!" He insisted on the matching wrap, hat and gloves, and at the club, where they ate a small bite before the show, he surprised her with a bracelet that complimented the outfit with aplomb.

"Oh!" Myrtle squealed when Celeste opened the velvet jewel case. "What exquisite taste your young man has."

As James latched the bracelet around Celeste's slender wrist, she leaned into his ear. "You're spoiling my mother for any other suitor."

His eyes crinkled with his smile. Kissing the inside of her wrist, he whispered back: "Now you know I am wise."

Her burst of nervous laugher tinkled across the dining salon, turning every head. She was confused by her mixed feelings for him: wanting to keep him at a distance yet simultaneously drawn to him. Was it the riches? Was it his Noel Coward style? Was it his assured self? Certainly all of her material wishes could be fulfilled by James, and she adored his refined taste and elegance. My god, his apartment and art made her swoon. Thank heavens she'd taken the art-history course Gamma had suggested and could talk intelligently about painters and art-nouveau design. But why didn't his presence spin her head or race her heart?

Throughout it all, she made a point to steadfastly observe his life and ways, as he had asked of her, calculating how she might fit into his world; a world so very different from her own. One thing she found especially odd was how much more interesting he was in the City. The noise and hubbub electrified him, while the never-ending crowds, trolleys, museums, restaurants and clubs somewhat overwhelmed her. His energy seemed boundless, and amped up as they ran from place to place, while she barely could barely catch her breath. Because of her conflicting feelings, she would only let him kiss her cheek, blaming her mother's presence … but it wasn't the full truth.

On the train ride home, confused by her daughter's apparent ambivalence, Myrtle probed her feelings. "Don't you like him?"

"Of course I like him. Who wouldn't? Charming, handsome, absolutely attentive."

"Then why were you so … removed?"

Celeste looked down at her magazine to claim a pause. She liked him, far more than she first thought possible. He was fun, sometimes funny, a good sport and didn't seem to mind her quips and challenges as they conversed. He had all the markings of a good mate – financial security, desire to be a father, social prominence – but she was bothered by what was missing … when they kissed, when they embraced. She felt warm and even a bit naughty sometimes, but not a smidgen of electricity raced through her veins, as it had when hugging Ron last summer.

"You haven't found a nicer catch, have you?" Myrtle asked.

Celeste would not reply.

∞

For her 30th wedding anniversary on the Saturday after Thanksgiving, Myrtle invited Estelle, Jack and James for a celebration supper. To set the tone, she chose a thick brown linen to display Gamma's finest tableware: the silver-edged bone china and gold-tipped crystal. None better could be found on the whole East Coast, Myrtle was sure, and it would confirm the quality of Celeste's upbringing, despite their modest home.

On the day of the party, after working all week on food preparations in addition to her other responsibilities, Celeste was dog-tired and had completely lost her appetite. As the hour of the Meadens' arrival approached, she was deeply thankful they had hired two maids to serve and clean up. But their presence added to her discomfort, as she was unaccustomed to household help, except for spring and fall seasonal scrubbings.

As Estelle entered the home, she immediately raised her nose in the air. "Oooh, smells heavenly," she chimed, slipping off her long mink coat into Celeste's waiting arms. "What are we having?"

"First course: vichyssoise with cheese straws and dry sherry," Celeste recited, having practiced the menu all day long. "Followed by petite rainbow trout and watercress sandwiches paired with cold Chablis and a salad of pineapple, grapefruit and greens." But then her mind went blank. Excusing herself, she dashed into the kitchen, mink still in hand, blustering to Gamma, who was overseeing the final preparations.

"Worry not, child." Gamma waved her back to the parlor. "Just toss your head, laugh and say: will be worth her waiting."

After gratefully kissing Gamma's cheek, Celeste hung Estelle's coat in the hall closet, checked her hair in the mirror and re-entered the parlor, where James waited to greet her with a surprisingly soft, long kiss on the back of her hand.

By the third course of filet mignon with mushroom caps, minted peas and rissole potatoes paired with a sparkling burgundy, James noted the wine "rounded the palate so nicely," and Celeste was having a giggling time. She couldn't help describing to Estelle how she nicked and burned her fingers preparing the potatoes. Estelle politely nodded as Celeste painstakingly explained each step of paring, frying, baking and dressing the potatoes with white sauce.

The evening turned a little raucous when Gamma's brother, Yazi, well toasted on seven-year-old scotch, demonstrated how to line up peas on his knife and slide them into his mouth without dropping one, and Jack decided to try to match him. Celeste almost fell on the floor from laughing!

Trying to recover the evening's decorum, Myrtle announced dessert would be served in the parlor, to best frame Celeste as she entered carrying a flaming pan of Cherries Jubilee. When her daughter's hair began to singe from the flames as she breezed into the room, Myrtle wanted to dive behind the divan in shame. But then James jumped up, crushing the flames nipping at Celeste's curls, and Estelle squeezed Myrtle's arm. "Look. See James' eyes? They're shining. I've never seen him enjoy himself more." That calmed Myrtle, and she even chuckled as James laughed out loud, along with his father, Gamma and Yazi. Even Martin let down his guard, guffawing with the infectious, tipsy giggles of his daughter. Toward evening's end, Martin stood and declared, "Myrtle, Gamma, Celeste: This was the finest meal I can remember! A most enjoyable and fitting tribute to the fruit of our marriage," to which everyone raised their glass, looking at Celeste.

After the anniversary supper, James and Celeste's courtship turned a corner. Their constant companionship at every holiday event in Gladden-bury fueled speculative chatter about their alliance. Neither Myrtle nor Estelle could go to the shops without being questioned about the budding young love. Even Jack was badgered by well-meaning ladies, offering their opinions and good wishes. So Estelle decided to host a New Year's party to formally introduce the promising couple to the town's most prominent families.

⌒

Resplendent in ice-blue satin, Celeste wandered through the Meaden house in a dream, nodding and smiling to the guests, drinking in the luxurious appointments. Her eyes lingered on the heavy, intricately carved rosewood furniture and the gleaming silver from every tabletop and niche: trays, bowls, chafing dishes, pitchers, coffee and tea sets and bone-handled cutlery. Examining a cocktail fork, Celeste admired its delicate, exquisite structure: tiny silver tines held by a luminous, alabaster handle.

"Fabulous, isn't it?" James said, slipping his arms around her waist from behind and lightly brushing her cheek with his lips. "Mother purloined that set in London, decades ago. I think they belonged to some famous actress and it was said that everyone who was anyone has eaten with them."

Replacing the fork in its perfect lineup, Celeste looked over the table. "So much food."

James barely heard her melancholy whisper. "Glorious spread! Mother outdoes herself every year." he waved at the stretch of platters, loaded with lobster-stuffed biscuits, beef tenderloin dressed with crispy bacon, small cornucopias of smoked salmon stuffed with cream cheese, a golden, roasted turkey breast encircled with wild rice, raisins and almonds, and at the far end of the table, a bowl of mixed greens with tiny Danish shrimp beside an oversized butcher block display of pineapple slices, apples, oranges, pomegranates and pears.

The opulence muddled Celeste's mind. She sat down to collect her thoughts. The abundance made her think of the shelter's soup kitchen and all the hungry people with hollow eyes, empty of food and hope. Overwhelmed, she began to cry.

"What? What's happened?" James immediately offered her a crisp linen handkerchief.

Dabbing her eyes, Celeste shook her head. "What will become of the leftovers?"

"The what?"

"Leftovers … of food," she whispered.

Turning to James with rounded eyes and soft face, she shared with James her work among the poor at the Catholic charity in Hartford. "Since I was six, I've been going with Gamma to cook and serve food and sort donated clothes. And now I teach the children a little art after school. You can't imagine their faces, bright and hopeful, coming to the center, in clothes you would barely use as rags. But it's never been as bad as now. So many people with no work, no money, no food. It breaks my heart, the lines for supper: around and around the block. So when I see this beautiful food, so much for so few, I can't help but wonder: What will become of the leftovers?"

James took the handkerchief from her clutched hand to dab her cheek, then wrapped his arms gently around her. "You and me," he whispered into her ear. "We'll package up all the leftovers and drive them to the shelter, first thing in the morning."

As he embraced her concerns, he was filled with a feeling of peace, more than he'd ever felt in his childhood home.

Relieved by his kindness, and oblivious to the crowd of guests surrounding them, Celeste let her body fall into his, deeply moved by his tenderness.

Across the room, watching the affection between her daughter and James, Myrtle sighed with relief and quickly said a prayer, resolved to maneuver their small spark into a quick betrothal, somehow, someway, as soon as possible.

After the party, Myrtle helped Celeste undress.

"He can give you a safe and solid life … especially in these times." She spoke quietly, taking the measure of Celeste's reaction. "Just think what you can do for your charities with the Meaden resources."

Climbing into bed, Celeste replied sleepily, "I wish Ede were here." She ached for her best friend's counsel. She was attracted to James, but somehow things were moving more swiftly than felt comfortable. And no matter how much her mother tried to conceal it, she could feel her intensity, her push, her insistence on this match. But Ede always knew how to help Celeste thwart her mother's plans. Without her, however, she felt untethered, floating on a ridge of wind, sweeping her further and further away from her own true desires.

And sure enough, over the next few weeks, dozens of well-meaning townsfolk sought her out at the store, on the street, at church and in the shops, sharing their observation as to how fortunate she was to have attracted such a good man, from such a fine family. It was a tsunami of opinion that overwhelmed her ability to reason with her own sensibility. Ede-less and vulnerable, Celeste felt helpless to resist her mother's insistence that they host a Valentine's cocktail supper.

24 Art

My Dearest Ede:
January 15, 1934

How I wish you were home! How will I manage until May? All Mama talks about is James this and James that. She won't let up and insists we host a Valentine's party! Eeee gads, another party! More cooking! She's so giddy; you'd think we were getting married tomorrow. Don't get me wrong. He's very nice. Wait 'til you see the sapphire necklace he gave me at Christmas and the matching dress for New Year's Eve: ice-blue satin with cap sleeves. I felt like a queen. But don't worry; I'm in no rush to marry. It's only been four months. We barely know each other. We spent one weekend in New York (Mama had to come along), but I've not met any of his city friends. Did I tell you he asked me to examine him as a prospective spouse? The way he put it was so odd. He said marriage is a contract or something like that. I think he meant it's not just kisses and flowers, but he certainly is doing all that, too, so I'm giving it a go. Why not, right? So far he seems smart, clever, sometimes funny, and underneath all his sophistication I see a bit of tenderness, but it's hard to be sure. I watched him from across the room at the holiday parties (there were a lot!) as he chatted up his friends, and I kept seeing a sneer on his face, which I don't understand because he's never like that with me. And when he's laughing, sometimes I'm not sure if it's real or if he's faking, to be polite. But then he'll do something wonderful, like drive all the leftover food from the New Year's party to the Hartford shelter the very next morning and even work the soup kitchen with me. That's special, isn't it? And I certainly wouldn't have to worry – about anything – no matter how many kids I have, which I would like, eventually. When I think of a houseful of children I feel light inside, and that's oh-so-different from my lonely childhood. If I hadn't met you I'd have gone out of my mind! But how do I keep Mama at bay so I can decide if James is right in my own time? Send your wise counsel – pronto! Miss you desperately.

Your devoted friend,
Celeste

P.S: New painter is fine but not nearly as good as you. Come home soon!!

In early February, Celeste heard back from Ede.

Dearest Celeste:

Only have a minute to dash off this note. It is crazy busy here, but I love everything about Hollywood and set designing. Learning so much from Mr. Moltano, and Mrs. Moltano keeps me even busier at the house. Can't wait to cook a proper Italian meal for you – so many courses and so much chopping! Regarding James, I don't know what to say except: Do you feel the passion? Remember our pact! The Art of Love is fueled by Passion and Inspiration. But don't worry, we'll sort it all out when I get back in May. In the meantime, do what I'd do: have some fun!

Hugs and Kisses,
Ede

For a week after receiving Ede's letter, Celeste walked around in a daze about the Art of Love. *Do I feel passion and inspiration?* If only she could answer yes. *But did it have to be just like that?* She liked James, he liked her, and, as he said, marriage is a serious contract that should not be based solely on lovey-dovey feelings. It called for the same cool-headed logic she used to build her business. Emotions don't consider the practical side of life, and raising children requires a secure home and financial soundness, which James could certainly provide. But she wasn't sure how he'd be as a husband. She didn't like the distance she saw between her mother and father. She wanted a marriage with warmth and zestiness, like she saw in Jack Meaden. So, she reasoned, maybe James will become more like his father as he grows older, and particularly after the children began arriving. That seemed logical enough for the moment, and in any event, Ede was right. She didn't have to decide right away. Why not have some fun?

⟡

Because business concerns sent James to the southern states, Celeste didn't see him for three weeks after New Year's. But immediately upon his return, he called, asking her to New York for the weekend, alone, and to her surprise, Myrtle agreed.

She saw him on the platform as her train pulled into Grand Central Terminal on Saturday morning, searching the windows until he spied her and running alongside until the train stopped.

"My Belle Celeste," he said, lifting her off the train steps and swinging her around. "How I missed that smile," and quickly kissed her mouth.

"Is that right, sir?" Celeste drawled, dabbing her lips. "Those southern belles didn't measure up 'nuf?"

"Not even close." James picked up her bag and hooked her arm. "Let's get moving, we've got a big day ahead." As he whisked her through the station to 42nd street, where his car and driver waited, Celeste craned her neck up and around, gaping at the grand, cathedral-esque hall, with columns of light streaming from the top windows, casting wide shafts of sunlight to the floor, peppered with dust and spotlighting the room and four-sided clock in the center. Every time she passed through the massive structure, she was struck with the same awe she felt at Prague castle, where she first met James. Today, she shivered at the coincidence.

As the long sedan pulled away from the curb, Celeste adjusted her hat and coat.

"Where are we going?"

"To see all my favorite spots, or as many as we can squeeze in before tonight's party. I want to introduce you to my crowd."

"You should have told me! What if I don't have the right clothes?"

"Un-Unh. No worries about anything. Just be yourself. They're gonna love you."

"Where to first?"

He leaned back in his seat. "Remember the painting in my living room?"

"My favorite? The Stuart Davis New York/Paris painting over the fireplace?"

He tapped her knee. "That's my girl! We're meeting him for lunch in Greenwich Village."

Celeste was flabbergasted. Although James had spoken often about the Village and his artist friends who lived there, she'd never been. Nor had she ever met a real artist before, other than Ede, and that didn't really count. "My lord, James, that's incredible."

"Well, he's a friend, now, and I hoped he'll show you his studio. Maybe bring us there after lunch; it's just around the corner. But we're meeting at his favorite haunt. I want to prepare you; both he and the place are a bit rugged and scruffy, but I'm sure you'll like both. I know you will. You fit in anywhere. And he's going to love you! Plus I'm counting on your charms. You are my secret weapon for securing his works for my gallery. Stuart is prickly about galleries. Doesn't believe in them. Thinks art should be sold in stores, like newspapers and magazines! Art for the masses, he says! But I think you could win him over to my side."

James took out his handkerchief to wipe his hands, and Celeste looked out the window to see where they were heading.

"He wants to make large, color reproductions of his work and sell them for five to ten dollars a pop. I doubt anyone would buy them with this Depression, but when things turn around, it might work – don't you think?"

Celeste barely heard him, lost in the scene outside the car window: her eyes drawn to the bedraggled people, block after block, some in doorways, some walking alongside the well-heeled. "Like Hartford," she half whispered.

"What's like Hartford?"

Pointing out the window, she said, "They look so cold and tattered, like at the shelter."

Barely glancing at the street, James reached for her hand. "Celeste, times are tough for many – but things are getting better. New work projects are starting. Government projects. Soon everyone will be able to buy a proper coat and hat and fill their stomachs to the brim." He squeezed her hand. "Just like you do for the Hartford children."

Nodding slightly, Celeste turned to the window to look again at the passing windblown faces and cold eyes. His words did not soothe her and they did not speak again until the car stopped on a small side street.

"Where are we?" she asked.

"In the bowels of Greenwich Village. Hadley, stay where you are," James instructed the driver as he slipped out, extending his hand to assist Celeste out of the car. "We'll be about an hour or so. Circle 'round, if you must."

Crossing the street, they entered a small restaurant named Ticino's. In the cramped entryway, their eyes adjusted to the dark, smoky room as James helped Celeste off with her coat and hung it on a wall peg. He took her hand and led her toward the back of the room.

"Davis!" he called out and waved to a lone man at a round table. "There you are. Sorry we're late."

The man in a rumpled jacket looked up from his sketchbook, his eyes foggy.

Celeste noticed his crooked nose and the wrinkles in his tall forehead as he peered in their direction.

"James, ahh, almost forgot you were coming. That Kate with you?"

James immediately drew Celeste in front of him, squeezing her shoulders.

"No ... I ... no. Stuart, this is Celeste, my girl from home, remember? I told you about her. She teaches art to children at the shelter in Hartford. Allow me to introduce you."

"Oh, right, sorry," Stuart said as he rose, sticking out his hand. "Stuart Davis. Pleased to meet you, Sorry 'bout my rough hands. Nature of the work."

Celeste slipped her small hand into his and clasped it firmly. "Celeste Howe. It's such an honor to meet you, Mr. Davis. James speaks of you often, and I've admired your work in his apartment. Some of it is ... a bit more than I understand, but I really like how it makes me feel." She patted her chest, finishing with a deep smile, her eyes sparkling. Something about him felt so familiar, but she couldn't quite place it.

Stuart ruffled his hair, grinning. "By god, you've got that right!" he said, patting his own chest. "It's the feeling inside that counts! Now call me Stuart. Have ya eaten yet?" Before they could answer, he waved to the barmaid. "Let's have some grub and get acquainted."

"Ok!" Celeste replied immediately, suddenly feeling a kinship with this man who a minute ago was a complete stranger. Without waiting for James, Celeste pulled out her own chair and sat at the round, heavy wooden table, ready for a delicious conversation along with the meal, feeling surprisingly light and free.

For the next hour she mostly watched and listened to James and Stuart banter while they all ate sausages and drank beer. There was something about Stuart that relaxed Celeste. His gravelly voice and laugh sounded like Uncle Yazi, but he most reminded her of Gamma, which gave her the courage to ask him a question.

"Excuse me, Stuart, would you mind if I asked you something?"

James looked surprised at Celeste as Stuart nodded.

"I wonder how it is you become an artist?"

Stuart looked at her quizzically.

"What I mean to say is, my best friend loves to paint and she's very good. Right now she's in Hollywood, learning to paint movie sets. And I also work with some children at the art center who make wonderful drawings. But I've always wondered how some people actually make art their profession. I understand how one becomes an accountant or a dressmaker ... or shopkeeper ... but how do you become an professional artist?"

While Stuart's speaking had been a little scattered throughout the lunch, his eyes suddenly cleared and his demeanor quietly focused.

"Some people have a natural aptitude," he began with a surety, "They are born with the gift to draw or paint with almost no effort ... from where ever that stuff comes." He emphasized his meaning by circling his open hand above his head. "And when you have it, you are compelled to use it, anyway you can. But the trouble is, most of those people spend their lifetime trying to replicate what they see. They strive to put on canvas exactly what's in front of their eyes, accurate in every detail. Now that certainly will make a pretty picture ... but – it's not art."

Celeste's chin cocked to the side. "No?"

"No." he said very calmly, folding one hand on top of the other. "Art is not about replication. Art is about inspiration, illumination, investigation. If I draw what you can see yourself, how am I contributing to your experience? What am I illuminating? A perfect copy – the exercise of recreating a round object on a flat surface – that's good for building one's skills – but it's not enough to qualify as a true piece of art."

"So, what-is-art?" Celeste asked with a boldness in her voice James had never heard.

Stuart leaned into the table, his eyes casting about as he spoke. "Art is found beyond the image. True Art captures the essence of an object, a place, a person. It brings you into a moment deeper than the eye can see, stirring up ... something inside you, deep, where your truth lies."

He quietly tapped his chest, just as Gamma did, Celeste noticed, when talking about the heart code. She gulped.

"Think about … DaVinci's Mona Lisa!" Stuart continued, looking at Celeste.

She nodded.

"Why do you think it's so popular?"

Celeste shook her head.

"It certainly isn't the woman's face. She's homely, in my opinion. But DaVinci wasn't painting a face. He was capturing a mystery, a mystique – putting on canvas the world behind her smile, her eyes … her being. He painted more than a normal eye would see. Now maybe it is something we all could see if we stopped running around like headless chickens, but most people don't see much, all caught up in our silly lives. But art, true art, wake us up." Stuart lightly banged the table, looked up and and caught Celeste smiling with an expression of fascinated wonder.

"See! Now that's what I'm talking about," Stuart nearly stood up with excitement. "Your face, your expression, your spirit, just now, that's what an artist must capture, far beyond the color and shape of a portrait. And when he's finished, you may not even recognize your self – like that crazy bastard Picasso – because an artist's job is to reveal the inside, the hidden, the overlooked, *making* a viewer take a second look, and a third, to see something new, something illuminating, something inspirational and true. That's how you become a professional artist. That's the work of it. It's *damn* hard but *damn* good, too – when you get it right."

Sitting on the edge of her seat, Celeste whispered, "Wow. So when you were drawing the Paris and New York series … ?"

He blinked.

She grappled to find the right words. "It seems you were juxtaposing the feeling of the two cities, so we can … I mean, I never thought about the difference and similarities of the two cities before I saw your drawing. Before, they were just two different places. But now, they feel like … mirror images of each other … opposite, yet similar."

Stuart leaned back in his chair, arms folded, pipe puffing, nodding at her, then looked at James. "You've nabbed a smart one, here."

Celeste's heart swelled. This was the most exciting luncheon she'd ever attended. She sat back and listened attentively as James and Stuart continued to converse about passion and art and painters, when the topic turned to the murals he was designing for a government work project.

"I thought the program was bunk," Stuart huffed, waving his pipe. "Like they were going to tell us what to do and how to do it. But I was surprised. They were hands off. Let us do our work, our way."

"What did you do?" Celeste asked.

"Just finishing one at Radio City Music Hall," he said, pointing his pipe at her. "But you can't see it 'cause it's in the men's room!" His eyes twinkled.

Celeste laughed. "I wouldn't dream of invading your bastion! What did you name it?"

"Men Without Women!" he said, puffing his pipe.

Celeste raised her eyebrows, asking for more.

"Icons of our customary diversions when not with the fairer sex. Smoking, cards, the barbershop, playing the ponies. Everything the itinerant bachelor pursues to evade loneliness."

Celeste poked her finger into James' side. "Like you?"

He smiled benignly at her.

Stuart puffed a few moments, looking at the two of them, and then poked the pipe stem at James. "Don't let yourself become one of 'em, Meaden. Even though we're loath to admit it, a man needs a woman, if for nothing else than reminding him to soften his hands. My Bessie, she was always fussing at me when my hands were too rough – on her skin, ya know. But she up and died on me last year. Now look at my hands: all torn up."

Celeste leaned forward "Oh, I'm so sorry Stuart. How awful for you."

Stuart momentarily shut his eyes. "She was a good girl. Always by my side, taking care of things, like a woman could. Took her to Paris in '28 and married her, proper. But then the butcher got her and … well. Meaden: don't be a fool and lose this fine lassie, if you're asking my advice. Which ya didn't, but I'm giving it, anyway." He rubbed his forehead and rose. "Best be going before I get on with anymore sad-sack stories."

In a flurry he was up, pulling crumpled bills from his pockets while James insisted on paying the bill and took off for the bar to do so.

Celeste rose and touched Stuart's arm.

He turned to her.

"Thank you," she said, taking and stroking each of his hands with her thumbs. "You don't know what this means to me, to meet you. You have … such a kind heart."

His eyes misted as she leaned in to kiss his cheek.

James returned and everyone walked out of the restaurant together to say goodbye.

"I was hoping you could show Celeste your studio …" James said but stopped as Stuart shook his head. "But it looks like another time would be best," he finished, shaking hands and parting ways.

Climbing into the car without another word, they drove north out of Greenwich Village and up Fifth Avenue in mutual silence.

Celeste was so busy thinking she hadn't even noticed James was quiet, too.

"What did he mean?" She suddenly blurted. "The butcher got her?"

James looked out the window. "The abortionist. She died of an infection. Don't know why she did it, either. Davis wanted the child, even in hard times. We all do, eventually." He quickly turned to her. "Don't we?"

"Y-yes, I think so. All women do."

"No, not all women," James said in a sullen tone, then turned away again. "Some women want a career and think it's impossible to have both."

"Mother certainly agrees with that."

Hearing the edge in her voice, he looked at her. "And you don't?"

Celeste paused, gauging his expression. "I'm not sure I do."

He winced but she pushed on. If they were going to be together, they had to get this straight. "Gamma did both. She enjoyed the work. Still does."

"Auff, Celeste, your grandmother doesn't run the business, she just fills in. There's a big difference."

Celeste bridle at his haughty tone. "That's not true! She knows everything about the shop. And it was Great grandmother who taught *her*. And Gamma was the one who taught my father! Plus, they both took care of husbands, children and households on top of that. Could you do all that?" She caught the beginnings of a sneer on his lip. "No," she answered for him. "I don't believe you could … so watch what you say about what you don't know." She turned away, addressing the window. "Both Grandfather and my father grew up playing in the aisles while their mothers ran the shop, and it didn't seem to hurt them any. And maybe it made them just a bit more understanding of what a woman can do." Her heart flamed as she turned back to him, unable to stop the words already formed in her mouth. "James Meaden, I think you have lived in a very rarified world and don't know one wit of what women are really about."

Surprised at her outburst, James knew he should ignore her remarks and regain good spirits for their weekend, but he felt agitated and couldn't restrain himself. "What are you saying? You'd have our children running wild in the aisles of a hardware store? Now wouldn't that look just ducky?"

"To whom?" Celeste snapped. "My clientele or your stuffy friends? I don't think Mr. Davis would have a problem with it. I bet he would have loved his child in the studio with him – with an easel of his own, even!"

The jut of her chin and steel in her eyes cut into James and he instinctively laughed. "Well, aren't you the little spitfire? So what are you saying? You want to keep working after we marry?"

Her jaw dropped as her chest inflamed. "Is that your idea of a proposal?" She drew a deep breath, trying to settle the jangling she felt inside. "*If* I ever marry, I promise you I'll work where ever and whenever I want. Your attitude galls me! How is what I want any different from your mother's charity work? Which I've never heard you complain about!"

"There's no need to bring Mother into this."

"Why not? She's the one who brought you into this in the first place!" Folding her arms, Celeste stared at him, hard and unflinching.

James blinked, recognizing himself in her resolve. If he kept up his banter, he'd ruin the weekend. It was time to retreat. Fishing out a handkerchief from his pocket, he waved it in the air. "Hold your fire, Miss. I didn't mean to set you off. Eee-gads, woman – you're a champion battler. Best remind myself not to take you on in the future." He grinned and was glad to see the tension drop in her shoulders. "It's just this whole Davis thing got me thinking."

Her arms loosened, but her voice held an edge. "About what?"

James reached for her hand. She dodged. He persisted. She petulantly gave in.

His voice softened. "I guess I am a bit spoiled."

"A bit?" Her eyebrows wiggled.

He wiggled his back. "I liked having mother at home growing up. Not that she was there all the time, but she was when I needed her. And I'd like that for my own children, a mother, at home, looking out for them."

Celeste shook her head. "That's very nice for your set, but not everyone has that luxury, and their children seem to do just fine, thank you very much. Anyway, a doting mother can have the opposite effect, too. Look at me. Between Mother and Gamma I've had two of them, and I'm a cheeky mess!"

As he looked at her puckered face and twinkling eyes, he twisted his face into a silly expression and they both burst out laughing, doubling over in mirth. She snatched his handkerchief to dab her watering eyes.

"Look at you," he sat back, admiring her. "Reason, logic *and* wit. Who knew?"

She shrugged with a chuckle. "You said take an unflinching look."

He nodded, crossing his leg away from her. "Celeste, you're probably right, and most of the world would likely agree. Necessity *is* the mother of invention. But if a woman had the choice, the option to … concentrate on one thing, don't you think it might be nicer for the children and still give the mother enough to do?"

Celeste lowered her head. "If that's all you like doing."

He rolled his hand for her to continue.

"Gamma worked all her life and always has a smile on her face. But my mother, who's never worked one day at the store, doesn't seem very happy at all. Not deep down like Gamma. So I wonder: Do I want to be more like Gamma or my mother?"

"Nothing makes your mother happier than your happiness."

"So she says, but I'm not so sure. In some ways I've been made responsible for her happiness, and I think she should find her own, regardless of what I choose."

"What does Gamma want for you?"

"Whatever I feel is right." Celeste instinctively tapped her chest. "That's all she's ever wanted. But with all the 'shoulds' in life, it seems the hardest thing to know."

"The shoulds?"

"Oh come on, you of all people know that: You *should* do this, you *should* do that. The list is endless: education, socializing, hobbies. Growing up we bounce from should to should, building up a good stock of interests. But then we get married and, at least for women, all those interests are supposed to collapse to nothing when you become a mother? Yours certainly won't, so why should I have to make that choice?"

Pursing his lips, James nodded, his foot tapping the air. "Ahh, yes. The maternal mantra: grow up, settle down, get married, have children – so we can do the same to them."

Her face softened. "Yes, something like that. So you understand?"

"The itinerant bachelor? Of course! Why do you think I traveled so long?"

"For the ladies, of course." Celeste giggled, softly pushing his arm.

"To evade the noose," James intoned.

She mocked a gasp.

He pulled her close, feeling her breath on his lips. "Until I finally found the right girl, for the right reasons." He leaned closer to kiss her when the car stopped. Glancing out the window, he sat upright.

Celeste followed his gaze. "Tiffany's?"

"Now don't get the wrong idea," he mustered. "I have to pick up Mother's birthday present, but since we're here, I thought it might be fun to look around. Maybe find a little something for your mother – and Gamma." He winked. "Come – let's see if we can find some art in there that inspires passion and inspiration!"

"Oh, You," she laughed, climbing out of the car. Clasping his arm, she felt regal and revived as they sauntered through the grand front doors of the finest jewelry emporium of New York.

25 *Valentines*

February 1934

Upon her return to Gladdenbury early Sunday afternoon, Celeste breathed in the woody smell of her house, a mix of polish, tobacco and cooking. Setting her valise by the front door, she walked directly to her father's study, hoping her mother was not at home.

"Papa?" She tapped on the door under the stairs. "May I come in?" Still wearing her travel cloak and gloves, she pulled out her hatpin as her father opened the door, his hair rumpled, sweater askew and eyeglasses in hand.

"Ohhh, did I interrupt your nap?" she asked.

"Celeste! You're here! Did I oversleep? Wasn't I supposed to pick you up in Hartford?"

She placed her hat on the hall table. "I caught the trolley." Brushing a kiss on his cheek, she entered his study and dropped on the settee under the window, pulling off her heavy kid gloves. James' cologne still lingered on the leather. "I need to talk."

Martin closed his study door and tripped the lock so they would not be disturbed.

"Did something happen?" he asked gravely, swiveling his desk chair to face her.

Celeste tucked her chin. "No, James was a perfect gentleman. Maybe that's the problem." She tweaked a small smile. "Where is everyone? Is Mama with the church ladies?"

Martin leaned back, rubbing his face. "Some one of them; I can't keep track. And Gamma's napping upstairs. Why did you come home early? What happened?"

"Oh, I don't know. There was a party with his friends and it was so full of frippery, when I woke up this morning, I just wanted to be home. The city's so fast moving. How did you grow up there?"

Martin clucked. "When I was young, the old neighborhood was not much different from Gladdenbury, only without grass, more horse manure and twice the watching eyes."

Celeste shook her head. "Papa, it hurt to see how bad off so many people are in the city, but when we went to the party with James' friends, it was as if nothing was wrong in the world, everyone laughing, drinking, dancing. I kept wishing I could do something."

"For whom?"

"All those hungry people."

"But you do, in Hartford. You think you have to save the world?"

"I didn't mean that, Papa, it's just … "

With his hands folded in his lap, Martin waited while his daughter fussed with her hair, searching for the right words.

"It seems selfish to be lighthearted when so many suffer, and I wonder if I should even consider marrying a man who doesn't seem to be bothered by it."

Martin scratched his ear. "So you're discussing marriage?"

Celeste shrugged. "Not directly, but – it's in the air."

"You're not to let your mother sway you. The decision is yours alone."

Celeste rose to remove her cloak, draping it on the sofa arm. "That's what I wanted to talk with you about." She spoke carefully. "I keep waiting for that certain feeling, that sureness I hear people talk about, and it got me wondering about you and Mama. I don't quite know how to put this, but when you married Mama, was it a decision you made – in your head, I mean – or was it a feeling? Or rather, how did you know she … was *right* for you?"

She'd never seen her father blush before as he turned beet red from forehead to neck, accented by his white collar.

Feeling the heat in his face, Martin swiveled away, pulled open a desk drawer and rummaged about. "I'm not sure I'm the best person to ask," he replied, pulling out a ragged bound notebook. "But I saved this in case you ever did, to remind myself what it was like back then and why …" He stopped, handing her the book.

Her fingers brushed over the creased, faded black cover and gingerly opened it, flipping over several pages of sketched ships, penned in neat lines, their sails unfurled. Each page had scribbles in the margins: names of captains and sailors, destinations and ports of call.

Martin's hand twitched as she perused the book, waiting until she came to what she was looking for: the page with Myrtle's name printed boldly across the top and a sketch of a young girl in a full skirt, tight-fitting bodice and long, dark, wavy hair.

It was an image of her mother, Celeste could see, but it also had something more, something like Stuart Davis talked about: the hidden and unseen.

She looked at her father. "This was Mother?"

"The best my hand could draw."

Celeste looked closer and then turned the page to find sketch after sketch and notes documenting their outings around New York City in the year they married: 1902.

"She knew the city like I knew the docks," Martin said. "Took me all around. Up north to the Dakota Hotel for a picnic, and east and south to places I'd never been. Between the hardware stores and school, I'd lived a sheltered life. Good, but smaller than I'd realized, until I met Myrtle."

She then came upon a sketch of a dance hall, with a fleeting figure caught in a whirl. "She seems so free."

"That's how I saw her back then. I could barely catch my breath when I was with her, so full of fun and chatter. And she listened to me as no one had before. All my stories and dreams of sailing seemed to enchant her as much as they did me, and she said she couldn't wait for me to become a sea captain and how happy she'd be to keep a good home for my return between the voyages, and before I knew it, we ran away and got married. And that was that."

"But then you never sailed."

"No, I never sailed. The baby came and … you know the rest."

Celeste stared at one drawing, a close-up of her mother's face: soft eyes with a bit of twinkle. Who was that girl and where did she go? She wondered as she turned the page and came upon another one with her mother holding a baby, wearing the deepest, widest smile.

Martin looked over the top of the notebook. "In those days she was as happy as I've ever seen her. Before I knew the truth about …" His expression turned dour.

"About what?" She closed the book, turning her full attention to her father.

Martin shook his head. "It's not mine to tell."

"Papa, you can't leave it like this. What about Mama? Her being orphaned?"

Martin shook his head slowly. "A long time ago I promised to leave it alone. But this much I'll tell you. Her life was harder than most; more than I could imagine, yet somehow she survived. When she showed up at my tutoring class asking for a chance to better herself, I don't know if what I felt at that time was love or a young man's lust, but I saw a lovely, broken bird to take under my wing, and … the rest you know."

He leaned back in his chair, hands clenched in his lap. "I don't know what help I can be to you in this matter. Except to tell you I'd do it all again, exactly as it was, to have you as my daughter."

Celeste's throat thickened with emotion as she shook her head, handing the book back to her father. "That's why Mama pushes so hard."

"I suppose, but you can't let it be your reason, Celeste. Your mother has her road to travel, and you have yours. But I will tell you this: Don't be thinking you can figure it all out from the start. Whatever decision you make, I promise there will be turns – changes you can't anticipate. Some rough, others sweeter beyond imagining. All you can do is follow what draws you, as best you can. And if you're lucky, someday you'll begin to see how all the pieces fit together, built step by step, by the good and bad alike, making up the full picture, the wholeness of your life. It's better than any puzzle you can dream."

Celeste ducked her head. "I think … " she began, then looked up. "I think James would make a good husband, but I wonder …"

Martin's shoulders dropped. "Wonder what?"

Celeste explained the conversation with James in the car about working and being a mother. "Mama thinks my business is just a folly until I marry and take on a woman's proper work. And I do want a family, Papa, a big one, which of course will take a lot of work. But something cringes inside when I think of giving up The Needlery. It's become so much a part of me now. What do you think? Am I foolish to want both?"

With his daughter's face as open as the sea, Martin read every sweet curve as easily as the waves he'd long studied. He leaned forward, picked up her hands and held them softly. "Those people you see on the streets of New York and Hartford? That could be us. Without the inheritance of the stores your great grandfather built and passed on, we could well be in the same boat. It was a great gift, which my father and Gamma and I have done our best to improve and sustain. Now you've added to it in a way I never could. Through The Needlery, you've made it your own and strengthened our offering to our community. That's not to be dismissed or overlooked. You've earned your place in the business. So, in return, I make this promise to you. If and when you marry, I'll train a manager who can run the store when I'm too old, so you'll always have it as your birthright and security. No matter what your station in life, I want you to keep it, because we never know what will come next. This Depression is a sharp reminder that no one can rely on past riches. So promise me you'll keep the store, for you and your children's future, no matter what else may happen?"

They heard the front door open. Myrtle hurried in, almost tripping on Celeste's valise. Then she saw her hat on the hall table. "Celeste? Are you home, Celeste?" she called, making a beeline to Martin's study.

Quickly rising, Martin flipped the lock and opened the door as Myrtle reached for the knob. "Here we are, just having a chat."

Myrtle poked in her head to see Celeste dabbing her eyes with a handkerchief.

"What's happened? Is something wrong?" Myrtle's heart dropped. She couldn't bear another setback.

"No, Myrtle, nothing's wrong," Martin answered, jingling the change in his pockets. "Just sorting out our ducks. Right, Duckie?" He winked at his daughter, who rose to kiss him. Squeezing her arm, he whispered. "Trust yourself, girl. You've got all you need inside."

"But why did you come home early?" Myrtle asked too urgently.

Celeste had so hoped her mother would not find them in Papa's study as she hated being left out of anything and would badger endlessly until she got a satisfactory answer.

"Everything's fine, Mother. I was just tired and have some Needlery work to finish. But we had a lovely time. I'll tell you all about it at supper."

Wrapping her arms around her mother, she gave her a lingering hug before gathering up her cloak, gloves and hat, and slowly climbed the stairs to her room.

Myrtle squinted at Martin. "What happened? You must tell me, now."

"Let's just say we've raised a good daughter with a mind of her own, and I think we ought to let her use it as she likes."

☙

After her conversation with her father, Celeste took a quieter approach to her mother's demands and wheedling. She did not resist her wishes anymore and tried hard to see beyond her mother's veneer, accommodating her annoying ways as a silent sacrifice, and working hard to agree with her requests.

As Valentine's Day approached, Myrtle became even more agitated, making sure everything for the party was just right. She wouldn't let up until Celeste confirmed every plan.

A week before the party, Celeste reported: "I was thinking about red linens, with a white rippled border for the tables and pink candles in the chandeliers and rosebud vases tucked into every corner." Myrtle was delighted.

Celeste also spoke with James, letting him know the party was her mother's idea and she was going along with whatever kept her happy, but she didn't tell him the conversation her father had shared.

She also kept looking for the right moment to ask her mother what happened in her childhood that Papa would not divulge, but the time never seemed right.

She also did her sums, numbering all of James's good points against those of every other eligible man she knew, and the math was clear. Their match, while not as passionate as she wished, would be pleasant enough, with its own bantering spice that would likely improve as their future children sanctified their union. Besides, she knew no one who could offer her better, except Ron, but he was off on his own adventure that might never be finished and she didn't feel her plans could wait. Not for six children.

So strong was her conviction, she felt a certain sense of duty to prepare the party meal herself. A test, she felt, a trial by fire, to see if she could stand the heat of a marriage contract, in the kitchen and otherwise.

The morning of the party she rose well before dawn to peel, grate and soak several dozen potatoes before mixing them with flour, milk and herbs. Then, with the diligence of a soldier in training, she poured small blobs of the batter onto a sizzling grill and closely watched the mixture congeal into small, toasty brown pancakes to be dressed with salty black fish roe and tangy sour cream. Testing one, Celeste smiled at the commingled flavors on her tongue. *So far, so good*, she thought. Perhaps this wouldn't be as difficult as she'd imagined.

Next, she tackled the shrimp toast, which was not at all simple; a fact she should have deduced, as the recipe was labeled "Conversation Piece" in the small cookbook James's mother had loaned her. The drawing of a muscular man holding another muscle man over his head should have given her a clue as to the herculean effort these little beauties would require. That fact only dawned on her, though, as she cut out heart-shaped pieces of bread, shelled and minced the shrimp, mixed the shrimp with eggs, herbs, sugar, salt, butter, cornstarch and breadcrumbs, then spread the mixture on the bread and deep-fried the pieces. She felt a bit frantic as the kitchen walls, counters and floor became spattered with flecks of batter and oil-soaked shrimp. Staying out of Celeste's way, Gamma followed behind, wiping up wherever she could.

A reprieve was granted with the spare ribs, which required only a dousing of an easily mixed sauce and slow roasting. But deep panic set in as she read the directions for paella.

- *Sauté chicken and sausage in oil in large flameproof casserole until browned.*
- *Add minced onion and mashed garlic and sauté until transparent.*
- *Add whole tomatoes.*
- *Steam clams until shells open.*
- *Add shelled/cleaned shrimp and lobster tails and simmer for 3 minutes.*
- *Discard half shells and add fish and liquid to casserole.*
- *Wash rice well. Bring to boil in stock with dissolved saffron thread. Cover and reduce heat to simmer 20 minutes.*
- *Add cooked green peas, cooked artichoke hearts and stuffed olives.*
- *Cook covered 20 minutes on top of stove and bake at 350 for 10 minutes.*
- *Serve in casserole garnished with pimento strips.*

She must have been out of her mind when she agreed to this menu. But in spite of nearly slicing off her finger when removing the artichoke bottoms and losing her balance when frothing the asparagus vinaigrette, she did not lose her resolve. Time, however, ultimately got the upper hand, and Gamma stepped in to make the six-layer heart-shaped chocolate cake so Celeste could dress the tables and parlor with flowers, candles and heart-shaped candies before tending to her own toilette.

Even though the cooking nearly beat her to a pulp, Celeste finished well, looking delicious in red taffeta with a wide skirt that flounced over soft crinoline and a sweetheart neck displaying her fine collarbones. Using Gamma's antique hair clip that James had admired not five months earlier at the church picnic, Celeste swept up her hair for a sophisticated silhouette.

❦

Despite the difficult preparation, the evening flowed with finesse. The food and drink were a smashing success, and the parlor glowed with ebullient guests, dancing cheek-to-cheek and stealing kisses in candlelit corners. Looking around at the good spirits, James decided the time was right. Before the cake was presented, he slipped his arm around Celeste's waist and asked to see what new plants she was growing in the conservatory.

Walking into the moonlit room, past the pots of orchids and protea and paperwhites, James admired the tall pot of spiky Spirea that Celeste had been growing since she was seven, and he carefully studied her clipped topiary of a small bird with upturned beak. Holding her hand on his palm, he stroked her long, slender fingers, admiring their delicacy and dedication, when he suddenly dropped to one knee, wincing as it met the cool hard slate.

"Celeste Howe, would you do the honor of bestowing on me the same loving tenderness these hands so graciously bestow upon these plants?"

Celeste laughed, half understanding what he said. "Is this some new cocktail game?"

He looked at her oddly. "No, I'm asking you to be my wife and mother of my children."

A welter of emotions arose in her throat and her chest swelled as her heart pressed out and her stomach contracted. She hadn't expected this. Not so soon, not just yet. They had been making good progress, but she thought she had time – at least until Ede got home. Staring down at his soft smile, a smile to soothe a distressed child, she felt an urge to pull away, but found her feet planted solid.

"So soon?" was all she could think to say.

"What more do you need to know?" he asked in return, shifting his knee. "I thought we had an understanding?"

"We do, but … I didn't expect … it's … such a surprise." She said, silently wondering if she declined, would he ever ask again.

"It's supposed to be a surprise. So will you? Be my wife?" His face pinched from the hardness of the stone beneath his knee.

A million thoughts rushed through her mind. *She liked him. She did. He was everything a girl could want, except a few odd bits, and did they really matter in the long run? She wanted to get on with her life. Looking around, she didn't see anyone who had everything tucked in place. There were always trade-offs. Look at her parents. Look at his parents! She didn't want to replicate either marriage. And she was sure neither did James. He may not be the most passionate of men, but he had good points. In the very least she would have an interesting life with him. Travel, society, art, and as many children as she wanted, without worry. Mama's right: Security is important, more than she realized when pledging with Ede to marry only for passion. There were more measures to consider than she'd originally thought, but most of all she worried he'd go away for good if she turned him down right now. But if she said yes, she'd have more time to make sure … before taking to the aisle.*

Pressing four fingers to her lips, holding back what she dare not say, she let her silence answer with a nod as a tear rolled down her cheek.

Smiling broadly, James presented an open ring box with the filigreed platinum diamond ring she said inspired her at Tiffany's in January. She gasped as he stood and slipped it on her finger.

"Good, it's settled," he sealed the deal with a hard kiss on her lips. Taking her hand, he turned, his voice vibrating with an electric charge. "Let's tell them now, before we cut the cake. Your father's already approved!"

Following him blindly into the parlor, Celeste found the cake on its crystal stand, waiting for them.

From across the room, Myrtle watched James carefully, waiting for his sly wink and nod. Her face lit up as she silently clapped her hands, then quickly turned away, regaining her composure so she could feign surprise at the happy news.

Celeste did not see her mother or anyone else in the room. Her eyes blurred as James squeezed her hand and cleared his throat, commanding everyone's attention. She could barely hear the words he spoke, or keep her balance as she felt the world slip beyond her reach, and the room began to whirl in a wobbly spin.

26 *Understandings*

March 1934

A few days after the party, in between the gushing customers at the store, Celeste cornered her father. "When did James ask your permission?"

Martin scratched his head with the nub of his pencil. "Earlier that night. But he didn't so much ask as tell me. I said it was your decision." He paused, his pencil poised to jot down the figures he'd been summing in his head. "Are you unsure?"

Celeste shrugged. "It just happened so quickly. I wasn't prepared … for any of it. I thought we were on our way, getting to know each other, but there's still a lot to talk about …"

Martin eyed his daughter carefully, noting the tautness around her mouth, which was usually soft. "Then take your time. Have a long engagement. Don't be afraid to change your mind."

The conversation at the Meaden household was very different.

After finishing her breakfast in the dining room, Estelle opened a folder to review plans for an early March engagement party. An hour later, James joined her.

"Welp, now the gallery can open," he said, pouring a cup of coffee. "There's a space I've been eyeing on seventy eighth, so I'll have the papers drawn up."

Looking over her reading glasses, Estelle cleared her throat.

"I said *when* you were married."

"Oh, come on Mother, don't be ridiculous. We're as good as married now."

She jutted her jaw. "Many a thing can happen on the way to the fair."

"No-no, that wasn't our agreement. Besides, don't you realize how much work there is to get the place ready?" He downed his coffee and poured another cup.

Estelle looked at him critically. His demeanor and pallor were rough from too much drink and too little sleep. It was not the time to start an argument.

"Alright," she said, returning to her papers. "On the condition it not open until after the ceremony."

"Then we'll marry next week."

"Don't be impudent."

"I'm quite serious, Mother. Set up the Justice of the Peace and we'll get it done. Lickety split! Let's see," taking out his pocket calendar. "Right. Saturday next. We can squeeze it in between a squash match at noon and drinks at seven. Can you make it?"

Estelle leaned back, lifted her teacup and slowly sipped. "Is the marriage only to procure the gallery? Because that's not a very promising start …"

James swigged down his second cup. "It's only fair you stick to the bargain you struck."

"Then be reasonable."

"How soon is reasonable?"

Estelle looked at her calendar, lifting one page, then the next. "May."

The tension in James' jaw drained. "May? I thought it took a year to plan."

"It can be done." Estelle set down her cup, smoothing the tablecloth with her fingertips. "In a simple, homespun manner."

James tapped his chin. "Well then, let May come quickly."

"MAY?!? I never agreed to May!" Celeste snapped upright at the kitchen table when Myrtle informed her of Estelle's suggestion.

Sitting next to her, Martin choked on a bite of apple and spat it out. "What's going on here? I thought long engagements were the protocol."

"Normally," Myrtle spoke into her cooking pots, stirring so as not to look at either of them. "But if everyone's in agreement, why not have a simple ceremony sooner rather than later? In uncertain times you never know what can happen. And times are certainly uncertain. Heavens, we can't even depend on the gold standard anymore."

"What does the gold standard have to do with Celeste's wedding?" Martin asked.

"Just another bit of evidence of how mad our world has become; everything turned upside down. Gold no longer backs our money. The banks closing. The bread lines. The work projects. Everything is too unpredictable. She should grab happiness when she finds it, quickly, before it's snatched away like everything else in this crazy world."

Celeste felt jumpy all over as she got up to set the table. "But Ede won't even be home by then, and she has to be my maid of honor. She has to be! Besides ... I was hoping to spend more time with James before ... before we even agreed on a wedding date. We've only known each other six months and already engaged?!"

"You've known him since you were 16," Myrtle chided. "What more do you need to know?"

Celeste dropped the silverware on the table. "What more? Everything! Most of the time we've been together has been in a crowd, either here or at his parent's home or church. I've got a lot of things I need to know before we actually wed." Her eyes cast about the room. "Like where are we going to live, how many children does he want and, and, and ... what's his favorite color?"

"Here in Gladdenbury. As many children as you wish. And he loves moss green," Myrtle replied succinctly as she stirred the boiling potatoes. "Which I know because he mentioned it when I admired one of his ties."

Celeste looked at her father with a crumpled expression and shook her head. "May is just too soon," she said and abruptly left the room, leaving her father to deal with her mother.

Myrtle continued facing the stove, her shoulders stiff, ready for a fight.

Martin waited for Celeste's footsteps to disappear into her room upstairs before addressing his wife with a quiet intensity. "She's right. They barely know each other. What's going on in your head, Myrtle?"

"We barely knew each other, and it worked out fine," she replied. "She has to trust her instincts."

"If she trusted her instincts, she'd be out the door as fast as she could. She's doing all this for your sake, woman, can't you see that? Do you really think she's ready? Just when she's finding her way with The Needlery? Just when she's begun to come into herself? I don't see the need for the rush.

She still very young. And I'm not sure of his motives, either. Last summer he was walking around town with another woman on his arm."

"Oh, that was nothing."

"Nothing to you perhaps, but a man doesn't bring a Broadway actress to a small town if it means nothing to him. That much I know. What happened to that?"

"I don't believe Estelle approved."

"But she approves of Celeste, and that's all you need to know? Myrtle, she's our only daughter. Why can't you think about what she wants, first?"

"My job is to look out for what's best for her, and I've been doing that." Myrtle said, turning to face her husband, one hand on her hip. "Honestly, Martin, what better opportunity is going to come along? James Meaden is the *crème de la crème!*"

"Ouff! Whose opportunity are you referring to? No doubt it satisfies your fixation on the self-anointed royalty of the Meadens', but what about Celeste's choice? How many times do I have to tell you to stop your conniving? She's a smart girl, but much younger in age and experience than James. She needs time. What is it you hope to acquire from all this … this … plotting?

Myrtle quickly shook her head. "The best possible life for our child and grandchildren."

Martin slowly shook his in return, not believing one word of it. "Best possible life for you, I think. Let's not pretend otherwise."

⁂

The next day, when James stepped into Celeste's vestibule to say goodbye before returning to New York, she confronted him. "What's going on? Why didn't *we* talk first?"

With hat in hand, James blustered. "About what?"

"About getting engaged, about a marriage date, about – any of it. When did you decide we should marry so quickly? One day you tell me to take my time, give it good consideration, and the next – whoosh, down the aisle we go! What changed? And why do I feel like there's something else motivating the rush? Something other than your wanting a life with me, I mean. What's going on that I don't know?"

"I thought it's what you wanted."

She eyed him menacingly. "Did you now? When did I give that impression? Wasn't it just Halloween when you said: take your time, Celeste."

As he rolled his hand in the air, trying to conjure an answer, Celeste caught it, tightly squeezing his fingers. "Is this how it's going to be? You making decisions with *your* mother and *my* mother and then informing me? Expecting me to happily comply?" Giving his fingers a last twist; she dropped it, turning away. "If so, you picked the wrong gal."

He quickly grabbed her shoulders, drawing her back to him. "Whoa, Celeste. That's not what I meant at all. It was just an idea that came up and … snowballed. Because … because … my traveling season begins in the spring, and I thought if we were married, you could accompany me. We could make it a grand honeymoon tour throughout Europe, showing you the world … and showing the world my beautiful wife."

The idea of a European tour momentarily softened Celeste to his embrace, but then she pushed back. "That's all very grand, but honestly, that's the cart before the horse. We have a lot of things to figure out. You can't just assume I'll go along with whatever you say. James, this is for the rest of our lives! There's so much we haven't considered, or even thought to consider. You told me to take a serious look. I have. So now I have a lot of questions."

"Absolutely. Absolutely! We will talk, I promise. But don't you see what a good thing we have here? It won't take us long to sort it all out. Make a list. We'll check it twice. We'll find all the answers, together. But we already know each other's families and backgrounds and have the same goals in life, so why should we wait a whole year to take Europe, and the world, by storm, as husband and wife? We're lucky to find each other, so why not take the leap and get on with it? Maybe our mothers have been a little pushy, but can you blame them? They see what I see: a perfect match. So do you, right?"

Before she could reply, he kissed her mouth, softly, then hard and long until she began laughing, pushing him away.

"What a rascal!" she said, keeping him at arm's length. "I bet you could talk the queen out of her crown."

"Maybe not a queen … but a princess, for sure. Done that before."

Celeste looked at him aghast, then burst out laughing. "You certainly are entertaining, I'll give you that."

"And I promise I always will be," he quipped, moving in for another kiss.

"No!" Celeste snapped back, holding up her index finger. "Just promise me you'll always be honest with me. That's number one."

James grabbed her finger, squeezing it softly. "Absolutely. Number One. Now make that list and we'll have it all sorted out before you know it. I promise. And do think about May, how beautiful it will be: the dogwood grove in blossom … you in white …. a stunning sendoff." He quickly kissed her nose. "I must run to catch the train. See you next Saturday, princess."

As he slipped away, down the steps, around the corner and out of sight, Celeste stood on her porch wondering why she still felt uneasy.

⟨∽

Estelle paused in the doorframe of Jack's study with a small tea tray. "Knock, knock. Care for some tea?"

"That would be nice," Jack replied, closing his periodical. "I need a break."

Estelle set the tray on the edge of the desk and sat across from her husband at the partner's desk. "Thought we might catch up. It's been so busy." She poured two cups, adding cream and a sugar cube to each, then handed one to Jack. "Earl Grey."

"Thank you. What's up?"

"You haven't said anything."

Jack removed his reading glasses. "About the engagement?" He shook his head.

"Aren't you pleased? I thought you liked the girl."

"I adore the girl, but I'm not so sure about James. It's all too nice and neat. Where's the fire? Where's the passion? It almost feels like … a business deal."

"Not all marriages begin like ours, Jack. Many are tepid at the start. Anyway, in the long run, even the most passionate marriages die down to a cozy ember – if you're lucky."

"Is that what we are now? A cozy ember?"

Estelle smiled, flirting her eyebrows. "We're more than lucky. But I would appreciate a bit more enthusiasm. It's an ideal match, in so many ways."

"Mmmmm," Jack murmured, sipping his tea, and then set down the cup with a clatter. "But why has he agreed so quickly? After all these years? It's unlike him. And what happened to Kate all of a sudden? I feel like something's missing here."

Estelle returned her husband's direct gaze as she fingered the pin at her neck. "I think there comes a time in everyone's life when they want to get on with things. James has a goal: to be taken seriously in the art world.

It's now important for him to appear solid, beyond his financial dealings. Having a wife and family goes a long way in securing that image. I think he finally realizes that."

Jack leaned back in his chair. "So it's all about the gallery, then?"

Estelle shrugged. "Does it matter? So long as he's come back to the fold?"

Still unresolved but considering a May date, Celeste sent a desperate telegram to Ede, begging for her early return to be her maid of honor. "You must come or I will renege."

But Ede replied she could not leave her apprenticeship on such short notice and could barely afford the telegram, much less the train fare.

Celeste dashed off several additional messages, pleading for her to come and promising to pay her way.

Hoping to soften her final refusal Ede sent a letter in return.

My Dearest Celeste:

I just hate not being there, knowing how much you need me right now. And even more, I hate having to tell you it's impossible for me to leave my position. Mr. Moltano depends upon me, and we are currently in the middle of building three different sets. And even though most of my duties are secretarial, I have been allowed to dabble in the set painting now and again. Please know I am deeply torn by your request, but I cannot risk losing either my place or the goodwill I've built thus far in a field where no other women are yet employed as artists. I have wept with each of your telegrams, anxious to be by your side, and I can only wish it were possible to postpone the wedding until early June, when I am scheduled to return. But even that is uncertain, as Mr. Moltano has indicated I might be hired as a permanent employee, if he has his way. So you see, both our lives are at turning points to which we must attend, to the best of our ability. I'm sure Gamma is right by your side with far more wisdom than I can offer. Dear friend, I send my best wishes and prayers for peace with your decision, whatever it may be.

Your faithful friend always,
Ede

With Ede's decision in hand, Celeste spent the afternoon crying in her room. Gamma brought her tea and toast, which she refused. Myrtle tried to comfort her, but Celeste snapped for her to get out and leave her alone. At the end of the day, her father knocked gently on her door. When there was no answer, he opened it a crack and saw Celeste sitting crossed-legged on her bed, scribbling in a notebook.

"Celeste?" he quietly asked, opening the door wider.

She looked over her shoulder with flashing red eyes and ruddy cheeks.

Approaching, he saw she'd been furiously sketching a design of something or other, almost ripping the paper with each stroke of her thick pencil.

"Celeste, what is it?" His voice was full of caution.

"I … have … to … finish … these … designs." Tears jumbled Celeste's speech.

"Whatever do you mean?"

"There's so much work to complete for The Needlery before …" she broke off abruptly.

"But darling girl, you needn't bother if you don't wish …" He ducked as Celeste pitched her pad at him and buried her head in the strewn pillows, muffling a wail.

Feeling lost on how to soothe her, Martin sat on her bed, waiting for her sobs to subside.

"Celeste?" he asked after she quieted. "Please tell me what you're feeling."

Sniffling, she rolled over, her eyes doleful. "I'm confused."

"About James?"

She sat up, leaning on her pillows. "Why do I have to choose?"

"Between?"

"My dreams."

Martin shook his head. "Who said you had to choose?"

Celeste rolled her eyes. "Everyone – except you and Gamma. But I don't see how I can possibly do both, given the social schedule James has in mind. He wants me to go to Europe with him after the wedding. How could I run The Needlery if I'm traveling, with Ede gone, too? And what happens when the babies come? Papa, I know you said you'd keep the store for me, but I don't see when I'll ever have time again. My heart rips at the thought of letting it go. Like I'm losing part of myself. But I do want children, and for that, James seems best. Mama was right. I'm already 20 years old." She blinked several times, holding back fresh tears.

Martin slowly wagged his head. "Celeste, I can't imagine what it's like to be a woman. I suppose you have some freedoms men don't even know exist, but I think you make more sacrifices than we do. Putting children and family first and your dreams on uncertain hold … maybe never to be realized … is a daunting choice. Especially when no one can predict it will work out all right. They'd be lying if they tried." He stroked her arm. "But I can promise you this: You need not decide right now. Let things unfold a bit. Get the lay of the land for the big changes ahead. And let The Needlery take a rest, too. It's not going anywhere. You can always bring it back. Because I promise to support whatever you want to do in that regard. Whatever you want to try; The Needlery or some other business you envision. If my son were alive, I'd not make him choose between creative dreams and having a family … and neither should you."

Martin's words cooled the room and calmed the air. He could hear Celeste's breathing and heart slow down. Reaching for a blanket, he draped it over her, along with a final thought. "One decision is just a step, one step in one direction that does not change who you are inside. Never forget that. You choose your steps, not anyone else, and I will always stand by you, supporting whatever you choose." Leaning in, he kissed her forehead as she snuggled under the blanket, finally calmed.

Returning to the kitchen, Martin found Gamma and Myrtle anxiously waiting.

"She was working on pillow designs."

"What?" Myrtle snapped. "Why does she even bother with that now?"

Martin sat down at the table with them. "Because she's torn, Myrtle. She doesn't want to give up what she's worked so hard to create."

"Augh, what nonsense." Myrtle rose, wiping her hands on her apron. "I'm going to set her straight right this instant. A married woman does not work outside the home."

Myrtle turned to march upstairs, but Gamma stopped her.

"For the love of Ogma, Myrtle, stop being a fool and sit down!"

The sharpness in her voice took them all by surprise.

Myrtle sputtered. "I'm her mother and this is a mother's matter."

"*No!*" Gamma barked. "Is Celeste's matter. Has she asked your opinion? Any more than you ask mine – when away you stole my son?"

Myrtle froze.

Gamma's steel blue eyes locked onto Myrtle's. For years – decades – she had stuffed her anger at Myrtle deep inside, for the sake of her son and her own dignity. But now her granddaughter's soul hung in the balance and all the pent-up fury she had denied burst forth like searing bolts of lightning. "No, you did not. Without saying anything to anyone, off you go and marry Martin … before we knew, before *he* even knew what happen. And just as quickly," Gamma snapped her fingers, "come a child. From love and unselfish devotion? I think not. Only to secure a place. I see how you eye the house down the block, needling Martin's father until he promise it for your own. Using my son to secure your future, regardless of his own desires. Is always how it is with you. And now you try the same with Celeste, using her for better position in town society. *Pfffft* – I won't have it. I … won't … have it! Not one minute more."

Myrtle gaped at Gamma, stunned and uncertain how to respond. Finally, she turned to Martin. "Are you going to let her talk to me like that?"

Although Martin felt a bit off balance by his mother's sudden vehemence, he pointed to a chair. "Sit, Myrtle," he said, slowly. "This has probably been coming for a long while." Then, to his mother: "Is there more?"

Gamma nodded sharply but softened her voice a meter.

"Out of respect for Celeste, so far I say nothing. But I do not like this so fast marriage. Something's not right. She is now grown and must make decisions her own. But to see you push her down the aisle, as you did my son, like a goat, is too much. Maybe this marriage is good, maybe a mistake … but must be hers. Leave her … to do as she choose: to marry or work, to have babies or not. Is not a decision for me or you or Martin. Is *her's* only. On this I insist!"

As Gamma was speaking, no one heard Celeste come down the stairs and stand out of sight in the darkened hallway. As she listened hard to Gamma's fiery words, she felt her own heart soar with each declaration. Then, in the stony silence that followed in the kitchen, only one sound emerged: the tinging of copper bracelets shifting on Gamma's arm. As it reached Celeste's ears, she clasped her own arm as her heart warmed, thinking of the gypsy's prophecy and James's chiding. He was right. If she wanted to have six children, she'd best get busy. Stepping from the hallway shadows, Celeste faced her family, tears dripping down her nose.

"Thank you, Gamma," she said with a breath of relief. "What you said means so much to me. I'm sorry I behaved so badly today. I am too old for such tantrums, and it is time I make my own decision and live the consequences."

Myrtle's body clenched, desperate that Celeste may be backing out of her grasp.

"All my life, all three of you have given me much to be thankful for. Such a fine childhood with so many gifts. Papa, working by your side has been one of my greatest blessings. The chance to create my own business is a treasure beyond words, for which I will always be grateful."

Still holding her breath, Myrtle felt a tiny crack of hope.

"Mama, for most of my life I did not think I was like you at all. I did not believe I could be content being only a wife and mother. Something in my blood called for more. To do and see and feel more than what Gladdenbury offers. More like Gamma, I suppose. I feel a wanderlust that draws me to adventure and creativity. It's why I so love Ede. She inspires me to be bolder."

Myrtle's heart dropped to her knees.

"But now that I'm to be married, I have different thoughts. I now see why you worry about my future; a single woman in a world where only men have the privilege to strike out on their own. And while I have the protection of our business, I am not equipped to take it over by myself, without my husband working by my side, as you had Gamma, and Great Grandmother Katrine. So I must admit that I am not well suited for the dreams I've dreamt. Better to be content with what I am able to do: support my husband, bear and raise his children. It's good work, sacred work, I think, with the hope that one day, one of them will be strong enough to rise beyond the challenges I am ill equipped to face." Celeste's head tilted down and to the left, matching her father's head position. "So I've made my decision. I will marry James Meaden and become the mother of his children. And hopefully, someday, I'll understand how all these pieces fit together in my unique path toward contentedness."

The three adults stared at Celeste as she nodded, turned and left the room to climb the stairs, wash her face, dress in one of her best outfits and walk five blocks to the Meadens, where James was staying the night.

Approaching their home, Celeste was confused by the sound of the phonograph playing and a hubbub of noise seeping though the windows. Normally the Meaden home was dead quiet, with everyone tucked away in private pursuits. But tonight the lights were gleaming. She knocked on the door and waited, reviewing the words she planned to say to James, to seal the deal and be married in May, when the door swung open and she nearly lost her breath. Standing before her, in a jaunty stance with a wide-open grin, stood her dear, old friend, Ron Meaden.

27 *Champion*

March 1934

Ron's green eyes glowed. His words tumbled without hesitation.

"Glory be to heaven! Celeste Howe, don't you look rapturous."

Heat instantly sparked throughout Celeste's body. A wide smile opened her lips.

They silently drank in each other, their faces full of wonder.

"Celeste is here?" James called from inside the house.

Celeste's smile vanished as James roughly pushed past Ron, with a smothering embrace, nuzzling her neck. She smelled beer on his breath and then saw a bottle in Ron's hand as he turned to walk away.

"What's going on, James?" she asked curtly. She'd come to soothe her nerves and confirm her resolve but was confused by the sounds of a soirée in full swing from the back porch.

Taking her hand, James led her through the house. "The champion has returned victorious," he announced, punching the air, then added flatly: "so we're celebrating." They stepped out onto the veranda, where a dozen or so people she didn't know were clustered, mostly on the lawn, in animated conversations. She recognized only Jack Meaden, who hailed from his chair at the far end.

"Celeste! What a grand surprise. James didn't tell me you were coming."

"Didn't know myself," James replied. "Hey, everyone!" his voice buoyed over the hubbub, "I'd like to introduce my gorgeous fiancée, Celeste Howe." He rolled his hand over the crowd as he turned to her. "Most of these ruffians are my little brother's squash mates, along with a few of their fine ladyfriends. Although what they see in these blokes is a gobbler's guess."

"Hey!" one of the girls objected, while the rest laughed and returned to their chatter. The redhead with a saucy bob sidled over to Celeste. "Sooo, you're the lucky one who snatched big boy. None of us thought it would ever happen, at least not by someone with class. I'm Lucy. Nice to meetcha."

Celeste was about to ask what she meant but was cut off by the brunette sitting on the wicker couch.

"I'll bet the same'll be true for the young one, as well," she said, eyeing Ron, slumped on a chair, absently swigging beer. Celeste noticed everyone had a bottle, and from their loose demeanor it seemed they had been drinking for some time.

The buxom brunette added: "Only Ron has a tougher mistress to combat. Whoever becomes his ball and chain will have a dickens of a time getting him away from his ball and racquet. You should have heard the grousing when he was a no-show for the Atlantic Dip."

"I beg your pardon?" Celeste asked, turning to James, but he was gone.

Ron, lounging with his feet propped on the wicker table, called out. "Jeannette, cut it out. She doesn't need your gossip and has no interest in squash."

"On that score, you're half right," Celeste automatically quipped, as she always had with Ron. "It's not that I don't care, I just don't know much about it. But if I'm to marry into this squash-crazed family, I guess it's high time I learned a bit." She turned to the redhead and brunette. "And I'd be a fool not to take advantage of your expert schooling."

Ron smiled at her cheeky reply but slowly shook his head. "It's your funeral."

Celeste smiled at the girls. "I'm plum blind about the sport. Haven't a clue what he's been doing all year except hitting a ball off a wall somewhere. I'd love you to fill me in on what I've missed!"

With a whoop, Lucy and Jeanette dragged Celeste to the wicker couch across from Ron, plopping her in the middle and flanking either side. Someone handed her a beer, which she looked at blankly for a moment before taking a sip. She immediately wanted to spit out the mouthful of foam but managed to swallow.

The girls began arguing over where to start, until Ron interrupted.

"Whoa! Ladies, slow down! She's right. All I do is whack a ball against a wall. No big deal. Why not leave it at that?"

"Hell no!" Jack chimed from his throne at the end of the porch. Although he usually removed himself early from his own parties, he always stuck around during his children's gatherings, no matter how old they were, knowing first-hand what follies youth could brew. "Celeste, my boy has made me prouder than … well; let's just say it's been a heck of a season. A *heck* of a season. Almost a grand slam. Unheard of for a first run. From the Tickon-Glidden to the Gold Racquets and topped off with a Windmill Double Boast! Unheard of! Yep, yep, I'm mighty proud."

Baffled by half of what Jack said, Celeste looked around for James but could not see him so she leaned across the table to Ron. "Whatever are they talking about?"

Before Ron could answer, Lucy commanded the floor. She had decided to start at the beginning. Pushing up her sweater sleeves, she explained to Celeste that the official amateur squash season began in November at the Tickon-Gliddin Round Robin Invitational in New Jersey and how Ron surprised the crowd by winning third place.

"Blasted right out of the gate. That's my boy!" Jack inserted, draining his bottle and calling out to someone in the lawn crowd to bring him a fresh one.

"The news buzzed up the eastern seaboard faster than the papers could report it," Lucy gushed. "And by December, the spectators doubled for the Gold Racquets; everyone panting to see the new boy on court."

"It's not as if I were new to the sport," Ron said dryly, downplaying his achievements.

Lucy made a face and waved him to be quiet.

"What's a Gold Racquet?" Celeste asked, holding her bottle with both hands.

Lucy brightened. "*Oh*, you really *are* a novice!" She then explained about the second tournament of the season, held at the Rockaway Hunting Club on Long Island, where the highest honor is called the Gold Racquet – which Ron won handily.

"You should have seen the sprint for the telegraph office," Jeanette added. "Shooting the news across the country faster than greased lightning."

"Is that why the house was decorated with gold-painted racquets at Christmas?" Celeste asked, having thought it odd when she saw them hanging everywhere at the Meadens'; from the ceilings and trees and around the entire porch. But she hadn't said anything, assuming it was an old family tradition.

Jack nodded. "It was a shame to take'm down."

Celeste giggled at the bizarre memory.

"Well," Lucy declared, snatching back control of the conversation. "Then there's the William White tournament in Merion, Pennsylvania, where everybody who is anybody comes to see and be seen; and our little Ronnie was the 'it' boy. The most dynamic squash player to hit the boards in years."

"Oh, yes-siree-bob," Jeannette chimed in. "It was a circus. The old men betting on Ron's odds, the young men measuring their prowess against his, and *all* the women engorging on romantic fantasies. And let's not forget the old biddies contemplating how to snag the young buck for their virgin daughters!"

Lucy snickered, and Jeanette burst into a guffaw. "What part of them is virgin?" they said in unison, peeling in laughter.

Celeste suddenly felt caught and uncomfortable.

Looking up, Ron recognized her distress. "OK, that's enough," he said sharply.

The girls shook off his reprimand, and Jeannette got up for another long-neck.

Celeste looked around again for James, wondering if she should go home.

"OK, OK, we'll behave," Lucy relented. "But we have to finish the story. You don't want her to show up ignorant, do you?"

Ron shrugged. He was already tired when he'd arrived home that afternoon, directly from the Canadian Invitational, which he'd won, in addition to conducting clinics for the younger players. He really didn't care what anyone said nor did that night, except when it came to Celeste. Keeping one eye open in case she needed him, he leaned his head back as Lucy resumed the story.

She explained that while the fans were disappointed with Ron's second-place finish at Merion and also at Washington D.C.'s Woodruff-Nee tournaments, he turned it all around when he wowed the crowds with a spectacular win at the Atlantic Coasts Tournament. "The roar of the crowd was wilder than the winter winds whipping Atlantic City's boardwalk. Everyone was parched for a champion, and Ron Meaden delivered! N'how, did he ever deliver!"

Just as Lucy finished speaking, James emerged from the shadows of the backyard, looking a bit disheveled and wearing a slow grin. Climbing the porch steps, he leaned on the back of the wicker couch, standing behind Celeste. "But then you nearly lost it, buddy boy, with a no-show on the beach," James said, staring at his baby brother, who looked away.

"Hey-ho!" Jack inserted. "You know damn well he had to save his strength for the Harvard Harry Cowles. Without his good sense that night, he might not have even taken second place in that tourney!"

"Yeah, yeah," James mumbled. "The reigning champ rides into the sunset." Without a glance at Celeste, James wobbled into the house.

Celeste started to get up to follow him, but suddenly Lucy was whispering in her ear. "By the way, there's a ritual at the Atlantic. After the tournament's formal dinner, everyone goes to the beach, still in fancy dress, for a huge bonfire until the winner arrives at midnight for the ocean dip."

"In winter?" Celeste asked, now feeling agitated and trapped. These were not stories she was used to hearing.

"Oh, yes! With the supposed virgin debutante," Lucy continued, her voice sliding into a conspiratorial tone. "A 'Lady of the Sea,' chosen among the young debs, is to accompany the tournament winner into the ocean for a complete submerged kiss. And the length of that kiss determines the strength of the champion's legacy. And for the girl, well, it's begun many a tryst and several, eventual, marriages. So it's a very big deal among the eligible ladies. And when they saw this one on the court ..." Lucy's eyes slid over Ron's sinewy limbs draped over his chair. "Oooff! Desire surged!"

"So, the selected maiden shows up on the beach wearing an extra-tight gown. White. Sequined. Ready to bedazzle Ron in and out of the moonlit waters. But he never showed. Sent his regrets via his brother, who was already tight when he came to the beach. And then *he* tried to convince the maiden that *he* should take Ron's place and starts dragging the girl toward the water and ..."

"*Lucy!*" Jeannette hissed, having just returned with her beer.

Lucy's eyes snapped to Jeannette, who looked at Celeste and then rolled her eyes toward the house several times until Lucy realized why she'd been interrupted.

"Oh, well," Lucy shrugged. "Anyway, that's what I heard, but you can't believe everything you hear."

With a slap to his knee, Ron swung his legs to the floor and sat up. "OK, ladies, that's quite enough. Celeste, let me walk you home."

"But where's James?"

"He's had a bit too much fun tonight and is probably off to bed," Ron said, rising with a commanding air. Celeste took his offered hand, stood and said goodbye leaving the veranda with all the dignity she could muster.

Silently, they walked the long hallway through the house, down the front-porch steps and strolled a block, side by side, caressed by the unusually warm March air. Celeste clasped her hands behind her back, turning her engagement ring around and around on her finger.

Finally, she spoke. "Quite a year you've had."

"You, too!" Ron replied. "Seems like I've missed all the fun."

"Oh ho! From what they were saying, you've had quite a ride! Besides," Celeste swung her arm, miming a racquet, "my fun doesn't compare with yours, Mister Champion."

"I wouldn't be so sure about that. It's kinda lonely on the road."

"You don't have to be on the road to feel lonely."

He nodded. They walked a while more in silence.

Then he spoke. "So, you're to be my sister-in-law."

Celeste averted her eyes, looking across the street to the Town Green. "Hey!" she pointed to the swings. "Let's go ... for old times' sake."

"Yes! Lets!" Ron said, placing his hand on her lower back, to guide her across the road.

A jolt ran up her spine and she bolted forward, racing to the Green. As she approached the swings, Ron caught up. They simultaneously slid onto the seats, pushed off, bending their knees, pumping their legs and furiously straining the chains to fly higher and higher; tilting back as they swept over the ground, peppering the night with whoops of laughter. "Oooooooooo" they alternately released, imbued by a delectable, simple freedom. Harder and harder they swung, back and forth until both were out of breath and, reluctantly, slowed to a stop. As soon as Celeste planted her feet in the sand, she swiveled to face Ron.

"I haven't felt that joyous since ... your creek swing!" She laughed out loud, feeling the warmth of his smile reach across the darkness.

He squeezed her arm lightly. Electricity crackled between them.

"Hey," she blurted, swiveling away from him, "what was Lucy talking about? That thing with the Atlantic kiss and that girl and your brother – was she talking about James?"

Ron grabbed the swing chain, pulling her back to face him. "Celeste, don't believe everything you hear, especially from that crowd."

"But aren't they your friends?"

"My buddies' girlfriends are not my friends. Or yours, either."

"But you are. So ... tell me. Was it James?"

Ron looked to the ground, his silence stilling the air.

"If it was," she asked quietly, "Don't you think I should know?"

"If it was," he answered quietly "Does it matter? All's well that ends well, right?"

Celeste cocked her head. "I'm starting to wonder what else I don't know. And why I wasn't included. I mean, if I'm his fiancée, shouldn't I be at those games and parties? By his side? And does James often drink a lot?"

Ron blinked at her. "I wouldn't know."

"No? He's your brother."

"He's my eldest brother, who was already out of the house when I was very young."

"But you suspect?"

Ron half shrugged. "He seems to enjoy himself on a regular basis."

Celeste looked down and began tracing a heart in the sand with her feet. A quiet hum filled the space between them. *How odd,* she thought, to feel more at ease in this moment, here, on the swings, with Ron, than she had in months. Still looking at her feet, she asked:

"Do you think I'm making the right decision?"

"About what?"

"Marrying James."

Ron swallowed hard.

So hard, Celeste heard him and looked up. "Ron, you're my best friend. You and Ede, but she's not here."

"Have you heard from her?"

Celeste nodded, her face prickling.

"What did she say?"

"She can't come back in time for the wedding."

"So move the date."

"Between your mother and mine, it feels as if I'm not even ..." her voice trailed off.

"You're not even what?" Ron asked.

His tone was soothing, but his words shot through Celeste like a truth serum.

"Oh, I hate this!" she spouted, dashing the sand heart as she stood. "I hate this ... this ... vacillation. I keep thinking I've made my decision. I'm resolved. I'm clear. I'll do what most women do: live through my husband and children – which is a far better lot than most people get. And maybe, when the children are grown, I'll pursue my creative side again ... if I want to ... I mean, it's not as if it's so strong to begin with." Grabbing the chains, Celeste stepped onto the seat. Rocking her hips and pushing with her legs, she got a good lift and swung through the night air, declaring to the sky: "I'll do as Gamma says: 'Create something new.' Children are something new." She looked down at Ron, and when he didn't answer, she slowed to a stop.

He sat calmly, his deep eyes fixed up on her.

"Besides, what options do I have?" She continued, flipping her hair. "I'm not an artist like Ede or an athlete like you. I'm just a shopkeeper's daughter who likes to needlepoint. Big deal. So I should be grateful, right? Like everyone says: snagging a Meaden! Who else could provide as good a footing?"

Ron's eyebrows drew in. "That's how you feel about him? A good footing?"

Celeste shrugged, twisting her swing left and right. "It's what everyone says. The suave, educated, handsome, debonair, worldly James Austin Meaden the Second, with the Meaden family fortune behind him! I mean, eeegads, who else has all that!" She stopped twisting and stared down at Ron. "Except you."

He stared back, unflinching until her eyes closed and her voice dropped.

"But you're off on your own adventure and who knows when you'll come back – if you'll even want to come back."

"I'm back now."

She opened her eyes, startled to find him standing on the swing next to her, eyeball to eyeball. She pressed her lips together. "But for how long?"

"As long as you want. I don't have to go back on the squash circuit."

"Yeah, right," she said, jumping down.

He jumped down and caught her hand. "No, I mean it. I don't have to go anywhere. I can quit squash. I can stay here."

She faced him. "And do what?"

"Work for the company … be with you."

Celeste's vision blurred. She looked beyond Ron's eyes, taking in his whole body. Tense, and wound tight from shoulders to feet, as if ready to spring to wherever the ball would land. Such a torrent of feelings surged in Celeste's chest she could not begin to sort them out. It was all she could do to push them back down.

"Don't be ridiculous," she said half-heartedly. "You can't give up squash any more than breathing." Tossing her head, she pulled her hand away, sitting on the swing.

Ron stood in front of her. "Why are you marrying my brother?"

"To have children." Her voice was flat.

"That's it? Why not with me, then?"

Celeste blurted a cold laugh, touching her head to her knees, then sat back up. "What are you talking about? Your dream is in the palm of your hand, everything you've wished for, waiting for you to seize it ... and you'd just leave it ... for me?"

"Gladly."

She looked away, across the Green, then down at her feet.

"You don't love him, do you?" Ron guessed.

She ground her heel into the sand, trying to stop the scramble inside.

"Do you?" His voice tightened.

"You shouldn't ask me that."

"Why not? I'm your best friend, right? Me and Ede? You'd ask me if I were in your shoes. That's what friends do, right? Ask each other for the truth?"

"But I'm not you. I don't have your talent or promise. If you let all that go for me, you'd regret it someday ... of what might have been ... and you know that."

"It's just a game, Celeste."

"Not for you. You can't tell me you'd be happy working for your father, locked behind a desk. Anyway, I wouldn't believe you if you did."

Ron grasped the chains on Celeste's swing, peering into her eyes, gently pulling her close until their faces almost touched.

She felt the warmth of his breath on her face and smelled the clean soap on his skin. Heat flushed through her body. The same heat she'd felt when he opened the door. The same heat when they hugged at the college. Only this time her loins were on fire.

"Tell me," he asked in a hoarse whisper. "How do you feel about me? Right now? Tell me true."

She closed her eyes, fighting the urge to kiss him, to wrap her legs around his slim hips and swing together, her hair falling onto his face as they sliced the air as one. Ron evoked in her what was missing with James: passion, fire, desire ... inspiration! She could deny it no more, despite her unspoken pledge to Ede, who was off on her own adventure in Hollywood. But Ron was right here, staring at her, waiting for her answer. Dare she let this moment slip away?

Without another thought, she reached for his neck, wrapping her arms tightly as he lifted her off the swing and collapsed softly to the ground, their hearts pounding, their bodies melding, rolling over the sand, onto the grass in one, long slow-motion tumble and then began kissing ... kissing, kissing kissing each other's eyes, nose, cheeks, ears, hair ...

again and again until they rolled again, back onto the sand, shrouded by the night and their blind passion, until they bumped into the post of the swings, halting with a thump. Startled, they both looked up and began to laugh, their limbs and hearts entwined, their breath as one. Clinging together as their breathing slowed, the nights hush filled their ears. Neither said a word and Celeste felt, for the first time in so very long, at peace. Slowly releasing their embrace, each laid back on the sand, their arms and legs touching, as they stared at the stars. No words did she want to speak or hear. Her mind was quiet. Her heart was happy. She felt open and curious and courageous. Everything Gamma talked about at the creek when she was only six. Everything she felt at sixteen, running hand-in-hand with Ron through the Meaden garden. It all added up, forming the word she dare not speak before: Love. It rang in her heart as lovely as the bells of Prague when riding the carriage to the Ball. The feeling she had most desired to know, to give, to understand … and it felt better than in her dreams. Lying next to him, eyes closed, every fiber of her body soothed, sweetened and encircled, she lifted her arms, reaching for the stars, and entwined her fingers above her head – when she felt the cold circle of platinum around her ring finger, and her eyes flew open.

What had she done? What had they done?

He felt her body stiffen. "What is it, Celeste?"

"This is crazy," she sat up.

He leaned toward her, still enraptured by their embrace. "Crazy good."

"No!" She said, pushing him back. "What were we thinking?"

He sat up, a slow grin on his lips. "What I've always been thinking – about you."

Her mind flashed on the same slow grin on James' face, at the party, as he stumbled away. She shuddered.

"Just like your brother."

"What?" Ron's grin vanished.

"This …" Celeste waved her hand between them. "What is this? The Meaden rule of lust? Get it while you can?"

Ron flushed. "No! I'm not like that. I don't do this with anyone, Celeste."

"Sure, that's what they all say," She countered, swiping the sand off her skirt.

"No," he squeezed her hand, his voice angered. "I don't. I haven't. I'm not like James at all. How could you think that of me? Grabbing any girl I can? I swear I don't. You are all I've ever thought about … all these years. You ... and me. Don't you see? You open my heart, Celeste, like no one ever has."

She stopped fussing, softened by his green, glowing eyes, but withdrew her hand from his grasp. She didn't trust what she was feeling, this overwhelming physical rush. Where did it come from? What did it mean? Was it true passion? Love? Or simply lust? *How could she know what was true?*

He spoke softly. "This is what the Heart Code is all about."

"What?" Her voice cracked.

"This feeling ... between us ... isn't it the heart's yes?"

She wanted to agree, but something stopped her. This rushing giddy ride into a blazing sunrise was what she'd been missing with James – but it was not the same as the heart code's yes. She felt a sudden clarity. No. This rush of feeling was not her heart's voice. It was passion, wonderful and consuming, but no matter how great her desires, Ron had dreams of his own. Dreams of places she could not go.

"No. The Heart Code isn't about romance. It's not about a tumble of feelings. It's about all kinds of love – for work, for family, for country, not just one person. It's about your path. And you know yours. What about the Squash circuit?"

"Come with me!"

She looked startled. "And do what?"

"Whatever you like. We'd be together. It's all that matters, right?"

No, the voice inside her automatically responded as she saw herself trailing after Ron from match to match. No different from following Ede to Hollywood. In both cases she'd be giving up on finding her own dream to follow theirs.

"No, it's not all that matters. I have dreams, too."

"And you can have them."

"How?"

Ron fumbled. "I don't know. We'll figure it out. But it's better than being with someone who doesn't love you like I do. Oh, sure, James can give you the big house and all, right now, but what we feel ... between us ... God, Celeste, we could take the world by storm!"

Why couldn't she just say yes? Plunge into his arms and life with all her heart and let the fur fly where it may. What was holding her back? She had so longed for the passion he aroused in her, but something was missing she couldn't name. Something calling from within ... an inner world reaching out.

"Ron, how do you feel about Squash?"

It was his turn to be startled. "What?"

"When you're playing, does it feel like you're living your heart's code?"

He blinked and involuntarily smiled. "Yes! I think so."

"How do you know?"

He blinked again. "Because I feel … alive … alert … more myself than anywhere else."

She nodded. "A passion of sorts?"

"Oh, yes!" he smiled wider. "I definitely feel passion for Squash."

"Even when you're losing?"

"Even more so."

"Why?"

"Because everything rallies inside me, everything slows down and I see it, clear as a bell and feel connected and open to something … bigger … I can't explain."

"No matter what else happens? Win, lose or draw?"

"No matter what else happens. When I'm playing squash, my heart is wide open."

"That's the feeling?"

"Yes! Just like I feel for you. And every day I want to live true to that feeling inside."

"So do I."

"So come with me!"

She slowly shook her head, picking up his hand in both of hers. "But if I do, I won't be living true to my feelings inside."

"No, no – I already said … whatever you want, we can do."

"And that's why it won't work. Because right now your Heart Code says you must play squash; which demands you be free, to go on the road, to see, to feel, to be open to wherever it takes you. You don't have a choice. You have to honor that true calling within. It's in your blood more than anything else. More than me."

"Not true!"

"Yes," she said quietly, "And the closest I have to that feeling, that fullness, right now, is wanting to create a family. It's not the same as how you feel about squash. Yet, I sense if I begin my family now, something more will come from that choice. Something I can't yet describe, but it feels like the right path, for right now, for me. I can't substitute your dreams for mine.

"But what about us?"

She slowly shook her head. "We've been dancing around each other since we were sixteen but never took the next step, until tonight! And while it feels more wonderful than I ever imagined, it also feels like we'd be running away to join the circus – all full of passion, but then what?"

Ron tried to interrupt but she softly placed her hand on his mouth.

"Passion comes in many forms. You can't make it up and you can't make someone else feel it. It comes from inside, from pursuing your dreams. Squash, the Needlery … a family. Each one of those takes time and concentration. I don't believe you can have everything all at once… so I have to choose. And right now, I choose to follow the dream in front of me … to begin a family of my own, with James. This isn't what you want to hear but I know it's what you need to trust … and follow the dream in front of you."

She cupped his face with her hands and kissed him, long and firm, pouring into his heart every bit of what she felt for him … like the whole universe was behind her, pulsating love. Pulling back, she swallowed hard and barely uttered, "You will always be my champion, Ron, but I'm so sorry, I've got to go." Scrambling up, she ran, speeding into the dark, two blocks to home and a million miles from where her passion for him might have led.

28 Clarity

April 1934

Running as fast as she could, from Ron and the feeling at the bottom of her spine, Celeste kept repeating to herself: "No good can come of it. No good at all." She slipped into the house, crept up the stairs and dove into bed, only to toss through the night, trying to escape the memory of his taut neck, angled jaw and green piercing eyes, searching for his place in her heart. In the morning, bleary-eyed and worn out, she sat in the bath and scoured away every fleck of memory, muttering "He isn't ready and might never be." But her protests did not quiet the thrilling memory of his hand on her back or the heat of his breath on her neck or the strength of his embrace. She kept the water cold but her body remained enflamed.

All day long, Celeste smoldered over last night's disaster. Those girls at the party made her feel small, unschooled and naïve, especially when James sailed past her without a hint of recognition. She'd seen their tutting glance and heard their smothered giggles. If she were a more experienced, more alluring woman, James would have taken her to those squash parties to show her off, untempted by any other. There must be something she lacked. Something she'd seen in the movie heroine, Clara Bow. The one they called the "It Girl," who turned heads and won hearts with flirty eyes, pursed lips, sly smiles, laughing grins and irrepressible joie de vivre. She then remembered the newspaper article by Elinor Glyn, about the *Quintessential Quality of It*. Determined to measure up to anyone in the Meaden set, she made a plan to find that article and learn everything there was to know about acquiring "It".

After a week's contemplation, Celeste made an announcement at supper: "I've decided to be married in New York City."

"New York City!" Myrtle could not have been more delighted. "Praise be in heaven – I've just booked the Hotel Carlyle for the bridal shower!"

Gamma and Martin exchanged surprised glances.

"The Carlyle in New York?" Martin asked. "Whatever for? Our friends live here."

"Most of James' friends and associates live there," Myrtle replied, pouring a neat swirl of gravy over her potatoes. "And since we're having a small wedding to which they won't be invited, it's only fair to host the shower closer to them."

"Says who?" Martin asked.

"Estelle," Gamma answered.

Myrtle shook her head. "No, that's wedding protocol." She turned to Celeste. "Ever since we had tea with James at the Carlyle, I've dreamed of serving their lovely Angel Pie Meringue." She looked at Martin and Gamma. "It's chock full of thickened sugar, egg and cream. Everyone will love it." she added, imagining a roomful of appreciative guests, savoring the luscious confection while Celeste opened a bounty of gifts. Myrtle turned back to Celeste. "Where do you want the ceremony? In a church or hotel?"

"Hotel, I think. It's more modern," Celeste answered instantly, replaying in her mind the movie scene of heroine Clara Bow at the Hotel Ritz. A hotel better suited the relaxed, devil-may-care attitude she'd studied among James' socialite friends. She'd lived a serious life for too long. It was time to break out and Manhattan felt more fitting to become Mrs. James Austin Meaden the Second; a woman who understood how to smooth her hair tight for the uptown crowd and wear it unpinned for a downtown soirée.

☙

Celeste's change of venue delighted James. When they gathered in his parent's parlor to sort out their plans, he hugged her "I never liked the idea of a quiet family wedding. A woman of your beauty should have a spotlight. What about the Plaza?"

"Or the Waldorf-Astoria?" Estelle offered, not caring except to have a proper standing.

"I was thinking the Ritz," Celeste said, imagining herself as Clara Bow, who brashly sashayed into the Ritz dining room, past all of grand society in her homespun dress. That's the kind of attitude she aspired.

"Any one is fine," Estelle said. "*If* they can accommodate us on such short notice. You realize the invitations must go out in two weeks?"

"Mother, with your magic, it won't be a problem." James quipped.

"Well, it might – given your expanded list. Why so many people, James? You had only a dozen or so before."

"For a New York wedding? Business, of course! A grand wedding will be marvelous publicity for the gallery opening."

Estelle shrugged, fingering the pin on her collar. She wanted no further complications.

"Before I make these inquiries, Celeste, are you sure this is what you want?"

Myrtle and Celeste nodded simultaneously.

"Alright then, I'll do my best – starting with the Ritz."

With everything in motion, Celeste felt a sudden compulsion to tidy up the things of her youth. She wanted a fresh start for her new life and packed away all her childhood treasures. Box after box she filled, stripping her bookshelves until she came to the top shelf where her old Birch Bark hat sat. Gently taking it down, she blew off the dust and held it over her head as she looked in the mirror, remembering the warm spring day with Gamma by the creek. "Someday," she said to her reflection, "Gamma will make these with my children, too." Carefully cushioning it into a hatbox, she stowed it away in her closet, along with the rest of her childish things.

She then tackled herself, becoming fastidious in her manners and dress … studying every detail of the movie stars, practicing their walks, talk, hairstyles and dress. She employed her elocution instructor to teach her the rapid, pointed patter of Noel Coward plays. And from watching the ladies in James' set, she dropped her guileless, straightforward ways and picked up the art of the quickly turned head, indicating displeasure without an utterance. It was astonishing how well it worked on her mother and James, although Estelle just looked at her with cold, narrowed eyes. And she didn't dare try it on Gamma.

Pushing further, she applied her keen observation skills to tailor her dress for various audiences. When accompanying James to Greenwich

Village, she added a touch of boho whimsy to her loose fitting dresses with scarves and drapes of beads that seemed to set the artists at ease. But with the uptown crowd, she chose fitted voiles, silks and satins with bosomy jewels. And with Estelle, she wore demure, high-collared blouses with an intricate pin at her neck. She even began keeping records of each person's favorite color and dressed accordingly.

At first she was only trying to make a good impression, to be familiar and pleasing, but soon realized the power it brought her: the success of quick acceptance and inclusion in the inner circle chit-chat, where everyone wanted to be. Then it became a game, being able to predict another's reaction based solely on her dress.

Along the way she also acquired an edgy temper, which threatened to spill at the slightest provocation. Gamma and her father both expressed concern at her unsteady temperament, but Myrtle shrugged off their alarm.

"With a squadron of details to attend, she's bound to be a bit snappish."

But Gamma was not assuaged. She could smell the fear driving Celeste's bizarre behavior, even though her granddaughter refused to discuss it.

"It's going to be fine, Gamma." Celeste insisted. "I'm just doing what you said: acting on my truth. Don't you worry a fingernail."

"Is not for me I worry, Celeste," Gamma replied, realizing it would be a while to wait before Celeste's true feelings resurfaced.

With Myrtle's grateful compliance and the precision of a drill sergeant, Estelle oversaw the ongoing details of the wedding. Anticipating the looming deadline for the invitation, she had them pre-printed with space left open for the date, time and hotel. But seven weeks before the wedding, with no suitable hotel able to accommodate their party, her back was to the wall and she summoned James home to meet with Celeste and Myrtle in the Howe's parlor.

"If the invitations are to arrive six weeks prior, we must make a decision today."

Panic rose in Celeste's throat. "It doesn't have to be the Ritz," she nearly cried.

"I only wanted a hotel to remind me of Prague – where James and I first met."

Hearing Celeste's cry, Gamma emerged from the conservatory. "I don't mean to intrude, but what about Narodni Budova?"

They all turned to her with quizzical expressions.

"Gamma, you needn't worry …" Myrtle began.

Estelle waved her quiet. "At this date, any suggestion is welcome. Where did you say?

"The Bohemian National Hall, is called Narodni Budova, on 73rd and 2nd Avenue. With a lovely ballroom on top floor. My husband and I make members, years ago. Maybe they can help."

"That's just across town from me!" James said. "What's it like?"

"Elegant. The ballroom is double high, and built nearly same time as Hotel Archduke Stephan … where first you meet," Gamma looked from James to Celeste. "Your grandfather and I, we dance there often. A place you like, I think."

With high hopes, James and Celeste set off immediately for the city while Gamma called ahead, making arrangements for a showing with the manager. Returning that evening, they were giddy as they joined their parents and Gamma at the Meadens for cocktails and supper.

"Oh, Gamma, it's gorgeous!" Celeste flounced on the couch, hugging her, then turned to her mother and Estelle in the chairs across from them. "It's an enormous building, nearly a whole city block. And the ballroom's double height windows reminded us of Spanish Hall," Celeste giggled, glancing at James by the bar with his father.

"Where we first danced," James added, delivering a tray of martinis to the ladies. "We both thought it would be a fitting way to parlay the magic of our first meeting on our wedding day. Wouldn't you agree, Mother?"

"Do they have a date in May?" Estelle asked, carefully lifting her glass.

"The last Sunday."

"Sunday? Who would come on a Sunday?" Myrtle asked.

"Anyone lucky to be asked." Jack mumbled to Martin, who both sat across the room from the ladies, knowing this was not their match to play.

"And you didn't tell us, Gamma, they had a roof garden, too!" Celeste squealed. "A perfect spot for the ceremony."

"On the roof? Out of doors?" Estelle was strident. "What if it rains?"

"Oh, well then, the ballroom is enormous." Celeste explained, fingering the filigreed pin on her collar, an engagement gift from Estelle. "We could easily partition off one section for the ceremony and …" She paused, looking at James.

He winked at her. "Or we could do it up grand and get married on stage!"

Myrtle looked confused and Estelle aghast.

"A stage? In a ballroom?" Estelle's voice sliced into Celeste, causing her to flush from head to toe, not knowing what to say. But James was unhindered.

"Hell yes! Those Bohemians know how to do it up right. We wouldn't even need a procession. Just open up the curtains – heavy, velvet, red curtains, Mother, dripping with gold fringe – and voila! The bride and groom revealed – ready to be hitched."

Not a sound was uttered as everyone looked to Estelle for her reaction.

After a long pause she replied. "Not amusing, James," tapping her neck pin.

Undeterred, James swept the air with his hand. "Not trying to be. And there's more good news. The room can hold eight hundred! What a grand bash we can host! A smashing party! The pip of all pips! It'll be the talk for months, hell, the whole year!"

Jack sat up in his chair. "Eight hundred? Have you gone mad?"

"No Father, it's perfect. All our social obligations met in one fell swoop: business, gallery launch and marriage – in reverse order, of course." James winked again at Celeste and looked around the room, assuming everyone's agreement.

Estelle sat stock still as Jack got up, heading for the bar while Martin's foot twitched and Myrtle began to hiccup, unsure if she should express her delight before Estelle commented. But only Gamma noticed the hooded glaze that had come over Celeste's eyes, as she repeatedly turned the stem of her martini glass around and around.

"I'll have to sleep on it." Estelle finally replied. "Let's go into supper."

Although pleased with having his son back in the fold and Celeste joining the family, the rush and bustle of the wedding plans did not feel right to Jack Meaden. Shrugging off his silk bathrobe, he sat on the edge of his bed, looking at Estelle, propped among her pillows, reading.

"Stelly, how did this wedding transpire from a small family ceremony to a New York bohemian bash for eight hundred?"

Estelle shut her book. "Every young bride changes her mind. And you must certainly understand James' business inclinations."

Shaking his head, Jack slipped his feet under his covers. "I don't like it. Not one bit."

"Well, neither do I, but it is their wedding, isn't it?"

"Are you sure this is what Celeste wants? She got awfully quiet after cocktails."

"I'm sure our reaction didn't help. See what happens over the next couple days."

⟨⟩

In the morning, Jack took a detour on the way to his Hartford office. As a rule he stayed out of the social fray, but discombobulated feelings forced him to seek out Gamma.

"Are we alone?" he abruptly asked when she opened her front door.

Gamma nodded, stepping aside to let him in. "Yah, they go. Come."

He strode past her, into the front hall, before turning back, hat in hand. "Gamma, what in blazes is going on? Can you make any sense of this ... this circus?"

Taking Jack's hat, Gamma set it on the hall table and led him to the conservatory. "Even a circus has more order. Come. Sit." Closing the doors behind them, she sat by her tea tray.

"Right you are about that. Right as rain. What in Sam Hill are we going to do?"

Pouring tea and adding two sugars, she handed the cup to Jack. "We wait."

Jack's head bobbed in agitation. "What do you mean – wait?" He didn't wait. He was a fix-it man. "Did you see the girl last night, a mouse all through dinner? You can't believe she likes the idea. But all James can see is the publicity it will garner his damn gallery. Why in hell did I ever agree to that? And Estelle – right behind him, pulling out all the stops, orchestrating this affair as if it were a royal wedding. We've got to do something before he ... before she ..."

"Before he or she what?" Gamma inserted. "Make a mistake? Marry the wrong person? Find their way later in life? And who is it you are hoping to protect? My granddaughter or is James your most concern?"

Jack was dumbfounded. "No ... I meant the changes ... the size and scope of the wedding. You know how much I like Celeste but I..." his voice trailed off. Up until that moment he had admitted to no one, especially himself, his distrust of the match because it was he who wanted the girl – the semblance of Gamma – to infect his family with good spirits.

Gamma laughed at his expression. "So what you think then? Is good match?"

Jack slowly shook his head, feeling caught in quicksand. "I – I – think she'd be good for James, but … yes, I have some doubts. But then, no one thought I was right for Estelle but it turned out quite right. Better than right. And now that James has …"

In a strangely sardonic voice, Gamma finished Jack's thought. "And now since James does your business bidding, how can you interfere with his choice?"

"Well, I suppose," he said quietly. "That, and Estelle …" His voice tapered off and again Gamma finished his thought.

"And with Estelle's dream complete, your life, too, is easier." Reaching over, Gamma took the untouched teacup out of Jack's hand. "No decision is without tradeoff. But you right. Is not ours to make. So we must wait. Until one or other ask for help. And if they ask, maybe they listen to what we say. But until then …" Gamma finished with a shrug and stood up, ushering the befuddled Jack on his way.

It took only a few days more before Celeste sought out Gamma. Returning early from the women's club meeting, she searched the house and found her in the garden, her gloved hands drawing a hoe firmly across the damp April soil.

As Celeste walked onto the porch, Gamma glanced up and saw the strain on her pale face. "Mmm, smart suit. Ladies meeting over so soon?" she asked, savoring the quiet when Myrtle was out of the house.

Celeste looked down at her new, dark-blue wool suit with white piping on the lapel, as she removed her matching hat and gloves. "No," she said, walking slowly down the porch steps to sit on the stone bench alongside the flowerbeds. Tilting back her head, she welcomed the sun's warmth on her face. She would have so preferred to have spent the afternoon with Gamma, preparing the black soil for the riot of spring color that would soon come. "When Mrs. Mackle turned to get more tea," she said quietly, "I just … slipped away."

Gamma glanced again at Celeste's sad face and slumped shoulders but did not stop tilling. "Well, the ladies must be a-gaggle over the news. Now, who is not invited to this wedding?"

Celeste lifted her head. "That's the problem, Gamma. It's become … enormous … more people than I've known my entire life, and most of them strangers."

Gamma nodded, still tilling.

"Gamma, am I doing the right thing?"

"What thing is that, child?"

Celeste straightened her shoulders, struck by the question. She meant the wedding plans but her mind suddenly flooded with thoughts of Ron. Had Gamma guessed? She hadn't seen him since that night at the swings. Not on the street or at his house. Not that she wanted to, having no idea what to say, but she kept looking for him. Her nostrils tingled as her throat began closing. "The ... wedding ... thing," she insisted, choking on her words.

Laying down her hoe, Gamma pulled off her canvas gloves and sat alongside Celeste. "Blow your nose – will clear your head."

Celeste slipped a handkerchief from her pocket and wiped her nose. "Eight hundred people, Gamma," she half whispered. "What have I agreed to?"

Gamma shrugged. "More lavish the wedding, more insecure the bride."

Celeste's mouth dropped open. "You think I'm insecure?

Gamma shrugged again. "You want my agreement ... or truth?"

Celeste quickly turned her head in disapproval, but Gamma did not react. Staring at her feet, Celeste acquiesced. "Truth. You're the only one who tells me what you really think."

"Or maybe you not listen with all senses. Tell me first: What you think of big show?"

Celeste drew in a breath, letting it out with a rush, causing her voice to pitch higher and higher. "Every time I imagine all those people in one room, I shudder. And then there's Mother, nattering about who will be there and how important they are and what it can mean for my future. Honestly, it's terrifying. I'm awake all night worrying about saying the wrong thing, acting the wrong way. What do I know? I'm not like those people. I get the feeling my wedding day could turn into one gigantic disaster ... and sink to the depths, like the Titanic!"

Gamma nudged Celeste's shoulder. "OK, OK now, no panic. I know how hard you work to make things right; your clothes, your speech. I see – how you try to fit with James and his friends."

Celeste did not feign surprise at Gamma's observation. She was rather proud of her efforts. "Yes, I had to. I needed to, for James' sake."

"Only for James? Not for your sake, too?"

"Without him, I wouldn't even know them."

"Maybe, but tell me this: Without James, you think they like you?"

"Me? OH, I don't know. Maybe. But how would we ever meet?"

"Och, so many ways it can happen, but not my point. Let's say you meet them, without James. You think you like them? And would you need them to like you?"

"No," Celeste instantly replied. "I have my own friends, but since I'm marrying James, I need to be accepted by them."

"Augh, there it is again."

"What?"

"The need problem."

"The need – what? What are you saying?"

"Need: Is big problem for many people – young and old alike."

Celeste's eyes narrowed, defensively. "Speak plain English, Gamma."

"What means 'need'?" Gamma continued. "In plain English it mean: necessity, compulsion, obligation – a *requirement* for life and happiness." Gamma dusted off her skirt. "The same as air and water and food, I suppose. So I ask you – is the same with James' friends? You *need* them for your life and happiness?"

Celeste's lips twisted. "Gamma! He's going to be my husband. Isn't that a wife's job? To need her husband's good favor? To be needed by him in return? Isn't that what makes a good marriage?"

"*Phefff,*" Gamma released a burst of air through her lips. "Your grandfather's love and company I want, not need. From very first day, when I see his goodness, I know I want to share a life with him. Without that, I turn around and find my own way. If I need him for my happiness, soon I be his slave and that –" Gamma pulled on her canvas gloves, "could never be." Rising, Gamma returned to her tilling. "But today, perhaps marriage is different. Only you can say."

Celeste rose, following her to the next patch of soil. "No, Gamma, I can't say. I've never been married before. It's just what everyone says: 'Oh, I need him so.' You hear it all the time in the movies." She put her hands on her heart and pantomimed a swoon.

Gamma smiled. "But life is not movies. So what you say? Need you James?"

Turning around in a full circle, Celeste stretched out her arms, looking to the sky. She didn't want to think about that again. She'd made her computation and James was the one.

"Need and want gets so mixed up." Celeste finally answered. "Gamma, I know I want children. No question there. And I'm already twenty, so James seems to be the right match for what I want, instead of waiting for –" She cut herself off, pacing to the other side of the garden patch. She turned back and spoke in a gust. "Instead of waiting for someone better to come along – who may never come – who may not even exist. So if I don't marry James now, I'll probably become an old maid, living with my parents, working for charities and my father's store … destined to become a crazy old hen like mother, feeding on gossip of other people's lives instead of living my own – that other's want to gossip about! So while it might not be perfect, I do need to take this chance – just like you did. James is my boat across the sea and I'm going to hop on board and hope for the best. Maybe it will be as good as your life. Maybe not. But at least it will be secure and have most of the things I love."

Celeste raised her hand to fend off any objections. "I know, I know – there are many ways to skin a cat. I think of Ede in Hollywood and how I could go out there. But Gamma, I *do* want children. Not just one or two, but a houseful of babies … and pets too. Cats sleeping on the radiators and dogs at my feet and birds – inside and out. And I want you and Mama to help make big Sunday meals and gather the family around the table, making more noise than I've ever heard before … although not by eight hundred strangers in a Bohemian Ballroom on my wedding day."

Gamma's snorted laugh caused Celeste to pause and laugh as well … the deep, bright, rounded laughter of unexpected discovery.

"Now *that's* what I *don't* need Gamma. That's the part that has me most worried. *Who* is that girl getting married on a stage at Bohemian National Hall?"

They both laughed harder, doubling over, leaning on each other.

"Can you imagine? Why don't I just put on a crown and a twenty foot train?" Celeste quipped, primping her hair and twirling around, flipping an imaginary gown behind her. "Oh the gaucheness of it all!"

At that moment, Gamma saw the uncertain girl of Celeste fade away and the self-assured, self-effacing woman emerge, who knew herself and her wants without pretension or permission. She had been peeking out over the last year or two but had disappeared completely since her courtship with James began in earnest.

"I like this," Gamma said serenely. "Your voice full and eyes clear. Now I hear the answer to your question."

Celeste stopped short. "What is it?"

"No big wedding for you."

"But what about James?"

"What about him? He ask you to marry, right? So marry as you want. To your comfort and pace: for wedding, for marriage, for your many children and pets. Celeste – to live life well is to live life true. Honor what beckons *you*."

Celeste blinked, feeling a moment of grace as her body flooded with peace. She felt, perhaps for the first time with such clarity, what Gamma described as the heart's nod. As clear as the first whiff of spring and the freshness of rain, she unmistakably heard her heart say: "Yes."

29 Conquests
April – May 1934

Rejuvenated by her new importance at the Social Club, Myrtle floated home from the meeting to find Celeste and Gamma in the kitchen, preparing supper.

"What a glorious day! I could barely keep up. Everyone wanted to know every little detail about the wedding." Myrtle basked, removing her gloves and unpinning her hat. "Where did you go off to so early, Celeste? Everyone was asking."

Scrubbing carrots at the sink, Celeste took a deep breath. "Mama, I've decided to cancel the wedding in New York. I want a small ceremony here in town."

Myrtle whirled. "You can't. It's too late. The invitations have been posted."

"Not until tomorrow. I've had them stopped," Celeste countered.

"But the expense! We'll lose the deposits!"

"Only on the hall, and Gamma thinks they'll give most of it back since it was for a Sunday. And we'll still need the florist and caterer in Gladdenbury."

"But the Meaden's business associates? Surely they've heard by now."

"With all the invitations they receive, it won't be noticed. Besides, they'll be invited to the gallery opening, which they'll like a lot more, anyway. They won't have to bring a gift!"

Myrtle's hat bobbled. "But ... but ... what will everyone think? Our friends? Our customers? The Meadens? We'll look daffy."

Celeste laughed. "Our friends will understand. Our customers' curiosity will bring them to the store, which means more sales for us. And as far as our in-laws go … they're already daffy. We're just adding ribbons to that hat!"

Gamma softly snorted and Celeste smirked. She felt a great relief from her decision and nothing was going to sway her. She wasn't a needy schoolgirl counting her lucky stars. James offered her means to higher society and commerce, and she knew the hows and ways of the heart. When commingled by their union, it was very likely they'd create something better and stronger than either now possessed.

Myrtle glared at Gamma as she snapped beans at the kitchen table. "Did you do this?"

Celeste turned from the sink. "No, Mama. It's my wedding, my decision."

Finally removing her hat, Myrtle sank onto a chair. "But it's not like anything we've talked about. Have you spoken to James?"

"I left a message with his secretary. I suspect he'll object, but he'll come around. It's best we start simply," Celeste spoke softly as she cut up the carrots, the knife slicing rhythmically. "There's no reason to make such a fuss. We have a whole lifetime for that." She glanced at her mother and suddenly saw the paleness of her face and the wisps of her hair standing on end. Her edges were clearly frayed and close to unraveling. Setting down the paring knife, Celeste dried her hands on her apron and sank to her knees in front of her mother, clasping her hands.

"Mama, please, listen to me. I know you worry what people may think. I did too, for too long. But I don't want to care anymore and neither should you. At the end of May, I will be married to the eldest son of the town's most prominent family. It's a dream come true for you and a new chapter for me. A good chapter. That's all that matters, isn't it? So be happy for that. Who cares how it happens? We're all getting what we want and the rest is just … poppycock!"

This bold, new Celeste surprised Myrtle to silence. As much as she wanted to protest, she was unable to disagree with her logic. Slowly, she nodded, wiping away a tear.

❦

Later that night, after Celeste spoke with James in New York, news of the wedding venue changes rippled through town, courtesy of the operator who'd placed Celeste's call. After James and Celeste rang off, the woman dutifully reported to coworkers and a few well-placed friends that James was very upset by Celeste's decision. She described in detail how he pleaded for her reconsideration, citing the many important people who'd be affected. And how Celeste held her ground, telling him if he still wished to marry her, it must be this way. With alacrity, the news sizzled across dinner tables and over fences and by the dawn's milk delivery, everyone in Gladdenbury knew the big New York wedding was off.

⌒

While many sympathized with Myrtle's disappointment, Estelle was much relieved. She didn't need the fuss and bother. But she was surprised by James' flushed anxiety when he arrived home that evening to reconstruct their plans.

"What has you in knots?" she asked several times.

He finally admitted his agitation. "The gallery publicity. I had so much riding on the wedding. It was a brilliant pre-launch gambit."

Estelle blinked, her mind in high gear. "It still can be. News is news." She rose from her desk and paced the parlor, twirling her hand in the air as she developed an idea. "Rather than news about a grand wedding, we can make news about an intimate family wedding, feeding all the little details that make people titter. With your social notoriety, the shy-bride angle might work quite well – making the press salivate for more. And ... if we invite the right sort of someone ... someone scintillating, who can stir the pot until it boils over with anticipation ... all the while sprinkling mentions of the gallery's progress ... we'll have them right where we want: panting for the wedding news and impatient for the gallery's grand opening ... the day after your honeymoon finishes!" Estelle brushed one hand off the other. "It's a recipe no one could resist. They'll gorge on it. Now let me think ... who fits that bill?"

Before James could respond, Estelle snapped her fingers. "Elinor Glyn!"

"The novelist?"

"Novelist, essayist, screenwriter, socialite. Without her, there'd be precious little to gossip about in Hollywood."

"Would she come?"

"Would she come?! Aunt Lucy was on the Titanic with Elinor's sister ... which led father to make some rather favorable financial dealings for Elinor's husband before he died. He was much older than her. So, I assure you, if I ask, she'll come."

Elinor Glyn telegraphed her reply the day the invitation arrived. "For a young man almost more notorious than me, how could I resist? Delighted to attend, with bells on."

○

Uncertain how Celeste would take the news, James cautiously broached the topic as they sampled wedding cake at the town bakery.

Seated at a table, Celeste orchestrated the tasting. "Lemon, angel food and yellow, each with buttercream icing." She informed James. "But if you'd like something more exotic, the baker said he'd be happy to accommodate."

"Celeste, I have to tell you something."

"You want a different cake?"

"No, about the wedding. Mother's invited someone special."

"Who?" Celeste plunged her fork into the yellow cake and held up a sample for him to taste.

"An old family friend … a celebrity of sorts," he said, obligingly eating the cake.

"That's nice. Anyone I know?" she asked, preparing a forkful of lemon cake.

"I don't suppose. Mother insisted. A family obligation, actually – Elinor Glyn."

Holding the fork midair, Celeste's mouth dropped open. "*The* Elinor Glyn? The author of 'It' is coming to *our* wedding?" Her fork clattered to the plate. "Oh good glory gracious, how did you make this happen?"

"You don't think it's too showy?"

"Are you daft? Elinor Glyn is every woman's heroine! I've read all of her newspaper essays and her movie – 'It' – with Clara Bow, is my favorite! Oh my heavens, I'll be Clara Bow after all! I can't believe I get to meet her, at my wedding!" Leaning over, Celeste smooched James on the cheek in the glare of a photographer's flash, who'd been waiting by the bakery counter for just that shot to accompany the news about Ms.Glyn, which Estelle had neatly seeded. The small mention and photo in the Hartford Society pages soon traveled to New York, where more reporters contacted Estelle for the scoop on the Meaden-Howe wedding.

○

After accounting for all the family members, plus special guests, the invitation list came to 100, which was far too many for the Howes' house but quite suitable for the Meadens'.

"Especially with the glorious blooms of the garden in late May," Estelle said.

Myrtle was disappointed but kept her lips buttoned because Celeste was delighted. "Mother, we've got enough to prepare without the fuss on our doorstep," she consoled.

Accordingly, the wedding shower guest list was also trimmed. But when word got around about the event, gifts began arriving at the Hotel Carlyle from many Meaden friends and clients. As it was another perfect publicity opportunity, Estelle arranged for a well-placed mention in the New York society pages.

> *Two weeks before the wedding of Mr. and Mrs. Martin Howe's daughter, Celeste, of Gladdenbury, Connecticut to James Austin Meaden the second of New York City and Gladdenbury Connecticut, a bridal shower was held at the Hotel Carlyle. Guests were treated to the Carlyle's famous Angel Pie Meringue along with cucumber and watercress tea sandwiches. As the Howe-Meaden wedding will be a family-only affair at the end of May, with some notable exceptions, including the author Elinor Glyn, the guest list for the bridal shower was limited to approximately 50. However, when news of the celebration circulated, well-wishers were prompted to action, and upon Miss Howe's arrival at the hotel, over 400 gifts awaited her attention.*

With their dining room and parlor and conservatory now covered with gifts, Celeste was doubly grateful to have the wedding ceremony and reception at the Meadens'. But she still had to resist all suggestions for a grand affair. Myrtle wanted a dinner and Jack wanted a platform for dancing and Estelle kept offering décor ideas, including swags of fabric running though the orchards where Celeste hoped to set the tables. Keeping true to her desire for a simple celebration, she chose a wedding luncheon instead of a formal dinner and tried to distract her mother and

Estelle by asking them to devise the menu, which they reviewed during her fitting at the Hartford Bridal Shoppe.

"We thought to start with a special potage," Estelle began. "Turtle soup."

"To take the edge off a hungry tummy," Myrtle quickly added.

Struggling to keep her face serene and unperturbed, Celeste imagined a pot of turtle claws and snouts while the seamstress pinned the sides of her dress.

"You're losing weight," she noted through a mouthful of pins.

"Even more at the thought of turtle soup!" Celeste replied.

"Followed by mushroom caps filled with cheese soufflé," Estelle proceeded, looking up from her notebook and nodding to Myrtle.

"To delight the tongue," she offered, as Estelle had suggested.

The menu was already more complex than Celeste desired, but she said nothing.

"Then veal Veronique," Estelle revealed. "Sautéed to perfection and laced with parsley and grapes ..."

"That burst in the mouth – a sweetness to counter the meat's savory flavorings."

Myrtle's enthusiasm was almost uncontainable as she imagined how the food would be received on the palate.

Celeste, who had stopped eating for fear of not fitting into her wedding dress, felt her stomach churn and dropped her head, counting the beads on her sleeve to distract herself.

"Head up, please," the seamstress cautioned, and Celeste straightened while Estelle described the fluffy almond rice, fresh vegetable salad and salt sticks. Then Myrtle described the finishing touches of champagne parfait before the chocolate wedding cake.

"Chocolate?" Celeste was surprised. "We decided on lemon."

"Chocolate is his favorite, dear. Do you mind terribly?" Estelle blithely inquired.

Celeste felt her temper rise. It was rude of Estelle to override her decision, *their* decision, on such an important occasion. Gathering up her skirt, she spun on her heel, nearly knocking over the seamstress to confront Estelle. But when she faced her piercing eyes, Celeste quickly turned back, her heart pounding and mouth dry. She would one day have to deal with a mother-in-law who was far more formidable than her own mother, but this was not the time or place. In a matter of days, she reasoned, it would be she would decide about all of their cakes, for the rest of their lives.

❧

A week before the wedding, with most of the elements tucked and tied into place, one more hurdle had to be cleared: where they would live as husband and wife.

"Do you really *want* to take over your great-grandfather's house?" Celeste asked James again, not convinced of his previous answer. His voice was bold but not his enthusiasm. As they stepped into the vestibule of the old Victorian, she waved away the dust waltzing in beams of sunlight and worried about how much time she'd be spending here alone, particularly after the children began arriving. While her mother thought the manse was a marvelous idea: situated on the Green, just down the street from Estelle and Jack's, and almost as big; Celeste considered the bigness a burden. She liked a cozy house, with everything near at hand. Here, the kitchen was miles away from the parlor, and ten bedrooms were far more than she'd ever know how to use. And it was already filled with Empire-style furniture that was not her taste, and it had that old, musty scent from no use in twenty years, since Estelle's grandfather died. Houses get sad when left alone too long, and she didn't want to begin her marriage in a sad house.

"Look at the bones!" James crowed, trying to infuse his voice with authentic sounding enthusiasm despite his own reluctance to move into the house. But Estelle had packaged the house with the gallery and marriage, and a deal was a deal. "Great-Gramps had a flair for architecture, spared no expense. Look at the curve on that wood!" he pointed to the ceiling beam, echoing the broad, elegant swoosh of the stair banister. "I marvel at how they made that."

Shaking her head, Celeste stepped into the parlor, her eyes adjusting to the dimness. The room was enormous, running the full length of the mansion and half as wide, filled with furniture covered in white sheets and rugs rolled up, stacked in front of the double-wide stone fireplace. "Like stepping into someone else's old shoes," she complained, loud enough for James to hear in the hallway.

He joined her. "Did you know he commissioned that stained glass on the stairway from a Bohemian artist?"

She shook her head again. "So you said. It's just …" At the far end of the room, she noticed the wall was completely draped by heavy curtains. Tapping across the parquet floor, she searched for the cord on the right side and gave it a yank. The drapes parted, flinging more dust into the air but also revealed a wall of glass, almost floor to ceiling. She kept pulling and discovered an enormous bay window with a window seat, from wall to wall, overlooking an overgrown garden outside.

"Well, now!" she exclaimed, turning to James with a smile, the first one today.

"Well, now! Does that make it work?" James replied.

"This is glorious." She said, turning to look at the long room, illuminated by sunlight, and, for the first time, began to imagine herself and her brood, tucked about with books and needlecraft and paints and tea and laughter.

Seeing her face soften and open, James slid behind her with a warm embrace, gently rocking her as they gazed at the grand room that would soon become the heart of their home.

"Gramps really loved this room. Every celebration, we had right here. I know if he'd had the chance to meet you, he'd be tickled pink that you were the one to bring his vision back to life."

"*Our* vision." Celeste corrected.

"Yes, our vision," James ceded. "Because we can do anything we want with it – new drapes, paint, furnishings – whatever you like. Mother's just going to have it cleaned up while we're away on honeymoon. But after that, it will be exactly as you like."

"I'll like to have you here, more often than not," Celeste countered.

James pressed his lips together, nodding. "That is our agreement. I'll only stay in New York when I have a late meeting. Or, you can join me."

"Until the children come."

James nodded again, squeezing her hard. "Yes! Think about the children! Can't you already hear their feet pattering up and down? Oh, Celeste, this is a family house! I can actually feel the bedrooms sighing with relief! Rejuvenated at the thought of the beautiful family that will soon fill its rafters with squeals and laughter!"

Celeste involuntarily shuddered and quickly turned to face him. "So you're in this for real? This is really what you want? All of it? The house, kids, noise, mess, garden, pets?

"Pets?"

"Oh, you bet! Lots of them. All kinds of them." Looking out the bay window, she pointed. "Look, we even have room for chickens and goats."

James' face froze, his eyes wide opened, his mouth in an O.

Celeste laughed. "Yes, goats. And you, mister, will learn how to milk them! This will be our own little Bohemia … from stained glass to barnyard. Now, all I need is a shed with a grass roof."

"All you need now is to kiss me and seal this deal." James said, pulling her close and kissing her laughing mouth.

She folded into his arms, releasing her resistance, letting him lift her up and swing her around and around the room, both laughing, both hopeful, both happy to have conquered the misgivings that began the day … and vaulted the final hurdle of their marriage plans.

30 *Connubial Mist*

May 26, 1934

The day before the wedding, everyone gathered at the Meadens' for a late-morning rehearsal and a luncheon on the back lawn, excepting the groomsmen, who would be departing for the bachelor party.

Celeste sat at Estelle's antique vanity in her chintz-lined dressing room watching Beatrice weave together a bouquet of ribbons from her wedding shower for her mock bouquet as they waited for their cue. With the door open, they could hear Estelle directing everyone downstairs until Katie, the house maid, came to the door and quietly said, "Ready for the bride."

Quickly assuming their places at the top of the long, curving stairs leading to the grand hallway, Celeste found her legs twitching without her consent.

"Alright Beatrice, come down," Estelle said. "Slowly now ... not like a herd of cows."

Glancing back at Celeste, Beatrice rolled her eyes and softly mooed.

"Come, come," Estelle called. "Don't dawdle. The boys have to get off to New York."

Holding the ribbon bouquet in front of her mouth, Celeste tried to hide her giggles at Beatrice's exaggerated sashay down the stairs.

"That's quite enough, Bea," Estelle chided. "Don't you dare pull any of your stunts tomorrow. All right, Celeste, when Beatrice reaches the doorway to the parlor, you begin. Step, hold, step, hold. Right. Lovely."

Suddenly noticing Martin was standing on the wrong side of the stairs, Estelle hooked his arm, pulling him over. "Father of the bride on the left," Estelle said, tapping his shoulders twice. "Now please remember! For tomorrow I'll be seated and won't be here to remind you." Estelle glanced up the stairs. "Eyes up, Celeste."

Lifting her head, Celeste caught a glimpse of Ron, standing just inside the parlor doors. His green eyes stared at her intently. They drew her in like a magnet and her body heated in a gust. They'd not spoken since the night at the swings. She looked down, trying to regain her composure, but she couldn't help looking up again. Still he stared, his eyes boring into hers. *What was he trying to do?* Distracted, her heel caught the step and she faltered, lunging forward, screaming and grabbing the heavy wooden banister just in time to avert a tumble, her ribbon bouquet floating away to the vestibule floor.

"Celeste!" her father cried, dashing up the stairs.

"What happened?" her mother yelled, popping out of her seat in the parlor.

Without a word, James swiftly strode into the hallway and up the steps, three at a time.

Recovering her balance, Celeste kept her eyes on Ron as he quietly slipped into the hall, picked up the fallen bouquet and held it high for her hand. Their eyes locked, their fingers touched, their hearts sparked, before James grabbed Celeste by her shoulders, crushing her to him.

Martin arrived at her side, and Myrtle stood at the bottom of the steps screeching: "Are you alright? Are you alright? What happened? Oh my goodness, is this staircase safe?"

Celeste turned her head away from James, her eyes following Ron as he stepped backward into the parlor and out of sight.

"I'm fine," Celeste protested, pushing them all away. "My heel just got …" She leaned on the banister, calling to Estelle. "I'm sorry. Can we keep going from here?"

But Estelle insisted they begin again, to secure the proper rhythm, and shooed them all back to their original places, lining up the groomsmen in the hallway, ready to march down the makeshift aisle into the parlor, which had been emptied of furniture and lined with rows of chairs. Returning to the top of the stairs, Celeste tried to catch Ron's eye as he stood at the front of the line, but he would not look back.

⌒

After the rehearsal was completed to Estelle's satisfaction, Celeste kissed James goodbye and stood on the porch, watching the Meaden men motor off to the bachelor party in New York City. She giggled at their spirited yelps, waving until the sleek Packard limousines turned the corner and were out of sight. Then she took a breath, not wanting to join the luncheon in the back yard just yet, as food repulsed her and chit-chat seemed even worse. Plus, she felt a circle of sadness squeeze her chest, which she didn't understand. Meandering back into the house, she slipped into the first room off the hallway, a dimly lit side parlor she'd never been in before, and dropped onto an overstuffed chair, tucking up her feet and leaning back, hiding from anyone passing by, and gave herself a long, pitying sigh. There she was, on the eve of her wedding, without her best friend to un-jangle her nerves. Beatrice had kindly agreed to be her matron of honor and did her best to fill the role, but no one gathered on the Meadens' back lawn could match what Ede did for her. She sighed again, looking about the dark, heavily draped room. *What is this room,* she wondered? It was one of the few in the Meaden mansion she'd never seen. For some reason or another, James always brushed by it. As her eyes adjusted to the dimness, she saw a museum take shape. A perfect representation of 1890 Victorian décor, with wood-trimmed furniture, potted palms, identically bound books, gold-leaf frames and … portraits. She sat up, looking at each wall, completely covered with dozens of portraits. No landscapes, no still-life fruits, no horses; only gold-brushed frames, encasing stern-faced men and women, in various eras of formal dress, staring at her with strict eyes and not a hint of smile on their lips.

"Jeepers," Celeste shivered. No wonder James steered clear of this room. Who'd want to answer to them? But her very next thought wondered if they weren't the reason for his formality and stiffness? In spite of his devil-may-care attitude and independent nature, was he really trying to measure up to their unspoken yet demanding principles?

"Did you *even know* how to laugh?" she spontaneously asked the portraits, then glanced over her shoulder. She could hear the luncheon party bubbling in the distance. Looking back at the paintings, she wished she could tickle them into a grin. Then she shook her finger in the air. "You may have gotten him, but I promise you, you won't get his children," she warned, adding, "And if at all possible, I'll find the smiles you doused in James, too." She nodded resolutely and suddenly felt buoyed. Laughter was something she *could* actually do; bring laughter to his world as he's never known before. The thought rang so true, she felt her body ripple, tip to toe. *Laughter* would be her measure, not the rules lying behind these grim faces. And she didn't need anyone else's opinion on that matter. In that very moment, feeling empowered by her own resolve, she decided to spend her last evening as a maiden by herself, to consider what other truths might make her chosen new life feel good to the bone. Finding her mother and Estelle on the back porch, she feigned a headache, made her regrets and left, slipping over the hill, out of sight and through the backyards of her girlhood to home, to enjoy the soon lost freedom of thinking and feeling in a bath, alone.

To ensure a civilized bachelor party, Jack Meaden took charge of the evening's arrangements. After the rehearsal, he transported James, his best man, four brothers and himself to Gallagher's steak house on west 52nd street, where they met up with several other friends. He had selected the restaurant for its proximity to a dance hall down the street. One he occasionally visited with colleagues and clients desiring a night's prowl. He liked it because of its upscale reputation, particularly the chorus girls who came on their nights off from a show and could actually dance. No fool to his son's proclivities with women, Jack was taking no chances for error on the night before the wedding.

After the hearty meal, cigars and cognac, and imbued with boisterous spirits, the men swaggered into the dance hall, encamped at a table, ordered a round of drinks and toasted the groom before each one slid away to find a girl to twirl. Staying at the table, Jack watched the young men scatter across the room. He was pleased with his choice and congratulated himself on making a good, safe bet the night before his son finally settled down … until he spied James's former sweetheart, Kate, dancing with a man in the middle of the room.

Soaking in a hot bath, Celeste kept thinking about the Meaden portraits in the parlor. Their haunting scowls and stiff poses were so off-putting. It was the vogue of the day, of course, but it didn't mean she had to carry on the tradition. Surrounded by rose-scented bubbles, she decided right then and there to create traditions of their own, beginning with her husband's portrait. "Smiling is a far better way to be remembered," she said out loud to the tiled walls. "We shan't have our lives ruled by their shoulds," she added, slapping the water and enjoying the ceramic echo of her declaration.

After a long, relaxing soak, she dried off and tucked into her coziest flannel pajamas, stroking the soft nap, sorry they'd be replaced tomorrow by satin and lace. "Along with all the other changes," she said to her bridal trousseau, displayed around the room. She admired the tiered white gown hanging on the closet door, its train trailing across the floor … and the antique veil spread across the window seat … and the opera-length gloves draped on the vanity, next to the betrothal jewels James had presented just before leaving for his bachelor's bash. "Sparkle and warmth, that's what you are," he said as she opened the hinged, velvet case. Gasping, she was startled by the opulent pink diamond necklace with a center opalescent pearl pendant and matching earrings. In her wildest imagination she'd never conjured all this, but here it was. The perfect costume for her starring role in what everyone said is a kismet union.

Yet she wondered, as she brushed her hair 100 strokes, how her new life might change her. Would the requirements of being Mrs. James Austin Meaden the Second completely erase the giddy girl she still felt inside? The one who loved to splash through the creek with a heart full of buttercups and daisies? Could that girl survive? That blithe young spirit? Or would she live only in her memory? Like her father's sketches of her mother as a young woman?

Tapping her palm with the back of her brush, Celeste shook her curls, flinging away such thoughts. She had already faced the fact that James, without a doubt, was perfect for a most desirable life. He was rich, cultured, handsome, smart, with undeniable *savoir faire* and ready, finally, to settle down. Everything a girl could want, except … she swayed momentarily, recalling the memory of Ron at the swings.

"No!" She snapped the brush hard on her hand. No more thinking of that! For what was passion without a plan? Gamma and Father had warned her: no matter one's choice, every path delivered both pleasure and pain.

Hearing her parents return, she tucked up her hair, pulled on a robe and went downstairs to review their plans for tomorrow. Who needed to be picked up at the Hartford train depot? Who would catch the trolley? Where would they freshen up before the ceremony at one? Celeste watched her mother's eyes shine, delighted by the detailed lists she'd made, documenting every step and turn. After picking at the cold supper Gamma had assembled, Celeste finally declined anything more and said her goodnights.

Myrtle followed her to the bedroom, wanting to talk about what tomorrow would bring between husband and wife. But after her first few platitudes, Celeste made her mother stop. Regarding the wedding night, she would hear nothing more. She had made her choice and would face, with grace, whatever came.

When Jack saw the elegant young woman swaying across the floor with a short, balding man, he about swallowed his tongue. He hadn't seen Kate since last summer, before James took up with Celeste. But frankly, he hadn't thought about her, either. Now, however, watching her tall, slender body move languidly to the music in the sweaty, stubby arms of some stranger, Jack felt compelled to rescue her. He instantly remembered how marvelous Kate and James had been together. Even though Estelle considered Kate beneath their social standing, Jack liked her spunk, thought her classy and delighted in how she and James finished each other's sentences. Glancing around the hall to spy if James had seen her, too, Jack was relieved to find him on the far side of the ballroom, dancing with a well-endowed blonde. As the song ended, Jack tapped the balding man on the shoulder. Seeing Jack's height and girth, the man scowled but quickly walked away. Looking directly at her next client, Kate did not recognize Jack until he spoke.

"Moonlighting with the mashers tonight?" he asked kindly, hoping for a laugh.

Her eyes cleared as she accepted his dance ticket. "Mr. Meaden," She spoke wistfully, as if waking from a dream, and looked around him quickly. "What are you doing here?"

"I could ask the same of you," Jack countered, drawing her eyes back to him. "And it's Jack to my friends. We are still friends, aren't we?"

Kate's dark hair brushed her shoulders as she shook her head. Although she felt a mix of opposing emotions, she couldn't help smiling. "I wouldn't have presumed … after James … disappeared so quickly."

Jack nodded, sweeping her up in his arms, enjoying her length and litheness.

"Yes. Very difficult I imagine, and I'm sorry, Kate. You two made quite a pair."

Her long lashes dropped, squeezing away the sudden sting she felt in her eyes.

Jack suddenly realized how weary she looked, compared to her vivacious complexion last summer. "What *are* you doing here?" he asked as they moved around the dance floor, keeping a safe distance from James. "Not enough work on Broadway to keep you busy?"

With a short laugh, Kate shook her head. "I haven't had a Broadway shuffle for two years now. I've been kangarooed. Once you bounce out of the pocket, it's hard to get back in."

"What do you mean? Weren't you in a production last summer?"

"Oh, that was a little private show for a company meeting. James introduced me to the producers. They needed a singer. I haven't had any real work … a job in the theater, I mean … for ages because … well, James … he wanted more and more of my time, so after awhile I stopped auditioning … as he provided …" Kate's head bobbed. She looked at the floor, washed with shame and sadness but desperate not to lose her dignity. "Look, Mr. Meaden, I want you to know I wasn't a kept woman. I earn my own money and have since I left my daddy's home. I'm not some silly girl. I know what kind of men are out there, but I thought James and I were onto something special. Steady for nearly three years when he introduced me to you. When we turned that corner, I began to believe we were going to spend our lives together, that we had the real deal, especially when James took me home to meet Mrs. Meaden after it went so well with you."

Jack squeezed her hand as they danced, keeping an eye out for James, not wanting to be interrupted. "I don't doubt it, Kate. I could see you brought something very special to James' life. He lit up around you, like I've never seen before … but sometimes …"

Kate would not let him continue. "I know, I know, you don't have to tell me. *Sometimes fate gets in the way of one's dreams.*" She repeated what James had said when he broke the news about his engagement and family obligations. Then he seared her heart with the words: "But I don't expect you to understand such matters," as if she were some country bumpkin, incapable of comprehending the code of the wealthy.

Kate's words resonated with practiced resignation, and Jack could feel her suffering. As they danced a few minutes more to the soothing melody of the orchestra, Jack felt time fold forward and saw, in his mind's eye, James and Kate as a married couple. The *bon vivant* and his vivacious wife, striding through New York, Paris, Venice, turning heads the world over with their dash and vigor. Two people who knew each other well, armed with common pursuits and equal footing, not one higher or lower but balanced and blessed with a child or two or more, living to their own measures and desires. In rapid succession, he saw how they became one of those rare, sparkling families, where contentment and passion never faded, seeping into the seams of their many friends and associates who sought their company. In the middle of a New York dance hall, surrounded by strangers, Jack realized Kate was more likely the true mate for James, far more than sweet, young Celeste. But once again, true joy is thwarted by fear … by compliance … by duty … for someone else's wishes and dreams. And that someone was him.

With a heavy heart, Jack lifted the girl's chin, peering into her wounded eyes. "I'm so sorry. I wish …" was all he could manage, in a voice thickened with regret, as the dance ended.

Nodding, Kate kissed his cheek and walked away, unwilling to cry any more about what might have been.

Sitting at her vanity, Celeste pushed up her pajama sleeves and methodically creamed her hands, elbows and arms while looking in the mirror at a face she barely recognized. Only her round ruddy cheeks and crystalline blue eyes were the same. All the rest had been plucked, penciled and coiffed to match the sophisticates of her fiancé's New York set. One of the many changes she'd endured on her way to the altar. Despite her momentary doubts, she could not dismiss her mother's repeated caution. "The logic is clear. James is solid and safe." In such bad times, who could disagree? The whole world had turned coldly ugly, hungry and desperate in four short years, with no relief in sight. Everyone said she was wise to be smart, but still, she felt occasionally unsettled. Climbing into bed, she pulled the covers to her chin and wondered: Was her life now a *fait accompli*? Or could her heart still surprise her? As Gamma said it would, somewhere, somehow along the way, revealing a passionate pursuit she couldn't deny? It didn't have to be as brilliant as Ede's painting or striking as Ron's sport, but surely something more than just a dutiful wife and mother. "Something of my own," she sighed out loud, turning over and over in the bed, searching for the sweet spot of sleep. "Something I can be proud of," she prayed. Finally nestled, she stared, for a long time, at the shadow of her wedding gown on the wall, flickering in the street's gas light, and deeply sniffing the sweet blooming lilac scent from the trees beneath her open window, until her eyelids finally drooped and her breathing shallowed and slumber arrived … along with a twisty-turvey dream.

There she sat, powdered and primped at Estelle's glamorous, dark-wood dressing table with a silk lined glass top; veiled, gowned and gloved in mounds of pristine white, peering moon-eyed into the gilded, tri-fold mirror, waiting for the ceremony to begin. Yet something did not feel quite right. The air was too still for the houseful of guests gathered in the parlor below. And why was she sitting all alone? Where was Beatrice, her matron of honor, and her mother, most of all? And just who is that woman staring back from the mirror? She looked over-plucked and a bit bizarre.

Impatiently tapping her toes, Celeste rose to go downstairs, when she heard a voice waft through the open window. "Wait!" It was James. Lumbering in her gown to the window, she drew back the gauzy sheath and saw him, running up the lane, chasing a lanky brunette. Reaching out his arms, he called again, "Kate, Kate, wait for me!" and nearly caught the girl's shoulders as they slipped out of sight, over the orchard hill and well beyond her screams for James to come back.

Unable to breathe, with heartbeats pounding in her ears, Celeste barely heard the knock on the boudoir door. "Come in" she called, swishing her twisted gown and veil straight. The door swung open and Ron stepped in, looking dapper in his morning suit, holding a tray of small, ceramic apples. "Mother thought you might like these to commemorate the day," he announced, placing the tray on the dressing table's edge. Leaning close to admire the fine blown porcelain, Celeste sucked in her breath. "Six!" she half whispered. "How did she know?" Ron shook his head. "Don't know that she does, but I wonder ..." he asked, dropping to one knee and holding out a small jewelry box, "would you trade my brother and six apples for me?"

The rush in her chest overwhelmed her reason. With a cry she surrendered to his outstretched arms, enveloping him in tulle and satin, whispering, "Oh please, oh please, oh please." The room glowed red as she hugged him tighter for what seemed an eternity. Then suddenly, he was gone, and she tumbled to the floor, smashing her face on an old squash racquet.

"Aaaieee," a piercing scream filled the room, followed by her mother's stomping feet. "What are you doing? My god, you are wrinkling. Get up, get up, get up!" Pulling Celeste to her feet, Myrtle snatched the racquet to swat the creases from her dress. Celeste stared at her mother's gown "What are you wearing? Are those apple peels?" she asked, touching the red and yellow skins, draped like petals on a chrysanthemum. She plucked one off, and her mother screamed again, waving the racquet over her head as she ran out.

Gathering up her dress to follow, a blare of bells and bleating drew her back to the window. She stuck out her head and gasped. On the hilltop, under the craggy old sycamore, a herd of green goats danced on their hind legs, two-by-two, *making a waltzing circle. Hanging in the branches above them was an enormous golden chandelier, like the ones in Spanish Hall. And standing to the side was the old gypsy woman, clapping to the dancing goats, with rows of copper bracelets jangling on both arms. And emblazoned on her chest was a bright green, dripping heart, as if freshly painted. Then above her head an airplane roared by, its wings happily dipping.*

"Helloooo," The gypsy waved. "Remember what I tell you when we met?"
Nodding vigorously, Celeste patted her arm.

"Good, then," the gypsy said. "God willing, someday my youngest daughter will meet yours in the field ... the prophesy revealed." Then she tossed six bracelets in the air, which slowly spun and rolled toward Celeste's reaching hands. But as each one neared, it slipped through her outstretched fingers, dropping to the ground with a thud. Horrified, Celeste looked back to the gypsy, but she was gone, along with the goats, airplane and chandelier. But standing by the tree was her best friend, Ede, hoisting a colossal brush on her shoulder, dripping the same shade of the heart green paint.

"Ede! Oh Ede, you came!" Celeste yelled frantically. "Please, help me! The bracelets fell." But without a glance, Ede marched across the grass, toward the orchard where James had disappeared. Just when she reached its edge, out popped Ron, grabbing her hand, and off they ran, laughing, with a melody of small green hearts dripping off the paintbrush, following behind.

Slumping on the window seat, Celeste did not notice her veil catch the ledge as the door opened again, revealing Estelle, wearing a broach the size of her head. "Do you like them?" She asked, nodding to the tray of porcelain apples. "So beautiful and delicate. So like you. Who could resist?" Unable to speak, Celeste picked up the tray and stepped toward Estelle, when the snagged veil yanked her back and everything tipped. Crumpling to the floor, she watched, aghast, as each apple slowly tumbled through the air and shattered, one by one, on the dressing table bench.

"Aaaieeee," her mother wailed again, sweeping down the hall, leaving a trail of apple peels as the yammering crowd of James' New York set pushed in. Dressed in cravats and silks, wielding long cigarette holders and hoisting martinis, they poked at Celeste, lifting her veil and ogling the diamonds and pearls gracing her neck and ears. Slapping away their greedy fingers, she cried for it all to stop, when through the cacophony she heard a child's laugh. Looking up, she saw her own face on a ruddy-cheeked girl with crystal blue eyes, cupping the gypsy's copper bracelets in her chubby hands. Beside her stood Gamma, wearing the birch-bark hat they had made by the creek, when she was just the child's age.

"Gamma!" Celeste cried, twisting her voluminous skirt and nearly tripping on the train. "Is this my child the gypsy foretold, or is this marriage a green-goat mistake?"

Gamma slowly shook her head. "The reason for our life, no one can know. Only to what we are drawn. Every step leads to the next, on the path we were born to take. So listen to the clues in your heart, and the rest will sort itself out. Is all I know of mystery thus far. Life has magic all its own." She then placed the birch-bark hat on the young girl's head and faded away, leaving Celeste staring at the child, offering her six copper bracelets with hopeful blue eyes.

After dancing with Kate, Jack lost his taste for the evening's festivities and sat at the table, nursing a gin. All he wanted was to get the boys together as soon as possible and go home. He kept an eye on Kate, who danced every song to make her weekly rent. But his blood ran cold when he saw James striding across the room, bee-lining to his former sweetheart. With a pain in his chest, he watched Kate stiffly greet his son and resist his request for a dance, repeatedly pushing away his offered ticket. But his grasp on her arm would not release, gently pulling her back until, reluctantly, she slipped his ticket into her pocket. "Bloody hell," Jack muttered under his breath as he followed their course. James danced her through the crowd with bold steps until her hair whirled and a smile graced her lips. Then he heard her laugh – bold, bright, unafraid, just before they disappeared, into the shuffling crowd, and then from the room altogether. Rising abruptly, Jack walked the perimeter of the broad dance floor, trying to find them, to no avail. Returning to the table, his stomach sour and tight, he dragged the crowd with his eyes, hoping to catch sight of them. One by one, the other members of the wedding party came back, having had their fill of dancing, asking for the guest of honor. Jack just shook his head, and soon everyone was looking about for the groom. But James was nowhere to be found.

It was nearly midnight when Ron spotted him ambling across the floor, top hat in hand, bow tie askance, wearing a sleepy, self-satisfied grin.

Jack walked directly to him, away from the party of friends.

"Where's Kate?" he asked, dispensing with formalities.

"Ahh, father, she said you had a dance. Lovely as ever, isn't she?" James replied.

"Where is she?" Jack growled.

"She wasn't feeling well, so I took her home. Shall we have a nightcap? Big day in the morning. Mother expects us to be fresh."

Waving his hat, James summoned the waiter to order a final round for his party, banishing all further talk of what might have happened with Kate.

"Nothing more?" Jack insisted as the party approached, joining them at the bar.

Twirling his hat on his finger, James winked. "Well, let's just say it was my last free night, ol' man. So … like you … I made the most of it."

A hot-triggered flash rose in Jack's chest and his body heaved with explosive anger. He tried to hold back, but his son's smirk filled him with an angst he could not contain. Pulling back his arm, Jack pivoted and plunged his fist deep into his son's belly, ripping his silk vest, jettisoning his hat across the crowd, and then watched, with twisted satisfaction, as James staggered back in slow motion and sprawled on the ballroom floor.

31 Courage

May 26, 1934

"Gamma! Gamma! Gamma!" Celeste cried awake, startled by the dream and twisted in the sheets. Stunned, she sat for a moment, collecting her bearings. This was her bedroom in her own home, but her birch-bark hat was not on the bookshelf.

Wriggling out of the bedding, she snapped on the overhead light, ran to her closet and searched frantically for the hatbox she'd stowed away. Finding it in the back corner, she clawed off the top and sighed, relieved her birch-bark hat was still intact. Sitting at her vanity with the box on her lap, she gingerly removed the dry, dusty bark and sniffed it. Somehow, after all these years, it still smelled like the creek: green and musky at the same time. Fingering its fragile edges and breathing its scented memories, Celeste felt herself transported to the afternoon when she had made it with Gamma, when she was only six and the world was simple and complete. Touching each side notch, she recited: "Truth, Courage, Openness, Curiosity, Creativity, Love." Gently placing the hat on her head, she peered into the vanity mirror, hoping to conjure the contented joy she once felt, when her bedroom door abruptly pushed open.

"Look, Gamma!" Celeste said without glancing up. "It still fits!"

"What on earth?" Her mother's voice ripped though Celeste's chest.

Instantly pulling off the hat, she turned to find her mother standing in the doorway, her nightgown rumpled and eyes half asleep.

"I thought I heard you scream," Myrtle said.

"I did, I had a dream … a nightmare, actually … I'm sorry," Celeste answered, not knowing how to explain her bizarre dream or the unsettled feelings it evoked. She wasn't expecting her mother. She didn't know how her mother could help.

"What are you doing with that?" Myrtle asked without moving, her voice sharp.

Looking at the hat in her hands, Celeste suddenly felt foolish and began to sob.

"What is it?" Myrtle swept to her side, trying to clasp Celeste's heaving shoulders. "What happened? Celeste, tell me, please."

Much to Celeste's surprise, out tumbled the dream, talking through her tears, barely understanding herself.

"I saw James running, with that girl, Kate, over the hill … and then Ron gave me apples, six porcelain apples, and asked me to marry him … and Estelle came in, her head was a huge broach, and you ran by, wearing a gown of apple peels … and green goats danced with the gypsy by the tree, but the bracelets fell, just below the window, I couldn't reach them … then Ede came but wouldn't help me and walked away with … oh, Mama, it was awful! I woke up feeling I'm making a horrible mistake."

Celeste dropped her head on her mother's shoulder as the birch hat slipped to the floor.

Myrtle puffed and tisked, patting her daughter's head, trying to think of what to say, swallowing hard and wishing, for once, Gamma would come through the door. Rubbing Celeste's back, she spoke in a half whisper. "It was just a dream, dearie, just jitters. Pay no mind. It will be alright. You'll see. Just too much excitement. With some sleep you'll –"

"No, Mama," Celeste snapped upright. "It's not alright. There was a girl in the dream, too. A little girl, who looked just like me, just like Gamma with blue eyes and ruddy cheeks … the girl the gypsy prophesied, *my daughter*. She held the six bracelets, Gamma's bracelets, looking at me with such eyes, like I was … like I am … if I don't marry James, she won't exist, won't be here to tell the world about the Bohemian Way and I'll be to blame!"

Just as Celeste was about to sob again, Myrtle snatched up her chin, looking hard into her eyes. "Now stop this. You're not making any sense. All this rubbish in your head. Marrying James has nothing to do with Gamma's bohemian nonsense …"

"Yes it does … *Yes-it-does!*" Celeste's weeping eyes stared back at her mother as she spoke in a gush. "I'm meant to have those children … I *am* … I can feel it in my bones. But how can I do this? When I don't feel for James what I feel for Ron?"

Myrtle's heart froze. Her hand dropped to her lap. The room seemed to echo Ron's name. Wobbling to the bed, Myrtle sank on the mattress, her mouth dry and breath shallow.

Watching her mother collapse, Celeste's sobbing ceased. Picking up the birch-bark hat at her feet, she placed it on the vanity and climbed on the bed, next to her mother. They stared at each other, both sets of eyes wide. One not believing what she heard, the other relieved at having finally said it.

"Mama," Celeste finally whispered. "Are you alright? Say something. Tell me something. Tell me anything."

Myrtle took a full breath. Her mouth opened, then closed. She shook her head.

"What, Mama? Do you need some water?"

Myrtle shook her head again. "No," she said weakly. "I need to know why you want to ruin your life."

Celeste blinked. "I'm not trying to ruin my life, Mama; I'm trying to save it. Can't you understand what I'm feeling? I'm not even sure about Ron ... but I know I feel something for him that I don't feel for James. Isn't that important? For a choice that affects my whole life?"

Myrtle took another full breath and closed her eyes. "What you don't know about life."

Celeste clasped her mother's hand. "Then tell me. Tell me what it is I don't know. About life. About love. About you." She shook her mother's hands to wake her.

Myrtle opened her eyes.

"Tell me, Mama, what I don't know, about your past ... why we never see any of your relatives ... and how you came to marry Papa ... and who you were before. Who was that girl ... in Papa's sketches? Was it really how you felt? So light and free."

Myrtle sat up. "Papa told you?"

"He showed me his sketches of you and I saw how different you were back then. What happened, Mama? Was that really you? I need to know. And why Papa? Was he like James? Safe and secure? Just like you want for me? Or did you feel for him like I feel for Ron? I need to know. Before I make a mistake I can't undo. Because Mama, as much as I love you – and I really do – I don't want to become like you ... or have the marriage I see between you and Papa."

Myrtle gasped, waving her hands in a fluster to stop Celeste. But she would not.

"Who were you, Mama? Before you married Papa? He said you have a secret about your past, but he wouldn't tell me what. Only you can tell me, he said. So please, tell me now. Tell me the secret you've kept all these years. Make me understand why and how you are now."

The room echoed again. Celeste sucked up a breath, shocked she actually spoke what she wanted to know. Just asking the questions released such a burden. Now all she could do was wait, and pray, her mother would answer.

Myrtle sat stiffly, eyes squeezed shut.

Celeste closed hers as well.

The night's silence filled their ears, until they heard a creak by the door and Gamma's soft voice: "Myrtle, is time."

They opened their eyes. Standing in the doorway, Gamma wavered in her nightgown and bed cap.

"It never should have been," Myrtle said dully.

Gamma shrugged. "Like many things but this was ... and she deserve to know."

"What good can come ...?"

"That you survived ... made good from bad. Hard truths will come to her life, too. Is good she know what her mother can do."

Celeste watched the exchange between Gamma and her mother with astonishment; expecting her mother to fly off the handle at any moment, squawking at Gamma's interference. But Myrtle only nodded slowly, wrapping one hand around the other, again and again, her lips opening and shutting, forming words not spoken, until she rose and crossed the room, gazing at the gloves, the jewels, the hat on the vanity, the dress hanging on the closet door, and the veil, draped along the window seat. Staring out the window, into the gas lit night, she finally spoke.

"I wish I had such kindness in my young life," she said, gesturing to the fineries behind her. "My dearest wish was to give you all the kindness life allowed. The beauty of life. A good meal. Fine clothes. A proud and safe home. Things I never had ...." Myrtle looked to Gamma, who nodded.

"But not just things," Myrtle turned to Celeste, holding her eyes with a gentleness Celeste had never before witnessed.

"You never see my relatives because they are not worthy of seeing you." Myrtle's lips curled in a sad smile as she paused.

"But," Celeste interrupted, "I thought you were an orphan."

Myrtle laughed sharply. "That might have been better."

Celeste's eyebrows crumpled, not understanding.

"Celeste, you are everything I wished I could be. But it was not possible because ... of his vileness."

Myrtle began to shake, causing Celeste to rise from the bed, but Gamma's slight wave of her hand caused her to sit again, holding her mother's gaze.

Myrtle sank to the edge of the window seat, careful not to sit on the veil. "How I wish I could forget where I come from. No one should know what I feel. Your father and grandmother do, but I swore them to silence long before you were born. If anyone found out, they would judge me worse then they already do."

Celeste opened her mouth to protest, but Myrtle raised her finger for silence.

"No, do not pretend when finally I have this courage to speak. I know they judge. In younger years, I did not think so. I thought I could make up what I want, what I dream, and push my way forward, ignoring what others thought of me; blind by my ambition. I did not know I was ... uncouth." Myrtle's eyes flickered to Gamma, who blinked once, deeply.

"I heard that word said of me in secret, and looked it up; as your Papa taught me to do. I did not like what I read but ... I knew it was true. Very brash I was, before you came."

Celeste looked again to Gamma, who held her face still.

"Don't look to Gamma. She knows the truth, better than I was willing to admit. I tried to learn to be less coarse but I won't ever have what you have ... because I didn't know kindness growing up; I didn't know grace. My mother tried her best, but she was no help against my father's rage ... an evil man. Evil and mean. So much so, I ran away at thirteen."

Celeste shivered. "Why, Mama?" she asked as softly as she could.

Myrtle clenched her teeth, looking at the floor. She couldn't bear to have her only daughter look down at her, once she knew. Raising her eyes to Celeste, seeing the innocence surrounding her like a halo, Myrtle began to cry. "Never did I feel like you, Celeste. Never a chance to be a child, to play by a creek, to dream of love. Never because ..." Her voice dropped to a whisper. "My father ... took me to his body ... his drunken, filthy ... even when my mother was home, asleep ... and then he try to sell me – to other men – like I was meat."

Celeste's mouth dropped open. "Mama," she breathed, instinctively hugging herself.

Myrtle held herself as steady as she could, but her head softly bobbed as she wept.

Gamma leaned against the door jamb, letting out a long sigh.

Confused, Celeste exploded with questions. "What are you saying?" she asked. "How could he sell you? Is that when you ran away? But to where? What did you do?"

Myrtle closed her eyes, unable to escape the memory flashes of those horrid days: *living on the street, frightened of every strange sound in the night, tucked away in alleys, praying she would not see the dawn's light.* Opening her eyes, fierce and wet, she cut the air with a sharp, curt laugh. "I got smart and found the brothel of prostitutes who knew my father well. Who hated him as much as I. And when I told my story to the one who hate him most, she took me in. Cleaned me up. Dressed me proper, as a girl, not a whore. I became her maid, and proud of it, too. Running her errands. Cleaning her room. Doing her hair. Whatever she wanted, except ..." Her eyes shifted to Gamma. "For three years she hid me, until I grew into a woman and it was time ... to find respectable work. So I wandered the city, looking for a good place, when I see the notice for a class your Papa was teaching. Helping young boys, street urchins, to learn and better them-selves. I persuaded him to let me learn, too, and then came to know him and all his kindness, and then, I want him, too."

"You fell in love?" Celeste asked hopefully.

Myrtle stopped short, momentarily confused, then shook her head. "Celeste, what could I know of love? All my life I was starved – for safety, for security – and to find your Papa, who had all of that to offer ... and your grandmother, too," Her voice cracked. "Of all the people I have ever known, they have been the most kind to me." Myrtle wrapped her arms around herself and bowed her head, her body swaying, her secret released.

No one said a word until Myrtle looked up with a contorted expression, afraid of Celeste's reaction.

Gamma saw her fear. "We learn, too, from you Myrtle."

Celeste and Myrtle turned to Gamma.

"Your story show Celeste no road is easy. No life perfect. You live courage. You believe in your good. And you find in yourself something worthy, something stronger than your father's cruel lies. You fight, to make life better with truth ... with courage ... with openness. You not collapse. I am made proud for what you did ... and what you do, then ... and today."

Crossing to the vanity, Gamma fingered the birch hat and winked at Celeste. "I think she deserve to wear the hat now, mmmm?"

Celeste popped off the bed. "Oh yes. Oh yes, oh yes, oh yes!" Carrying the hat to her mother, she looked at her lovingly and raised the hat above her head. "Truth, Courage, Openness, Curiosity, Creativity, Love. You've lived it, Mama, in so many ways I never knew and never could. Thank you, for bringing to me ... all that should have been for you. So now it is yours to wear – the birch bark hat – and be proud!" Then Celeste hugged her mother hard, refusing to let go.

Clasping her daughter's arm, Myrtle held out her other hand to Gamma, who joined them, wrapping her arms around them ... daughter, mother, grandmother ... three generations, at last entwined with immutable love, melting away the long standing generational divide.

"Oh, Mama, I'm so sorry," Celeste spoke into her shoulder. "*I've* misjudged you all these years. *I* didn't understand ... anything ... I'm so very sorry. Why didn't you tell me sooner?"

Gamma stepped away, walking toward the door.

Myrtle stroked Celeste's hair. "It's not a bedtime story, Celeste. I want for you the childhood I did not have. So do you see now? Why a life with James is right for you?"

Gamma swiveled, surprised.

Celeste pulled her head up. "But ..."

Myrtle would not let her interrupt, her eyes soft and blurry. "Listen. You have kindness in your blood. Not like me. I work hard to find some; harder to give some. For you, I wish much more. For your Papa, I wish a gentler wife than I was able to give. But for your children, these six children Gamma's gypsy say you will bear, I wish a deeper kindness ... and with James, I know it can be. With James, you can do so much more, in a life far beyond anything I could dream."

"But ..."

Myrtle shushed her, ignoring Gamma's shaking head. She fingered the tips of Celeste's hair. "Children can make more kindness, like you did for me. And through them, more children come with more kindness, more love. This is the good in life and can make right all the bad I endured. You and James can make it right – with the six children you will bear. "

"The six children I will bear," Celeste repeated tentatively, appeasing her mother.

"The six children you will bear," Myrtle confirmed, her eyes now bright and focused.

"Myrtle," Gamma cleared her throat. "For *your* life, what you say is true. But for Celeste, I must correct. The gypsy *not* say she would *bear* six children."

Celeste released her mother's embrace. "Yes she did. You said she did."

"Ne. She say you *raise* six children."

"What's the difference?" Myrtle snapped her head. The birch bark hat slid back, bouncing off the window seat to the floor. Celeste's surprise caused Myrtle to immediately soften. "What I mean is: many children are raised by someone other than a parent ... even with a parent," she looked at Gamma. "Like you did for Celeste."

Gamma did not smile. "Is true," she replied. "So we agree: marriage or birthing is not necessary to do such work?"

Celeste saw her mother staring at Gamma, her lips pressed tightly together.

Gamma stared back. "The gypsy's words do not make fate. There are many ways to make a prophesy true. What the gypsy say may be different from what you hear. The only way to know your truth is to honor what beckons *you*."

An angry cloud passed over Myrtle's face. She grabbed Celeste's arms, pulling her close.

"You do want children, don't you?" Her voice tinged with urgency.

"Y-Yes," Celeste replied. "But is James my only chance?"

Myrtle's shoulders stiffened, her eyes hardened and bored into Celeste. "How can you even ask that, Celeste? How can you lose sight of the best opportunity *any* girl could *ever* have?"

"I – I'm not sure, Mama. Is it? The best opportunity for *me*? Or the best opportunity for *you*?" Celeste pulled away, backing up to the bed and sliding onto it, pulling a pillow to her chest. "James is what *you* need; safety and security. But you and Papa and Gamma gave me a wonderful childhood. The kind I want to give my children and I do want children, but ... after that dream, it feels like something's not right. Everything's happened so fast, there wasn't anytime to think about ... anything. Now I'm more confused than ever." She squeezed the pillow tighter, her chin quivering.

Myrtle stepped to the bed. "Listen to me, Celeste. Listen. All this talk about feeling and passion – it's not what makes happiness. It's not what you build a marriage on. Your Papa and I have respect for each other – that's what lasts. That's what gave us the ability to see it through, to make good in spite of the bad. And you are the very best of what we've done. Don't forget that. Now it's your turn to make a future; a good future, for generations to come. If you remember nothing else I say tonight, remember this: This choice is not just for yourself. Your children will begin the best part of the Howe's, the best part of the Meadens, and bring out the best in you and James as well." Myrtle pulled back the covers and shoed Celeste under them, kissing her forehead goodnight. "Now you dream on that and we'll see you in the morning."

Myrtle waved Gamma out, snapped off the overhead light and shut the door behind them, leaving Celeste alone, illuminated only by moonlight and the gas lamp from the street below. Staring blankly, her stomach twisting from her mother's last words, her eyes were drawn to a shimmering on the floor ... something round and softly silver. Slipping out of bed, she gingerly tip-toed over and found ... her birch bark hat. Half crumpled from her mother's discard yet still intact ... like her own thoughts and feelings about the life she was trying to find: a little crushed, but glowing in the moonlight ... as if lit from within.

32 *Hows and Means*
May 27, 1934

As the early morning light streamed into James' eyes, he awoke with a splitting headache and an aching body. Pulling a pillow over his face, he groaned, unsure of where he was, and didn't hear the knock.

Ron cracked open the door. "James? You up?" he asked gruffly, then saw his brother still in bed. "You'd better get moving."

Pulling the pillow aside, James squinted at Ron. "Oh my god. What time is it?"

"Nearly eight. Everyone's at breakfast."

Rolling over, James groaned harder, his abdomen ripping with pain.

Ron waited a few moments then asked, "Why did Father slug you last night?"

James glanced up then dropped his face into the pillow. "Didn't he say?"

"Not a word. After we got you to the car, you passed out and he said nothing."

"Where's he now?"

"On the court, hitting balls, smashing out the boil, I'd say. What-did-you-do?"

With great effort, James sat up, holding his head. "I'm trying to remember."

"Was it Kate?" Ron asked.

James turned his head too quickly, wincing at the sharp pain. "I thought he didn't say anything."

"I guessed ... after seeing you dancing with her before you disappeared. Here," Ron moved toward him, carrying two cups. "Drink some juice and coffee. Then answer my question."

Unable to fight with anyone, James quickly downed each cup. "So whatdaya want to know? How I screwed up again?"

"Why are you marrying her?"

James closed his eyes. "You too? ... hell, I dunno ... because it's time, I suppose. And everyone gets what they want ... you got a better idea?"

"So you don't love her?" A hard edge had crept into Ron's voice.

James shrugged. "I wish I knew what that was. Maybe she'll teach me and make me a better man." Looking up, he saw fierceness in Ron's eyes. "Whoa, what's that about? Are you in love with her? You itching to take my place?"

Ron clenched his jaw and hands. "Shut up. She made her choice – and god help her for that – but fair warning: You treat her right, 'cause I'll be watching." Leaving the door open, Ron strode down the hall.

James automatically jumped up, wrapping the sheet around his waist, and rushed into the hallway, bursting to hurl a caustic retort at his brother, when he saw his mother marching up the staircase, sidestepping the workman fixing a bower of flowers along the banister.

"James," she snapped her fingers. "Whatever you did last night to put your father in a spin is done and over. Everyone will be arriving soon. Get yourself ready. I'll have some breakfast sent up." Without giving him a second to reply, she disappeared into her room.

At the Howes', Celeste woke to a commotion downstairs. Recognizing Uncle Yazi's booming voice, she didn't think twice, jumping out of bed, grabbing her robe and racing down the steps barefoot to leap into his arms.

Yazi squeezed her tight. "Awww geez, how can my bitty golden girl be gettin' married today?" he said, pulling back to look in her eyes. "Look at ya – all grown up and settin' for a family of your own. Are ya sure that art dealer is good enough for ya?"

Celeste giggled as Yazi tickled her neck with his full whiskers.

"Cause if he don't, you just calls me up and I'll take care-a-him for ya."

"Yazi, don't muss her skin," Myrtle fussed, pulling Celeste away.

Releasing her, Yazi scooped up Myrtle and whiskered her face instead, sending Celeste into peals of laughter.

"Stop it! Stop it! Put me down!" Myrtle cried until Yazi did, patting her behind.

"You're never too big for a squeeze," he said, wagging his head as he strode to the back of the house, calling for Martin.

Taking Celeste's arm, Myrtle steered her toward the kitchen. "You need some breakfast before you get ready." But Celeste squirmed away.

"Aren't Gamma's friends here? Didn't they come with Yazi?" she asked, looking around the parlor, then heard the chatter on the back porch and ran to greet them.

Standing at the door, Myrtle watched her daughter hug and kiss Gamma's three friends from New York with a twinge of jealousy. Two of them were not much older than she, yet she didn't have a single old friend or family member coming to the wedding. When she left them all behind upon their move to Connecticut, she never thought of what it might mean in the long run of their lives.

"OK, now, OK, enough of this foolery," she interrupted, taking Celeste firmly by the arm. "Celeste must get ready. Gamma, Estelle is expecting your help at the house this morning. Perhaps your friends could go along?"

Walking Celeste to the staircase, Myrtle released her arm. "Go on up and I'll bring some juice and a roll. You must put something in your stomach."

Undeterred by her mother, Celeste pecked her cheek and slipped around her, heading toward the kitchen. "As soon as I say good morning to Papa."

She found him at the side door, bringing in the friends' overnight valises.

"Hello my beauty," he said, kissing her cheek. "Heard you had quite a night. How do you feel today?"

The familiar, loving crinkles of his eyes filled Celeste with warmth ... and uncertainty, at the remembrance of her mother's confession and subsequent insistence on what she should do with her life.

"I'm ..."

Martin tucked a valise under his arm, giving his daughter full attention.

"...a little jittery, but good."

"Sure?"

Celeste nodded, her eyes misting.

Martin set down the suitcases and enfolded Celeste. "I am going to miss you, every moment of every day. You mean the world to me, Celeste. Whatever you need, wherever life takes you, I will be here for you. I hope you are always happy."

With her mouth muffled into his chest, he did not hear her sigh: "I'll try Papa."

Kissing the top of her head, he held her out, carefully examining her face. He had acquiesced to her decision but wasn't placing any bets on James. Something about the boy never felt right, besides his being so much older. Having seen Gamma's pain at losing her husband so young, he didn't wish the same for his daughter. But even more, he didn't like the glibness of James. He was not at all like Jack. More like his mother, slick and social, which wasn't how he'd raised Celeste. Nor did he like his daughter's sudden changes, molding herself to suit her fiancé's tastes. It smacked of pretense. He'd done what he could before leaving the decision to Celeste. But seeing her beautiful face, Martin felt the pinch of lost promise. However, after futile years of battling his wife's schemes, he'd made a rule not to interfere with the plans of others. "One last time: You're sure this is what you want?" he asked.

Celeste nodded, solemnly. "To see you as grandpop – you bet."

"Well then, there's nothing more for me to do but walk you proudly up the aisle and celebrate your choosing." But as he squeezed her tightly, he silently prayed for something, or someone, to intervene.

Still wearing her apron, ready to help with the wedding's final setup, Gamma arrived at the Meaden house with her three friends in tow, at the same moment a long limousine pulled up to the curb. A chauffeur popped out of the driver's seat and ran around to open the passenger door, where he pulled out a tall, round-topped cage, covered in heavy, white silk with a wide satin ribbon tied in a floppy bow. By the loud squawking, there was obviously a bird of some size inside.

"Quiet!" A raspy reprimand came from within the car just before a large woman emerged, attired from head to toe in emerald-green silk.

One of Gamma's friends gasped. "That's Elinor Glyn," she whispered.

"Who?" the other two friends asked in unison.

"The Hollywood columnist," Gamma whispered back. "The author of 'It'."

"Ohhhh," they replied.

The large woman looked up and smiled. "Hello. I'm here for the wedding. This is the Meaden house, isn't it?

"Yah," Gamma answered, about to introduce herself when Elinor waved toward the car. "Good enough. You'll find the birdfeed and sundries in the car, but don't forget the large cage in the trunk. He hates that small one." Turning on her heel, she sauntered up the walk, followed by the bird-carrying chauffeur.

The first friend began to laugh. "She thinks we're the servants," she said loud enough for the chauffeur to hear, who looked back with such a burdened, apologetic expression that Gamma laughed even louder. "Well, we come to help, so let's get to doing! Girls, see what you find in car. I check the trunk."

With the front door wide open, Elinor Glyn swept into the Meadens' vestibule, now draped in silk and flowers, and bellowed, "You-hoooo, anybody home?" The bird squawked even louder. "Shush!" Elinor reprimanded again as Estelle appeared at the top of the stairs, hairbrush in hand.

"Good Lord, Elinor, you're here already? The wedding's not 'til one."

"Yes, yes, it's such a bore to be early," Elinor waved away the complaint. "But I didn't want to be late. Besides, what was I to do with Hector?"

"Hector?" Estelle asked tentatively as she quickly descended the steps. This was one aggravation she did not need just now.

"Their wedding present," Elinor announced as the chauffeur stepped forward, swept off the silk and presented the large gray bird with a red tail and hooked black beak.

Estelle gasped. "What is that?"

"Hector present! Hector present!" the bird exclaimed in a raspy voice.

"I tried to teach him to say 'Hector wedding present,' but this was the best I could manage on such short notice," Elinor explained. "Hector's a Congo African Grey Parrot. I thought he'd make a lasting present. They live up to 60 years, you know."

"Sixty!?" Estelle had to stop herself. What on earth was she going to do with that bird for this day, much less the four weeks of the honeymoon? Slipping out a handkerchief from her sleeve, she patted her upper lip as Gamma came through the front door, carrying a birdcage almost as tall as she. "Gamma, what in the world are you doing?" Estelle rushed to take the cage from her and then saw three other women on the porch, laden with baskets and bags. "And who are they?"

At the same moment, Jack appeared in the vestibule, still wearing his squash togs. He stopped in his tracks. "Could it be?" he called in a loud voice, adding to the bedlam. "*Is* that *really* Elinor Glyn under that *awful* green turban?" Then he charged, swiftly picking her up with a grunt and twirling around as she and the bird squawked. Setting her down, he stepped back, looking at the bird. "Holy Moses – is that Hector? Who are you trying to foist that bird on now?"

"James and Celeste, it appears," Estelle said with raised eyebrows and pursed lips. "By the way, so long as we are all standing around, Elinor, may I introduce you to the bride's grandmother, Bertra Howe – but we all call her Gamma."

Wiping her hands on her apron, Gamma smiled, nodding to Elinor. "Pleased to meet you, Miss Glyn. My Celeste admires your writing works very much."

Elinor's mouth opened and shut before she spoke. "Oh my goodness, I'm so sorry. I didn't realize." Then she turned to the three ladies carrying her packages on the porch. "And those are your friends?"

Gamma nodded. "No worries. Come, I introduce you and we all be friends."

As Elinor made her apologies to Gamma's friends on the porch, Estelle turned to Jack. "What on earth are we going to do with it?"

"With Hector? Damned if I know. That's up to James and Celeste."

"But what do we do with it for the wedding and reception?"

"Hell, put him right in the parlor to witness the ceremony. It's only fitting, since he's gonna be with them a long, long time. I'm going to shower," and he bounced up the steps.

"Jack Meaden!" Estelle called to him, "We'll not go through the day this way."

"What way?" he feigned ignorance at the top of the stairs.

"I'll have none of that from you. Whatever happened last night – I don't want to know. Just make sure you talk with your son and clear it up before the ceremony. He's in his room."

As Beatrice parked her car in front of the Howe's house, she was struck by the calm. Compared to the swarming bustle at her mother's, it looked deserted. Rapping on the screen door, she peered in, but no one came. "Hellooo, Mrs. Howe? Celeste? It's Beatrice." She switched her dress bag to her other hand and rapped again.

"Yo ho, can I help ya?" a husky voice came from the side of the house.

Turning around, Beatrice laughed nervously at the sight of the large, whiskered man. "Hi, I'm Beatrice, James' sister, looking for Celeste – to get ready."

"Oh, nice to meet ya. I'm Celeste's great uncle. Everyone calls me Yazi." He gave her hand a vigorous shake. "I helping Martin around back, but let's go inside and find the girls."

Beatrice followed Yazi and stood behind him as he yelled up the stairs.

"Celeste, Myrtle, ya got some company here. Should I send her up?"

Two doors opened upstairs. "Who is it?" Myrtle called.

Yazi nodded to Beatrice.

"It's Beatrice," she laughed. In her mother's home such informality was just not done, but she rather liked it.

"Oh, Bea! Come up," she heard Celeste call and thanked Yazi as she headed up the steps.

Hanging her dress in Celeste's closet, Bea sat on the bed across from the vanity where Celeste was applying her makeup. "Oh my god, your uncle Yazi is a panic. Those whiskers! He looks like a wild-west man."

"Sailor." Celeste said. "He was the one who brought Gamma here."

Beatrice looked confused. "From Bohemia?"

"Yep. Without him, I wouldn't even be here."

"Wow. So he's a Bohemian, too?"

"Ohhh, more so than any of us!" Celeste laughed. "I could listen to his stories forever. … So what are you going to do with my hair?"

Beatrice popped open her travel bag stocked with combs, brushes, clips, hairpins and large, cumbersome heating wands. "Well, to go with that gorgeous veil – whose was that?

"Gamma's."

"Did she make it?"

"Her grandmother."

Beatrice examined the finely detailed lacework. "I just can't believe how exquisite this is. How can hands make anything so fine and small?" She then lifted the large tortoise-shell comb, lined with pearls, that was lying on the vanity. "And where did this come from?"

"My grandfather – he bought it for Gamma on their trip to the Orient."

"Geez, Celeste, your family has tons of interesting characters and stories. All we've got is dusty old insurance money."

"Not true! I think you're very interesting, Beatrice. Before you, I didn't even know women played squash."

Bea waved the air, dismissing the compliment. "That's just another form of knitting. I mean, Gamma left her country to come here, for gosh sakes, and then traveled to the Orient and who knows where else. You are so lucky to have her as a grandmother. Mine only wanted to drink tea and gossip. I gotta make me some bigger dreams," she muttered, rummaging into her bag and pulling out a curved comb. "But first, I've got a masterpiece to create. Bride: face the mirror, please."

After his shower, Jack stared in the mirror, combing back his wet hair, thinking about the night before. What had James actually said? He took it to mean he'd bedded Kate, but could it have been a false boast? One prompted by liquor and the weight every man feels the night before their options shut down? Flinging off his towel, Jack quickly dressed in his morning suit and set off to find James to see if he could set things right.

In the Meadens' backyard, Gamma and her friends were finishing tying bows on the chairs when Ron came out on the porch and called to Gamma.

"Gamma, mother asked me to let you know it's nearly 10 and you better get home to dress."

"Yah, yah, won't take me much. But come, I need your help for something."

Ron bobbed down the steps and crossed the lawn as Gamma told her friends to go ahead to the house. She'd be along shortly.

"Ahh, how handsome you look," Gamma said, brushing Ron's suit lapel. "I like a minute with you to talk."

"Sure," Ron agreed. "Glad to escape! Mother's going crazy with the caterers."

"OK, then, let's walk to see your creek."

As Gamma and Ron strolled up the hill, Estelle spied them from the back window and wanted to call them back, but something held her tongue.

"James? You decent?" Jack called, rapping on the bedroom door. He heard footsteps, then the door yanked open and James stood before him, tucking in his shirt.

"Come for another round?" he asked in a surly voice.

Jack cleared his throat. "I came to apologize. I may have overreacted."

"You may have?"

"Well, you led me to believe …"

"What did I lead you to believe? I haven't any idea what I said."

"Let me in" Jack said, not wanting their conversation to be overheard by the many workers still circulating in the hallway beneath the banister.

James walked to his dresser, and Jack shut the door behind him.

Clearing his throat again, Jack jiggled one leg, his hands plunged into his pants pockets. "I thought you intimated that you and Kate had …"

"Father, I was rather drunk, so I don't know what I actually said, but I can assure you …" James stopped speaking and looked at his father. "Did you actually think I'd …?"

Jack scratched his neck. "It was a bit disconcerting. You were … rather glib."

"We all know I can be that way." James turned back, picking up his cufflinks. "But I simply took her home."

"That's it?"

James turned sharply. "If you won't believe me, why not ask her?"

"No, I just …. Well, frankly, when I was talking with her, I was struck by how right you two had been together, and I guess …" Jack stopped fidgeting and stood tall. "James, what I'd really like to know is: Are you sure you want this marriage?"

The anger in James' shoulders slumped away as he dropped onto the chair by the window. Rubbing his forehead with one hand, he loudly exhaled a lungful of air.

"I'm not a stupid man, father," James said, exasperated.

"I didn't say you were." Jack replied, sitting on the edge of the bed. "I just want you to know the deal's not done until you say yes to the minister's question."

James huffed. "Seems to be a conspiracy. Ron asked me this morning if I love Celeste. I couldn't even get angry. Somewhere along the way, I seem to have misplaced my ability to feel. For everything – Kate included. But I haven't lost my mind. I know a good woman when I see one, and Celeste is most definitely that. If life is a set of circumstances from which to choose, I think she's my best choice. Maybe even better than I know. I'm sure she'll teach me a thing or two – being joyous, maybe – something I don't believe I've ever known how to do, at least not well."

Jack shook his head. "There was a time."

James huffed again. "Yeah, but I'm no longer ten."

Jack nodded. "I think you're right… about Celeste, I mean. Her *joie de vivre* is … refreshing. So long as your heart is in it …" Jack kept looking at James with a probing eye, searching for any nuance of his deepest desire.

"Of course, of course," James agreed. "We suit each other. I have the means for the life she desires, and she'll show me how to become the man she thinks I can be."

"Hmgh, – hows and means, " Jack said, slapping his leg as he got up from the bed. "Howes and Meadens – well, that's not a bad outcome, anyway you look at it. Finish getting dressed, then. I'll go smuggle some hair of the dog that bit us last night so we can get this show on the road."

At the door, Jack looked back at James, who sat unmoving in his chair. "Son, it'll be alright."

"I know father." James nodded once. "I know."

Standing at the top of the hill, overlooking the creek, Ron stuck his hands in his pants pockets.

"Is nice, no?" Gamma said. "Sweet creek memories?"

Ron grinned. "It's where Celeste and I first …" He cut himself off. "What did you want to talk about, Gamma?"

"Maybe I step too far, but last night, Celeste say something you should know."

Ron's ears pricked and his heart quickened. He nodded for her to continue.

"You and Celeste have special feeling for each other, no?"

"We're friends."

"More so, I think," Gamma checked his eyes and saw they were round and full. "But somehow you never got going too far, yah?"

Ron shrugged. "I didn't realize until … too late."

Gamma shook her head. "I think maybe you both not so good at that."

"Well, anyway, the best man won."

"For somethings … not for all things."

Ron looked confused. "What?"

"Last night Celeste tell how much feelings she have for you."

"She did?" Ron's heart leapt.

Gamma nodded. "I think maybe she change her mind today, but seems not."

"What do you mean? Should I go to her?"

Gamma shook her head. "I don't know. I only felt to tell you she say for you she feel special passion. But she won't let her desire get in the way of your dreams."

Ron wagged his head. "But she wouldn't! I told her that."

"So you know already?"

"Yes, we ..." his face flushed.

Gamma waited.

"Two months ago, I told her how I felt and I know she felt something too. But."

"But?"

"But ... she said just what you said – even though I promised we could work it all out ... but she ran away and I didn't know what to do, Gamma."

Gamma nodded. "Two months, hmmmm. Is some time. So, I think Celeste has made her choice. But, I hope you stay her friend. Someday, I think she will need you."

Ron did not reply, staring down the hill at the creek, chewing his lip with regret.

Placing her hand on his shoulder, Gamma patted him softly, turning him around to return to the house.

By 11 a.m., all the wedding plans had come together. The house was clear of workmen, the glasses set out for the wedding toast, the caterers finished banging around their pots, and everyone was dressed, ready for the ceremony.

Celeste and Beatrice arrived just after 11 in the back of Martin's car. He left them at the curb to go inside and make sure the way was clear to the stairs without running into the groom.

"Oh, I sent them all to the back a half hour ago," Estelle assured, closing the doors to the parlor, and went out to help the girls into the house. Myrtle jumped out of the passenger seat to open the back door, and Celeste carefully stepped out, one hand gently gathering up her gown and the other holding her father's.

"Careful, you're wrinkling," Myrtle cautioned.

Celeste blinked rapidly, remembering her mother's same cry in the dream.

Then Beatrice scooped up Celeste's veil and train before it hit the ground, and together they paraded up the Meadens' front steps and grand stairway, directly into Estelle's boudoir.

Seated at the dressing table, Celeste inspected herself in the tri-fold mirror, then noticed the silk-lined glass top and flashed on the dream again. If Ron opened the door holding a tray of porcelain apples, she was going to faint.

"Champagne!" Beatrice burst into the room with four filled glasses and distributed them to Myrtle, Estelle and Celeste. "To our beautiful bride!" she toasted, lifting her glass and clinking all the others. "How wonderful to have a new sister!"

Celeste giggled and sipped lightly.

"Your hair is beautiful, Celeste. Perfect for that exquisite veil." Estelle said, then held out a small, turquoise box tied with a white ribbon. "I found a little something to commemorate the day. It was so delicate and exquisite, so like you, I couldn't resist."

Celeste's jaw clenched. *Oh my god,* she thought, *how prophetic was that dream?* Setting down her glass, she took the box, but her gloves got in the way, so she handed it to her mother.

"A little something from Tiffany's, I'll bet," Beatrice quipped. "Mother's favorite little shop around the corner."

Myrtle untied the ribbon and loosened the top of the box before handing it back to Celeste. With trepidation, Celeste opened it. "Ahhhh," she sighed, trying to mask her relief that it wasn't an apple.

"What is it?" Myrtle insisted.

"Two porcelain lovebirds in a silver twig nest," she said, handing the box to her mother. "It *is* most exquisite. Thank you, Estelle, we will treasure it always."

"Well, Myrtle, we should go down now, to greet the guests. Beatrice will look after our bride."

"That's my job, matron of honor!" Bea replied, downing her champagne.

Myrtle hesitated before leaving, taking Celeste's hands and squeezing them hard. "I'm so happy for you," was all she could manage to say before tears choked off her voice.

"Thank you, Mama. I love you, too." Celeste said, releasing her mother's grip.

After the mothers left, Beatrice slipped down the back stairs to fill their glasses again, leaving Celeste alone. Unable to do anything, Celeste peered at herself in the mirror, wondering who that woman was staring back.

"Celeste?"

She looked up.

Ron stood in the half opened door. "May I come in?"

She almost couldn't breathe. "Hello," she whispered.

He stepped inside, closing the door behind him. "You look beautiful," he said, one hand fidgeting and the other behind his back. "I just wanted to give you … something," and presented a small jeweler's box.

She blanched, clutching the bench to steady herself. "What is it?"

"Nothing, really. Just a little memento I've been meaning to give you for some time now … to let you know how much your friendship has meant to me."

Shaking, she took the box and opened the lid to find a small, flat, white stone – like the ones she had often stacked in the creek – with an inscription on each side.

"To Our Creek Days," she read aloud. "Our Heaven on Earth." Blinking away tears, she looked up as he crouched alongside and took her hand.

"To be honest, I wish it were me … but I understand," he said softly. "Our timing was just all wrong, but I want you to know I will always be your friend. The very best, for whatever you need."

Letting out her breath, she wrapped her arms around his neck, clutching the stone in her hand. "Me, too … always, always, always," she said in his ear and kissed his cheek.

"Aieeeee," Beatrice screeched as she came through the door.

Celeste jumped at the sound of her mother's cry in the dream and pulled back from Ron.

"What are you doing, Ron?" Bea snapped.

Ron stood, flushed with embarrassment.

"I was just …"

"You were just mussing her dress. No one sees the bride before! Now get out."

As Ron scuttled out the door, Celeste called: "Ron – Thank you."

"Men have no sense," Beatrice declared, setting the glasses on the vanity.

Celeste looked down at Ron's stone. "No sense at all," she murmured.

"You should see it down there. Everyone's arriving! It's a mad crush. And the hats, ohmygod! Elinor Glyn has a green-silk turban that's as tall as the Empire State Building! It's hilarious!"

Beatrice bustled about the room, picking up the empty glasses and setting them on the tray by the door, searching around for her gloves, glancing in the mirror at her hair." "Gawd, it's hot in here," she said, opening the window just behind Celeste. "I've got to go ... powder my nose. Can't be squeezing my knees during the ceremony! You OK? Do you need to tinkle?"

Celeste smiled, the picture of calm perfection. "I'll be alright."

Beatrice opened the bedroom door, making a face at the gust of crowd noise bubbling up from the vestibule, then closed the door behind her.

Alone again, Celeste tenderly touched Ron's stone sitting on the glass top. Through the open window, she heard the band rehearsing in the distance. Closing her eyes, she conducted her own rehearsal of the upcoming wedding in her mind's eye ...

At precisely 1 p.m., she'd begin her descent down the Meadens' grand staircase, its wide, curving planks and carved balustrade perfect for her grand walk, each drop of her satin train on the stairs reminding her of a similar descent down the hotel stairway in Prague, gliding toward her first taste of independence and freedom at the Ball. Only this time she would enjoy the extra weight from the gown's train and long lacy veil trailing down her back, held in place by the heavy, pearled, Balinese comb. It was as close as she imagined Royalty to feel, as she stepped toward her destiny, her eyes on her father below, waiting to present her with the bouquet of fresh-picked white lilacs from Gamma's garden, and escort her up the parlor aisle, accompanied by Mendelssohn's wedding march played on the piano.

She would enter the parlor, and despite Estelle's repeated caution to keep her eyes and head straightforward, she would look around, at a room filled with most everyone she knew and loved. She'd smile and nod to her dancing teacher from first grade and her favorite neighbor on her block and the bright smiling faces of Ede's parents, which would cause a twinge of regret at Ede's absence, and she'd grin at Uncle Yazi and hope not to cry at the sight of Gamma's brimming crystal-blue eyes. Even her mother's controlled countenance would warm her to the bone, for never had she felt so lovely, the air pulsing goodness. Then she would be presented to James and would feel at peace, knowing every step she'd taken along the way had led to this day and the future she embraced. And after the minister pronounced them married, James would sweep her in his arms and kiss her with such passion as she'd never before felt, and the guests would applaud and she would laugh out loud and impetuously kiss James again and again as they glided down the aisle – officially husband and wife.

Celeste left her reverie with a deep breath, letting it out slowly, keeping her mind as still as possible, ready for this next step in her life – when she heard a rather loud, male voice just below the open window.

"Hey, Buddy Boy, Mr. Groom – that was some party last night."

Must be one of James' friends, she thought, who still sounded a little tight.

"By the way," the man continued, "saw that little vixen of yours this morning, before we headed out here."

Celeste's ears perked up. She rose from the dressing table bench and shuffled to the window. Peeking out, she saw James standing in the garden, talking in a low voice to a man who looked familiar, but she wasn't sure of his name.

"Yeah, we saw Kate!" the man said, even louder than before. "She was waiting for a bus."

She could not hear James' reply but saw him grab the man's arm. She leaned farther out the window, straining to hear what James was saying.

"Well, hell, what can I tell you?" the man countered, chucking James under his chin. "Whatever you did with her last night, she sure was glowing this morning. You are one mighty lucky son of a bitch. Kate *and* Celeste: Two gorgeous women on a string, in different cities! What a perfect setup!"

Celeste gasped a sharp, pitiful cry. James' face snapped up to the window. Their eyes locked.

"Bloody hell," the friend said. "Sorry, old man."

In a panic, Celeste pulled back from the window, oblivious that her veil had caught on the latch. She moved swiftly, desperate to escape the room, the house, the town – this life! Suddenly the veil went taut and her head snapped backward, her hands flying up to the headdress as she crumpled to the floor. Stunned, she heard footsteps pound up the stairs, and then the bedroom door burst open.

"Celeste," James pleaded. "Please, let me explain."

33 *The Space In-Between*
May 27,1934

"Celeste, please, let me explain."

The words hardly seemed real to her ears. She could barely recognize the sounds or the man in front of her. Her eyes blurred, her ears slurred, her limbs were limp. She felt her arms being grabbed and pulled up, but she soon slipped out of his grip, crumpling down, falling forward, her head on the floor.

"Celeste … Celeste," she kept hearing her name, but from a far-away place. Then she saw feet surrounding her. Shoes with pointed and peep and round leather toes. Nothing made sense. Then she was lifted, her whole body heavy with silk and satin, and moved across the room and rested on – *what was it? Oh, yes, the chaise longue*, she realized. She began to see faces hovering, felt hands touching her arms, neck, face. The thick cloud encircling her head muffled every sound. She kept trying to shake it away, shake herself awake. *Who kept calling her name?*

"Celeste? Can you hear me? Celeste, it's your mother …. it's Papa … it's Gamma … it's Beatrice … Celeste? Celeste?"

Then other fragments floated by: "What happened?"… "What do you mean you …? Why did you come up? … Well something must have happened …." The voices became progressively sharper, but she couldn't tell if it was male or female, as she floated in the space in-between.

Still, she could feel the intense energy wafting around her. Some hot, some cold, some warm, circulating from one side to the other, wavering over her, along with the cocooning cloud that wouldn't disperse … until she heard one particular word.

"Kate."

In a flash, her vision cleared. Her mind focused. Startled back to reality, she saw them all at a glance: Ron, James, Papa, Mama, Estelle, Jack, Beatrice, Gamma – all staring at her anxiously.

"What …" she began, trying to push herself up, to move them all away.

"Ohmygod, don't get up!" Beatrice grabbed her arm.

Celeste shook her off, zeroing in on James, standing at the foot of the chaise.

"What," she directed to him, "did-you-do-with-Kate?"

James' eyes swept the room. Martin, Jack and Gamma on one side … Estelle, Beatrice and Myrtle on the other, Ron leaning against the wall by the window. He rubbed his forehead. "Nothing, darling. You misunderstood."

Celeste's leg spontaneously kicked under her heavy gown. She shook her head, whipping the final bits of cobwebs away, instantly remembering every detail that happened before she hit the floor. "No," her voice firm. "I was at the window. I heard what he said. What do you have to explain?"

James slipped his hands in his pockets, shifting from one leg to the other.

"Go on, James," Ron sneered. "We'd all like to hear this."

James sneered back. "What the hell are you even doing here?"

"None of us would be here if you hadn't …"

"What?" Myrtle squealed. "What happened? What did you hear, Celeste?"

Celeste pushed herself up farther, not even glancing at her mother. She continued to address only James, slowly and methodically. "I was sitting at the dressing table and heard someone call to you. He spoke about Kate. I moved to the window and saw the two of you talking, and your friend said …" Celeste tilted down her head, remembering, "You're one lucky son of a bitch – Kate and Celeste – two beautiful women on a string in different cities." She looked up. "Is that about right, James?"

Myrtle gasped.

Estelle squeezed her lips together.

Beatrice swiveled with her hands on her hips, glaring at James.

His expression did not change. He stood tall, face drawn, stiff and frozen, but for his fingers, which would not stop twitching inside his pockets. In the prolonged silence that ensued, the room's energy began to turn in a tight, downward spiral.

Finally, James cleared his throat. "Yes. That's what he said, Celeste. But it's not true. He was talking out of turn."

"Really?" Ron jumped in. "What's not true? You bastard! Last night! Just last night you saw Kate! You took her home – during your bachelor party! What the hell is anyone supposed to think?"

"I took her home … just like I said. That's all," James retorted.

Then everyone began talking – everyone but Celeste.

"What the hell did you do that for? Unless you wanted something more?"

"James, is this true?"

"Why would you risk something like …?"

"I knew it, I knew it – you are so sleazy, and now everyone can see."

"This can't be … this can't be happening."

"I asked you directly, last night and this morning, and both times …"

Estelle's voice rose above the fracas. "I can't imagine what you see in that …."

"What he sees is forbidden fruit," Jack countered his wife.

"Now don't you start blaming me for this," Estelle retorted.

"Why not? You're the one who set it all in motion. If you'd just let the boy make his own choice."

The others fell silent as the volley escalated between Estelle and Jack.

"His own choice? I do believe we were all doing everything we could to accommodate *your* choice, darling – *your choice* to retire."

"That's got nothing to do with it."

"No? You wanted your boy back in the fold and I made that happen."

"It wasn't only me who wanted him back!"

"You precipitated it."

"I don't think …"

"*Excuse me,*" Martin loudly interrupted.

Estelle and Jack snapped their mouths shut as everyone turned to Martin.

"What am I hearing? That Celeste was part of some … package?"

All eyes looked from Martin to Celeste, then back at Estelle, who looked at Myrtle standing next to her.

"Well, I wouldn't call it a package …" Estelle said.

"No, Mother?" James seized the opportunity to deflect the accusations from him. "You certainly made it clear that the art gallery was attached to my letting go of Kate and choosing Celeste. Beginning with those cookies at the church picnic."

"I knew it, I knew it, I knew it," Beatrice muttered with glee.

"Damn it to hell!" Ron smacked the wall behind him.

"Watch your tongue," Jack warned Ron.

"My tongue? Where's *his* been lately?"

"Now there's no need for that …"

"Geezus Christ, there it is – the way it's always been – all hail the black prince!"

"Ron!" Jack spoke sharply. "That's enough."

"No, it's not." Ron held his ground. "He's gone about and done exactly what he likes, all his life, without any consideration for anyone – except Mother, his unswerving benefactor – and it always brings us back to the same place: bad boy ruling the roost."

"Anything I like?" James replied, in spite of knowing better. "You haven't worked a day in your life, Mr. Squash, and *you're* throwing barbs?"

"*Stop it stop it stop it!*" Myrtle screamed, unable to control herself, holding her hands over her ears, slumping onto the dressing table bench, sobbing.

Martin crossed the room and rubbed her back. "I think everyone needs to calm down," he said quietly.

Estelle looked at her watch, then opened the bedroom door. The hubbub of the crowd gathered in the vestibule filled the room. She shut it with a snap.

"I think we need to remember why we are here," Estelle asserted. "It's nearly twelve-thirty. We need to determine what we are going to do." She folded her arms. "Celeste, would you like us all to leave so you can work this out with James?"

Celeste blinked, having quietly watched the words being hurled back and forth, feeling almost disengaged from the action in front of her; as if she were in a darkened theater, watching a movie. But Estelle's question snapped on the overhead lights in her head. *What-had-she-been-thinking? How-did-she-get-to-this-place?* In rapid succession, the past nine months rolled out in front of her: *The art cookies at the picnic. He was right, that's where it began. The Halloween Dance, when he first wooed her. The anniversary dinner – the holidays – the dress – the jewels – New York City – High Society and Bohemian Artist – the Valentines Party – seduced by the new, succored by the shiny and – whoosh – she was engaged and planning a wedding – sooner than she wanted – trying to please everyone around her – ignoring the clamor she felt inside: the constant knot in her stomach, the cramping muscles, the gnawing unrest in her brain, poking her to stop – look – listen – from inside to out. Until she found herself on the day of her wedding, shocked awake – and deep in the muck of her own denial.*

Folding her hands on her lap, she looked at Estelle. "What exactly would we be working out?" she asked calmly.

"Well, whatever was agreeable between the two of you. To come to an understanding ... as we all do in marriage ... when facing such circumstances ... so you can get on with things. We've a houseful of people waiting for you downstairs. What do you want to do?"

Yes, that was the question, Celeste said to herself. *What do I want to do?* She looked down at her gown for a minute, then at James, then at Ron before turning back to Estelle.

"I don't think I can do that," she said quietly, glancing at Gamma, who tweaked a small, encouraging smile. "I don't think there is anything to work out."

"What?" Myrtle glared at Gamma and moved to Celeste's side. "You can't mean that. You need to work this out. He said it was a misunderstanding. You should at least listen to him."

"Or," Ron suddenly blurted, striding to the side of the *chaise longue*, dropping to her side, reaching for her hand. "You can marry me, Celeste!"

She blinked at him, surprised, but did not offer her hand in return.

James let out a tortured laugh. "So this is where we've come to! Believe a pack of lies and then switch out the groom!"

Celeste calmly looked past Ron to James. "Is that what you want, James?"

"What? No! I agreed to marry you. I mean – I want to marry you. We're right for each other, we agreed."

"We also agreed to be honest. So can you tell me truthfully, now, about the art gallery? Was I part of a packaged deal?"

The question rattled James. He turned around; rubbing his forehead, then looked plaintively at his mother.

Jack also turned to his wife. "We need to know."

Estelle shook her head several times before answering in a gush. "Oh, good gracious. This is ridiculous. You were going to give him the art gallery anyway ... but at the time it seemed ... well ... I ..." Estelle stopped, then defiantly threw out her arm. "Alright then, it's true. I swapped out the horses ... so everyone could get a bit of what they wanted. Children for Celeste, Gamma's bloodline in the family, a gallery for James, and society for Myrtle. I believe that about covers it all." Estelle drew a finger down the center of her neck. "I'm sorry this has caused such an uproar, but I did what I thought best for all parties concerned. And not, mind you, without a lot of complicity on most everyone's parts. So that's the truth and do with it what you will, but … I'm finished trying to make it all right for everyone. It's all up to you, now, Celeste." Stepping back, she sat down on the straight-backed chair by the door, folding one leg over the other and crossing her arms on her chest.

A shroud of silence enveloped the room … no one looking at anyone else, until they heard a small knock on the door.

"Celeste? Are you in there?"

Everyone shifted.

Estelle and Myrtle shook their heads vigorously.

Jack, Martin, James and Ron looked at the door, then back at Celeste.

Beatrice almost laughed out loud.

Gamma smiled, recognizing the voice.

Celeste slid her legs to the floor, disbelieving her ears.

"Come in!" she said hopefully.

The door swung open, and there stood Ede, a bit rumpled in a grey travel suit with a valise in one hand and a broad smile on her face.

Celeste's skin popped with goose bumps. She blinked her eyes, wanting to rub them. Was it a mirage? No – it really was Ede, her gloved fingertips at her lips, blowing Celeste a kiss.

"Surprise! I couldn't find anyone downstairs, so I just came up!"

"Oh my lord, Ede." Celeste tried to rise, but her gown was twisted around her legs. "When did you get here? Come in! Come in!"

Standing outside the doorway, Ede could only see Celeste on the chaise longue, but as she walked into the room, she saw everyone posed like bizarre statues, and instantly felt the clotted tension.

"What's going on?" she asked, setting down her valise. "Did something happen? It feels like someone died."

"You can say that again," Beatrice quipped.

"Shut up, Bea," James snapped.

"You don't get to tell anyone to shut up," Ron countered.

"All of you stop it now!" Estelle demanded.

Ede's mouth dropped open. "What in the world …?"

"Ede, you shouldn't be here," Myrtle said, standing, rubbing her hands. "This is a family matter."

"No, she shouldn't," Estelle echoed.

Martin grabbed Myrtle's arm. "That's quite enough. Ede's more family to Celeste than anyone in this room right now."

"Yah," Gamma finally spoke. "Perfect time to come."

"I think we should all leave," Jack added.

But Celeste said, "No," tottering to stand as she untwisted her gown around her legs. "No. I don't want anyone to leave. Not when I finally know what I need to say." Ede's arrival had released something bound within her, like a first breath from a long, underwater submersion. She felt her heart pulsing a new rhythm, syncopating with her own truth. She felt imbued with a simple surety that lightened her arms and chest like helium; and the clarity of a child's eyes, uncomplicated and free to see what was really in front of her. Looking around the room, she caught every eye until she rested on Ede's.

"Ede," she began, her tone grave. "I was about to make the biggest mistake of my life. Turns out, I was not about to marry a husband, I was about to become the consolation prize in a big, big scheme."

Celeste turned to face James. "Seems my so-called fiancé here, wanted an art gallery more than a wife – but to get it, he had to strike a deal with his mother."

Celeste faced Estelle. "His mother wanted him to give up the actress … you know, the Kate-girl everyone whispered about, and the one I think he actually loves but won't admit it … and marry me. Why?" She sighed. "I'm not sure but I suspect it's because then she'd have more control over him because we all know what a push-over I am," she looked sharply at Estelle. "Right?"

Looking down, Estelle pursed her lips, her head slightly shaking.

Celeste shifted back to Ede. "Now why did James agree to this scheme? Because then he could play big shot with all his artist friends … and all his big shot friends as well – justifying his natural interest in art with a big time gallery. Plus," she held up her finger, circling the room with her eyes, stopping on James. "Turns out he wasn't really going to give up Kate because he saw her, just last night. Oh so innocently he claims but I don't believe that for one cotton-pickin' minute."

James took in a breath to answer but Celeste held up her hand, stopping him.

"But, so long as we're getting all the truth out – the truth is, I wasn't in love with him, either. I was just as guilty in this dream of schemes, trying to please everyone in the mix and ignoring my true feelings."

She looked down at Ron, slumped on the floor by her feet. "And in the middle of it all, sweet, wonderful Ron asked to marry me, as well."

She looked back at Ede and saw her face blanch.

"Ede, I'm sorry. I promised myself never to get between the two of you ever again, but I can't be half way truthful here. I do have feelings for him. Crazy, mad, passionate feelings that zing my body all over ... but," she glanced at Myrtle. "My own mother convinced me those feeling weren't important, that they don't last, and being safe was the only valid consideration ... given the economic times and all."

She turned back to Ron, who sat up now, his eyes hopeful. "But you already know why I won't marry you. I could not live with myself if I became the reason you gave up your squash career."

Ron tried to speak but she shushed him. "Refusing your proposal may be the only decent thing I do in my life ... because this is your chance to see how good you can be and nothing should stand in the way of finding that out. And I know you would leave it all behind to have a chance with me and, quite frankly, that's as crazy as me marrying James right now."

Celeste returned her gaze to Ede, presenting her case to her jury of one.

"But, if I did marry Ron, and ruined his dreams, and maybe my own as well, – my mother would still be happy because he's also a Meaden and her craving for high society would be satisfied, delivered by the Meadens' noblesse oblige, regardless of how it twisted up the people in between."

Ede's mouth gaped at Celeste boldness. She could barely believe her ears.

With arms akimbo, Celeste gazed around with mockery in her eyes. "The lack of forthrightness in this room is astonishing ... including me. It's startling how easily we delude ourselves. Even you, Jack, whom I love and adore, got swept up in the scheme. ... Heck, Ede, the only person in this room who actually lives true to their heart is you! And the only other two people who tried their best to get me to do the same were Gamma and Papa."

She looked between them. "But you both kept quiet, giving me a chance to figure it out for myself, so I could learn how to do it ... but somehow I couldn't hear you, or my heart, in the clattering noise of everyone telling me what to think, what to feel, what to do ... and I let them!"

She began snapping her fingers in the air. "Marry James – marry Ron – wear a broach on your neck – French twist your hair for the social set – leave it loose for the bohemians – become a debutante – wear this gown, ditch that one, – stuff down your feelings – create the perfect home for perfect children – forget your own dreams, live through your children. And one day, maybe, just maybe, you'll find a smidgen of time to hear your own thoughts, feel your own feelings, find your own passion and live your life true."

Celeste threw back her head and howled, startling everyone. "Aieeeee! What a fool, I've been, Ede. A blasted fool! Thank god you showed up.

Because just seeing you gave me the strength to ask myself the questions I've been too afraid to even think."

She gulped for air, kicking away her train and faced her parents behind her.

"Who am I? What do I love? Where do I most feel myself? And how do I find more of that?"

Celeste stopped, feeling a shock roll through her body. "Ohmygod, what a dunce I've been. *Howe!* My very own name!"

She went to Gamma, grabbing her hands, kissing each cheek. "*How* is what you've been trying to teach me all these years, and I just didn't get it! I kept hoping for someone to come along and tell me what to do. And they did and nearly succeeded, too! But that's not *how* you learn, is it?"

Gamma shook her head, her eyes smiling.

"Only by doing can we learn! Trying, taking risks, falling down ... and learning." Celeste sucked in another breath of sudden realization. "Learning how not to marry from fear of facing yourself!" Celeste stamped her foot victoriously, scanning the room again. "And for that reason alone, I guess ... I have everyone here to thank!"

"Gamma!" Her voice vibrating. "I never understood when you said: 'Things may not turn as you want, but always as they should.'... But now I think I finally do."

With new and a quietly strong energy, Celeste stepped up to James. "You don't love me, James. In fact, I'm not even sure you like me."

He opened his mouth to protest. She shook her head.

"Don't even try. We all saw who you love, besides your artists. You never looked at me the way you looked at Kate, strolling around the Town Green, blatant as can be, declaring to the world with every fiber of your body; and hers, too. Don't be a fool and let that go ... for anyone or anything."

James reached his hand toward Celeste's face but she caught it, squeezing just hard enough, and dropping it before abruptly turning to Estelle.

"I don't hate you, Estelle, for what you've done. I think I've admired you most because of how you ran your household and charities and still had a marriage worth keeping. If anything, I hoped my marriage to James would become like yours and Jack's ... but that would require having Jack as a husband, I think." Celeste winked at him. "Someone who loves you for who you are, not just a well-chosen accessory."

Jack raised his eyebrows in agreement, nodding to Estelle.

"And Ron," she slowly crouched beside him. "I want to feel about myself and my life the way you feel about squash. I don't know when or how that will be, but I know I can't marry anyone until I find it. But you have to keep going, make that dream come true, become the champion of your own life. We all believe you can do it and I'll be cheering loudest, every step of the way."

Rising, she moved back to Gamma, clasping her hand on the six copper bracelets. "The way things are going, I don't know if I'm ever going to raise those children the gypsy prophesized."

Gamma shrugged. "No one can know what future will bring, but what you do today is more important and come first. And these bracelets are not only for prophesied children. They also are symbols of the Bohemian Way – same as the notches in your birch bark hat – and is time for you to carry them forth – for whatever your life may become." Smiling, Gamma took off one copper bracelet and slipped it on Celeste's arm.

"First, for Truth: which only you can know."

Celeste's eyes brightened, giving the bracelet a squeeze.

"Second, for Courage: to follow your heart whispers," Gamma slipped it on.

As she presented the third bracelet, Celeste said:

"Third for Openness: to embrace what comes your way."

Gamma winked. "Fourth for Curiosity: of what beckons you."

"Fifth for Creativity in all you do," Celeste spun the fifth one on her arm.

Gamma held up the last bracelet and Celeste clasped her hand around it.

"Sixth for Love," they said in unison, laughing.

"First for yourself, from inside to out," Gamma finished, slipping on the last bracelet and closing Celeste's fingers into a fist, pressing it on her chest. "These are the roots of our Bohemian Way, yours now, forever, from this day."

Celeste tapped her chest with her fist. "The roots of contentment." Running her finger across the six bracelets on her arm, Celeste shivered at their 'tinging,' and realized she now carried all the measures she ever needed for knowing her own heart's code. Bowing her head, she momentarily wept.

"Thank you," she whispered to Gamma, dabbing her eyes with her fingers, then turned to her parents.

"And thank you, Papa, for loving me more than I knew how to love myself."

Seeing her mother's terrified face, she reached for her hand. "Ah, Mama, don't worry. I still love you. Thank you for trying to undo what had been done to you. I know you did what you thought best ... even though ... but never mind, I forgive you. But please, forgive your own parents, too. Do not carry this burden anymore. Because in spite of it all, their actions brought you to Papa ... and you both made me ... and despite how crazy it's all turned out – it brought me to the one person I've been searching for all along: myself ... for that, I thank you most of all." Kissing her mother's cheek and squeezing her father's hand, Celeste felt complete and looked around for Beatrice.

"Bea, my almost Matron of Honor, would you clear everyone out of the vestibule and close the parlor doors behind them? Have the pianist play something to entertain them."

"You bet!" Bea answered, slipping out the door.

Moving to the dressing table, Celeste pulled off the Balinese head comb and released the veil down her back. Gently gathering half of it, she held it out to Gamma. "Sorry, I think it got a little torn."

"No matter; serve purpose!" Gamma softly balled up the yards of lace.

Facing the mirror, Celeste looked at herself, then quickly unhooked the diamond necklace and pulled off the pearl earrings, laying them on the tabletop. As she did, she saw Ron's engraved stone and quietly snatched it up into her gloved hand.

Swinging around, Celeste pulled up her train, wrapped it over her arm and stood tall. "Shall we?" she said to Ede, motioning to the door.

"We shall!" Ede said, scooping up her valise and sweeping the door open.

In the door frame, Celeste paused, hearing strains of the band outside, practicing the song that began it all ... so many months ago. Laughing, she sang along.

"Blue Moon ... now I'm no longer alone ... without a dream in my heart ... without a love of my own."

Then she was gone.

Looking over her shoulder, Ede kicked up her heel. "Ciao, Ciao," she said, shutting the door behind her.

34 Yes

May 27, 1934

Sweeping down the Meadens' grand stairwell, Celeste heard the murmuring behind the parlor doors, felt the weight of the bracelets tinging on her arm, and saw Ede catching up behind her. But it all felt surreal, cloaked in a gossamer cloud.

"What happened?" Beatrice called from the vestibule.

"She sang Blue Moon then vanished – poof!" Ede called back, "Open the door! Open the front door!"

Beatrice yanked the oversized door

Celeste glided across the hallway.

"What are they gonna do now?" Bea asked.

"Hells bells!" Ede replied. "Maybe Ron and James will marry each other!"

Beatrice's laughter pealed as Celeste and Ede stepped onto the porch, saw some late arriving guests coming up the walk, and reeled left, cruising to the back of the house, almost colliding with a huge bird cage containing a red-tailed grey parrot.

"Yikes!" Celeste side stepped around it.

"Hector Present, Hector Present," the bird squawked.

"What in the world? My god – madness!" Ede cried.

"Don't I know it," Celeste muttered, her gown swaying with her strides. "Where are we going?"

"To the safest place I know: The Creek!"

As soon as Celeste rounded the porch corner, Beatrice raced up the staircase, nearly out of breath as she whipped open the door to her mother's boudoir. "Wow, was that ever keen!"

A stony silence returned.

Most everyone was still. Myrtle cried softly into her handkerchief. Martin stared out from the window seat. James perched stiff-backed on the dressing-table bench eyeing the abandoned jewels. Ron slumped on the *chaise longue*, next to Gamma, who silently tapped her toes. Estelle was still upright in the chair by the door but Jack paced the room.

"Shut the door, Beatrice." Jack said, planting his feet wide, hands on hips. With a swift glance and boisterous voice, he addressed everyone. "Who would have thunk it? She took us down and built us up in a matter of minutes! It was magnificent! Martin, Myrtle, Gamma: I've got to say – that's quite a gal you've raised – quite a woman! I will forever rue this day she got away but ..." his finger raised in the air, "I think we would be wise to follow her lead."

"Whatever are you talking about?" Estelle asked dryly.

"Seize the day, just like she did: face into the disaster, make a choice and move on, lickety-split, head high! We've got the band, the food, the party's all ready to go ... Sooooo, let's put it to good use."

"How on earth are we supposed to do that?" Estelle asked.

Jack bent down on one knee in front of Estelle.

"Well, well, my sweet bride Estelle ... we could ... if you would ... agree to marry me again, today!"

"Ooopmh! Go on with you." Estelle waved him away, trying to hide her smile.

James, Ron and Beatrice looked up, horrified.

Myrtle and Martin were shocked.

Gamma smothered a laugh.

"You can't be serious father!" James sniped. "You'll make a mockery of me."

"I'll save you if your mother says yes."

"Really? And what am I supposed to do?"

"Be our groomsman!" Jack quipped then shifted his tone, wagging his finger at James. "Wipe that smirk off your face, stand up straight and tell the truth, for once in your life. You got jilted – by the best woman in the county. Take your lumps and move on. And the best way to do that is to beat 'em to the punch."

Jack turned to Martin and Myrtle. "I know this must sound strange. But honestly, Celeste is not one to waste a festive occasion; nor would she want the whole town prowling after her right now. If we do this, we give her some time to – I don't know – clear her head and decide her next move. I'm not trying to disrespect Celeste in any way."

Myrtle held her handkerchief to her nose, unable to speak. But when Martin squeezed her shoulder, she looked to him and briefly nodded.

"We understand, Jack." Martin confirmed.

Jack slapped his hands together. "Right, then," and turned back to his wife. "So what-do-ya-say, Stelly? Will you have me all over again?"

Estelle laughed long and low. "You always surprise me."

"Just like the first time. Yes, then?"

"Of course yes," she took his hand, standing with him.

He hugged her hard. "Lucky me!" Then he pointed to James.

"Now, Son, here's your chance. Go down to the parlor, tell them to sit tight – there's gonna be a wedding but a change in the program. Then tell the pianist to play a long introduction to the Wedding March. You'll cue her when to begin the actual march." Jack turned to Ron. "Ron, round up your brothers. Line them up on either side of the minister, half and half, age order. James and Beatrice will pop in after the procession. Got it?"

Ron nodded. No one argued with Father in command mode.

Jack shifted his gaze to Gamma. "May we borrow that veil?"

She smiled, handing him the soft ball of lace.

Jack held it out to Beatrice, "Can you fix this on your mother? With that fantastic comb?" he looked to Gamma for approval, who nodded.

"Oh no-no-no, I don't need ..." Estelle protested.

"Oh yes you do!" Beatrice said, taking her by the arm to the dressing table.

"Let me help," Gamma said.

Everyone started moving while Martin and Myrtle looked on.

When Estelle caught Myrtle's contorted expression reflected in the mirror, she paused Beatrice and Gamma and swiveled around to face her.

"Myrtle, you should be proud. Your daughter's finally stood up for herself, as I always hoped she might! I know it looks a little grim right now but believe me, it will all work out in time, just as it's supposed to, you'll see. But for now, what's done is done. We can't change the past, and since we ... well, most of us, anyway ... had a hand in this, why not begin the next chapter together, too? As proper friends this time, not prospective in-laws. Now that we know each other's follies … won't you join us? Be our witnesses?"

"Excellent idea my love!" Jack cheered, "Yes – yes – stand up for us – the most stand-up couple we know, truth be told!"

Myrtle straightened up, feeling hope spark in her belly. "But what about Celeste? Shouldn't we …?"

Estelle shook her head. "I suspect Celeste wants some time to herself right now, and she has Ede with her."

Myrtle saw Gamma's nodding smile then looked to Martin, who confirmed with his eyes. With a controlled half-smile, Myrtle finally felt whole and equal in stature to the Grand Dame of Gladdenbury. Had she been alone, she would have hugged herself. Nodding gravely, she confirmed the offer. "As proper friends? That would be lovely. Yes."

When Celeste reached the backyard, enchantment befell her eyes: white satin ribbons entwined every orchard tree above linen-swathed tables, set in family-style rows beneath the flowering branches.

"Holy cow, what a bash," Ede sighed as she caught up with Celeste. "You OK?"

Spinning on her heel, she lightly bumped Ede's face.

"Oooops," they both laughed.

Ede squeezed Celeste's arm. "I'm so glad I made it in time. You were fantastic!"

"Thank gawd you showed up!" Celeste threw her arms around Ede, hugging long and hard. "I had no idea you were coming!"

"Me neither!" Ede exclaimed. "It was all last minute. Out of the blue, Mr. Moltano presented me with a train ticket and told me not to return until the end of June. I suspect my father called him about the wedding and all, but … oh, I forgot to say – he's given me a job! A full-time job! Still as his secretary, but he promised to let me work on the sets – undercover, of course. But in white overalls all the painters look alike. So I just throw on a cap and leave off the lipstick those days."

Celeste blinked. "Wow. Lucky you!"

"Yeah … And you too! A clean escape, in the nick of time … so glad I saw it!"

They simultaneously turned, gazing over the yard as workers and waiters brandished last-minute touches.

"Wooooha! Those Meadens' sure can throw a party!" Ede muttered.

Celeste wavered, recalling the copy Estelle had shown her that would appear in the Hartford Courant's evening edition, reporting news of the reception in progress.

> *After cocktails and a few posed pictures, the bride and groom led the wedding party to the Meadens' pink dogwood grove, where luncheon tables were dressed. The dropping blossoms speckled pink kisses on the strictly white table décor. The sumptuous four-course meal was served family style on long tables set among beribboned trees. In between courses, James and Celeste graciously walked among their guests, giving personal thanks for their attendance and good wishes.*

"Sorry to be passing on all this?" Ede waved to the festooned backyard.

Celeste gulped. The temptation of riches was what got her in this mess in the first place. She shook her head. As if on cue, a rousing introduction to the Wedding March began pulsing from the parlor.

"What the heck?" Celeste looked back at the house.

Ede grabbed her hand. "Let's get outta here before they lasso you back!"

Laughing and tripping across the lawn past confused waiters, Celeste dragged along her gown, following Ede to the top of the hill, where they stopped again, leaning against the towering, craggy sycamore tree, her breath heavy from the weighted run, her heart pounding in her ears.

As the new wedding party gathered in Jack's study making final plans, Martin looked around, astonished by the abundance of family memorabilia. The taxidermy alone was overpowering. Then he noticed Gamma closely examining a picture on the wall of photos.

"What is it Gamma?" Martin asked quietly as he approached.

Her eyes were round and eyebrows furrowed. She pointed to the picture of a young man, holding a diploma, flanked by an older man and woman, next to a sign for The Free Academy. "My eyes play trick on me," she said. Martin looked closer.

"Grandma Katrine?" he whispered.

"Yah, is what I see, too."

Across the room, finishing up his pep-talk with James, Jack saw Martin and Gamma huddled by the photo wall. He strode over. Seeing the photo they were pointing to, he announced: "That's my great grandfather on his graduation from The Free Academy – which became City College!"

"What?" Gamma looked even closer.

"The first Meaden in this country to graduate—"

"Jarden Mederheim?" Gamma blurted.

"What? Yes! That was his name before he … but how did you know?"

"Because Katrine –" Gamma pointed to the woman in the picture, "is my mother-in-law. And Martin's grandmother. She tell me about a boy she help – a Jarden Mederheim – who work at their hardware shop in New York."

Jack's mouth dropped open as he snatched the photo off the wall, flipped it over and pointed to the inscription: *1853 T.Harris, K. Howe.* "K. Howe – that's your mother-in-law and Martin's grandmother?"

Gamma and Martin both nodded, equally astonished.

"Yes." Martin answered. "Jarden began working at my grandfather's store when he was around 13 and my father was 6, I believe. They played together sometimes, in the aisles of the store. And Grandma Katrine helped Jarden enroll in the Free Academy. T. Harris – he was the man who created the school for poor boys who had no other option. Then when Jarden's parents died in an accident during his last year, Grandma Katrine took him in, helped him finish."

"Well I'll be a monkey's uncle! Estelle! You're not going to believe this —"

"She also helped him get a job, at a hotel uptown, in his last year of school. That's where he met the insurance people who offered him a job. After his graduation he moved away and they lost contact. But she knew he was going to change his name from Mederheim–"

"—to Meaden! In 1854." Jack declared, squeezing Estelle's hand. "The year he moved to Connecticut, married and gave birth to my father. Well, I'll be … Stelly! I just knew there was something about this family that made my heart happy! Now I understand that feeling!" He pumped Martin's hand then swung his arms around Gamma, lifting her in a bear hug. "Your ancestors helped my ancestors become what we are today. That makes it official – you're as family as family gets!"

Estelle was speechless, barely able to comprehend the news. But Myrtle instantly felt her fortunes change with the bliss of a good surprise and a secured promise of a rising tide.

❧

Standing in front of the closed parlor doors, James hesitated. He did not want to do this. He'd rather have walked away ... out the door ... back to New York ... disappearing for good from this small-town whirl. But somewhere deep inside his pinched heart he knew he had to close this chapter, head on and head high.

Glancing over his shoulder, he saw Beatrice, Myrtle, Martin and his parents lined up in the hallway. Catching his father's eye, a jolt went through him, steeling his resolve. Yes, he could and would do this ... stand up and own his behavior ... perhaps for the first time in his life.

Sliding back the pocket doors, he stood straight as an arrow, facing what felt like a firing squad; a roomful of intimates: neighbors, friends, family. People who didn't necessarily like him but would claim to love him, as part of their social code. The pianist stopped playing and the crowd turned in their seats en masse, staring at him.

"Ladies and Gentleman," James began with an uncertain voice. "You came for a wedding and a wedding you shall have ... just not the one you thought."

He paused, fighting the urge to be glib. The room was heavy with smothered silence, as if no one was breathing. His instinct to cut-and-run surged but he fought it back, committed to his confession. "I need to tell you I have been a dishonest man and caused unnecessary pain, for the benefit of my own ambitions."

One hundred pairs of questioning eyes widened. He pushed on.

"But it may please you to hear that ... through my own indiscretions and questionable ethics ... I have been humbled. And as a consequence," he bowed his head, clearing his throat, "and as a consequence, I have been jilted by the best woman in the county, and rightfully so."

The guests shivered but remained silent.

In the vestibule, Estelle and Jack touched hands, surprised by their son's forthrightness. Martin put his arm around Myrtle, who leaned against him.

James looked up. Pain etched his jaw. His lips dry.

"Once the details of my conduct became evident, Miss Celeste Howe, with astonishing graciousness... " His voice cracked, "made her goodbyes, choosing to pursue her own dreams. And I applaud her for it."

A murmur rolled. James dismissed it, unconsciously tossing his head.

"Unaccustomed as I am to admitting my faults, I feel compelled to confess my deep regret ... and embarrassment ... at my own behavior. Not only for the awkwardness I have caused all of you, but for how callously I treated the kindest young woman we've all ever known." With a tilt of his head, he could not stop himself from adding: "For which I should probably be put in the public stocks and flogged."

Brief laughter twittered in various corners of the parlor, the sharpest one drawing James' eyes to Ron, who stared back, his mouth unforgivingly twisted.

"To some, such a punishment would never be enough. I do, however, make a solemn promise to find a way to make amends with Celeste ... if she'll allow it ... and to all of you, as well."

He shifted his stance, glancing at the pianist, who sat up, her hands ready.

"At this moment, however, I hope you will accept my deepest apology for the confusion and ..." he moistened his lips, "my failings."

James glanced over his shoulder at his father, who nodded once with an expression of reserved pride. He took a breath. The hardest part was over. His voice rose with renewed strength. "While we gathered here today to witness a union of two hearts, which I am now incapable of delivering ... my family invites you, instead, to witness a renewal of vows between two people I would be wise to emulate. They are, by all accounts, quite remarkable. Separate yet conjoined, opposite yet equal, and despite the social disparities at the beginning of their relationship, they have been devoted to each other's success. I ask you to join in the celebration of their continuing legacy ... exemplifying unwavering esteem for each other. A reminder, particularly to me, that enduring love is still possible."

Before anyone could respond, James nodded to the pianist, who energetically launched into the beginning chords of the Wedding March as he strode up the aisle, looking neither left nor right, his forehead glistening with beads of perspiration as he took his place on the far right of the minister, alongside his brothers.

Beatrice immediately followed, stepping in time to the music, carrying a bouquet of lavender lilacs that complimented her pale-tangerine dress. Smiling boldly, she proceeded as if nothing had changed in the day's plans.

As Beatrice took her place next to James, the guests turned, trying to guess who would be coming next, and everyone gasped when they saw Martin and Myrtle, strolling up the aisle arm-in-arm, their facial expression a bit awkward but smiling as best they could, taking their places on either side of the minister.

Finally, Jack stepped into the doorframe, cocking his arm with a flourish as Estelle stepped into view, clasping it, looking resplendent in an icy-silver, tea-length dress, silhouetted by Gamma's long, lacy veil, crowned by the Balinese pearled comb and carrying Celeste's white lilacs.

Marching slowly up the aisle, Jack and Estelle nodded and smiled as spontaneous applause burst across the room. When they reached the bemused but approving minister, Jack shook Martin's hand, and Estelle squeezed Myrtle's before passing her the bouquet, and the pianist punctuating the moment with a rousing finish.

With all eyes fixed on the new bride and groom, Gamma chose not to enter the parlor and quietly slipped across the hallway and out the front door. Rounding the porch to the backyard, she saw the silhouettes of Celeste and Ede on the hilltop and stood in the shadows to watch them.

❧

At the burst of applause, Celeste faced the house. "What are they doing?"

"Making lemonade!" Ede replied, sarcastically.

"How?"

"Do you actually care?" Ede turned Celeste by her shoulders, away from the house. "Let's talk about you. What the heck are you going to do now?"

"I have no idea…" Celeste said, glancing back at the house.

"Hey," Ede tried to distract her, "you could come to Hollywood with me! With a full-time job, I'll be getting my own apartment! We could share! Wouldn't that be slapping?!"

Celeste looked wistfully down the hill, at the creek. "Maybe" she half answered, "But maybe a visit first … to see what beckons me." She absent-mindedly clasped her armful of copper bracelets.

"Brilliant idea!" Ede nodded, holding Celeste's arm and walking her fingers along the bracelets. "Truth, Courage, Openness, Curiosity, Creativity – hey, you know what Gamma once told me when I asked her about true love?"

With emotion thickening her throat, Celeste nodded for Ede to continue.

"She said:" Ede imitated Gamma's voice, "Eeedeee, Love is a verb, not just a feeling. Is what you *do* that makes love *true*."

"What you *do*," Celeste repeated. "Well, I guess I truly loved myself, today."

"Amen to that, sister!"

"Gawd, Ede," Celeste shook her head. "I may have just passed up the best chance I'll ever have in life."

Ede began to protest, but Celeste stopped her.

"No, no, I'm not reneging. I mean ... well, bets are, this was likely the most expensive decision I'll ever make! Monetarily, at least ... unless I come up with some brilliant idea, hahaha. But the cost," Celeste pointed back to the house. "The emotional, physical, mental cost of being someone I was not – pfffft! Epic disaster! A marriage of lies!" She grabbed Ede's arm. "Did you know his mother chose the cake? We picked lemon and she changed it to chocolate – without a by-your-leave! That could have been my life! Chocolate cake! And I don't much like chocolate!" Celeste spit a laugh.

Ede released her breath in a rush, laughing loudly. "Nooooo, you've always been a lemon head!" She poked Celeste in the ribs.

"Yes, I have!" Celeste declared, casting her eyes down the hill.

Standing close to the house, Gamma watched the girls on the hill, studying their postures and gestures, trying to read clues of Celeste's wellbeing. But when Ede's big laugh bounced into the yard, she knew all would be well and returned to the parlor, where the ceremony was waning into sentimental mush. Slipping into her seat next to her girlfriends, she nodded to them, her eyes twinkling, anticipating the zinging gossip that would gush like an uncapped oil well after the ceremony, prompted by the first sip of champagne.

Staring down the hill at the creek and surrounding trees, Celeste's vision blurred into a watercolor impression as her thoughts congealed. "It wasn't just the little things like the cake. There were plenty of signs I ignored along the way." Her head snapped up. "Even Gamma's bracelets – these very bracelets!" She cocked her arm over her head, shaking the bracelets. "They hung over me like a sword!"

"The Damocles sword." Ede supplied.

"Right!" Celeste smacked Ede's shoulder. "Just like the Sword of Damocles hanging over the king's throne! No one can enjoy being a king with a double-edged sword hanging overhead. And that's exactly what it felt like for me! The Meaden Fortune and the Gypsy's Prophesy dangling over the throne of marriage! As if money and children were the source of happiness! Gawd! All I felt was constant fear! Trying to anticipate what

wrong move I'd make that would crash that sword and slice off my head –
disappointing everyone and wrecking my life!"

She pointed to Ede. "Had you been here, I'd never have gotten near
that throne in the first place. It wasn't a choice … it was … an escape!
From myself! By agreeing to the marriage, I didn't have to consider other
options. Options I was already doing, and loving!" She ruffled her dress.
"Eee-gads, Ede! Isn't it funny how the worst day in my life is actually
the best?! I feel something opening up inside – like I can finally breathe
again!" She inhaled deeply.

The burst of applause and rousing recessional from the house whirled
both girls around again. They gaped at each other.

"What the heck?" Celeste began. "Oh stuff it, you're right. Who
cares? That's not my life anymore!" Shaking her bangles in the air, she
declared: "Sixth for Love! First of yourself, from inside to out." Gathering
up her skirt, she cantered down the hill to the creek, her wedding dress
billowing behind.

"To the Bohemian Way!" Ede cheered, following with a lanky,
happy gait.

On the mossy bank, Celeste stood on the crescent of rock jutting out
from the creek's edge and slowly released her gown, feeling it cascade around
her feet. Staring at the soft-flowing, gray-green water, she sniffed deeply, her
nose filling with the scent of mud and new green. Wiggling her toes in her
shoes, she glanced up at the houses on the hillcrest overlooking the creek.
*News traveled fast in small towns and those glassy eyes would report them on the
grassy slope, shoeless, sockless, skirts pulled up to their knees, splashing their feet.*
But nothing would stop her now. Wrinkling her nose like a rabbit, Celeste's
laugh gurgled in harmony with the stream as she slipped off her heels, hiked
up her voluminous skirt and tiptoed in, sucking small breaths at every step.

"Too cold?" Ede asked blithely, rolling up her waistband.

"Oh, noo," Celeste said, biting her lower lip as Ede plunged in.

"Eeek! It's freezing! You *are* a pixie!" She retreated to the bank.

Celeste teetered in the water, turning fully around, admiring every
stone, stick, bush, tree and the crystal-blue sky above, puffed with
white clouds.

"Where it all began …" she reflected. "This very creek … my birch-
bark hat … our friendship … and Ron's, too. It feels like … no other place
I know." Lulled by the babbling water tumbling over the rock clusters,
Celeste swayed to its melody.

"It's where your heart sings," Ede dabbled her feet over the water.

"Yes, that's it!" Celeste replied quietly, studying Ede.

"And where does yours sing?"

"Anyplace I'm holding a brush, loaded with paint."

"Ahhh! Have brush will travel."

"You bet."

"And when you're painting? How do you feel inside?"

"Awake," Ede kicked, splashing the air. "Alive, alert, free and … open."

"Open." Celeste instantly responded. "That's how I feel when designing for The Needlery! And that's almost exactly the same words Ron used about playing squash."

Ede glanced away. "Makes sense."

Celeste caught her eye. "Hey, are you … OK … with all that?"

"Ron?" Ede fixed her gaze across the water on the rope swing. "Sure. It was a long time coming. I just didn't want to believe it."

"And now?" Celeste asked tenderly.

She shrugged. "You can't help who or what you love, right?"

Following her gaze, Celeste looked at the large rock where the rope swing hung. The sun shimmered on one side, shading the other. Celeste twisted her head, blinked her eyes and looked at it again. "Ede? Am I seeing things? Look at that."

"What?" Ede craned her neck around the tree on the embankment.

"Our rock! Come here and see. I can't believe I never saw it before!"

Ede quickly waded over, looking with her and instantly saw. How had they ever missed it? Their creek rock, their jumping off rock, the anchor of their sacred hide-away was … heart shaped! On the very top, a crevice split the rock in two, rounding out on either side, curving down to a point at the bottom. All these years, yet never noticing … until this very day!

"Jumping Jehosaphat!" Ede said.

Celeste laughed. "Come on!" she cried, wading to the smaller rocks leading up to the heart rock and swing.

Wobbling at each step, Celeste grunted. "I worked so hard to fit into the Meaden clan and lifestyle … to be the perfect catch for James … but what was *I* catching? A man in love with someone else?"

"Certainly someone you didn't love," Ede followed Celeste, trying to hold up the train of her dress.

"Precisely! Sure, I'd have the children to love, but never a real partner … never a true mate." She twisted to Ede, her eyes pained. "And how could he? When I'm essentially a stranger to myself! That's the question I have to answer: Who am I?"

Turning back, she stepped onto the top of the heart rock and felt a magic course up her feet and through her body. Releasing her skirt, she made a slow circle, looking up and down the creek. "Look at this ... just a little nothing creek ... in the middle of nowhere ... yet standing on this rock, I feel I could be overlooking the Vltava river ... surrounded by the Bohemian mountains. Is that who I am?" she queried the sky, then pounded both fists on her chest, vibrating her voice: "Yes! I-am-Bo-he-mi-an"!

Ede laughed out loud, dangling her legs off the rock's edge.

As soon as the wedding service completed, Jack invited everyone to the reception and Ron immediately pushed his way through the giddy throng of guests, all clamoring to uncover scintillating tidbits of what had happened to Celeste. Disgusted, he dashed to the backyard, racing past the tables and up the hill to the craggy, old sycamore tree, sure the girls had gone to the creek. Just as he reached the top, he heard Celeste's voice yelling "... I am Bohemian," followed by Ede's unmistakable laugh. Dropping back so as not to be seen, he peered around the sycamore, hearing their words echo off the water. He just wanted to know she was alright. Seeing his two friends at the top of his rock made him feel calmed and jealous at the same time, wanting to be with them but something held him back, something he knew he had to honor. Then he saw Celeste reach for the rope swing.

Drawing the round, wooden swing towards her, Celeste continued her self-discovery. "But I'm a business woman, too. I love The Needlery! And I've gotten good at designing. Can't wait to show you. Even some abstracts, like your paintings."

"Abstract? Really, Miss Realism?" Ede teased.

"Yep!" Celeste said, twirling the seat in a circle. "James is a jerk, but he did introduce me to Stuart Davis and opened my eyes to ... well, lots of things, including abstract art. New York's energy made me crazy but ... it was inspiring, too! Shook out my cobwebs. I've sketched a couple dozen patterns so far and can't wait to make more!" She'd barely spoken the words when her body shook with a sudden realization. "My gawd, Ede, it's been here all along, hasn't it!?. Who-I-am! What I love to do!

I kept thinking the hardware store was an obligation but it's not! It was a doorway to what I most love doing! This is crazy! All this time I kept looking for 'it', and I was already doing it! Making new out of nothing! Exactly what my ancestors did … those crazy Bohemians, millenniums ago. Why-why-why has it taken me so long to figure this out?"

Ede shook her head. "It comes when it's supposed to, I suppose …"

"But all this wasted time?"

"Not wasted. Without James, you wouldn't have explored the abstract … or New York … or the artists … or – heck, he not only opened your eyes, but gave you a foil to push against. Woke you up – albeit abruptly – but look what you got in return – look what you're finally discovering. He showed up – you paid attention – and it brought you to … yourself. Pretty good deal if you ask me. We can't know who is going to show up or for what reason, but there's *always* a good reason. Our job is to pay attention and stay open."

"Really, Gamma?" Celeste smirked. "It's that simple?"

Ede smirked back. "And crazy scary sometimes – trusting your heart."

"Hmgh," Celeste mused. "I'm beginning to think my heart sees an entirely different world than my head. Like it knows me better than I know myself!" She pointed to Ede. "Like a best friend who's always there!"

Ede tapped her chest twice. "Count on it."

"Eeeegads, Ede, I haven't been a very good friend *or* listener – to you *or* my heart. But from now on I vow …" She held out the swing like an offering to the gods and spoke in a clear, bold voice. "From now on I promise to stay alert and open to my heart's whispers. To let it have the last word and lead me along the path I most want to go, even when I don't know where that is, and trust – trust! – it will help me find the contentment that is truly mine!" Then with a whoosh she launched – hoisting her body with the rope, throwing her legs around the swing, and sailing over the water, her gown rippling wildly and bracelets tinging.

"To the Heart Code!" she hollered.

"To the Heart Code!" Ede echoed.

As the swing twirled her around, she spied a fat strip of birch bark bobbing towards her, bathed in sunlight, glowing as if lit from within … just like her birch-bark hat last night, lying on her bedroom floor half crumpled yet glowing in the moonlight. *A sign!* Celeste thought as a laugh gurgled up her throat. *Oh, Gamma, you and the gypsy were right! Signs are everywhere … but if there is no laughter, I know it's not for me!*

The swing slowed and Celeste leaned back, her body perpendicular to the deep pool beneath. After a long silence she blew out a breath.

"Ede: I know what I'm going to do next."

"What's that, Celeste?"

"Something I should have done a long time ago ... just . . .let ... go!"

And she did,

... with an exuberant "YESSS"

... and a billowing splash

... into a life of her own!

Still in the shadows at the top of the hill, Ron watched Celeste's fall in slow motion ... rolling off the seat ... arms flung wide ... an explosion of water ... her muffled cry. Leaping into the light, he instinctively howled with the joy he felt, witnessing the baptism of Celeste ... to herself!

The Heart Code is the first of the Bohemian Hearts Series. The next book will continue to follow Celeste's life and journey as she seeks to live true to her Heart's Code.

Author's Note

The idea of a Gamma, a wiser person to help you figure it all out, was seeded in me very young.

Growing up, I was an adventurous girl, trying out whatever I found interesting. My mother kept a sharp eye for what might inspire me – as she did for each of her eight children and subsequent grandchildren. She'd select specific gifts and experiences to cultivate our curiosity and creativity, including, but not limited to: an art easel, wood burning tool (which I still have), glass cutting kit, zither, sewing lessons, a vanity (for which I had to sew the skirt), dance classes, tickets to the ballet, opera, symphony, theater, simple blocks, roller skates, trips to the park, zoo, woods, lake, ocean, camping, hiking, cooking, dining, dancing and books, books, books. I had lots of inspiration in my youth but, as I got older, I felt somewhat ill-equipped for the world at large. Our family was big, noisy and cozy-safe. But the world beyond was a mystery and I wanted a little more help in figuring it out.

As I began to discover myself apart from the family, I remember longing for a mentor who would discover me and tell me what I was meant to be and do. But no single person showed up for that job. No Svengali for me! Instead, several people came along, one by one, at just the right time, for just the right reason and helped me see myself. Bit by bit, I began to realize and trust my instincts and notions.

Somewhere along the way, I decided to live my life according to those instincts and notions. I wanted to discover how life would unfold when I trusted my sense and sensibilities. It felt risky, but it felt better than giving my life over to something safe but not true to my spirit. Early in my career, while waiting for the Cable Television Industry to come into the market where I lived, I took on a series of jobs that each gave me a different skill/experience. I accepted each of these jobs in low-level sales, television production, marketing and performance with a conscious evaluation of how that skill would be useful if I ever got the Cable TV Local Origination Production job I sought. When I finally did land that job, I asked my new boss why he chose me. "Because," he said, "You had all the skills we were looking for." That was the moment that solidified my commitment to follow my instincts, my heart voice, and whenever I have, things work out in a whole and balanced way – even when the waters turned choppy.

While I knew since I was ten that I would write a novel one day, I also knew life had to be lived in order to have something worth writing. As a result, I've sampled a smorgasbord of life and relationships, spanning the world and delivering a colorful palette from which to craft stories. While this work is not autobiographical, it is informed by my interests and experiences.

I hope to continue the story of Celeste, as she steps into the responsibility of creating her own life, along with following up on all the characters from *The Heart Code*. Please share your thoughts and experience of reading *The Heart Code*. I am also available to be part of your reading group – in person or via skype.

Thank you for your interest and lend your support by buying a copy of the book for your like-minded friends!

Best to you,
LAURA

Laura Matson Hahn
TheHeartCodeBook@gmail.com
www.TheHeartCode.com

Acknowledgements

One of the reasons we are all together on earth, I believe, is to help one another grow. The creation of this book was only possible because of the help and encouragement of many people. Never having written a novel, I enrolled in the school of trial and error and trial again. So the final draft took many years and many readers to shape.

The final form of this book is due to a very talented designer, Caryn Newton, who gave me much patience along with a layout, font, maps and design that rang true to the material. The cover was a blessing from artist Julie Costanzo, who intuited the essence of the book and loved it to fruition. When we first spoke, she shared her love of book covers that were so rich in detail that she'd be compelled to study it after each chapter. That's when I knew I had the right artist.

My heartfelt thanks to everyone who risked reading the early manuscripts: My sister Patti McHugh's book club in Glen Rock, NJ, and Marie O'Neill's Brick, NJ book club, and Sharyn Soifer Keiser's New Hope, PA book club and Robin Hepp's New Hope, PA book club. Each one provided a range of valuable feedback, from multiple ages and perspectives, much of which greatly influenced the final manuscript. But most of all, it was a most joyous process.

Thanks also to the fearless friend readers for their support and excellent critiques:

Isabelle Almeras-Heyraud de Vos, Betty Benton, Wynne Caldwell, Mindy Camp, Tracy Coulson, Adrienne Crombie, Keith David, Ellen Emerson, Gail Enman, Judy Eustace, Joleen Fitzgerald, Meg Fitzpatrick, Marliese Ganellen, Gerry Grassia, Eleanor Hahn, Kate Kaiser, Clare Kendall, Karl Laundre, Donna Lehmann, Sarah Lipoff, Maura MacNamara, Cynthia Matossian, Helen Matossian, Sarah Matossian, Ellen Melchiondo, Wanda Nadal, Krystina Nickle, Laura Pearson, Barb Peterson, Harald Poth, Chris Reynolds, George Saunders, Bethany Sawyer, Mark Sebree, Carol Short, Sharon Stratton, Mark Talbott, Suzy Tomai, Kathy Tomai, Evula Vopalcka, Florence Warner and special thanks to Karen and Paul Craig for use of their RI home to restructure the manuscript, Scott Edwards of *Bucks Magazine* for the article and Will Lippencott for his kind assistance.

Special thanks to my cousin Dee Sarchet, who read and re-read and read again, all the while picking up the phone to hear a plot idea or brainstorm or buck me up. My Aunt Therese was another repeat reader and when I finally heard from her "You did it!" it was a happy day, indeed. And to Jennifer Levine, who devoured the final manuscript, then read it again, shooting back to me all the lines she was sure I'd written just for her.

I am forever indebted to my husband, John, for his patient endurance while I was consumed by the words and plot and characters for years on end. Also for his wise counsel as I worked my way through the drafts. Everlasting blessings to you, my best love.

Similar thanks to his sister Jeanne Bertke, who went far beyond the call of duty as a sister-in-law, lending her wisdom, razor sharp perception and editing expertise and time, illuminating just what was needed along the way.

Much appreciation to Bernadette McBride, editor of my first draft; and to Beth Leiberman, whose early review set me on the path featuring Gamma; and to Francis Vitulli who checked and double checked my people, places and things. Special thanks to my final editor Gerald Monigan, who applied his insight and understanding of my style to challenge me to expand and expound in just the right spots.

Last, but by all means not least, to my mother, Barbara Nugent Hahn, who shared with me her passion for story and reading. She was the smartest reader I've known, with tough, literary standards and is solely responsible for introducing me to my top favorite books. When she finished reading the first draft of this novel, she called me, thrilled and delighted with the story and especially Gamma. That call turned out to be our last as she passed on a few days later. It remains one of the most memorable and cherished phone calls of my life.

My most heartfelt thanks to all.

Reader's Guide

Questions for self-reflection and sharing.

Gamma's Philosophy

1. Who's your Gamma? When you were growing up, who saw and appreciated who you are and tried to help you find your way? More than one? What would you say to your Gamma(s) now?

2. To whom have you been a Gamma? How has it impacted both of your lives?

3. In Chapter 15, LEGACY, Jack muses over the questions Gamma posed to him (P. 146): "What had he chosen? What did he let pass? To what was he now being drawn? Has it turned out as you dreamed?" How would you answer those questions today? Ten years ago?

4. In Chapter 16, GRADUATION, Gamma explains the feeling of "beckon" as what one is naturally drawn to between the ages of 7 and 11 (P.166). What beckoned you at that age? What feeling did it invoke? Do those feelings arise today when doing something you really love?

5. In Chapter 9, TRAVELING BLOOD, Gamma recounts her experience with Charles Dickens in an English Dockside Pub (P.90). Celeste hopes something like that would happen to her one day. What special experiences have you had in your life that you consider a rare moment?

6. Gamma believes one should pay attention to everything that shows up in one's life as the bad stuff is as much a blessing as the good stuff. How can that belief make a difference in how you handle life's difficulties?

7. In Chapter 30, CONNUBIAL MIST, Gamma's last words in Celeste's pre-wedding dream (P.331), asserts that no one can know the reason for our life, only to what we are drawn and that each step leads to the next on the path we are born to take. Do you think each person has a reason to be here on earth? Or, is it just a random mix of DNA and circumstance through which we have to muddle? What is the consequence and benefit of either one of those beliefs?

8. In Chapter 22, HOLLYWOOD, Gamma shares with Celeste about her father's dream to be a sailor (P.235) and urges her to follow what

beckons her before "circumstance take your choice away, too." Do you believe that anything is possible at any time? Or are some things only possible for a specific window of time (like child bearing), after which, the door is closed? How does this impact one's choices throughout life?

Heart Code Concepts

1. Do you believe modern science's postulation that the heart has the capacity of intelligence separate and unique from the brain? How about the possibility of the brain revolving around the heart? How might that discovery change your choices in life?

2. At the end of Chapter 11, HOMECOMING, Gamma defines the Heart Code (P.114), and how to hear its "yes". Have you heard the yes of your heart? At what age did you first feel your "yes". How would you describe that feeling? Where else in your life do you feel that feeling?

3. Do you recall a time in your life when you absolutely relied on your heart instincts? How did it feel? How did it turn out?

4. Has your heart ever steered you in a direction that did not have the approval of important family or friends in your life? How did it turn out? Would you do it again?

5. Do you believe things show up in your life at the right time for the right reason? How has this manifested in your life?

Relationships and Ideas

1. In Chapter 1, BIRCH BARK HAT, Gamma agrees to honor Myrtle's parenting choices (P.23), but reserves the right to answer any questions Celeste may ask. What do you think of that rule? Is it important for a grandmother to be free to speak her truth to her grandchildren?

2. In Chapter 7, EDE, Celeste became upset when someone referred to Ede's "obvious talent" (P.70). Do you think everyone has an obvious talent or only a few, with most people discovering their particular talent over time? Do you have an obvious talent? What have you done with it? What would you like to do with it?

3. Celeste had a hard time figuring out what Gamma tried to teach her, until the end, when she truly heard her heart's "yes" when she made

a choice that felt true. Why do you think it took her so long? How does our society make hearing our own "yes" difficult?

4. In Chapter 18, CHOICES, Gamma shares with Celeste that after this life, she would like to come back as a bird (P.184), for a resting time, with not so many choices to make. Many people believe in a God who directs life's circumstances that they are to follow. But the Heart Code suggests that while you have a map to contentment through your heart code, a person has the right of free will and choice to create their own life. How do you approach life: as a creation of your own doing or as a follower of the will of a higher being? How does your belief impact your actions?

5. In Chapter 22, HOLLYWOOD, Gamma discusses dreams with Celeste (P.235-6). Ultimately she says: "Dreams are just something to do while we learn how to live." In the modern western world, finding your dream and passion is often focused on celebrity and entertainment. But are dreams/passion limited to only outward, showy behavior? Is the dream of raising a good family and being a positive person just as valid and important? And what if it really doesn't matter WHAT we do – only HOW we do it? If that were the case, how would it impact your life choices – past and future?

6. In Chapter 28, CLARITY, we witness Celeste making herself over again and again to please others(P.302): dressing and acting one way for James' mother, another for the high society set and yet another for the bohemian set. Do you know people who act this way in modern day life? What are the benefits and consequences?

7. In Chapter 24, ART, Celeste meets the contemporary artists Stuart Davis and they discuss artists and art (P.260). Stuart asserts art is not about making an exact replica of what can be seen, but about creating "inspiration, illumination, investigation … that contributes to another's experience." How does this definition interplay with your own experience with art … and how might it also have applicability to how one lives life.

8. In Chapter 31, COURAGE, Myrtle comes clean about her life and actions (P.337), noting that in her younger years she believed she could "…make up what I want, what I dream and push my way forward, ignoring what others thought of me." Modern day Reality Television

displays a lot of people "acting" in ways that seems false and inauthentic in situations that seem "made up" to boost ratings. In many ways, Myrtle was in her own "reality show," when she was plucked from the New York slums and relocated into Connecticut society, where her "wants" list became longer and longer. With so much attention placed on false behavior and external "wants," how much harder is it to be true to ones heart? What are the costs and benefits of being true in a society that celebrates pushiness, showiness and falsity?

9. In Chapter 13, DANCING, in a conversation with Celeste (P.131), Gamma says "No matter what say your mouth, the body speaks truth." Most young children, and animals, can instinctively "read" the energy of the people around them and they react accordingly – with or without words. They feel and "see" positivity and negativity in the other's body, regardless of what words are used. While we all retain that ability, somewhere along the way, we learn to rely less on what we see and sense and more on what is said. How does this shift in attention impact us and our relationships?

10. Who were your favorite character(s) in *The Heart Code*? Who and Why?

11. What do you think Celeste will do next? Ron? Ede? James? Martin? Myrtle? Jack? Estelle?

12. What more do you want to know about *The Heart Code*? The Bohemians? The Meaden's and the Howe's?

13. Do you consider yourself a Bohemian in spirit? How does this show up in your life?

14. Of the six elements of the Bohemian Way (Truth, Courage, Openness, Curiosity, Creativity, Love) which one means the most to you at this moment? Which ones have you already integrated into your life? Which ones do you want to focus in on next? Why?

15. Who will you share this book with and why?

Thank you and Happy Heart Code Discovering!

Author's Biography

"What dat, Mom?" and "Why" were Laura's favorite questions from her earliest days and she has never lost that inquisitive nature. Raised in a large family filled with drama – both on the stage and within the home – her love for understanding the world through art and literature was nurtured early.

Throughout her education she was fortunate to find mentors who cultivated her appreciation for creative writing, performance, literature, human nature and the world of commerce.

After earning a BA in Oral Interpretation of Literature and Urban Affairs from the University of Rhode Island, she completed her Masters of Communications at the University of Michigan, specializing in the new industry of Cable Television. She then embarked on building a career which took her around the world as she morphed from Television Production to Business Writer to Change Communication Strategist. After twenty years in the corporate side of life, she left to focus on writing for magazines, periodicals and children's history books. In 1999 she was inspired to begin what became *The Heart Code*, when standing at a window of a stone monastery in the south of France at early dawn, listening to the whine of a motorbike approaching the village. A voice came into her head, which she followed for ten years until the novel was completed; a very nice voice, indeed.

Laura lives with her beloved husband, John Matson, in New Hope, PA, where she is active in the community and her days are filled with walking her dogs, tending her home, enjoying friends, creating projects and writing – in that order.